I0757902

Hunting the Witch

Book 7

Witch of Appalachia Series

Francesca Quarto

Hunting the Witch ©2021, Francesca Quarto

Tell-Tale Publishing Group, LLC

Swartz Creek, MI 48473

Tell-Tale Publishing Group supports the right to free expression and the value of copyright. The purpose of copyright is to encourage writers and artists to produce the creative works that enrich our culture. The scanning, uploading, and distribution of this book without permission is a theft of the author's intellectual property. If you would like permission to use material from the book (other than for review purposes), please contact: permissions@tell-talepublishing.com. Thank you for your support of the author's rights.

Printed in the United States of America

"When the Green Mother calls ye home
Home to her verdant rolling hills and moss-covered castles
With their howling shades and breathing walls,
Ye dare not refuse.
Nay, when the Mother whispers yer name,
ye will rise above all else, and fly to Her
To stretch yer naked body upon Her beating heart."

From the Book "The Bastard's Lament" 1527AD

(As dreamed of by Francesca Quarto) 2020

Chapter 1

Cathleen crept from the muddled fog of unconsciousness. Struggling to focus her eyes, she found herself looking into the flickering light of a single torch. The bundle of stalks burned in an ornate iron sconce hanging directly above her. Her eyes drifted shut with the effort of watching the quivering flames, and she slipped back into the waiting darkness.

When her eyes blinked open again, she watched trembling shadows dance across the rough ceiling. They resembled sleeping bats. *No. This is wrong.* Jarred by that random, rational alarm, she gave her head a small shake. She must dislodge the strong urge to float back into comforting nothingness. Somewhere in her scrambled brain, she realized the smoke from the torch gave off a strange odor. It worried at her consciousness. Her head felt wrapped in cotton batting, and a heavy sensation radiated throughout her body. When she tried to move, sharp pains shot up both arms, into her shoulders. The jolt shook off any remaining stupor, bringing her to a full realization of her condition. The first information she processed was easy; she was bound hand and foot. Calming her chaotic thoughts, she determined she was stretched out on a cold hard surface. She methodically began to sift through her memories of movements up to this point, starting with following her eccentric host through his fabled wine cellar. She remembered looking around while he pointed out rooms dedicated to certain vintages, droning on in his high, irritating voice about the ideal soils to grow the specific grapes needed for each type. They passed a partially open door. There was no gold vintage plate, but a quivering light from within leaked into the hallway. Curious at her host's silence about the room, Cathleen pushed the door slightly as she walked past and poked her head in.

No orderly shelves of dusty bottles, only a long marble table under the wavering light of a sputtering torch. Cathleen was instantly reminded of a sacrificial altar. Even for her unusual host, it seemed odd that in this ultra-modern building, a room was lit by torch light. Curious, she checked that her host had moved ahead. He was still playing tour-guide, likely enjoying the superior tone of his own voice. She stepped a foot into the room. Her eyes were drawn to symbols deeply etched into the creamy face of the marble. She instinctively jumped back from the opening when she recognized them as cyphers unique to the Black Arts. Her host turned in time to see her pop out of the mysterious room, but he never lost his bland expression. Cathleen smiled sheepishly, hoping her curiosity would appear innocent. When she caught up with him, she casually mentioned that his wine collection was thought to be worth millions of dollars, and the critics considered him a true connoisseur of rare vintages. As in all his other comments, he was disdainful of what the critics thought, even the complimentary views. She was careful not to mention the marble table and its unsettling engravings as they moved on.

She felt the cold slab under her body but forced herself to concentrate only on remembering how she came to be there. It began with a phone call. Mason Mirage invited her to interview him at his newly completed estate, during an out-of-the blue phone call. She was driving over rough mountain roads toward the highway, and on to Pittsburgh International. She'd been planning a ten-day trip to her ancestral home in Ireland for months. Curious at who besides Jason and her assistant had this number, she pulled to the shoulder to answer.

Having a face-to-face meeting with the reclusive multi-billionaire, Mason Mirage, was a real temptation for any member of the news media. He knew she owned WHIP Radio, Iron Mountain's local station. He seemed to have other, more intimate background on her, casually dropping tidbits into their road-side conversation. He nonchalantly mentioned he understood her purchase of the station was the happy result of an inheritance from her paternal grandfather. Cathleen was too shocked to respond when he followed this by complimenting her for increasing sponsorship and boosting its listening range. She did recall his tone was more patronizing than praising.

"You have a *head* for business it would appear, Ms. O' Brien. I'd like to give you another opportunity to achieve something truly unique and invite you to interview me at Mirage Mansion."

Cathleen hemmed and hawed before agreeing but knew there was plenty of time to make her plane, and his private compound was on her way out of town. Following his directions, she drove the forty-five minutes to the sprawling estate. She tried to reach Jason as she pulled onto a nearly invisible road leading to the heart of the compound and the manor house. As Sheriff of Iron Mountain County, Jason was likely patrolling some remote part of the mountains he called his beat. She gave up the effort, thinking to tell him that evening when she landed at the Dublin Airport. She didn't bother leaving a message because Jason rarely checked his personal cell and hadn't sent a text in his life.

She parked the Jeep near the wide skirt of steps leading to the front doors of a hulking stone building. Cathleen noticed the double mahogany doors were etched with some odd symbols, but as she bent closer, the doors swung inward. The servant looking back at her startled face appeared as if he'd been recently exhumed. He stared mutely at her and with a curt nod, lead her to a spartan sitting room to wait upon her host. Sitting in a chair worthy of a museum, she reflected on what she already knew about this man.

When Mason Mirage began to build his extensive compound, Cathleen did some in-depth research on him, uncovering precious little on the elusive billionaire. All she knew was that he purchased the remote two-hundred-acre tract of land in Iron Mountain County, over a year ago and hadn't lived there until quite recently. His reputation as an extreme survivalist and avid hunter were well documented. She found numerous pictures and commentary on his hunts of the most dangerous species that roamed the planet. He reportedly used his fabulous wealth like a pry-bar, opening otherwise protected preserves, hunting many species most countries deemed endangered. By funding private safaris, he routinely skirted hunting regulations. One unflattering story stated he'd been accused of corrupting whole villages with his money, so he could bag whatever quarry caught his fancy. She'd only found a few dated photos of the man himself, most of those in hunting gear and holding big rifles.

Before the great man himself moved to Iron Mountain, the place was crawling with large teams of construction workers, hard landscaping experts, and engineers in multiple specialties. These were all under the supervision of his Architect, Byron Bledsworth. Mobile work lights could be seen filtering through the woods round-the-clock. The talk buzzing among the locals was of secret rooms and underground bunkers. The less fearful put this gossip down to superstitions and an innate distrust of strangers. By the time Mirage stepped foot onto his mountain hideaway, most of the work was completed.

At the outset of construction on the massive building project, Cathleen was told by her local news reporter, all on-site workers had to sign confidentiality agreements. This would assure their silence on the layout of the vast estate. In return, they each received half-a-year's wages as a bonus, plus their normal pay. After several weeks on the job, some of the workers drifted into town for the five-thirty breakfast at the café. It was noticed by the waitresses that some of their regulars didn't return after making off-the-cuff comments about some aspect of the work to a friendly local. Cathleen suspected Byron Bledsworth had an effective spy network among his crew, and maybe even among the citizens of the small town of Iron Mountain. Money can be a potent influencer on behavior, even for simple-living folks. All the things she'd unearthed about the enigmatic Mason Mirage stirred Cathleen's determination to accept this invitation.

After an hour of enduring his self-aggrandizing interview, Mirage clearly lived up to his public persona as an egotist. At one point, he referred to himself as being "a superior hunter of magical creatures." While this comment perked up her ears, Cathleen was unsure what he meant by the odd phrase. She discounted his knowing anything about her alter ego of Green Wizard and the Sworn Protector of the Green. Her wizarding abilities were as hidden from public view as the Mirage Compound.

Mirage took a welcome break from touring the seemingly endless cellars to show Cathleen his Gun Room. This occupied a spacious corner of the lower level, incorporating a huge taxidermy studio. Cathleen felt like she'd stepped into a graveyard with the bodies on top of the ground! She was surrounded by the heads of trophies as well as several fully preserved specimens. Among these was a pack of dingoes in a very extensive diorama. Cathleen knew these feral dogs, indigenous to the Australian Outback, were considered endangered. The large pack were loosely arranged in aggressive, snarling poses, around a wounded red kangaroo. Cathleen couldn't believe how realistic the bloodied creature was, right down to its fear-crazed eyes. She was studying this unsettling display, when she sensed the man responsible for all the frozen slaughter come up behind her. She started to turn when there was a sudden prick on the side of her neck. The last thing she heard before losing consciousness were his whispered words as she fell into his arms, "I shall now name myself, *The Witch Hunter!*"

Reliving that moment jolted Cathleen back to her current situation and the tight restraints around her limbs. She struggled quietly to test how securely she was bound, able to stretch her neck to identify the type of bindings used. *Chains? Pretty medieval!* she thought, checking them out from the awkward angle. Her alarm tripled when she realized the lustrous white gleam coming off the links could only be one kind of metal. Titanium! Another jolt to her system! Her magic was useless while she was shackled by chains forged of this material. Titanium was the only alloy that could block her from accessing her magic. She couldn't break the links without magically enhanced strength. In reality, titanium was stronger than steel for all its light weight.

She squeezed her eyes shut, fighting to control the wave of despair that threatened to engulf her. Her body was bound, but she was still free to use her disciplined mental training. She turned to a power that couldn't be chained and would free her Spirit Body into the ether. It was a rare use of magic and would leave her completely vulnerable. This cell would become her tomb until her life-essence returned to her and that would be after it delivered its message. Cathleen mastered the delicate art of out-of-body travel after much training. She knew Jason had experienced many such mystical journeys in his life and been declared an 'Oracle and Seer' by the Council of Green Wizards. His Waking Dreams had been a part of his life since early childhood. She knew, with his sensitivity to magic, her husband would recognize her mystical body, and hear her urgent message.

The last task she had to perform was nearly complete. Cathleen opened her mouth in a long exhale of breath. She watched with dimming eyes, as her Spirit Body drifted above her. The ethereal being looked down, studying her for a brief moment before vanishing from space and time. The flame burned less intensely in its sconce, altering the shadows pooling on the stone floor until they reached the table and the defenseless woman. Like dark wraiths, gauzy fingers of shadows crabbed-up the marble legs and began to cover the beautiful Protector of the Green in their inky embrace. Oblivion claimed her and Cathleen couldn't know someone had entered the room. Even the touch of his cool hand along the soft curve of her cheek was not enough to rouse her from a death like slumber. This lack of response alarmed the visitor.

"What fun will this hunt be, if she's already dead?" he murmured angrily. Panicked at the idea of being cheated of his perfect quarry, Mirage began using his Dark powers to rouse Cathleen from her stupor. His companion Byron Bledsworth, stood by silently watching. His tongue darted between his full lips every few seconds, tasting the air like a reptile, licking them in anticipation.

The last word of his spell was chanted, but Mirage's anxiety was the only thing to rise. The lovely wizard continued to lie as unresponsive as a corpse. Mirage touched her face again. *Warm.* He reached for a forearm, *Pliable, not stiff. She's alive.* Mirage leaned close to Cathleen's ear.

"I know you have done something to yourself Protector. Something that makes you unable to participate in the hunt I've planned in my Labyrinth of Lies but know this witch…I shall not be denied my pleasures!"

Staring down on her impassive face he snarled, "You will find me a most patient man, which is why your little ploy will be unraveled soon enough."

The two men began to turn toward the door when Mirage stopped and added another thought. "Then my dear, like all the other witches and sorcerers I've hunted and bagged, your beautiful head will grace my Wall of Magic Users in my *real* Trophy Room."

Chapter 2

Jason sat at the kitchen table, willing his cell phone to ring. He'd been moving a half-eaten muffin around on his plate, watching the old flip phone as if he could stare life into it. The only sound was the crackle of burning logs in the fireplace, warming the chill off an early spring morning. He rubbed a sleepless night from his right eye and adjusted the black patch more securely over the left. Looking over at the large flagstone hearth, he met the sleepy, long gaze of Cromwell, his wife's Irish Wolfhound.

"So, why do you think Cathleen hasn't called yet old son?"

He got the answer he expected, silence and the rolling of the large hound's golden-brown eyes. Jason went back to sipping distractedly from his cooling mug of coffee. He smiled to himself, thinking Cromwell's nonchalant attitude toward his mistress's absence proved he'd finally outgrown separation anxiety. Jason knew he was still low human on the affection scale when Cathleen was about and even when she wasn't around, he suspected he ranked as mere food provider in Cromwell's opinion. The sky was beginning to lighten and a weak wash of light was showing through the windows and he'd stewed long enough!

"Time for a walk, Cromwell!" Jason said firmly.

He slipped into his boots and grabbed the dog's leash off the hook in the mud-room. Pushing his arms through, he zipped up the heavy wool jacket with the cloth decal *Iron Mountain Police Department* encircling a purple-blue mountain crowned with snow. The logo characterized the once booming Appalachian coal mining town of the late 1800s. As Sheriff, it meant home and duty.

The big hound watched Jason's preparations closely. Once sure of the plan, he scrambled to his gangling legs, a deep bark showed his agreement with this new arrangement. Jason fastened the lead onto the dog's thick leather collar, and they stepped into the brisk air of a rising dawn.

Winter was melting in the rugged mountains of Pennsylvania. Except for the dense forests ringing their stately old house, the ground was beginning to thaw, showing the first signs of budding life. Jason spotted a half-foot of snow snugged up against the broad tree trunks and boulders scattered haphazardly by time and weather events. He loved the first light of day inside the heavy woods around their home and set off toward the denser part of the forest. Here, the silence was deep and the air was heavy with pine scent and the earthy smells of a living woodland. He'd moved into Cathleen's one-hundred and sixty-five-year-old rambling house after they married, almost three years ago. He was thrilled to give up his bachelor cabin on the outskirts of the town of Iron Mountain. He'd been Sheriff for the wild, far-flung county and small town, for nearly six years. It was a job he looked upon as a noble profession. He had seriously considered studying law when he finished college, but when he returned to Iron Mountain, he found himself running for Sheriff. He smiled to himself thinking how he would have been keeping the bad guys out of jail, instead of putting them in. He knew Cathleen would enjoy that little joke and he's mind drifted back to his lovely Irish wife.

She was never really out of his mind. Not since the first day he met her at the old bakery shop, on a morning like this. He felt a profound connection with Cathleen from that first moment, when he was drawn into her beautiful hazel eyes. It was her first day in the rustic town, six years ago. He discovered in her a forever kind of love, not to mention a secret that would change his life completely. He'd married a Wizard whose beauty was only matched by her mind-blowing powers. He was mulling over their exciting and happy life, as he and Cromwell hiked further into the green shadows and breathless stillness of the forest. Suddenly, Jason jerked to a halt. Cromwell looked inquiringly over his shoulder at him, immediately taking advantage of the halt to sniff around a mossy log. Jason stood still. He felt a distinct chill running down his spine, raising the hairs on his neck. He knew that tingle well. Cathleen was nearby! But how could that be? Cathleen left for Ireland nearly twenty-eight hours ago. He stretched all of his senses to understand what was happening. While the dog walked to the end of the leash, searching out un-sniffed territory, Jason ran through the plans they discussed.

Cathleen was leaving work early the day before, to make the three-hour drive to Pittsburgh International to catch her flight. It was scheduled to land in Ireland around midnight his time, with the eight-hour difference. After renting a car, she'd drive to the small cottage she inherited from her mother, like she always did during this annual trip. Cathleen used this time to address any issues that sprang-up over the year at O'Brinnion Keep, her mother's ancestral castle over many centuries. It had become a favorite tourist attraction under her care, keeping the local village thriving with welcome activity. Jason knew Cathleen would have limited cell service while she trekked around those areas, but she'd make every effort to let him know how things were going. While he reviewed these facts, a stronger chill ran down his back. He moved his head slowly from side to side, checking out the area around him. The black patch was no real impediment after many years of self-training to compensate for the loss of that eye. He was certain he felt her presence. His response mechanism always provided him a jolt whenever Cathleen was close. Somehow, this alert felt different to him, weaker as if it was a mere echo of her presence.

"It's her, but it's not her," he whispered. His words clung to the fog of his breath in the cold air.

The big dog looked up from the ground at the sound of his voice. Even though Jason couldn't understand his deduction, he was certain he was right. He pulled on the leash signaling Cromwell to his side. The Wolfhound immediately responded and sat close to his leg. Jason glanced down, seeing Cromwell also waited for whatever was coming. The dog pricked up his ears, his gold-flecked eyes glittered with intelligence and expectation. Neither the man, nor the dog, felt anything threatening stirring around them, but there was a definite energy source close by. Jason unconsciously laid a hand on the Wolfhound's head where it leaned into his thigh.

"She's near, boy," he murmured as he again scanned the dense woods surrounding them.

"Jason...I'm here!" a thin voice floated toward him out of the muted shadows.

Cromwell shot to his feet but stayed close to Jason's side. His ears pointed forward, confirming his own location for the voice. Cathleen stepped away from a clump of tulip saplings, looking as unsubstantial as the young trees among the large pines. She didn't approach the waiting pair, holding her hand up to stop Jason from coming closer. Jason realized he was seeing through his wife's translucent body. *This is no hologram*, he thought. He'd seen those on other occasions. But it definitely wasn't his wife standing in front of him, either.

"Are you a messenger from my wife?" Jason tried to hide a rising apprehension, but his tone betrayed him.

"Jason, it's me sweetie. Cathleen. I've had to use an out-of-body charm to come to you, but it's vital I return quickly to my physical being."

His voice was strained when he asked, "Where *are* you, love?"

Jason's alarm at what he'd heard so far from this spectral figure, grew with every passing second. Cathleen's image began to fade in and out and he almost thought he was imagining her. She was struggling to hold on to her ethereal projection.

"Not much time!" she continued as soon as she stabilized, but her voice was weaker. "I was kidnapped by Mason Mirage! I'm being held somewhere in the wine cellars of his mansion on the Mirage

Compound. I think he knows who I am, Jason. He called himself the *Witch Hunter*."

"Can you call on the Colossus Faeries, or one of the other Fey clans until I can get to you Cathleen?" Jason asked, an edge of panic creeping into his voice.

"I can't use my magic! This projection is all I can manage. You have to find me, my love. And Jason...bring the Historian!"

Those where Cathleen's last words before her body shimmered and disappeared, leaving Jason and Cromwell staring into the trees. Jason stood for a second longer while the surreal exchange settled into his brain. Pulling on the leash he said firmly, "Let's move, Cromwell. Your mistress is in trouble!" The Wolfhound whined softly acknowledging they were in crisis mode.

When they returned to the mud room, Jason quickly unhooked the leash from the dog's collar. He watched as Cromwell returned to his bed in front of the stone fireplace. Pulling off his wet boots, he put on sturdy hiking boots. Grabbing the cell phone off the table, he called the Vet's home office and left a message to arrange for the Doc to drive by the house and collect Cromwell for indefinite boarding. The Vet was an old friend and had a key for just such impromptu requests. Jason remembered to switch to his old wool hunting jacket after a quick call to his Deputy informing him of a family emergency. He shoved the cell phone into a pocket from force of habit. He knew there was no way to reach their friend Will Farley, by simple phone call. The only alternative flashed through his mind; *Magic will have to be used if I want to reach him in time.*

Will Farley had returned to the Outlander Wizard Scouts a few years ago, as the Master Scout. His predecessor had been murdered on the dangerous job. Known to the wizarding community as the Historian, Will formed a close friendship with Jason and Cathleen. They worked on several investigations involving the paranormal and had come to value their close relationship over the years. Contacting him if he was on patrol hunting Demons would prove difficult, but not impossible. For these kinds of emergency trips, Cathleen created a charmed space in their house, where they could catch a Time Thread to travel anywhere on a moment's notice. "A private jet for magic users," she called it.

Cromwell was already asleep by the hearth. The logs glowed warmly from Jason's earlier fire and he added a few more before leaving the sleeping dog to race upstairs. When he got to the end of the hallway, he pulled down the ladder to the attic. After a minute of searching through the dust motes, he sensed the Time Thread's location by its energy signature. Cathleen had tied it to an old headboard tucked under the eaves. He reached out to grab it. In the gloom of the low-ceilinged room, it immediately glittered like a string of diamonds, waving in the gentle air currents his movements stirred in the crowded space. He didn't relish trips on the Time Thread, but this one couldn't be avoided. He felt the pulse of magic in the shimmering rope as he secured it firmly around his waist and grabbed it tightly in both hands. Mentally focusing on Will Farley's rugged face, he sent out a thought command to communicate his destination.

The Thread blinked out of sight with a muffled popping sound. He had to trust the Thread would deposit him in the vicinity of his friend, if not on his doorstep. The pressure of the shift through time, and the space between, felt like it was crushing the living breath out of him. Suffering through the initial disorienting seconds, he consciously loosened his muscles for the coming drop. There was the expected muted pop and Jason knew he had arrived. He was in a half-crouch when a deep voice rasped out of a thick ground mist that swirled around him.

"Don't move a muscle! Don't even breath hard."

Chapter 3

Jason recognized the voice immediately but decided not to provoke any unwanted reaction by spinning around.

He said, "Greetings, Historian!"

A large hand grabbed his shoulder, forcing him to turn. Jason was face to face with a tall, swarthy man, wearing a distinctive uniform. The fit of the green jacket and brown pants emphasized the heavy musculature of his legs and broad chest. His shoulder-length dark brown hair was tied in a tail with a leather strip.

"Jason! By the Mother's green love, it's you!"

The reserved Historian sounded downright jubilant to see his friend. Theirs was a friendship forged by deep mutual respect, and in the fires of many shared experiences of danger and regrets.

"No one has called me by that moniker since our days together hunting the Deceiver! I am called by my official title these days, my friend; a title I both enjoy and am honored to be named."

"I'll try to reschool my brain Will, but I guess you'll always be the Historian to me and Cathleen."

"Whatever you name me, it's truly good to clap eyes on you once again, my friend! And where is the lovely Protector, Cathleen O'Brien?" Will asked, looking intently at Jason.

Jason lost his smile and the worry he held in check replaced his wide grin. "Will, that's why I'm here. Cathleen's been kidnapped by a man calling himself the *Witch Hunter*. His name is Mason Mirage and Cathleen's being held somewhere on a remote compound he built in the mountains around Iron Mountain. Cathleen came to me in her Spirit Body, because she can't use her magic to free herself. She told me to bring you along on this rescue mission, Will..."

"If the Protector of the Green has summoned me, my duty is to answer her call, my friend! Give me leave to contact my Scouts to make them aware of my coming absence. My Second can oversee Scout expeditions for however long it takes us to free the Protector and capture or destroy this so-called Witch Hunter!"

He stepped away from Jason to reach out to his subordinates via hologram. He told Jason he didn't want to divulge his presence to anyone, especially any Demon-Spawn that might have crossed the borders into First realm.

"You'd make tempting prey my friend, being the Protector's mate."

While the Historian spoke to various aides, Jason reflected on what he learned over the years about this elite band of Defenders. The Scouts were all specially trained wizards with enhanced powers, mostly geared toward military encounters and creative espionage tactics. Their job was destroying demons infiltrating from the Fourth Realm and the Dark Pit of the Sleepless Dead. He knew Cathleen's mother Brighid had been an Outlander Wizard Scout when she met Liam O'Brien, the youngest sitting member of the Council of Green Wizards at the time. Brighid had a broad range of gifts, making her stand out in the ranks and become a well-known target of the Dark Ones. The perfected hologram charm the Historian used now was one of Brigid's many contributions to the Scouts and wizarding community. Cathleen was well schooled in this spell, giving Jason shivers whenever she suddenly appeared to him in that gossamer state.

The Historian was speaking with his Second, after alerting his Personal Aid of his plans to absent himself on a special mission. Jason wasn't used to hearing such dated language and had to remind himself this man was probably over five-hundred years old. The Historian looked as trim and vital as any active man of forty. The longevity of the wizards of the Green was one of the gifts they enjoyed from the Green Mother. Naturally, their great age colored most aspects of their lives, including their formal manner of speaking.

"I am ready to accompany you, Jason. Since you are still tethered to the Time Thread, we'll just use that for this trip. Where will you take us?"

That was a good question and Jason hoped his target was the right one.

"Cathleen's somewhere in a two-hundred-acre area of wild mountain country. When she came to me, she said she was being held in Mirage's mansion. It's set nearly in the center of that area. I'll get us to within two or three miles of the property boundaries. That should give us time to do reconnaissance around the area before we make a move toward the main buildings."

With a curt nod, the Historian grabbed the shimmering Thread and looped part of it around his waist. Jason fixed the picture of the rugged ground around the estate in his mind. He realized that his exploration of the area over the long period of its construction would be paying off. He focused on the last spot he visited within a few miles of the compound's border, where it nudged up against the unpopulated outskirts of the town. The sudden weightlessness and compression of air from his lungs lasted less than a minute, but as always, made him feel like he was drowning. The welcome popping noise announced their arrival. Both men landed in crouched positions as they looked around themselves. Jason led the big Scout to an area the construction crews used as a dump site inside a shallow valley, ringed with heavy forest, and well-hidden from view.

It was a cluttered burial site for several hundreds of old-growth trees, and tons of dirt and mountain foliage, clawed from the earth to make way for the numerous buildings on the compound. The site was peppered with enormous debris mounds, added to by the many bulldozers parked nearby to make way for more of the devastation they visited upon the woods. Jason felt uneasy walking through the uprooted vegetation and displaced rocks and boulders. Everywhere he looked, nature had been torn away from its created habitat to accommodate this arrogant billionaire. The Historian must have had a similar response to the forest graveyard. His face was dark with anger as he stepped around recently felled trees, and still-smoldering ash piles several feet deep.

Jason interrupted the Historian's somber thoughts with, "We need to cover about two miles before we reach the compound's outer fencing. From what I saw, they've installed a mechanized perimeter fence in that area. Once we get past that, I'm pretty certain there's a secondary barrier to get over before we can get to the grounds around the mansion."

As they moved away from the debris field, Jason filled the Historian in on what he found during his earlier reconnaissance.

"When the advance team of construction workers arrived, I started to investigate the man building in our backyard. There were no recent pictures of Mirage, but several news items showing photos of him hunting. I did find one story by a reporter who interviewed him ten years ago. He called him a ruthless egotist, who bullied everyone. The reason it caught my eye was because that same reporter was found dead a few days after his story was published. Apparent heart attack …he was thirty-four."

They shadowed a rough-cut road that led down the side of a hill, and to a smaller burn site. Just beyond was the first perimeter fencing, a stretched barbed-wire barrier that looked like it went on for miles. Except for small black boxes set at intervals, high and low along the fence line, it didn't look as if it would be much trouble to get through. To test that theory, Jason picked up a stout limb to simulate a man's body mass. He heaved it directly into the fence. The black boxes spun simultaneously in the direction of the limb, where it hung off the barbs. Each box released a knife-thin red beam at the pseudo-intruder. The limb burst into flame and before either of the men watching could take their next breath, it disintegrated into a fine gray ash. Jason looked over at Will who registered a similar reaction to the toasty reception they would have received if he hadn't been cautious.

"Guess we'd better double down on our precautions Will. This guy uses some seriously lethal methods to guard his privacy."

Jason recalled a wide stream to the north of the main buildings. He mentally filed it away as a possible access path into the heart of the sprawling grounds if the need arose.

Before they moved too far, the Historian asked, "Jason, do you suspect this man has any magical abilities? I've been sensing some power surges in the atmosphere as we draw closer to his manor house. It's definitely not the Protector's magical trace."

Jason admitted that while he'd kept tabs on the construction of the compound, he'd only gathered local gossip and speculative Internet information about the man himself.

"He's definitely unconventional, but nothing of a paranormal nature has ever been reported. He's a ruthless hunter of rare game. That reporter who turned up dead also wrote that Mirage was suspected of bribing tribal leaders and heads of governments so he could hunt with impunity. The guy has no moral compass. I did some friendly questioning of the workers I bumped into on the occasions they came into town. A few of the older guys mentioned a trophy room they'd seen, after it was furnished. They said there were easily a hundred heads on the walls. There's also as many as seventy-five animals on display that he's had preserved by a taxidermist. The workers couldn't identify most of them."

The Historian listened closely as they trekked toward the stream. Finally, he shared his thoughts.

"Jason, using her Spirit Body to reach-out to you, indicates the Protector is being held in some sort of magically secured cell, prohibiting her access to her powers as she indicated to you."

Jason thought about that possibility before saying, "My snooping didn't turn up anything pointing in that direction. No mention of him dabbling in the occult or hinting at any interest in the mystical."

They walked on a few minutes before Jason added, "There is one thing though. I heard that a few of the regulars that visited town, suddenly took off without giving notice to their foreman. Guess it's possible something in that place spooked them."

"My friend, I don't wish to alarm you unduly, but it occurs to me this man may have turned his rapacious eye on another rare child of the Mother. If somehow he's uncovered Cathleen's role as a Wizard of the Green, it may have ignited his greed to the point of acting to capture her."

A sickening vision of Cathleen's beautiful head hanging on a trophy wall, flashed across Jason's mind. He groaned aloud, "No!"

Chapter 4

Cathleen felt the jarring presence of her Spirit-Body, sluggishly seeping into her rigid form. It felt like ice splinters flowing through her veins. She hadn't done an out-of-body journey for quite some time, and then, only to gather intelligence. Her very life depended on its outcome this time. Her mind prickled with anticipation of becoming fully alive. When she felt whole once more, she stretched her muscles as best she could without being obvious. She didn't want her captor knowing she was fully awake. It was better to keep him guessing about the sudden onset of her comatose state. Cathleen sensed she was alone, but the sharp odor of Mirage's distinct after-shave jumped out of the gloom behind her eyelids. She fought the urge to wrinkle her noise at the musky undertones of the fragrance. *Mirage must have been checking on my condition.* After listening for any footsteps outside the room, she decided to try a new approach to escaping.

Being double jointed would be her key to success. *The chains can't be broken, but if I can get one hand lose…*Cathleen pulled her right hand slowly, until it stopped at the cuff attached to the titanium chain. Her dad used to say her magically enhanced, double-jointed ability, was worthy of a circus act. She used this gift sparingly because of the pain that inevitably followed.

By concentrating on the bones of her hand she began the deliberate, torturous process of compressing them closer and closer together. The shape of her small hand became elongated. The fingers appeared to be fused, until gradually, with one last pull, the hand slipped through the restraining cuff. She froze, wondering if anyone observed her action. Only the soft hum of a generator somewhere in the vicinity reached her acute hearing.

Cathleen performed the same process on the left hand. When they were both free, looking deformed and throbbing with pain, she rested before murmuring a healing charm and pulling the bones back into proper alignment. Keeping her arms at her sides gave the appearance of still being bound. She was careful not to come into contact with the titanium chains. Because she still wore her boots, she could work on her feet without being seen. Three minutes later, sweat glistening on her forehead, Cathleen slipped both feet out of her boots. Not able to use her magic yet, she cringed when they dropped the floor. They sounded like canon shots, one, then the other, blasting the quiet into shards of echoes. She knew someone was bound to come, but now she was ready! Her healing spell quickly mended the compressed bones and she shoved her throbbing feet into the soft leather boots and ran to the door.

She was right in guessing she'd been held in some sort of cell, but she underestimated its size. Like the rest of Mirage Compound, it was overly large. Most of the room was hidden in shadow, and Cathleen wondered if there were other tables like the one she just escaped. She took a second to scan the cell using her Inner Eye, spotting six other tables, their titanium restraints dangling idly. *He must have thought I'd bring company*, she thought grabbing the handle on the door and poking her head out. Once outside Cathleen took a moment to orient herself to the layout of the cellar. She thanked the Mother that her magic had been fully restored, but something nagged at her. She felt it had to do with her powers as a Celtic Wizard but had to let it go and focus on her escape.

Mirage brought her down here on the pretense of touring his wine collection. Cathleen remembered the elevator they rode in. Things were still somewhat blurry in her memory from whatever drug he injected into her, but she recalled the elevator opened into a hallway with numerous closed doors. A picture of the first door flashed in her mind. *Bordeaux* on a fancy gold plate hanging above a wood door. Her thoughts were interrupted by a muted sound coming from somewhere in the subterranean complex. Hurrying down the hall, she finally located the Bordeaux sign among the countless door plates she passed. Stepping into a climate-controlled room, she was relieved it only held rows of bottles nestled into snug wooden beds. Cathleen peaked through the narrow opening she left, checking for any movement in the hallway. The air in the room resonated with the heady fragrance of recently uncorked bottles. *Wonder if he was celebrating my capture*? She realized with a jolt, her mind was wandering, still under the influence of what must have been a powerful drug.

It was only a matter of time before Mirage would return to check on his prisoner. Cathleen shivered when she recalled the gleam of blood-lust in Mirage's eyes as he described his hunting expeditions. He insisted on showing her his Gun Room, with its mounted heads of glassy-eyed animals staring out upon their own oblivion. The vague memory of how she'd been taken prisoner, suddenly pierced the fog left by the drug. She'd been morbidly fascinated by the death staring back at her, like a witness to an awful accident. And then she felt the sudden jab of a sharp needle enter the side of her neck. What had been nettling her since she regained consciousness, now floated up like a soap bubble. *He said he would hang my head on the Wall of Magic Users in his* real *trophy room!* "Dear Mother," she whispered. "Are there others like me here?"

Before her imagination could conjure a scene of mounted wizard heads, the sound of the elevator making its decent close by jarred her into action. Calling the shadows scattered around the rows of bottles, she used a spell to weave them into a Shadow Wrap. She threw this over her head like a tent, completely concealing herself before stepping back into the hallway. There was no way she wanted to be trapped in that room with him or any of his henchmen. She heard the gentle whoosh of the lift door. A second later, the tall, corpulent figure of Mason Mirage stepped into the hall.

In her ill-fated interview with him, Mirage wore a dark, scrupulously tailored suit. She pegged him then as an over-fed, self-important man. Watching him now, it was as if he'd been concealing his powerful physique under the double-breasted business suite. Ominously, he wore the khaki pants and shirt, with the iconic numerous pockets and flaps, of a safari hunter. His shaved head reflected the recessed lighting in the hallway, appearing too small for his body's girth. He turned his head slowly, checking the hallway in both directions. Cathleen noticed the large diamond stud he wore in his left ear. It looked out of place earlier with his fine-worsted suit, and more so now, in his hunting gear.

Although she knew he couldn't see her while the Shadow Wrap was in place, she felt a moment of panic when he looked around the hall. She couldn't allow herself to forget for a minute he was a man with a hunter's instincts and would be alerted to changes in his environment. He also had a clear understanding of how titanium would impede her magic. Cathleen took a deep breath as the big man passed close to her. He disappeared around the corner and would reach the cell she escaped in less-than three minutes. She couldn't take the elevator, not knowing what would await her upstairs. It opened into the foyer where guards were probably posted. Cathleen spotted several uniformed men from a distance as she waited for the wrought-iron gate to open. They must have been on the lookout for her arrival. Several other guards were moving around the immediate grounds of the mansion. It had taken a few minutes to drive the private road to the mansion, and she counted at least fifteen guards along the way. *They sure aren't here to add glamor to the place!* she thought grimly, moving along the hallway, willing herself to be absorbed by the shadows.

She passed several rooms with plaques naming a rare vintage and wouldn't have noticed one more except for the absence of the gold plate on the door. Instead, this door had very distinct markings and looked out of place among the others. There were beautifully carved runes, deeply embedded in a dark black wood. Cathleen stopped to decipher them. They were clearly a mix of Druid and some kind of mystical symbols unknown to her. She was able to make a rough translation from the context of the familiar words. Her voice came out in a strangled gasp, "Sidhe sean. Magical Treasures!"

Chapter 5

Cathleen decided the room marked Magical Treasures might offer her the unexpected benefit of hiding in plain sight. It would also give her a chance to determine if Mirage held other Magic users. She didn't relish taking the risk, but it was her duty as Protector to help those who served the Mother. She was certain Mason Mirage was a total psychopath who used the Dark Arts. She speculated the use of such darkness was a contributing factor in achieving his tremendous wealth.

She returned the Wrap to its natural state and watched as the dark shadows dropped away from her, scuttling like mice toward a corner. With a flick of her wrist the door swung inward and she stepped inside. When the door closed with a huff of air behind her, she found herself in a small antechamber. Her entrance likely triggered the fiercely bright light that sprang into life. Squinting against the eye-searing glare, she surveyed the six-foot-square foyer. The walls appeared seamless, with no obvious door leading into the main room. Even the door she used to enter had vanished into the starkly white walls. Cathleen had an unsettling sense of being inside a gift box. A vague notion entered her head, that this was some kind of de-tox space before being allowed to enter the room beyond. Her suspicions proved correct when a soft droning tickled the air, followed by several flat-headed nozzles dropping down directly overhead. She looked for other surprises, finding a recessed storage area where two dazzling-white coveralls hung like newly risen ghosts. Thinking of the hazmat suit Jason kept at the Sheriff's office, she wondered why Mirage would go to such lengths to ensure the purity of the trophies. Or was all of this an effort to protect himself from whatever was in there? She likely used-up any time she had to deactivate any alarm set by entering the scrub-room. Cathleen had a hunch that anyone going beyond this point would need to wear a coverall, and then punch in a pass code before entering. If that sequence wasn't followed within a few minutes... She dropped a Dome of Protection over herself. If those nozzles sent jets of some kind of paralyzing toxin at anyone entering without the proper authorization, she was ready.

There's no way I can trust this guy not to set a death trap, she thought as the Dome sealed around her. She stirred the outside air with a quick, fan-like sweep of her hand. The nozzles instantly released a yellow vapor that clung in tiny globules to every surface including the protective sphere. She waited a minute for them to turn off. Working from within the Dome, she used a cleansing spell to rid the room and air in the small space of all trace of the mustard-colored spray. Assured it was completely safe, she dropped the Dome.

Cathleen still had the key-pad code to crack. There was a charm her dad used successfully to enter restricted areas around Verdant Keep, the castle headquarters of the Council of Green Wizards. As a newly accepted and youngest ever Council member, he denied access to secret parts of the enclave until he'd been properly initiated. The wards set in place were complicated for the purpose of frustrating any curiosity. Liam O'Brien was up to his ears in curiosity! Cathleen murmured his unique spell now.

"Deiseal Caoi...open the pathway hidden within."

Numbers on the pad began to light up. Cathleen smiled when the wall to her right slid into the narrow pocket that concealed it. The Magical Treasures collection lay beyond. She hung back, not sure she wanted to go rushing in. Her hesitation gave her time to spot a narrow red beam slowly sweeping the area. There were only seconds before it would reach her. *Another way to identify visitors.* A heartbeat before it would move across her body, Cathleen dropped to her stomach. Jumping to her feet when it cleared the space, she darted into the room. The door closed with a hiss behind her and the red light vanished. Cathleen stood up but felt a twinge of concern when she heard a clicking sound, realizing the door automatically locked behind her.

"Hope that won't be a problem," she whispered to herself.

She knew Mirage would have discovered her escape by now, and a search had likely begun. Before she could think of her own safety, Cathleen had to establish if there were others here like her. Mirage had all but said there were other magic users taken prisoner for a hunt. She moved further into the room to start her search.

The lighting was scant, leaving much of the room in a murky state. She'd had the briefest glimpse of the interior when she stood on the threshold for that split second. It appeared empty except for several large, glass-fronted display cases. As she moved closer she saw their shapes more clearly. They were lined up like silent sentinels in two rows. She counted ten but figured there were others under the shadows at the back of the room. Cathleen walked over to the nearest case for a closer look. Peering in, she discovered it was much deeper than it seemed at first glance. Whatever was inside was lost under a masking of darkness the low lighting couldn't penetrate. She pressed her face closer and gently taped on the glass. She swallowed a scream and jumped back when something hit the heavy viewing window before returning to the depths of the case. *He's keeping live specimens in here?* she thought frantically.

As she was about turn away to investigate the next box, a low moan came out of the darkness, sending a chill down her spine. It was not the frightened distress of a caged wild animal, but the keening of a human. Needing to see more clearly than the inky interior allowed, Cathleen called for the Sacred Green Fire. A small green flame flared into life, nestled inside her palm. She raised it slightly to see into the depths of the case. The face and upper body of a woman floated out of the murky recesses. Her hair was very black. A stark white streak ran back from a widow's peak and was woven into a long braid lying on her shoulder and reaching her waist. Wide dark eyes stared boldly back at Cathleen. They were filled with fear and desperation.

And something else.

Hate.

Chapter 6

Jason shadowed the Historian as they moved along the outer-perimeter fence surrounding the Mirage compound, searching for a weakness. Will was hesitant to use his magic and draw unwelcome attention to their presence. The pair already discovered it was more than just a barbed, electrified fence. It was rigged with some kind of high-tech lasers that would incinerate anything, or anyone, trying to get over it.

Will's irritated tone revealed his frustration as he said, "This man Mirage is more than a little serious about his privacy! We can't waste more time trying to find a way in without making our intrusion obvious. I'll take care of disarming a part of this fence and we can proceed."

Jason nodded his agreement and Will raised his arms toward the deadly barrier. Some of the words he whispered were very familiar to Jason after six years of life with a wizard, but he wasn't prepared for the spectacular results. A section between two of the ominous black boxes began to shake violently. Sharp snapping sounds crackled in the air and a shower of red and yellow sparks sprayed the ground around them. A burst of bright light bloomed at each end of the section. The boxes shimmered as a rainbow arc linked the two units. Jason squinted his eye against the intense flares of light. When he looked again, both boxes were reduced to puddles of black sludge smeared over heavy gage wire and ground. He was shocked to see a small doe lying among the scorched material. As the Historian crossed over the downed section, he called back to him.

"Something had to create this mess Jason, hence, the doe. But have no fear, I sacrificed none of the Mother's creatures. This one is merely a useful conjuring. I hope the next barrier comes down as easily.

I fear the closer we get to the main compound, the more resistance we'll meet."

Jason blinked away the shock of the flashes and wondered if any guards witnessed the tiny cataclysms that occurred along the line. The whole unit was likely hooked up to a bank of computers somewhere inside the compound.

"Let's head west, Will. As I recall, the workers were preparing a small airstrip closer to the main buildings. We need to make sure Mirage won't take off in his private jet with Cathleen on board."

The Historian gave his companion a sobering look saying, "Jason, like you, I've been a hunter my whole life. I believe Mirage will not harm Cathleen until he's enjoyed the thrill of hunting her. He must have uncovered her true identity, and the only way that was possible was through the use of the Dark Arts and torture."

His words hit Jason with an unthinkable possibility and he asked, "You think he's captured other Magic Users, and they told him about Cathleen?"

"It's highly probable my friend. She said he referred to himself as *The Witch Hunter*. Once he uncovered the existence of Cathleen O'Brien, and her role as Protector of the Green, sheer ego would drive him to bag the greatest prize of all, the Witch of Appalachia!"

They passed carefully through the dense woods barely breaking a twig underfoot. Arriving at a prominent drop-off with a view of the valley, they huddled behind a mound of uprooted vegetation, left in earlier excavations by the ground crews. Jason was pleased to see how quickly nature reclaimed the hill, with newly reseeded wild berry bushes and tree saplings. Searching for a way down to the valley floor, he spotted what he recognized as a well camouflaged bunker. Cleverly built into the easiest descent, a trespasser using this route would have to pass directly in front.

"We need a diversion so we can get down to the valley without being picked-off," Jason said.

"I think I have just the thing, my friend," the Historian replied, a sly smile softening the hard lines etched into his handsome face.

Jason watched as the big man closed his eyes, inhaling deeply. His exhaled breath carried a hum into the stillness, while he moved his hands like a music conductor. A blurry form began to take shape and by his last word a tawny buck stood nearby, twitching his tail and ready to flee down the incline in front of them. Jason heard the Historian hiss, "Run!" just before the conjured deer sprang into life. It made enough noise in its flight that by the time it neared the bunker, two rifle barrels were jutting from concealed window slits like thorns on a stem. With Jason leading, they took off down the slope, their movements masked by the buck's. They were deeper into the woods when the sound of rapid gun fire sent a few roosting birds into flight. After several minutes hiking downward, Jason stopped. The Historian stepped closer. His thick eyebrows furrowed with a question and concern.

"Will, something just occurred to me. My Deputy told me he overheard some workers discussing how Mirage brought in two specialized teams for the sole purpose of installing barriers. We'll likely be coming up to another one soon, and it may be more difficult to get around."

Will responded with a curt nod and they moved on until they stepped out of the thinning tree line, slightly above the valley. Staying near the fringe of tree cover, Jason studied the sweep of the land's depression, spotting a stream and several areas dotted with huge boulders. He estimated the valley encompassed at least one-hundred acres of idyllic landscape. Early spring field grasses, flowering trillium and thick patches of wood-nettle carpeted the area. A few azalea and rhododendron bushes were starting to bloom where the sunlight was most intense. It reminded him that spring was settling among the rugged mountains of Appalachia. Bird calls and chittering squirrels punctuated his thoughts, giving him a feeling of normalcy. He was still vigilant in these forests. Along with the resident black bears, he guessed the extensive compound grounds were now crawling with mercenary guards.

The Historian slipped into the lead. Jason knew his friend was a truly skillful woodsman. He carefully picked his way over anything that might give away their presence. A rolling rock, bent tree branches and footprints were avoided, moved, or wiped out with a wave of his hand. Fortunately, his Outlander Wizard Scout's uniform was a combination of forest hues, perfect for a trek through the woods. He noticed earlier the insignia of the Scouts was displayed on the jacket's breast pocket, showing the Druid's Sacred Yew Tree, with bolts of green lightning shooting from its branches. Jason was impressed with how quickly Will adapted to this environment. He'd come directly from the rocky borderlands he'd been patrolling, but seemed as comfortable here, where he had to negotiate territory heavily covered with trees, boulders and wild vegetation. With the fast-paced Will kept, Jason knew his friend was likely at home in any environment, natural or otherwise.

He nearly collided with the fast-moving Historian when he stopped abruptly. He crouched to one knee, grabbed Jason's forearm, and dragging him down with him. Without a word the Historian pointed straight ahead at a deer blind several yards off, tucked in among a thick cluster of spruce. As well blended as it was with the surrounding foliage and fir boughs, Jason knew a less astute eye would have missed seeing it altogether. As if proving that point, a white tail doe, followed by two yearlings, passed between the blind and their position several yards away. The doe was alert, but gracefully bent her head to browse among the mosses and any grass shoots she nosed. She clearly did not sense any danger.

There was no hunter of deer inside that blind, but Jason was certain there was a presence. As he studied the rough shack for movement, he saw the doe jerk her head up. Alerted to danger, all three deer bounded off in the direction they came from. Jason nudged the

Historian, gesturing with his chin to a slight incline on their left. They searched for whatever caused the deer to panic. Their eyes settled on a large oak at the top of the rise. The lower branches swayed sharply in the windless air. Jason looked over at Will Farley as he silently mouthed a spell. A few seconds later, Jason felt the chilling sensation of a Shadow Wrap dropping over them. They were now invisible while they waited to see who, or what, materialized.

Watching the area around the big oak tree, they saw the branches sway again. This time it was as if a swing was attached. Suddenly, a shrill whistle cut through the silence. The Historian slipped his hand down his thigh, pulling his long knife out of its sheath. Jason knew the many symbols decorating the blade meant it had magical attributes besides being deadly sharp. Jason's weapon was the gold signet ring of the deceased Arch Wizard, Sir Alex Portchamp. It was awarded to him by the Council of Green Wizards, in recognition of his contributions in Cathleen's last mission. As beautiful as it was, he only wore it during investigations of a Paranormal nature, and strictly for defensive purposes. It allowed him to access deeply rooted powers within himself, transforming that power into a formidable weapon.

After the high-pitched whine, Jason felt the ring heat on his finger. Looking down, he saw that the emerald set into its wide gold band was beginning to throw out shafts of green light. He quickly covered it, turning it around on his finger and making a tight fist. *A Magic User is coming*, he thought. He didn't need to mention this to the Historian who would have picked up the trace of magic just before he slid out the long knife. Jason knew it wasn't Cathleen trying to move into the present time and space as they watched. He had no sense of her nearness. But he knew when magic was in play and the chances were good whoever was in the deer blind was going to have a visitor.

Chapter 7

"Jason," the Historian's hushed voice cut through the deep silence. "This is not magic I'm familiar with. Whoever is crossing into our time knows how to manipulate space and time movement but is using an unfamiliar magic to bend these to their will. They must be very powerful. Be ready to protect yourself." He looked over at the hidden deer blind adding, "This is bound to stir-up some response from the guards."

The oak tree's sturdy branches were still bare, just beginning to show their furled leaves. The branches shook like a child's rattle, making loud swishing sounds as they battered the silence. Jason wondered how long it would be before the mystery sorcerer was revealed, when the shaking abruptly stopped. A thick, reddish vapor filled the area under the still trembling branches, gradually resolving into a shape. By the time Jason blinked twice, the magic user fully materialized.

A strikingly beautiful Native American woman, perhaps in her late thirties, stood like a newly installed garden statue. High cheek bones and a small straight nose emphasized wide, dark eyes. A startling white streak ran through her hair, back from a sharp widow's peak and woven in a thick braid of blue-black hair. The lustrous braid brushed the intricate beading across the bodice of a knee-length, deer-skin dress, falling to a slim waist. She wore thick-soled moccasins with the same colorful beading around the tops. A leather pouch hung from a wide beaded belt. Jason noticed her protective gesture when she pressed it close to her side. Familiar with several Native American cultures, Jason studied the beadwork patterns and concluded she was a Navajo Medicine Woman. If so, the pouch was her medicine bundle. He glanced over his shoulder at the Historian expecting some kind of response to this lovely magic user. Will had a far-off look and seemed lost in his thoughts as he stared. Jostling his arm to get his attention, Jason jerked his chin at the hidden guard post after hearing some stirring from that direction.

The camouflaged door boldly creaked open. Two men stepped into the sunlight that dappled the ground between trees. Their backs were to the watching men, but it was clear the tall guard was in charge. He motioned for his shorter companion to move further away, likely to keep his shooting field unobstructed. The smaller guard was quick to scuttle off like a crab. Jason noted they were armed with semi-automatic rifles. He got a good look at their para-military uniforms after they spread out to face the woman. There was a distinctive logo of a bloody scythe on the khaki jackets. Under that, the slogan *Live to Kill, Kill to Live*. A not-so-subtle message of these death bringers. *No Semper Fi, for these creeps*, he thought. He immediately redirected his attention back to the mysterious woman, thirty feet from the two guards.   She looked supremely indifferent to their threatening presence. Jason followed her line of vision, realizing her eyes were riveted instead to where he and Will Farley were hunkering down. She wore a slight smile. The guards raised their guns higher when she finally looked in their direction.

"Step a…way…from… the tree. Put…hands on…head!" the leader shouted.

He had a curiously accented voice. The command sounded choppy and guttural, like he was strangling on the words. Jason watched the pair as they shuffled their feet to get closer to her. He realized they both moved with a kind of jerky motion, as if they found walking unnatural. The armed men shifted closer to where Jason and the Historian hid. As they stepped into a brighter patch of sunlight, Jason was struck by their sickly pallor. Instead of the weathered look of mercenaries used to fighting in any climate, there was a greenish tinge to their complexions. When the leader looked over at his comrade,

Jason was able to see his eyes more clearly. They were as lifeless as a fish's hanging from a pole.

The woman was not intimidated in the least by the guards. In a blur of movement, Jason saw her hurl a disk-shaped object at the leader. A split second later his head fell to the ground, quickly followed by his twitching body. Before the other mercenary could react, another disk launched. A surprised look etched across his face as his newly detached head rolled under some scruffy bushes. His body made a soft thud accompanied by the sound of snapping twigs when it tumbled backward, hitting hard among a scattering of large rocks and stumps. Several bones jutting out of the torn fabric of his uniform. The bones were yellowed, as if they'd been buried and disinterred after many years. The Historian watched intently as each guard was taken down and leaned toward Jason, never taking his eyes off the exotic beauty.

"This woman has extraordinary abilities. I sense her magic is bound to the Green Mother."

"Is she a friend then?"

Before Will could reply to the whispered question, the woman was standing within touching distance. Both men jumped up and backward.

"I'm a friend. Cathleen O'Brien rescued me and asked that I find you both," she said in a soft voice.

Hearing his wife's name, Jason stepped closer, saying, "Before we go further, who are you and where is Cathleen?"

Her voice was calm and pleasing to the ear as she said, "My name is Star Fire among my people. Others call me Starla White. I am known as a *hataalii*, or *singer*, to my clan, the Coyote Stone People. Simply put, I am a Navajo Medicine Woman."

She turned her dark eyes on the Historian adding, "And to answer your speculation, Will Farley, my powers are linked to Shima Nahasdzaan, the Great Mother Earth, just as yours are. You both have many questions, but we need to return to the main compound. Be prepared, we will encounter others of these obscene creatures patrolling the woods before we can reach the big house."

The Historian blocked her way as she began to move. Looking down at the petite woman, he spoke unhurriedly in his rich, deep voice.

"Starla White, while I am unfamiliar with your powers as a Medicine Woman, I trust what I have seen. However, you need to answer some questions before we can follow you. First, what are these guards you dispatched so effectively?"

The Medicine Woman looked into Will's dark brown eyes. She seemed to be considering how to respond to his curt manner.

"The creatures you saw me destroy were two of the Undead, hand-picked and brought back as Zombies by Dark Powers. They were part of a small army formed from among the most violent and evil humans to draw breath. Many were put to death for their crimes. Most were military elite who savaged their own country's citizens on the orders of some dictator."

The Historian asked, "Are all of Mirage's guards from among these…Undead warriors?"

"All except his right-hand man, Byron Bledsworth, the Architect of this hellish place. I suspect he's more than an architect though. I believe he practices the Dark Arts along with Mirage and is the one responsible for calling these Undead into service."

Jason had heard enough and turning to the Historian, "Will, I don't want to waste any more time. We need to get to Cathleen before she runs into these two maniacs on her own!"

"Yes, my friend. Where will the Protector be?" Will asked, looking back at Starla.

"Cathleen told me to bring you to the wine cellar where Mirage has created a diabolical trophy room. That's where she found me. I believe she'll try to rescue any others she finds alive down there."

They moved at a brisk pace. As they traveled deeper into the woods their comments were muffled by the closeness of the surrounding trees. Jason followed directly behind Starla, with Will, close on his heels.

"What kind of trophies is this guy hunting, Starla?" he asked, his rapid breathing breaking into the words.

She hesitated for a moment before saying, "The Magic User kind!"

Chapter 8

Starla was gone a few minutes when the high wail of a siren exploded the silence of the underground warren and penetrated the thick walls of the Magical Treasures room where Cathleen listened to its blaring call. Roughly a half-hour had passed since her kidnapper walked by her while she hid in the dimly lit corridor. She assumed Mirage was on his way to check on her and wondered why it took so long to sound the alarm once he discovered her escape. It was as if it added to his thrills, to have her on the run. *Was he giving me a head start?* She felt a shudder at the thought of being no more than prey to this sociopathic predator.

Discovering the Magical Treasures room was a stroke of luck and releasing the Navajo Medicine Woman gave her one more ally in this deadly game. Cathleen was horrified to learn the large cases were meant for live captives. Special lighted mounts dotted the walls, ready to illuminate trophy heads from among these future victims. Using a tiny shoot of Sacred Fire, Cathleen read a plaque over the case that once held Starla. *Star Fire, Native American Shaman.*

"They're all lined with titanium," Starla confirmed earlier as they looked at the many cases.

Cathleen read a few more, moving down the line. She recognized the names of two highly ranked members of the Council of Green Wizards among them, relieved they remained empty. She wondered how many of the remaining wooden cages she'd find occupied.

Though their time together was brief, Cathleen felt an immediate trust for Starla White Fire. When she heard Jason and the Historian were likely heading for the compound, Starla volunteered to find them. "We'll need their help to face the Dark Powers that Mirage wields," she told Cathleen firmly.

Before she left, Cathleen asked if she knew how Mirage planned to hunt his prey.

"I found it helpful to pretend unconsciousness when the Dark Ones were nearby," Starla said. "I overheard Mirage tell the architect the time was drawing near for their hunt in the *Labyrinth of Lies*. In all my years of training to become a tribal Shaman, I've never heard of this evil place. Not until I was taken from my home and awoke in that wooden case."

Cathleen said Mirage mentioned the place while boasting after her capture.

"It sounds like a maze created exclusively for Mirage and Bledsworth, a confusing environment where they can hunt their quarry. I suspect I was to be the first trophy in their sick game, since I wasn't put into one of the holding cases."

When the siren stopped its wailing, Cathleen hurried to finish checking the remaining wooden cases. She peered inside the next one, using her Inner Eye to catch any signs of movement. The titanium lining had been covered in a black material, adding to the inky environment inside the deep containers. She knew her search would be a rushed job. Mirage would have his thugs scouring the grounds and buildings for his runaway Witch. Outside of two uniformed men that waved her through the gate as they watched from a distance, Cathleen had no idea how many guards roamed the estate. She knew Mirage would have no trouble hiring an army of mercenaries for his little kingdom.

The second case was empty, as were the next three. She was giving the next a hurried check, when a flash of movement caught her eye. Whatever it was moved into the darker recesses, six feet back. Cathleen brought the small green flame close to the thick panel of tempered glass and was rewarded when it found its current prisoner. A small man, clutching a long yellow robe around his spare frame stared back defiantly at her. The robe was covered in astrological symbols and signs for the elements, air, water, earth and fire. Cathleen was unsure of his age, but the few strands of wispy hair were white and his skin had the color and look of aged parchment.

"I'm here to free you," Cathleen said as loudly as she dared.

The frail man seemed to float to the front of the case. Closer, Cathleen saw he was indeed very old and likely a practitioner of an ancient Asian Mysticism. Her knowledge of these early magical arts was limited, since much of its practice was shrouded by time and lost to memory. As her father's apprentice, she was taught about every kind of magical practitioner known to the Wizards of the Green Mother, but this area of primeval magic was very sketchy. Cathleen was working on limited time. She murmured her spell and the heavy glass door swung wide. She extended her hand to help the frail looking man climb out of the case, but he ignored her, and with a thin smile floated out unassisted. He was no more than five feet tall, hunched over with the weight of his years. After a low bow to Cathleen, he introduced himself. His voice creaked like an old mill wheel. Cathleen bent down to hear him clearly.

"I am Li Shaoweng, servant and Wu in the Magical Occult in the Court of my Master, Liu Che. But this is dust and bones history. Identify yourself young wizard!"

Cathleen already had a memorable experience with a Chinese Sorcerer on a case involving a particularly nasty Chinese wizard named Fang. She dismissed any concerns with Li, as he wouldn't have been chosen by Mirage if he shared his dark side.

"With respect, Master Li, there's no time for long introductions. Just know I am one of the Mother's Wizards of the Green. Are there still others here?"

He studied her for a long moment as if weighing his response, "There is only one other, directly next to my prison box."

Cathleen went to the case. The room's dim lighting added shading, and the depth of the case made it black as pitch inside. Cathleen called up another small flame. She jumped back when a heavily muscled arm shot out, the palm of a huge hand smashing against the heavy glass. That shock was followed by another when she heard the muffled calling of her name.

"Cathleen O'Brien. You have come."

Cathleen came close to the glass door and face to face with a magic user she called friend, and in the past, had called upon as an ally. Her face and his were pressed close to the glass door when she breathed out his name.

"Geilt."

Chapter 9

The three were wrapped in the unnatural stillness permeating the woodlands they moved through. A small army of Undead was likely crawling over the two-hundred-acre compound. The Historian slipped into the rear position as they trekked single-file through a densely wooded area. From that distance, he could easily observe the Medicine Woman, Starla White. She set a fast pace for them, moving self-assuredly over difficult terrain. She proved so light-footed that even his keen ears never picked up more than an occasional rustle of dead leaves under her moccasin-clad feet. To a guard alert for noise of an intruder, her movements could easily pass for wildlife. He noticed the forest floor had taken on a gentle grade and wasn't surprised when Starla signaled a stop. He moved up beside Jason to find they stood at the edge of a sharp incline.

"The valley you see is well shielded by the forest here, and by the part of the mountain that its tucked into, like a Papoose strapped to its back," Starla said describing the scene below.

The Historian smiled to himself at her choice of analogies, thinking it an endearing observation. He refocused his attention as she continued to speak in a soft voice, as if wary the noticeably stronger wind-gusts would carry her words to unseen ears.

"Before I found you, I was able to study the area surrounding Mirage's main house and buildings. He has chosen this lowland carefully, and I suspect has created his hunting grounds somewhere in the valley itself. He named those grounds The Labyrinth of Lies."

The Historian and Jason exchanged concerned looks. Jason's voice was firm despite his anxiety for his spouse. "Starla, are you saying Mirage built some kind of *maze* to hunt humans in?"

"That is what both Cathleen and I believe. The grounds surrounding the main buildings will be heavily patrolled. We need to proceed with extreme caution as we get closer. The big house will be within view in a short while. From what I observed, it's well hidden, even from aerial view, by natural and man-built camouflage."

The two men had more questions, but Starla told them there was little time for asking them. She explained once they reached the sprawling mansion it would mean slowing their pace considerably if they were to remain undetected.

Their progress was already vexingly slow to Jason, as they started their descent to the valley floor. He watched Starla's back as she carefully climbed over some jutting rocks. He knew the Shaman was capable of using her magic to travel as she'd already proven, but guessed she probably wanted to stay close in case of other guard encounters. The Historian's baritone voice broke into Jason's thoughts.

"Starla, will there be other captive magic users in need of our help?"

The Medicine Woman stopped walking. She turned, letting her dark eyes rest on Will's face for a second before she responded. Her own face betrayed her anger.

"There are only two others left. Yesterday, before Cathleen found me, two guards took the red-bearded Warlock they called Peacock from the Trophy room. I saw them place a bracelet around his right wrist before they dragged him out. I'm certain it was fashioned from a thin strip of titanium. He won't be able to access his powers as long as he wears it. That will be one of the challenges facing the captives. To free themselves of the bracelet...any way they can."

Jason had a sickening vision of the man with the red beard trying to slice off his own hand. He asked Starla if Cathleen was wearing one of these on her wrist.

"Cathleen is free of any impediments to her magic, or I would not be with you now."

They stopped beneath a cluster of boulders when they reached the valley floor, keeping to the shadows of the rocks while scanning the area ahead. Several small buildings dotted the area where guards shuffling about in that strange gait of the Undead they noted earlier. Closer to the edge of the boulders where they hunkered down were two enormous garages, as wide as airplane hangars. The double-doors were open on both, showing pieces of heavy equipment parked inside each. The sunlight winked off the metal bodies. Jason could make out a dozen bulldozers, a number of smaller earth-movers, and at least three cranes attached to eighteen-wheel trucks. He remembered seeing some of this equipment being used on his exploration of the area at the outset of construction. A thought struck him that with the building completed on the Compound, only the Zombie guards would be left. The human workers would be paid and long gone. *At least I hope they were paid and allowed to leave,* Jason thought. He leaned over to whisper to Will.

"This is enough equipment to build a small town!"

"And a labyrinth to hunt in," the Historian whispered back grimly.

Jason felt a twinge in his gut, realizing his wife was one of those chosen as a live pawn in this game. He knew she was free now, but for how long? Starla turned to the crouching men.

"The guards are too many to confront, and we can't risk an alarm being sounded. That would bring other Undead flooding into this area. We need a diversion that will pull many of these Zombie creatures away from the road leading to the main house."

"I will supply such a diversion," the Historian offered. A ghost of a smile crossed his tanned face.

"Be ready to sprint toward the first small storage building down the road. Take shelter by the far wall. I'll meet you there," he added.

Seeing both his companions give a nod, the Historian moved slightly to the right of them. He had to work fast. The sun was higher, and the shadows on their ledge would be thinning, exposing him to any guard who might look in his direction. Breathing deeply of the clean mountain air, he could taste the tangy pine scent and smell freshly turned earth. His incantation was brief. He held his arms out stiffly, pointing them toward the open garages where the big equipment sat like sleeping animals inside their dens. His voice was low and commanding,

"Earaid toghairm!" The air stirred around him, blowing the loose dirt at his feet.

Jason and Starla watched closely, turning when the deep rumbling of an engine turning over burst from the closest equipment garage. They watched as one of the massive trucks carrying a crane, rolled into the sunlight and onto the dirt road. This truck was followed by the other two crane trucks and various dump trucks emptying that garage. As a smattering of guards began to move in that direction to investigate, the second garage began a similar exodus of machinery. Heavy trucks of every description roared into life and began rolling out of the area. They followed the first group, heading straight toward the woods opposite the boulders. Jason and Starla watched a moment longer until all of the guards abandoned their posts and moved awkwardly to intercept the odd parade. Glancing back at the Historian, Jason saw he was absorbed in maintaining his spell. Taking off at a run, he and Starla headed toward the designated building. Starla was surprisingly fast and easily kept pace with Jason's long strides. They made it to the side of the metal shed undetected. The confused guards were entering the woods, pursuing the truck convoy as it plowed its way through the trees. The Historian took advantage of their frenzy, as they moved clumsily in the wake of the rampaging equipment. He raced across the open ground until he reached the waiting pair.

Not even slightly winded, he calmly said, "Let's go while they're still distracted. The Undead are incapable of reasoning there is magic at play and will focus solely on the trucks. These will only keep moving for another five minutes, but that should give us ample time to reach the manor."

The Medicine Woman took the lead. She quickly moved them off the open road and threaded a path through the trees where the heavy firs gave way to more stands of oak and maple. Jason wondered aloud why the equipment was so far from the main house. The Historian suggested the elusive billionaire couldn't risk any curious human workers seeing, or hearing, anything that might suggest the paranormal and start rumors of magic. *That probably included hearing any screams* Jason thought.

They'd been moving almost fifteen minutes when they spotted another guard station. Unlike the first one, this was no more than a lean-to made up of cut branches. They carefully moved out of visual range of anyone inside, circling well behind. Oddly, Jason had a strong feeling their movements were being observed. The hairs on his neck stirred with the sensation. As soon as they were well-clear of the rough outpost, he reached out and tapped the Historian on his shoulder stopping him.

"We're being watched," he said in a hushed voice.

As softly as he spoke, the Medicine Woman must have picked up his comment. Jason glanced over at where she stopped several feet in front of them. He turned away and began searching the shadows cast by the tall trees, half expecting to find a guard pointing a gun at them. Tilting his head back he began to study the sky. The others waited quietly. The sun glinted off the black patch covering Jason's eye as he turned his head slowly to search the trees for possible snippers. Suddenly, he yelled in a strained voice.

"Crows... thousands of crows!"

The large birds filled every tree as far as they could see. After his discovery the birds set up a raucous squawking, bobbing and shaking their sleek dark heads like metronomes marking the pulse of their synchronized cawing. Their yellowish beaks were much longer than most crows to Jason's trained eye, but then, there was nothing natural about this murder of crows. As quickly as they appeared and their cawing began, the birds fell silent. As if acting on a single impulse they shot up, high above the treetops into the open sky. Coming together in a coordinated movement, they formed a wide V-shaped wedge. Swinging in a graceful loop until directly above the humans, they fell into a steep dive. Watching their choreographed actions, Jason had the impression of a single beast coming directly at them.

The Historian shouted and a Dome of Protection slammed down over them. Starla was too far away to be covered by the invisible shied, but as soon as she saw the birds rising, she became enveloped in a red mist, and vanished. The flying wedge fell upon the Dome with the force of Thor's hammer. All the lead birds were instantly pulverized on impact, and the rest of the wedge dissolved. The crows returned to the trees, their beady yellow eyes peered into the shimmering oval-shaped fortification, bright eyes studying the humans inside. The Historian looked around at the trees, seeing they were blackened with the bodies of the unnatural creatures. He glanced over at Jason.

"This is indeed a unique barrier to keep strangers from exploring further."

Jason looked over to where he'd seen Starla stopped ahead of them, saying, "Will...Starla's gone!"

"I saw the Medicine Woman enveloped in a red mist just before the birds attacked. She disappeared seconds before. Looks like we're on own again."

<h1 style="text-align:center">Chapter 10</h1>

As a very young child, Starla began her training in the healing arts, as well as the more subtle arts of spiritual and community leadership. Star Fire was considered a prodigy. From birth, marked by the auspicious streak of white hair shooting from her forehead into a thick black cap of baby hair, those in her clan would whisper and speculate on her place among them. She began instruction in the sacred magic used by tribal Healers almost as soon as she could talk and hold a ceremonial rattle without playing with it. Her father Hooting Owl was the clan's Medicine Man. He was held in high regard by the tribe over many seasons as Shaman. Along with her paternal great-grandmother Listening Woman, he gave his young child intense tutoring in the secrets of the mystic life known only to a select few in the tribe. Star Fire learned several centuries worth of folk medicine and spells from her two elders. For their part, her teachers scrupulously guarded her progress as she refined her skills. They kept all aspects of her training a closely held secret, even to the exclusion of family members.

But there was another who would enter the girl's life as a mentor, as Star Fire passed into womanhood. When the young Healer turned thirteen, she bravely approached an ancient woman known as Red Cloud. According to the folk lore that clung to her old bones like moss, she was so named for an uncanny talent she possessed. She might to be standing in front of a person, then abruptly disappear into a cloud of reddish mist whenever it suited her. This remarkable occurrence brought about an implicit bond of silence among any of the clan actually experiencing such a mysterious event. Most felt they wouldn't be believed. Others, didn't want to stir the ire of a Witch!

No one could say with confidence when Red Cloud came to be among the Washee. In the memory of Little Feet, a clan elder of ninety-six summers, Red Cloud was among memories from his earliest recollections.   He sometimes braved sharing a story with the youngsters who found tales about the wrinkled woman more terrifying than getting close to the shriveled Little Feet. He was often inspired if she happened to pass by his favorite napping spot, and he was certain she was out of earshot. Star Fire was a frequent listener in his audience. She was most fascinated by insinuations that Red Cloud was actually a Skin Walker who survived the Navajo Witch Purge in 1878. This event was brought about after years of hardships and calamity. The Navajo blamed their misfortune on the evil machinations of the Witches they called Skin Walkers. Forty men and some women were hunted down as suspected practitioners of witchcraft and killed to restore harmony in the life of the tribe. Little Feet told of how Red Cloud would simply disappear when a hunt was under way for these magic users among the clans. Now, she walked freely amongst them having amazingly outlived all those who instigated the killings during the purge. Little Feet pointed out that many people still made secret signs against evil when she passed or her shadow fell across their own.

Star Fire had no fear of the diminutive woman in the shabby deerskin dress that looked like an outer skin ruined with age. In fact, the girl's natural gregarious nature encouraged her to engage the ancient woman in conversations about times past. At first, Red Cloud shunned her overtures. After three or four persistent tries, she relented, beginning to enjoy the rare, positive attention, and succumbing to the open smile, and inquisitive mind of the young woman. Soon after, Star Fire began training in the magic known only to Initiates of the forbidden. Though she was coached in the secrets of the Skin Walkers, Red Cloud made it clear she would never share their darker powers with her. She herself foreswore them in the time of the Great Purge. Star Fire knew the years between the present and that long-ago incident, were too many for any mere human to survive. But the frail appearing Red Cloud was no ordinary human.

Countless times Star Fire would sit across from the old crone, a small campfire flickering between them. Shadows pranced like Spirit Dancers across the dirt walls of the cave used for her clandestine training. Reflected flames painted the shriveled face of the ancient Witch in the dead color of rust. Hungry for the arcane knowledge possessed by her, Star Fire listened closely. Her secret training continued over four years. By the time of Star Fire's seventeenth birthday, she had mastered more magic than both her father and great-grandmother combined.

Her ancient teacher gave her a rare toothless smile and sharp nod of approval the day Starla reappeared in the small cave. The magic red mist was still falling from her slim body when Red Cloud told her she was now in command of her mystical powers. Pleased, she was opening her mouth to speak when a sudden darkness entered the cave, smothering the light from their small fire. She looked over to where Red Cloud sat, expecting an answer to the phenomenon. In the meager light from a sliver of rising moon, she saw the woman's expression had dramatically changed. A look of terror swam in the pools of her rheumy eyes. Red Cloud reached out and wrapped a boney hand around Star Fire's firm arm, pulling her closer to her creased face. She told her she had a sudden vision into the girl's future. Star Fire listened intently as she foretold that soon after Star Fire passed thirty-eight summers, into the fullness of womanhood, all her powers would be denied to her.

"You will remain as an infant until the white Witch rescues you from the lair of the hunting beast. Other fearsome challenges await, but first you will be lost again inside a place with trails to nowhere."

Starla hadn't given that warning any thought for many years. Standing inside the Magical Treasures room where she materialized from her red fog, she was struck by its accuracy. She tried to ignore the last part of the prophesy and focus on present needs. When her eyes adjusted to the dim lighting, Starla spotted Cathleen in the far corner of the room. The Protector had freed two more prisoners while she was gone. She was about to reveal her presence when something in the atmosphere of the room made her hesitate. She learned long ago to listen to these warnings. Keeping to the deeper shadows, she moved closer to the small group. Standing a few feet from Cathleen was an ancient Chinese man. His diminutive frame was draped in a yellow robe, probably silk. It was embroidered with astrological symbols marking him as a Sorcerer. Starla didn't remember seeing him being put into any of the boxes while she was held prisoner, but he might have already been there. Nevertheless, her instincts put her on guard.

The old sorcerer and Cathleen were dwarfed by a second, newly released prisoner. Looming almost three feet over them was a bearish looking man, wearing so many furs and skins, he appeared to be part animal. He was surely an untamed creature of the wilderness. He looked strong enough to crush boulders between his heavily muscled arms, but when he spoke his voice was surprisingly gentle, almost melodic coming from his thickly bearded face.

"Cathleen O'Brien, I am indebted to you yet again," he said looking down into the Protector's upturned face.

Starla turned her attention back to the Sorcerer. He moved slightly apart from Cathleen and the Wildman as they spoke softly to one another. There was something about the diminutive Chinese magic user that felt off to her...like curdled milk that still appears sweet. She wondered if Cathleen picked up the same peculiar vibe from the man, but she seemed preoccupied with the fur-clad giant. The Medicine Woman decided to keep to the shadows of a tall case for a bit longer. Studying the small wizard, she saw him slip his hands deep inside the wide, drooping sleeves of his robe. She wondered if he had something hidden there. Starla turned her attention back to Cathleen and the bearish man. Cathleen was trying to interrupt the giant with hand gestures, but he talked on, vividly relating how he was captured, followed by graphic descriptions of how he would rain down revenge on those that put him in a box and took away his powers. Cathleen listened for a moment, then stopped the tirade of blood-curdling threats with a few soothing words. Starla guessed she used some sort of voice charm to calm the big man until she could speak.

"Geilt, there will be time for talk of revenge. Right now, we have to find a way out of here undetected. Jason and the Historian are somewhere in the area. They'll join us to stop Mason Mirage before he can harm any others like us."

Cathleen turned to the Chinese Sorcerer, noticing how silent he'd became since she released Geilt. Not only was he not speaking, but he also seemed only slightly interested in Geilt who usually caused a considerable stir with his size and feral looks. Li's detached behavior made him appear almost bored.

"Li Shaoweng, do you have any knowledge of the design of these cellars that might be helpful in our escape?"

The little man made a gurgling sound deep in his throat. He smiled, showing broken yellow teeth, and bobbing his head energetically. He seemed pleased to have her full attention.

"I do indeed, young wizard. I was able to study the route while I was being moved through the halls to this room of boxes for the soon-to-be dead. I shall lead the way if that is your wish."

As this conversation drifted over to her hiding place, Starla thought his phrase about *the soon to be dead,* was more than a little strange. Almost as if he wouldn't be one of them. She decided to follow the three through the wine cellar undetected. That way she could intervene if her suspicions of the Chinese sorcerer proved well founded. While the big man called Geilt would be a formidable opponent, his size hadn't prevented his capture. Also, Starla had no knowledge of any magical powers he might possess. It was obvious he too was susceptible to the weakening effects of titanium, however. Starla whispered her spell, making certain the others were unaware of her presence. A dense red mist swirled around her, and she vanished. The shadows from the tall cases masked any movement as the vapor rose, hovering at the unlit ceiling. In this state, the Medicine Woman easily moved from place to place, but she'd be relying on her best guess to reappear behind the group.

The door to the Magical Treasures room clicked open and the three moved into the empty hallway. The Chinese Sorcerer led the others down the long, diffusely lit hallway and directly to a freight elevator around the corner. Starla couldn't enter the lift in her present form, so waited to learn their destination, to get there ahead of them. As they stood in front of the stainless elevator door, she heard the sorcerer speaking to Cathleen in his whinny voice.

"This is how they transported my numbed body. It will take us to the main floor, where it opens into an area for provisions and cooking."

The red mist entered a ceiling vent and hung suspended there as the pale-yellow finger pushed the elevator button.

"Will there be anyone around that area?" Cathleen asked as the lift descended.

"Only the cook and his staff. They all busied themselves when the guards entered with my body strapped to a table," he answered with a sneer.

Geilt had been silent up to this point, but when the elevator door whooshed open, he took a step back from it.

"This is a box, Cathleen O'Brien. To enter is to step into another trap."

"This is our way out of these cellars, Geilt. We won't be in it for more than a minute." Cathleen noticed the Chinese Sorcerer had a small smile on his creased face which he quickly lost when he caught her glancing over at him.

Geilt relented, and the door smoothly closed behind them. Cathleen saw Wizard Li push the button marked Kitchen. They rose silently, but when it flashed past the first floor and kept rising, so did her apprehension.

"Li, why haven't we stopped?" she asked, watching as they rose to the third floor of the sprawling mansion.

Li didn't answer. Instead, when the door slid open a second later, he was first to exit the elevator. He looked back at the confused faces of the others, a smug look on his face. Cathleen and Geilt faced a harshly-lit area that could have been the sterile waiting room for a corporate office. The light made Li's face appear like well-worn parchment, with deep lines and creases. In the glare bathing his small form, Cathleen knew he was much older than she originally thought.

"I'm afraid this isn't *your* floor Protector, but the Wildman can accompany me as my newest pet!"

Cathleen wasn't sure she'd heard correctly. Before the impact of his strange comment fully hit her, the wizard lifted a hand, making a fast-spinning motion. Geilt was airborne in an instant, turning like a roast on a spit, as he floated out of the elevator car. The wizard dropped a ropey net of woven titanium around him as he hung above his upturned face. There was no struggle on Geilt's part. He never uttered a word, but Cathleen saw the stricken look in his eyes. Murmuring a few words, Green Fire sprang to her hand. She heard Li's high-pitched laughter as the sorcerer threw up a shimmering, golden shield. Green flames hit it squarely, spattering like molten liquid to either side, and setting the nearest furnishings alight. Cathleen called for a powerful wind to be directed at the sorcerer's charmed protection. He was caught off guard by its force when the shield shook violently and began to waver. The smirk on Li's wizened face was gone.

Geilt was spinning overhead at a dizzying speed. Cathleen kept up the powerful wind charm as she worked to remove the titanium net from around the Wildman. Her spell was quick and neat, just like her father had taught her. She recalled his words as she chose her next magical move, *Simple is underestimated by the boastful.*

"Fortach!" she screamed over the winds' howl.

The titanium net vanished from around Geilt and the big man fell heavily to the floor, rolling once before springing to his feet. His arm shot out to grab Li's puny figure, but his big hand only grabbed empty space.   As soon as she saw he was safe, Cathleen dropped her wind charm. Geilt had a confused look on his face and snarled at his empty hand. He turned to Cathleen, her sacred flames still shooting from her fingers.

"Cathleen O'Brien, I will enter no more boxes," Geilt said firmly.

Chapter 11

After hearing the Chinese wizard urge Cathleen and the Wildman to use a freight elevator to the first-floor kitchen, she waited until the door swished closed to follow. She'd been so preoccupied she almost missed the signs that her body was trying to revert to its natural state. Opening her partially forming mouth, she swallowed more of the red mist. The moist particles altered her body until she was once again more fluid than solid. Over the years, Starla perfected the powerful charm, and was able to shift into this form at will while retaining her self-awareness. She entered the narrow opening of a return air vent in the hallway. Rising to the next floor, she passed through the kitchen's extensive venting system, to hover over two massive, gas stoves. Starla could maintain this form for only a few more minutes before the energy it took became too much to hold.

The place was empty of any of the bustling staff she expected to find. The pantry doors were closed, the keypad locks next to each of them glowed red, set against being opened by any but the absent cook. Anxious when she realized the three never exited the elevator, she reentered the air ducts. Her mist form searched the floors above, thinking she may have misheard the Wizard Li. Muffled sounds floated around with the dust motes in the duct work. Human voices. This was followed by a tremendous thump, as if something heavy was dropped from a height. The shapeless red haze seeped through a metal grate on the third-floor. It poured out in a bright room that appeared to run most of the length and width of the building. Even in this state, Starla could taste the stale air, as if this room was never opened.

In the corners, the pale walls were beginning to color a dingy gray as shadows deepened with the shifting sunlight filtering through squares of skylights. Starla could feel her spell weakening with each passing second. The red mist settled itself onto the floor, shuddered several times and resolved into the body of the Medicine Women. Dressed in the knee length deerskin shift, Starla opened the pouch hanging from the beaded belt at her waist. She murmured in the secret language for the conjuring of objects. When she pulled her hand out of the bag, she was holding a skinning knife, its bone handle brownish with age and rubbed smooth with use. She knew it was razor-sharp.

The small Chinese Sorcerer had his back to her. He was focused on launching orange bolts of fire, spinning and sizzling like burning firecrackers, and aimed at the Protector and Geilt. Starla saw the pair was shielded by a wall of Green Fire that easily deflected the fiery bolts, but they made no counterattack. Suddenly, Cathleen launched herself over the burning wall, making an unexpected frontal assault. She spun something above her head before hurling it. It spread like a stain as it flew from her hand. Starla realized it was a net, peppered throughout with deadly looking spikes. These made sharp clicking sounds when the wide net landed on the empty space where the Chinaman had been lobbing his missiles. Cathleen jumped back over the wall of fire, her adversary nowhere in sight. He popped into view a second later directly in front of the crouching Medicine Women, ignorant of her presence. Cathleen and Geilt spotted the Medicine Woman at the same time as she stood from a crouch. Their attacker remained unaware of her standing behind him, resuming his assault. His wheezing laughter echoed throughout the nearly empty space and stung their ears like stirred hornets. He shouted insults across Cathleen's fiery barrier, scorning her attempts to capture him.

The air was filled with the crackle of Li's burning missiles as they smashed against the fiery wall. The booming noise effectively covered the sound of Starla's knife as it traveled at the speed of a bullet, toward the back of the yellow robe. A piercing screech bounced around the cavernous room when the blade found its target. The Sorcerer's withered hands shot upward, scorching the ceiling with his orange bolts. He lurched forward a few feet, falling face down a moment later.

Cathleen dissolved the burning barrier. She and Geilt warily approached the still body. Coming forward, the Medicine Woman moved to join them. Geilt studied this new ally closely. He turned to Cathleen, raising his heavy eyebrows with unasked questions.

"This is Starla White, Geilt. She is known by her people as Star Fire and is a Shaman with many powers." Cathleen made this last comment as she turned to look at the striking woman.

Starla said, "You saved me, and now I am happy to return that favor, Protector."

She leaned down to retrieve her knife from the body of Li Shaoweng. There was no blood on the blade as Cathleen was quick to note. Another question that would need answering. The Medicine Woman looked up at the colossal figure of the Wildman. Rather than shrinking back when he moved closer, she stood still, her stare frank.

Finally, she said, "You have been touched by the Great Spirit, Geilt. I sense your power and something else besides. I see courage and loyalty in your aura."

Geilt's mouth shifted under his heavy beard and Cathleen realized he was smiling. She was pleased with his response but had to break into the amicable mood. "It's obvious the Chinese Sorcerer was placed among the prisoners to keep tabs on them for Mirage. We can't know if Li informed Mirage of our escape and location, but we should assume he did. Where did you leave Jason and the Historian, Starla?"

Starla related the attack by the crows adding, "I vanished to avoid attack, but saw the two men sheltering under a clear dome just before I was enveloped by my mist. They may still be pinned down by the unnatural birds."

As they moved through the third floor, it appeared to be mostly unfinished space, with the exception of the area in front of the elevator. Cathleen walked slightly ahead of her two companions and they exited the vast hall. She used her Inner Eye to scour what were likely storage rooms, searching for any hidden enemies. They climbed a short staircase leading up to a metal door that opened onto the roof. When they stepped outside, they found themselves within a few yards of a black helicopter parked on its pad. With the sun burnishing the sleek body, Cathleen had the fleeting impression of a giant mud wasp. *Everything about this place seems abnormal*, she thought as she looked around.

"Geilt," Cathleen said looking into his attentive eyes.

"I need to take Starla to help Jason and Will, but I can't take you too. Can you follow us on your own?"

"Cathleen O'Brien, you know my powers are many," he shot a look over at Starla as if confirming her assessment of him.

Cathleen had Starla lock arms before she called out a Wind Charm. Whisked off the rooftop like fallen leaves, the pair quickly became spots in the daytime sky. Many years before, Geilt had formed an indelible character marker for Cathleen upon his most primordial senses. He was bonded with her magic so deeply he could sense any threat to her. Finding her on the vast grounds was merely a matter of tapping into this unique connection and translocating to her side. He waited on the precipice of the heliport, the helicopter sitting silently behind his back. As soon as he felt Cathleen was stationary, he too vanished from sight.

A few dark clouds scudded overhead, pushed by a chilled wind, when a low hum stirred the air around the black chopper. The sound permeated the clouds and bounced off the hard pad site. The blades whirled faster and faster, sending vibrations through the thick body at the controls. Mason Mirage smiled contentedly at this new twist to his plans. The three magic users would join the would-be rescuers, increasing the addictive challenge of a hunt through his Labyrinth of Lies. He was excited with the unexpected bonus of adding the two men to his wall of trophies, along with the other three. He suspected they had unique powers as well. The sorcerer Li deserved his final destruction, Mirage thought, frowning. *But I would have liked to have his head for mounting.* Mirage detested failure, and the sorcerer had failed in his mission to capture the escapees by pretending to be a friend. Instead, he tried to destroy them for his own reasons, foiling Mirage's plans in the process. *I never should have called him back with the other Undead. Ah, well. Time to play!* The helicopter blades disappeared in a blur of speed as it lifted from the roof. Mirage ordered the architect to where the men were like flies under a glass. He was responsible for turning the birds into killers. The sun bounced off the bald head and white teeth of the man at the controls. The large diamond stud in his ear lobe flashed like the sharp edge of a sword.

Chapter 12

"We can't outwait these crazy birds," Jason said tightly. His voice showing his frustration at yet another delay in getting to Cathleen.

"I know my friend. These creatures have been manipulated to act violently by a Dark force, and whomever wields that power is likely to be close by. I'm hoping they'll show themselves before we leave our safety."

Jason clenched his jaw against his impatience, but he knew Will was right to be cautious. He looked around the grove at the trees encircling their Dome of Protection. Every branch was blackened with the abnormally large, aggressive crows. The Dome itself sat in the middle of the undulating sea of birds. The air was filled with raucous cawing, making it impossible to hear without shouting close to his friend's ear. The bird's numbers seemed to have grown by a few hundred more, with others darkening the sky with their wide wingspan. They continually swooped down, pushing their way to the Dome where they used sharp beaks like mallets, smashing against the smooth exterior of the sphere. The din penetrated the curved wall, and Jason had to fight the urge to cover his ears. The Historian looked as cool and calm under the siege as he would on a walk through the woods.

As the two men waited for something to happen, a sudden stillness fell over the chaotic scene. The crows stopped moving and squawking. The silence was shattered by a high-pitched whistle. The call continued, rising in pitch until even the Historian's enhanced hearing could not detect the sound. The birds began to drop from the trees like rotted fruit. Those already on the ground tumbled onto their backs. The area around the Dome became a carpet of scaly yellow legs, jutting up from stiff bodies. As they watched the littered ground was suddenly empty of every black bird. Not even a feather was left behind as proof they ever existed. Jason scanned the area for whatever had caused the mass killing and disappearance. The Dome remained in place and Jason figured Will's senses were warning him of more danger, just as his own were. The two men didn't have long to wait to identify the source of the new threat.

A slightly built man wearing carefully pressed khakis with a matching belted jacket, festooned with pockets and loops, stepped out of the woods. He held a pith helmet in his hand, completing the look of a safari guide. His compact body moved with the fluidity and grace of a cat, as he approached the Dome and its watching occupants.

The Historian whispered, "He looks like a peacock trying to impress us with his plumage."

Watching the stranger closely Jason said, "This guy is trouble. I can smell a mountain lion a mile off and they aren't particularly big either."

The Historian harrumphed in response. When the man got within six feet of the Dome, he coolly studied the trespassers, making a slow circuit around the sphere. Jason began to study the stranger as well. Safari man, as he dubbed him, never stopped smiling. Jason was familiar with that kind of cocky grin; he'd seen it on some seriously nasty creeps on his job. Safari man had a mass of curly, sandy colored hair. With his yellow-brown eyes, Jason was reminded of the crows, almost expecting him to peck at the Dome. The cherubic face notwithstanding, Jason put him in his mid-forties. He was definitely comfortable in the presence of magic, looking over the Dome of Protection with keen interest. He turned his small eyes back to its occupants, giving each in turn a broader smile.

"Very impressive fortification, gentlemen. Unfortunately for you, it has now become your prison."

He raised the hand holding the Pith Helmet above his head, and the trees directly behind him trembled as if awaiting his cue. A long tremor rolled under the Dome as they watched the trees bend outward, many splintering under the force of whatever pushed through. A black-feathered beast the size of an earth moving machine lumbered into view.

"So, that's where the crows went," he said quietly.

This creature was more dragon than bird, he realized. The slightly elongated head, with its yellow beak and glittery black eyes bobbed with the constant movement of a bird but sprang from the thick neck and body of a dinosaur. Jason was amazed the spindly bird-like legs could support its massive body weight. He noted that the layers of overlapping black feathers were actually a form of body armor. The legs appeared to be the only weakness he could spot. Like the crows, they were covered in muddy-yellow scales. The transformation of thousands of crows into this monster signaled the power of the unimpressive figure that called it. Jason knew his first instincts were correct. This was a true hunter in the misleading guise of a safari geek. While Jason was searching for vulnerabilities in the monster that watched them with hungry eyes, Will didn't move. He's been confronted with monsters many times in his life as a Scout. To his mind, this one didn't rise to the level of even the least formidable.

"Why don't you tell us your name, or are you simply called, *servant?*" Will asked the stranger.

The taunt resonated inside the Dome. Jason wondered if the Historian was stalling to buy them time. Safari man stiffened his back. Answering slowly, his words as sharp as the crease in his pants.

"I am no man's *lacky*! One of your last memories will be my name, the name of your killer, Byron Bledsworth."

Jason turned the gold signet ring he wore, letting the emerald stone show. It had begun to pulse with energy, since the birds attack. He watched the Dragon Bird's fidgety movements during this exchange, seeing it back up several yards to the man's left. Without turning toward the beast, Bledsworth shouted, "Take them!"

The Dragon Bird exploded with blinding speed, launching itself at the pulsating skin of the Dome. Thick yellow talons would have pierced the shimmering wall, if the Historian hadn't predicted this move and with a few words, turned the hard shell into a yielding elastic covering. The bird's sharp talons curled around the pliable wall, without ripping the fabric of the spell. The creature's excited screeching was deafening inside the close space of the Dome. Jason shot a worried sideways look at the Historian, wondering why he wasn't acting. He was raising his arm to aim a laser-sharp beam from his ring at the Dragon-Bird's exposed underbelly, when Will's firm hand stopped him. He leaned close to Jason's ear, using the Dragon-Bird's squealing to mask his words. "I have sealed our Dome around us."

Jason looked down to see the iridescent sparkle of the Dome under their feet. The Historian continued speaking with a firm resolve in his voice.

"We'll let the beast carry us to the destination this man has chosen. We need to get to the heart of this evil and I suspect that will be found in the maze called the Labyrinth of Lies. That is where it will likely deliver us."

Jason didn't respond as he turned the ring into his palm and made a fist. He watched apprehensively as the creature took a firmer grip on the Dome and rose into the sky. Circling once, the ball of quivering light swinging like a captured sun beneath it, the Dragon-Bird took off in a northernly direction. When Jason looked back down, Bledsworth was gone. He wondered if Safari man was preparing a warm welcome for them wherever they got deposited.

Moving inside their bubble, Jason was using this airborne view to study the lay of the land below. Will pointed to an area ahead of them where the trees were removed, creating the shape of an enormous square. It was ringed by virgin woodlands, and beyond that, the rugged mountains, making it appear even more out of place. The Historian looked over at Jason after committing the aerial view to his incredible memory.

"I judge that abnormal swath of land to be a mile or two from that small lake. The Dragon-Bird will likely place the Dome somewhere in its vicinity."

"Will, that dead area looks to have trails cut throughout. I think…"

The Dragon-Bird began a slow, spiraling descent. It made tight circles over a patch of sandy earth, close to the lake Will spotted. The beast released his burden seconds before it landed, causing the elasticized Dome to bounce several times when it hit the ground. They came to rest close to the muddy shore. When they recovered their footing, Jason finished his comment.

"I think we've been dropped near the opening to the maze. If we can get out of here, we can try to disrupt Mirage's plans to begin his hunt!"

After depositing his burden, the Dragon-Bird moved toward the lake. The men figured its role now was to keep a beady eye on them. They watched as it folded its scaly legs under itself. Once it was settled on the rocky shore, it swiveled its large head in their direction. Jason commented that he now understood how a worm felt.

Chapter 13

It couldn't be more than a few minutes since they were here Cathleen decided. She felt the familiar tingle when Jason was close, but this wasn't quite as strong. More like a whiff of his after shave. She and Starla stood in a small clearing surrounded by the hushed forest. Cathleen registered the use of magic where Starla said the Dome appeared, a trail of mangled trees led directly toward it. She glanced over at the woman who turned in slow circles studying the empty ground.

"Cathleen, I know those birds could not do more than keep the men inside their protection. The torn appearance of the ground and trees points to something more formidable joining the attack on them."

"I have a hunch the Historian allowed whatever that was to carry them off, otherwise they'd still be here. Nothing moves a Dome of Protection once it's fixed unless the magic user who conjured it allows such a thing."

As she looked for possible clues to the Domes new location, Cathleen shouted out, "Here!"

Starla crouched beside her to study several prints. They agreed one was clearly a giant avian creature. Cathleen pointed to where its talons gauged deeply into the winter hardened ground. The other prints led from the woods and went up to the spot that still held Will's magic.

"These boot impressions look to be made by a slightly built man," Cathleen said.

Starla leaned in closer, "I'd say it was Byron Bledsworth, Mirage's henchman. The guards all called him the architect. It was he who designed this evil place. He is a small, compact man who enjoyed showing off his magic to me after I was brought here. He's as twisted as

Mirage, and in some ways more dangerous because he appears so unthreatening."

Cathleen felt a mental pinprick when she heard the word 'architect'.

"He would be the one who designed the Labyrinth of Lies as well," she said, confirming the truth in Starla's dark eyes.

The Medicine Woman nodded, "He is a vile man that one. Where Mirage is driven by his egotistical needs, Bledsworth is more cunning. I believe he subtly uses Mirage for his own wicked ends."

Cathleen didn't meet Bledsworth when she arrived at the compound, but Starla's insights rang true. There was a lack of self-control in Mirage, like a child who threw tantrums unless he got his own way. That kind of personality is blinded by ego-shine and could never see beyond self- glorification. Bledsworth, would be the cold-blooded, calculating adversary, capable of disciplined patience. Both qualities would help him achieve success in carrying out a quest for ultimate control.

"Starla, if the architect wants to wrest power from Mirage, it's likely he designed the Labyrinth with some secrets he withheld from his boss."

"What kind of secrets?"

"The kind that ensure the outcome of the hunt, where he ends up as king of the hill!"

A warm wind blew up around the women, followed by a loud thrumming sound. Starla blinked away the dust and when her eyes cleared the Wildman towered over Cathleen.

"I am with you now, Protector."

"I see you, Geilt. We need to stay together from now on. I suspect Jason and the Historian have been taken to the Labyrinth of Lies. Mirage is likely hoping to use them to draw me into a trap."

Cathleen turned to Starla adding, "I don't think they know you've been freed Starla. That will be to our advantage when we enter the maze. Though I'm sure it's nearby, can you recall any hints to the exact location?"

Starla was quiet for a moment before answering, "I heard Mirage say of me, "I can't wait until this one is wandering inside my puzzle box." I don't know if that will help you, Cathleen."

"Protector," Geilt said, a deep frown drawing together his heavy brows. "I have seen this strange box in the forest! Coming here, my eyes passed over a place where many trees had been ripped from the Mother's arms, leaving an unnatural square. Inside this false box were paths, with twists and turns laid out like many long-used animal trails. I saw no way out before I swept past."

"Geilt, did you see any sign of Jason or the Historian down there?" Cathleen asked hopefully.

"I saw no sign of your mate, or our friend, but my passage was swift."

It was decided Geilt should lead them to the area he spotted within the green shadows of the woodlands. Cathleen was convinced this would prove to be the Labyrinth of Lies. It would be carefully prepared for the contrived hunts of captive magic users. If Jason and Will were inside the maze, Cathleen prayed they'd find them safe inside their Dome. If they were wandering the maze...*Only the Mother knows how I'll locate them before they are taken as trophies!*

What kind of magic was at play within this huge puzzle box was another unanswered question. Cathleen wondered which of the two adversaries, Mirage, or Bledsworth, used the powerful Dark Magic she felt prickling her senses as they moved closer to the sinister Labyrinth of Lies.

Chapter 14

Jason's idea of how they might escape the watchful eye of the Dragon-Bird guarding them made the Historian grin. Concentrating on the shimmering water several yards from where the Dome sat like an unhatched egg, Will began his enchantment. The placid face of the lake was shattered when a big silvery fish jumped out, two feet into the air, and fell back with a loud splash. The Dragon-Bird jerked its huge head around at the sound, spotting another leaping fish. It took to the air in a single leap before the lake water settled into ripples. Soon the creature was circling the lake and diving like a torpedo into the deep water, over and over. The beast clearly enjoyed these headlong plunges, always coming back up with a fish dangling from its deadly beak. It would take short breaks from its cavorting to land on the muddy shore, throw its dragon like head back, and toss the squirming fish into the air before catching and swallowing it whole. Jason and Will waited patiently in the Dome watching the game being played by their jailer.

Not long after they were dropped on the sandy ground, the architect, Bledsworth, checked that his prisoners were secured. Upon his arrival, the intimidating Dragon Bird moved to hover over the Dome. It was clearly meant to keep the men under its golden gaze like two worms. Something the architect said before he left, however, convinced Jason they were meant to escape. *"The hunt shall begin with you two. Mason will enjoy your puny attempts at survival, as much as I have."* Jason filed that comment away, at the time; it resurfaced now. With their guard busy diving for fish, they finally had their chance and quietly slipped away. The dense shadows in the woods swallowed them as quickly as the Dragon Bird dropped the fish down his dark gullet. They kept a fast pace, putting several acres of heavy woodlands between them and the beast. Jason remarked how the trees were beginning to thin-out and there was a subtle change in the terrain. The Historian led the way toward a large swath of cleared-off area he spotted while they swung beneath the Dragon-Bird. Jason agreed Will was better suited to deal with any magic they might stumble across. Privately, he had confidence the signet ring would do well if he needed its power. Jason felt the ring's snug fit, recalling how he came to own a magical artifact while he followed the Historian's broad back.

He'd been awarded the ring by the Council of Green Wizards, for *Outstanding Bravery* as the inscription read inside the wide gold band. This reward acknowledged his part in helping Cathleen defeat the Deceiver, a singularly evil Dark Magic user. Jason would walk into fire to help his beautiful Cathleen, but he was glad for the magic he seemed able to control while walking through those flames.

He was drawn back to the present when they abruptly exited the trees. They hiked over uneven ground for several more minutes until the Historian moved toward a precipice jutting out from the rocky earth like a crooked tooth. Both men dropped to their bellies, not wanting to be spotted by any alert Zombie Guard patrolling the area. There appeared to be at least two miles of clear air between the over-look and the ground below. From their vantage, the twists and turns of an intricate pattern of trails, appeared like a woven carpet spread over a great swath of land.

"The Labyrinth of Lies," Jason murmured.

After Will studied the area around the maze he said, "We'll need to climb down without notice, my friend. I would guess going by foot would take a good two hours with this terrain. Ready for a short jump?"

Jason knew the Historian meant to call up a Time Thread to transport them further along the time continuum. It would get them close to the maze, while avoiding exposure while climbing down the side of the mountain.

"Let's do this Will. I have a strong hunch Cathleen and Starla will be heading this way too, especially if they believe we've been taken captive."

"Yes. The attack of the birds was the last thing Starla witnessed. Also, it's logical to think we'd be moved to the Labyrinth since it's staged to be the killing grounds."

The Historian called for the Time Thread, and standing shoulder to shoulder, the Historian focused on the intricate puzzle brazenly cut from the Mother's forest. Jason felt the pressure along the length of his body as the cliff fell away and they vanished inside a space in time itself. His breathing became restricted to shallow breaths as the weight of time pressed heavily on his chest. He squeezed his eye shut against the swirl of colors rushing past at a dizzying speed. A few heartbeats later he heard the popping sound of their arrival. He knew they were now a few seconds ahead in time and he was a few seconds older. He waited until his body became acclimated to the normal gravity of earth before opening his eye. Will was detaching the vibrating rope from around his waist, looking around cautiously for any imminent threat.

"Jason, I believe we've been set down on a path somewhere inside the extensive maze. I must have miscalculated the starting point in my mind."

"Do you think we should try to make our way back to the opening? Cathleen and Starla would likely start there. It could be our only chance of meeting up with them," Jason said, his voice subdued and strained.

Before he got his answer, a rustling sound nearby diverted their attention. It came from the interwoven hedges bunched in front of a thick line of trees, tightly snugged against the path. Extraordinarily tall brambleberry bushes lined both sides. On closer inspection, the men agreed that the thorns were unnaturally long and sharp. They both froze, watching as some lower branches and shrubs thick with berries, swayed slightly. Something low to the ground was passing through the foliage. Jason shot the Historian a look. He saw him mouth the words *don't move*. The bramble bushes stopped trembling. Jason sniffed a pungent odor wafting through the stirred air. It was the scent left in the wake of whatever passed by them, heading deeper into the maze. As familiar with the woods as he was, he had no idea what manner of animal just moved within smelling distance of them. From the look on Will's face, he knew he'd smelled the foul scent as well. Jason nudged the Historian's arm leaning close to his ear.

"Whatever that was, it headed away from us. Let's take the opposite direction and try to locate the entrance to this place."

The trails were shrouded in darkness, especially where the trees branched overhead, intertwined like the arms of conspirators. Will used his Inner Eye and after several minutes of walking and pointed out a particular thicket of brambles. These had attached themselves to the huge trunk formed by two oak trees growing from a single wide base. Jason caught a faint movement under the dead leaves pressed against the bottom of this living wall. *Snake!* He raised his right hand, the signet ring already hot. A slithering sound cut through the silence behind the wall of vegetation, followed by an anvil shaped head being pushed through the brambles. The snake confronting them was far larger than the enormous South American anaconda. Its mouth stretched wide; its two curved incisors flashed in a frightening grin. Jason saw the reptile launch itself and Will was its target! A beam of bright green solidified as it shot from the ring, driving through the huge snake like a javelin. The force behind the shaft was so great it carried the creature several feet, impaling it on the front of a tree, deeper in the woods. The pale body twisted, coiling and uncoiling its incredible length several times around the trunk, while it continued to hiss and spit. Jason watched as its eyes went from a deep red to a muted golden color. After a last spasm, the snake went limp.

"Well played, my friend," a startled Historian was saying. Jason felt the adrenalin rush he experienced begin to drain away.

"That monster must be what passed us earlier. I guess it doubled back on us," Jason was saying, trying to sound calmer than he felt.

"The snake was only a small problem compared to what I have just discovered among these trails," the Historian said ominously.

"We are back where we started, Jason. I left a small mark at the base of the twin tree," he said pointing down to a knife scratch made on a mossy bark.

"I have suspected for a while the path we are on is either circular or the trees are being subtly shifted as we walk, preventing us from making any real progress. I fear we are further from the beginning of this Labyrinth of Lies than we thought. The Protector and Starla will surely fall into the same trap as they undoubtedly search for us in here."

Jason felt his stomach clench. If he and the Historian used a Time Thread to escape the Labyrinth now, there would be no way to warn Cathleen about the shifting paths and the predators that likely roamed the maze. He knew Cathleen's magic was powerful, but Mason Mirage was an unknown actor in this deadly game. Starla told them he wanted to hunt magic users for the thrills he sought and planned to fill his trophy room with their heads. Jason knew that would make Cathleen a prime target.   He unconsciously rubbed the cooling stone in his ring thinking, *Not while I draw a breath...*

Chapter 15

The two women stood at the edge of the forest. The thinner winter limbs provided them little concealment, and the breezes began to pick up, constantly shifting even the meager cover. Their heads were close together as they spoke softly. Geilt stood nearby, alert to any threats. The Wind Charm Cathleen used to bring them to this spot, provided her and Starla the same birds-eye view Geilt reported on earlier. The forest here had been supplanted with a carved out square, encompassing a huge swath of what should be densely wooded land. When viewed in the fly over, the area inside the engineered shape revealed countless twisting paths. There was no doubt, they had found the Labyrinth of Lies. The three were near the entrance to the maze, but there was no sign of Jason or the Historian.

"I can't feel any trace of Jason passing this way into the maze, or any indication of Will's magic being used," she said quietly.

The Medicine Woman saw Cathleen's concern clearly reflected in her eyes. She felt a similar worry when she visualized the Historian and felt the danger all around him. She wanted to dismiss this growing connection she felt to the big man but couldn't deny thoughts of him kept creeping into her mind.

Cathleen knew Geilt could hear every word but was grateful her hulking friend wasn't hovering over them. She turned back to study the archway into the maze. The words *Labyrinth of Lies,* hung over the yawning entrance, blatantly boasting of the devious nature of Mirage's riddle. The arch itself was constructed of stout tree trunks. Stripped of their bark, the wide boles gleamed perversely like pale, dismembered bodies propped-up naked in the diffused sunlight. Cathleen realized the place was having a subtle effect on her mood. *Mustn't let the atmosphere here effect my focus,* she reminded herself. Coming closer to a trunk, she ran her fingers over cyphers that were burned deeply into the dead wood. Her eyes traveled up the matching ten-foot trunks. Grotesque masks looked down from the top of each pillar. The eyes suddenly caught her attention.

Starla said softly, "The eyes are moving."

Nodding her head Cathleen said, "Anyone stepping through the arch is likely seen by Mirage, triggering the hunt."

"Protector, if Will Farley and Jason hurried to join us here, they must be somewhere inside, searching for us as we speak," Starla pointed out.

Cathleen needed information about this giant puzzle-box they were about to enter. She tried reading the symbols carved into the pillars for clues. So far, she'd only translated a few phrases of the cyphers. *"Lies to lead you to the truth,"* and *"All you see within is never real without."* She repeated them out loud for the others.

"That's just the ones I can figure out. Only the Green Mother knows what the rest of it portends. We need to go into the labyrinth. I agree with you, Starla. Jason and Will must have gone inside, thinking I entered earlier."

They both turned when Geilt's broad shadow blocked the sun and he said, "This Wildman has traveled many unknown paths, Protector, and I shall lead the way into this strange place."

Cathleen saw her friend was correct. Who better than Geilt, his powers forged by the perils of the untamed Third Plane?

"Yes, Geilt. You will lead, but do not engage in any magic unless absolutely necessary. We don't want to draw attention to our presence. Our priority is to locate Jason and the Historian."

"I will prevent the eyes in the masks from seeing us, Cathleen," Starla murmured into their huddle.

She held up an arm, pointing her hand at the first mask. A heavy red mist shot from her fingers, covering the mask completely before she turned to the other.

"Hurry! While they are blind!"

They rushed between the towering columns, into the unknowns awaiting inside the maze. They looked up to see the mist falling away from the spying eyes. Cathleen looked over at the Medicine Woman, giving her an approving nod. Geilt began to move off as quickly as the twists and turns in the trails allowed, leaving the women to keep pace with his long strides. Cathleen looked over her shoulder, checking that Starla was close behind. She saw her pull a thin leather rope from under the top of her dress. A charm, likely made from a flat piece of bone dangled from the end. Even under the smudging shadows of overhanging trees, Cathleen saw the phases of the moon had been carved into the yellowed disk. She suspected this would hold some powers for the Medicine Women, along with the Medicine Bag snuggly secured at her side. Cathleen felt a welcome surge of confidence in their readiness to face the unknown traps inside the twisted paths they had to follow.

The neat path from the entrance narrowed and curved, gradually transforming into a hard-packed dirt trail, with no obvious ending point. Geilt stopped abruptly when their path ran directly into a high wall of thorny bushes. The row of tightly clustered Poplar trees behind it, were clearly meant to reinforce this barrier. It was unlike anything Cathleen had ever seen in a woodland setting, but this was not a natural forest. Geilt studied the blockage carefully before speaking.

"This is not the Mother's woods Geilt knows. These trees and thorny bushes have little feet."

Cathleen thought she misheard him until she looked down at the long scuff marks cut into the dirt trail. They indicated shifting among the surrounding shrubbery and trees lining the pathway. This subtle movement forced their path in a new direction altogether.

"What on the Mother's Green Earth are we into?" she asked to no one in particular.

Starla stepped closer, saying in a hushed voice, "This is Magic of the Dark Spirits that roam freely through these twisted lanes, and they do the bidding of a powerful master."

They looked around themselves for the path they'd been following, now lost somewhere behind the thorny wall. Cathleen and Starla started to turn back in the direction they had come when Geilt's deep voice cut through the silence.

"There is another way, Protector," he said excitedly.

The women saw Geilt had dropped to his hands and knees. He was in front of an opening at the base of the barrier. He said the little feet of the bushes and trees suddenly shifted, leaving this low passageway through the green wall. Cathleen realized there was nothing for it but to take this unexpected exit from the dead-end confronting them. She didn't want to retrace their steps, losing significant time in their search for the others. Starla hitched up her dress, securing it with her belt so she could crawl through the opening. Before starting this expedition, Cathleen warned them both they would have to restrict their use of magic to defensive action or risk alerting Mason Mirage to their location. She was relieved Starla didn't simply disappear inside the red mist she could conjure, and likely become separated from them in the process. *This crawling like an insect doesn't appeal much to the Medicine Women's sense of dignity*, Cathleen thought when she saw Starla's mouth set in a tight line of disapproval.

Geilt took the lead, shoving his more substantial body through and widening the hole, as the three scuttled like field mice through the tunnel of trees and brambles. Cathleen followed directly behind him, while Starla scooted behind her, muttering to herself. They were covered in dirt, with thorns sticking to various parts of their clothing and pulling at their hair when they finally emerged onto an open trail. As they stood together, Geilt raised his hand. He tilted his head and turned it from side to side. Cathleen realized he was sniffing the air. She picked up a nasty smell herself, thinking it had a feline character to it. No more had that thought penetrated her senses than they all heard the muffled yowl of a big cat. Cathleen shot a look at Geilt. He pulled a large hunting knife out of a fur-lined boot.

She signaled they should move back. She wasn't afraid to confront whatever was skulking in the shadows, but now she picked up signs that Jason and Will were somewhere nearby. Her focus was on finding them, not doing battle unless necessary.

They moved on, watching for movement among the hedges enclosing the trails. They needed to retrace their steps whenever they ran into solid walls of thorn bushes, or trees, tightly bound together with thick, ropey-vines. The surrounding woods appeared transformed into a living, barred cage.

Cathleen slipped into her Inner Eye earlier, when she picked-up the scent of the beast tracking them. After a few minutes of torturously slow progress, she tapped Geilt on a fur-clad shoulder.

"I need to lead, Geilt," she whispered.

With a curt nod, the Wildman shifted into position behind Starla and Cathleen moved ahead. She didn't want to tell them what she saw moving parallel to them, in the patches of shadows. She'd keep a furtive eye on the stealthy threat, just as it kept a sly eye on her. Without the Inner Eye, her friends couldn't detect the beast trailing them through the tangle of foliage. It blended perfectly into the jumble of hedges and vegetation enclosing them. The creature moved when they moved, stopped if they stopped. Cathleen recognized it had the keen instincts of a top predator and was capable of remaining patient and concealed as it stalked them. Suddenly, she glimpsed more of the cat-like form when they came around a bend on the path. A grotesque head stared out at her from the greenish undergrowth. The trio passed with just a few feet separating them. Cathleen saw the glittery black eyes shift off of her and fasten onto the tall Geilt bringing up the rear. She knew it had marked him as the biggest threat. She shot a glance at the Wildman, seeing he picked up the presence of the invisible beast. A scowl turned down the corners of his mouth, and his nose made his beard twitch as he sniffed the air. *He's ready*, she thought, relieved, afraid giving a verbal warning would surely trigger an attack.

They'd been moving faster for a few minutes and Cathleen hoped they were headed toward the heart of the labyrinth. The feeling that Jason and the Historian were nearby faded considerably, causing her to fear they were actually moving away from each other. Starla's soft voice cut into her thoughts. Cathleen slowed down but didn't turn to look back.

"Protector, I think the creature stalking us is closer."

"I know. I've been watching it." Cathleen was pleased her companions felt the hunter at their back.

They came to a T-crossing in the trail. Cathleen glanced into the shadows on her left, checking on the position of the beast. It was nowhere to be found. Geilt moved to join Cathleen and Starla.

"We cannot proceed to the right, Protector," he said in a worried, hushed voice.

Cathleen looked in that direction. The trees and hedges had come alive with bolts of current, snapping with a weird electric energy. A voice cut through the web of electrified brambles.

"You can't go that way, my dear Protector! Too bad you'll have to choose to face my beast! Are you ready?"

There was no time to call for a Dome of Protection. Cathleen immediately brought Green Fire to both hands. The three stepped further apart. Cathleen heard Starla hiss words to some kind of charm. She snapped a quick look in time to see the Medicine Woman crouched low to the ground. Watching the petit form, she was shocked as her clothing melted away, replaced by a thin veil of red mist. A deep groan erupted from the crouching figure as she began to shift. The lovely face stretched until it elongated into a tooth-filled snout. Her body contorted in unimaginable angles, covered in thick, reddish fur, marked by a single white strip running down the hunched back from the slopped forehead. When it stood, it towered over Cathleen. Rather than panic at having this monster within arm's length, Cathleen moved to give the seven-foot beast room to fight. A side-long look back to where Geilt stood assured her he had readied himself. Besides the deadly looking knife, he now had a tight grip on a huge club studded with long spikes. If he was disturbed at seeing the lovely Medicine Woman change into a creature resembling a werewolf, he didn't show it, but he watched this new creature closely. Mirage's voice rang out once more, hanging in an echo over their heads. "Let the games begin!"

Chapter 16

After the incident with the snake, Jason and Will kept a sharp eye on the twisted vegetation outlining the paths. They stopped when the Historian reported smelling the sharp odor of a big cat in the vicinity. Jason said he smelled it earlier, telling Will it might be a mountain lion unlucky enough to have wandered into the confusion of paths.

"It's unlikely though. I'd bet we're smelling one of Mirage's pets."

Will nodded and they moved on. Coming to a T in the trail, they opted for the left-hand path, seeing it was longer and might lead to the center of the labyrinth. Jason remarked that the trail they were on seemed less maintained than the others they'd followed. Branches with sharp thorns sprang out to scratch, unseen along the shadowy trail. The packed dirt of the path was strewn with small rocks in places, making footing uncertain and slower.

"Do you think maybe this part of the Labyrinth isn't finished?" he asked Will in a low voice.

"Oh, it's finished, but in such a manner as to make our going more difficult, and perhaps to encourage us to take an easier trail."

They walked on for several minutes until the Historian jolted to a stop, holding out his arm to keep Jason at a distance. His voice was strained with alarm.

"Don't come any closer, Jason! The ground here is not solid under my feet!"

Jason looked down, noting the dirt a few yards away from where he stood had a glittery appearance. By the time he looked back, Will had sunk into the sparkly earth half-way up his boots. The Historian murmured in the Old Tongue, but Jason saw a look of concern pass over his face when nothing happened.

"Something blocks my powers," Will said tersely.

Jason looked frantically around himself for a long branch. With all the trees over-hanging them, not a loose limb was in sight. He cursed the maze under his breath all the while hearing the sucking sound of the glittery muck pulling Will deeper. Needing something to lop off a branch, Jason remembered the signet ring and pointed it on an old oak with stout limbs. A thin green light shot out from the large emerald, sheering the branch cleanly off the tree. Jason rushed back to where his friend was now submerged to his chest, with only his arms and shoulders free to move. He judged the circle of sludge extended three-feet out from where it captured the Historian. Dropping to his belly, Jason stretched out his arms, his muscles straining to support the heavy limb so he didn't lose it in the muck before it reached Will. The Historian managed to push his weight sideways, to lean closer to Jason's branch, wrapping his strong hands and one forearm around the thick limb. Jason slowly backed up, wriggling his lower body from side to side to haul the big man out. He could feel the constant pull of the sludge through his aching arms. It took all of his strength, but he was soon rewarded with the wet sound of Will's body being released. They sat on the dry path, both drained by the exertion and near calamity. The Historian spoke in short gasps.

"Thank you...I... owe you...my life."

"What just happened, Will?" Jason asked. "Why didn't your magic work?"

"My powers were as dead to me as that limb you used is to the tree."

Jason looked back at the dangerous spot; the faint glimmer traced its edges.

"I'm just relieved my ring's power doesn't seem to be effected by the titanium particles. Look."

The Historian raised his eyebrows in surprise. The ground that nearly swallowed him appeared solid and safe again, as it laid in wait for the next unwary footstep. Studying the surface closely, he picked out the occasional sparkle of finely ground titanium mixed into the dark earth.

"The leaves and rocks must have concealed the titanium's presence. Time to find a different path, Jason. Let's back-track to that fork in the trail."

They were almost to the split when they stopped. The light breeze inside the maze had picked up noticeably, and it carried the sound of others moving along the confusing trails. Jason felt a familiar jolt and heard the faint sound of Cathleen's voice riding the wind. The tree branches stirred madly, causing them to push bare limbs into the thick brambles. It sounded like wooden chairs being dragged along a floor to Jason's ears. The Historian's enhanced senses picked out the words being battered by the breezes.

"The Protector is doing battle within the labyrinth! I detect an unusual magic besides hers in play, and it is not the Medicine Woman."

As they moved down the left pathway, two men stepped away from the shadows behind them. Mason Mirage grinned widely as Jason and Will disappeared around a bend in the trail. He removed a snowy white handkerchief from a pocket and began mopping beads of sweat from his bald head. The architect twitched his nose and looked away from the rotund man.

"This hunt is proving even more delightful than the one we had for the Giant Panda. Boring stuff next to human prey, wouldn't you agree, Byron?" His round face glowed with a sheen of perspiration and excitement.

Bledsworth nodded, thinking to himself how his employer was a fool, filling the air with his annoying voice and comments. He knew he was a more skilled hunter than Mirage, and recognized stealth was as important as a loaded gun. He also understood his employer was an egotist, incapable of using sound judgement, especially if it meant denying his insatiable appetites. He stupidly insisted they had to dress in khaki, appropriate only in the seething jungles. The architect knew they looked ridiculous among the forests surrounding them. As usual, Mason needed to create the *illusion* his name suggested... he needed to appear more than he actually was!

Yes, he was wealthy beyond imagining, and powerful enough to buy and sell life cheaply. He was also weakened by his own narcissistic nature, constantly self-aggrandizing, and missing the subtle signs of plots boiling in the heart of his kingdom. Bledsworth detested the portly man with every fiber of his being. When Mirage glanced over at his minion, he saw a slight smile on his face. The architect knew Mirage was far too arrogant to think his henchman was scheming his demise in the maze he created for him. Afterall, Bledsworth knew where every trap existed and purposely didn't include some on the map clutched in Mirage's sweaty hand.

"The Labyrinth of Lies will prove most entertaining," he said, turning that thin smile to his employer. "Most entertaining, indeed."

Chapter 17

Starla shifted into the two-legged wolf-creature known as a Werewolf to those who lived long enough to describe it. It moved closer to Cathleen. While Geilt witnessed the shift, its meaning was unclear, and when it moved toward Cathleen, Geilt brought up his spike-studded club. Cathleen's voice cut through the air.

"No, Geilt! See, the white streak in the fur? Starla's shifted to fight against the big cat!"

Cathleen picked out the beast from the depths of the muddied shadows using her Inner Eye. As the three waited, a large tawny head poked out from between the bushy hedges in front of them. This was followed by a second head, the four ears flattened and pointing forward, getting ready to charge. The snarling heads were followed by its massive body. It muscled way through the undergrowth in a low crouch, readying itself to pounce. The beast was a hybrid of African lioness and prehistoric Saber Tooth Tiger. *This abomination is the work of Dark Magic*, Cathleen thought. She watched the animal creep toward them, its belly scuffing the dirt trail as it exited the brambles. The pungent odor coming off the cat was nearly suffocating in the close confines of the pathway. The jaws of the twin heads partially opened, revealing four deadly incisors and huffing the smell of other kills into the thick air.

The Green Fire jumped on Cathleen's palms. The slight breeze became a strong wind with Cathleen's urgent charm. It tugged at her long hair, whipping it across her pensive face. As the fans of her fire swayed, they got the response she sought from the beast. It froze in mid-step. She hoped it had the same fear of fire any natural beast would have. After that split-second of hesitation, it appeared this creature was only appraising the challenge the green flames presented.

Cathleen saw the ears tighten against its heads. A glint of sunlight bounced off the long curve of an incisor. Geilt shifted slightly, putting him closer to Cathleen. His club rose menacingly. Ignoring the Wildman, the wolf-creature growled deep in its throat. It stood as tall as Geilt, even with a slightly hunched back. The stiff rust-colored fur covering its body didn't conceal the grey skin beneath, or the bunched muscle in arms and legs. Its human-like hands had tapered fingers tipped with thick, hook-like claws. Flecks of white froth seeped between the teeth of the elongated jaw. Any humanity in its eyes was lost in a blood-red sheen.

Before the others could move, the Werewolf launched itself at their adversary. The roars from the twin heads made Cathleen's neck hairs stand on end. Her Sacred Fire became shafts of green flame directed it at the pouncing creature. They left long scorch marks along its side but didn't slow it down. The shifted Medicine Woman smashed midair into the chest of the two-headed monster. The force of the collision brought them to the ground where they rolled over one another, teeth and claws tearing into flesh and bone. Cathleen couldn't direct her fire accurately while the two creatures clutched each other in mauling grips. One of the cat's heads had fastened its jaw onto the Werewolf's left shoulder. The long incisors penetrated deeply into muscle and tore at the arm. Geilt moved toward the battle, searching for an opening to apply his club to one of the Saber Tooth heads. He stepped back when the Werewolf sunk its claws into the throat of the head clamped onto its shoulder, causing it to open its jaws in a howl of pain.

Cathleen found an opening and was able to send a bolt of fire into the other head when it lurched back. The body of the beast began to spasm. The Werewolf leaned in for the kill. Rolling the beast onto its back it raked the massive chest with its claws tearing it open. The exposed heart was still beating when the shifter tore it out and held it up like an offering to its gods. Both heads flopped lifelessly from their thick stems. The dying muscles twitched once before the gutted beast lay still.

Geilt stepped back to stand beside Cathleen. They were waiting for the Werewolf to shift back into its human form. The creature turned pitch black eyes on the pair. The heart dripped dark ropes of blood onto the ground. In a single heartbeat of Cathleen's own pounding heart, a red mist began to seep between the jaws of the lycanthrope. It thickened and began to swirl around its blood-spattered body until only the white streak showed at the top of its head. Cathleen's Fire was down to candle-size flames on her palms. She waited until the shift completed before daring to lose her defenses entirely. She'd just witnessed how single-minded the destructive power of the shifter was, and until she understood it more, couldn't chance becoming its next target. She felt Geilt go very still as they waited to see who, or what, would emerge from the red fog. His heavy club was still raised. The red mist evaporated, revealing Starla. Slightly hunched over, she straightened and stood to face the waiting pair. The heart ripped from the gutted cat was dropped beside the body. Geilt moved to stand beside her while Cathleen raised a hand and opened the ground beneath the bloodied carcass. Starla arranged the belt around her deer skin dress as Cathleen approached.

"There will be others like this one, I fear. Because my energies are drained by a shift, I can't promise I can make another until I've rested."

"Starla, I don't think you should risk using your Warrior Spirit again while we're inside the labyrinth. It's clear that you can't return to your human form without consciously calling on your powers. Your human spirit will be at serious risk if Mirage takes you down in the Werewolf form because your strength will be too depleted to shift back."

The Medicine Woman made a small nod, but otherwise didn't respond to Cathleen's comment. Her face revealed nothing of her feelings, leaving Cathleen to worry as they started down the path. She hoped the other woman's silence didn't mean she would call on the wolf-creature, without being strong enough to control it. This was something that created a danger to friends, as well as enemies.

The trail ahead made a drastic twist, where tightly knit trees hovered above a thick tangle of low privets. As they got closer, Cathleen could see this hedge was studded with long thorns and some kind of bulbous fruit. The same mass of ropey vines and berry bushes was mirrored on the other side of the lane. The trio was forced to walk with their arms pressed to their sides as the passage visibly narrowed inside the curve. Geilt suddenly bellowed out a warning.

"Beware the thorns!"

Cathleen turned in time to see the big man sink to his knees, and fall heavily, face forward, onto the ground. Warning Starla to remain perfectly still, she squeezed past her, trying not to connect with the barbs. They narrowly missed her face but snagged at her long hair as she shuffled past. A sharp hiss of words disentangled the long strands. Geilt hadn't moved since she saw him drop. From the position of his body, she couldn't see his face. Kneeling beside him, she whispered a charm, rotating her hand over his still body until he flopped over. Cathleen drew in her breath with a sharp gasp. Geilt's face was the color of the dark red berries hanging from the brambles. His breathing was shallow, barely audible even to her enhanced hearing. Cathleen checked his arms, bare except where the furs hung loosely around his neck and back.   She discovered a barb deeply imbedded in the Wildman's left arm. His broad shoulders must have rubbed against the bushes in passing.

Geilt struggled to take each breath. Digging a fingernail under the flat stem where the thorn had broken off, Cathleen carefully wiggled it, loosening it enough to pull out, while avoiding the sharp end. Holding the barb between thumb and index finger, she saw the tip was shaped like a hook, insuring it stayed in place once it pierced a victim. It was covered in Geilt's blood. Cathleen felt the evil tampering with nature yet again, in this Labyrinth of Lies. The bramble bushes had been altered by Dark powers, turning their annoying but harmless thorns into lethal weapons against the unwary. Cathleen held her hands over the prostrate form of Geilt.

"Slan leigheas. Health and healing to this being, Mother."

The Medicine Woman came closer, murmuring her own prayers for the Wildman. The two women watched as the sickly color drained from Geilt's face and his breathing steadied, gradually returning to normal.

His eyes fluttered open and he said, "Are we ready now, Cathleen O'Brien?"

Chapter 18

Two bodies dangled from gnarled limbs of a giant oak. Jason stared, not acknowledging Will when he came up beside him.

"What has captured your attention, my friend?"

"My parents. They're hanging from that tree! They've been dead for almost thirty years! What's happening?"

"This is a trick, an illusion, Jason. I see nothing here but an old oak, its branches moving in the breeze. Mirage has named this the Labyrinth of Lies for good reason. Nothing can be trusted as real."

Jason blinked, unconsciously touching the black patch over his left eye. He didn't speak but studied the two bodies swinging in a slow rhythm as if they'd just been hoisted. *Just in time for me to pass by them*. His parents still looked in their early forties. Both wore the awful injuries and broken bodies they suffered after the truck accident that mangled their young lives and orphaned their two young boys.

"How could he know about my parents? I'd never heard of Mason Mirage before he moved to Iron Mountain."

"He obviously has intimate knowledge of your background because of your relationship to Cathleen. I would guess with his immense wealth he was able to unearth much personal history about you and the Protector and your life here." He continued in a sober tone, "He likely knew about the Witch of Appalachia for a goodly while. It may be the reason his compound was built here. It's remote, and his small army of guards can go unnoticed and unchallenged. And you, my friend, well, it appears you are considered collateral damage in his evil campaign to capture Cathleen O'Brien for his Trophy Room. He'll torture you only because he knows how."

Jason grew more incensed with every point Will made. He was being manipulated in the most hurtful way Mirage could conjure. He turned his back on the tree and the gruesome parody of his parents' deaths.

"Let's go," he said firmly, moving past the rustling oak and its burden of nightmares.

They came to the first substantial opening in the trails a few minutes later. A stone water fountain stood burbling in the middle of the open ground. Approaching cautiously, both agreed it was remarkable to encounter this tranquil setting in the dangerous maze. The bowl, filling with a flow of crystal-clear water, was wide and shallow. The figure of a small boy wearing overly big coveralls stood at its center. He poured the recirculating water from a pitcher, too large for his small hands. At the heal of the barefoot boy, a young dog pawed at the spray as the child emptied his pitcher in an endless loop. Jason's voice sounded out-of-place even to his own ears in the peaceful surroundings.

"Will, I wonder if the water is fit to drink. I didn't realize how thirsty I was till I saw the fountain."

He interrupted the Historian from his close study of the beautifully carved figure, drawing Jason's eye to the remarkably fine work. The stone was elegantly detailed, right down to the serene smile on the boy's plump face. As Will looked back at Jason, his peripheral vision caught the boy's stone eye's shift downward for a split-second. *He's looking back at me,* he thought, alarmed by the notion.

"Don't drink the water, Jason," Will replied calming, not wanting to give away his concern. "In fact, don't touch the fountain at all."

The Historian moved briskly to the path where it resumed behind the gurgling waters. Jason was quick to follow. A chill ran down his spin when he heard the sound of a child's giggle, and the loud splash of water from behind them. They followed the path until it dead-ended at another wall of impassable brambles, knotted like tight fists in the path.

As they backtracked to find a different trail, the Historian said, "It's likely the water in that fountain back there is enchanted, just as the statue of the boy is. I caught it looking down at me and saw the darkness glitter in its stone eyes."

"This maze is like a human-sized mouse trap," Jason remarked soberly.

Eventually they came to a fork in the path. Unlike others they'd encountered, a wooden sign had been nailed to a post where the trail split. A small leather bag hung below it. *Roll the dice to find your way.*

Jason looked over at the Historian saying, "This seems like another invitation to get some help, just like the water in the fountain."

"Yes, but this one we'll need to take. There is a good chance if we choose our path incorrectly, we'll end up back where we started. Let's see where the dice takes us."

He slipped the bag's string off a rusty nail. Emptying it into his hand, they saw a single die, but rather than dots carved into the sides, each side was blank. Will turned the ivory piece over and over.

"No marks, or indication of how to play this game. I'll roll and see if that triggers a message."

The Historian bent a knee, tossing the cube onto the hard-packed earth. It rolled until it butted-up against a thick tree root.

A messaged appeared. Jason read it in a low voice, *"Dead right."*

"That could mean we're correct to go right, or we'll be dead if we go right!" Jason said, clearly exasperated with the mixed message.

Will looked thoughtful before he spoke. "I would try to roll again, but I fear the results would be the same. Let's go right, my friend. Our chances of surviving one of Mirage's creatures are better than wandering aimlessly through this evil place."

They rehung the bag with the die in case Cathleen came this way. It was possible she'd get the same message and make the same choice. Jason knew Mirage wouldn't help his quarry in any way. He toyed with them as he stalked them through the muddle of trails. He guessed Mirage used the beasts and endlessly perplexing trails to shake their confidence and eventually extinguish all hope in his victims.

Will was several paces ahead when he remarked, "see how the trail is narrowing? The trees are more tightly clustered, and the bramble bushes interwoven with them appear taller and more substantial. The canopy they have formed above us, effectively blocks much of the sunlight."

He scanned the living roof, then looked ahead at the path they needed to follow. It was full of shadows, shifting with any breeze that weaseled its way under the tightly interlaced limbs and prickly bushes. The Historian was reluctant to use his Green Fire, believing it would alert any hunters, human or otherwise, to their position. Jason was concentrating on avoiding the incredibly long thorns protruding from both sides when a thought occurred to him. He reached into a pocket of his jeans, pulling out a slim, plastic lighter.

"Will," he called softly, "I always carry one of these...never know when I'll find myself in a dark place around you Wizards." He flashed a grin, handing it to the Historian.

Will spun the flint and a small yellow flame sprang up. Its effect immediately magnified in the tight confines of the trail. He nodded back his approval to his companion and held the lighter higher, searching the path in front of them.

As Jason followed, he was sure he saw some of the bordering foliage shrink away when Will passed and the glow from the lighter fell directly on them. He tucked away that bit of information, not wanting to break into Will's concentration as they negotiated the difficult path. They walked for ten minutes, turning back at each impasse, then retracing steps until they found open trails. They moved carefully, reluctant to trust solely in the small flame to spot danger. When a loud rustling came from above both men instinctively went into a crouch.

"Looks like we disturbed something," Jason whispered, looking up.

"Jason, I'll go forward a short distance to try to tease out whatever is laying an ambush. When I do, use your ring on it! I believe my own magic is sorely diminished in this cursed place."

Another commotion shook the knot of tree limbs, sending down a shower of dead leaves and thorny twigs. The Historian crept ahead. Jason clearly heard the Old Tongue, recognizing a few words from Cathleen's own use of the old Druid spells. He was watching Will's shadowy form inching down the trail when his warning shattered the dark air. "Jason, stop!"

Suddenly, the small flame from Jason's lighter became a yellow column, illuminating a horrifying scene. The Historian had walked into a gigantic web. The intricate round design was instantly familiar to Jason as the common Orb Weaver. He'd never seen a web so extensive, and certainly none strong enough to snag a grown man! His friend's attempt to free himself made the strands of webbing shiver with every frantic movement. Jason knew this would telegraph Will's presence to the spider that likely waited nearby for just such a message. His thoughts evaporated when something heavy dropped out of the canopy, directly in front of the snagged Historian.

An enormous spider soundlessly emerged from the dark green shadows. It had the bulbous shape of an Orb Weaver. Eight crooked legs bristled with the same spiky black hairs covering the round body. This beast was an ordinary garden spider, altered to become the monster approaching his friend. Several small red eyes fixed like lasers on Will. It reared back slightly, releasing a spray of luminescent silk that began covering the Historian while spinning him around and around with dizzying speed. Jason realized Will wasn't fighting back while the beast threw out more and more of its sticky silks. It dawned on him this webbing might be laced with the magic-suppressing titanium.

A stunned Jason finally swung up his arm. The signet ring shot a jagged beam directly into the exposed underbelly of the creature, followed by its piercing screech. He spotted oily smoke pouring from the area of his direct hit. Rather than letting go of the encased Historian, the beast reared back further, still screeching as it pulled on the sticky strings looped tightly around Will's body. Another green bolt shot from the ring only managing to sear the darkness that swallowed both spider and his victim. Jason stood shocked for a moment then cautiously approached the spot Will had been trapped. Traces of sticky threads were still attached to the limbs and bushes. He felt a new vulnerability as he stood alone, but that was quickly replaced with a determination to find his friend. There was a sparse light coming from the hole in the canopy where the monster likely pushed through. Jason studied the ground where gooey filaments from the web glistened like threads of spun gold. Knowing he couldn't follow the creature through the woven ceiling where it dragged Will behind, he hoped he might be able to track it from below. He needed to search for signs of the Orb Weaver's food storage location. It was a gruesome thought but strengthened Jason's resolve never to allow such a fate for his friend.

Moving down a series of crooked paths, Jason occasionally experienced the subtle chill of Cathleen's presence somewhere nearby. He wanted to shout out to her but knew that would only invite trouble for both of them. He figured Cathleen would eventually discover what was left of the spider's webbing. *She can take care of herself,* he thought. *I have to find the spider's lair before it's too late.* Jason looked ahead, finding the path he followed cut off by yet another dead-end. He was about to turn around to retrace his steps when he noticed something. Having to rely on one eye, he was habituated to constantly scanning with his right eye and missed very little. He was sure he saw movement among the tangle of tree limbs and bushes. *There it is*, he thought, reaching carefully into a nest of thorns and pulling free a piece of cloth. He was certain it was ripped from the Historian's uniform. Jason scrutinized the surrounding area along the path. There was no other trace of the spider dragging off its prey except for the cloth, but he was certain it passed here on its way to wherever it would stash Will. He had a sobering thought that brought the situation into stark reality. If Will was unable to access his Magic because titanium was laced into the spider's silky web, his survival depended solely on him.

He began turning the signet ring around on his finger when he became aware it was heating up with that cold heat that warned of danger nearby. He moved closer to the dark hedge wall at the end of the path. It felt different to Jason's sense of the natural. Moving closer, he studied the tall block of twisted greenery. When he got within a foot, he reached his hand into the mass of brambles and leaves and watched it vanish. He jumped back. His fingers were almost numb with cold.

"What the…" he gasped, rubbing the feeling back into his hand and fingers.

He studied the hedge closely, making up his mind.

"It isn't really there and what I felt was the void of its absence," he said under his breath. The sound of a human voice gave him some reassurance, even if it was his own.

He rushed at the dark wall, dropping his head like a charging bull. The cold was nearly unbearable for a breath, as his body passed through the void. When he opened his tightly shut eye to look around, he was still on the path.

"This must be how the spider vanished so quickly. There must be other voids tucked in among the hedges." Jason's whispered words were lost inside the black-green walls of the labyrinth. He was studying the network of limbs above his head when a reedy voice broke into his thoughts.

"And then, there was one!"

Chapter 19

Cathleen kept an eye on Geilt for any residual effects from the thorn's poisoning. He appeared to be somewhat embarrassed by almost dying because of an innocuous scrub bush, and not by some enormous beast. The path led them into a spacious clearing. The sound of a bubbling fountain bounced around pleasantly, inviting a respite for the weary. A statue of a young boy pouring endless streams of water from a pitcher into the fountain's shallow basin, looked serene, almost playful. Starla and Geilt began to reach into the inviting water with cupped hands when Cathleen shouted a warning.

"No! There's magic at play here! There's no way Mirage would supply his quarry with water. We need to stay on the trail."

Walking around the fountain, they were all keenly aware of the vivid smell of fresh water, as the angelic boy continuously poured it from his jug. All of them were suddenly overcome with a maddening thirst. Starla was the first to tentatively reach a hand into the stone basin as she passed it. She scooped out a drink, gulping it down, and was reaching in for more, when the statue of the sweet-faced boy spun around to face her, his innocent look warped into open hate.

"You dare to take what is mine, Star Fire?" He used her given name, just as he had when he first captured her.

"Mirage," she managed to croak as her throat began swelled and close off her breathing. Seeing the Medicine Woman fall to her knees, clutching at her throat, snapped Cathleen's attention away from the water. She moved to stand protectively over Starla, who rolled onto her side. Cathleen heard a whisper of the strange language used in Starla's spell casting. Her face darkened while she gasped for air between words. The stone boy leaped from the fountain; his mouth opened wide. His high-pitched laugh burrowed into Cathleen's head like leaches sucking at her brain. The Wildman was suddenly beside her and she heard the solid whoosh of his massive club. Scrambling nimbly out of range, the imp's piercing laugh buzzed through the air when the club struck the ground with a jarring thud. The scampering boy began to spray Geilt in a wide fan of water from his pitcher. There was a hissing sound as it touched flesh and ate holes in the furs and skin alike. This enraged Geilt and he hurled himself at the smirking gray figure. Gathering the squirming boy into a bear-hug, Geilt clearly meant to crush him.

Cathleen yelled out a warning, but too late. The pitcher hanging from the small gray hand came up to explode against the Wildman's brawny back, the contents running down his bare legs. The burning was more than a few drops and enough to break his hold as he growled in pain and outrage. The imp jumped back into the fountain and vanished inside a wave of water. When the water settled back into the bowl, the corpulent figure of Mason Mirage stood there. He still wore his khaki hunting gear and had the same leering smile of the stone boy.

"That was such fun! Your magic is considerably weakened in my Labyrinth of Lies as you've all discovered by now."

He looked down at the gasping Medicine Woman and the scorched spots on the Wildman's furs and exposed skin. His delirious grin widened.

Cathleen stared up at him shouting, "You are truly a coward, Mirage! You have to weaken your prey before you're willing to hunt them. You are no great hunter, but a pathetic little man!"

Cathleen hoped her words would prick his bloated ego, making him respond without thinking. Instead, Mirage cocked his head to the side, staring down on her with a blank expression.

"What did you call me, Protector? Do you dare to repeat your insult?" he jumped back to the ground, standing a few feet away.

Cathleen had to back up in order to fling the Net of Nettles she conjured while Geilt was attacking the devilish stone boy. Mirage took her movement as a show of cowardice just as she hoped.

"I shall make these the last words you'll hear, Witch, before I collect your lovely head! Perhaps I'll have your whole body preserved and set on display. How does that suit you?"

Mirage began murmuring under his breath. Cathleen recognized a few of the words as an incantation of Dark Magic. She waited until he seemed engrossed in his spell-casting, then threw back her arm. The Net of Nettles flattened itself as it spun over his head, dropping to cover him in heavy ropes of vine and poison berries.

"If you struggle, Mirage, the berries will burst and you'll die an excruciatingly slow death. Reverse the effects of your curses on my friends, or I start breaking berries. There's one close to your left eye that looks appealing to me..."

Mirage spoke between gritted teeth. Geilt's burned flesh immediately began healing. Starla sat up, her complexion returning to its healthy bronze tone. They joined Cathleen, staring daggers at her prisoner.

"I'm not who you think I am, Protector, but a pale copy of the more powerful Mason Mirage." He sounded haughty when he added, "Shall I prove your mistake?"

Before Cathleen could answer, her captive stepped through the tight loops of the Net, the berries bursting and staining his face and clothing. He stopped moving and the three watched as the red juices dripped onto the ground.

"A clone!" Cathleen hissed.

Her words brought on more maddening laughter just before the body-double of Mason Mirage fell face forward onto the ground.

"The coward would never risk his own hide! He only saved Geilt and me so he could continue these sick games." Starla's voice reflected her rage as she watched the clone's twitching body.

Cathleen moved around the fountain to return to the path. The others followed silently, skirting the body as the berries took effect and melted it into a dark red puddle before soaking into the hard ground.

Several minutes passed before Starla interrupted the heavy silence with, "the paths are much darker now that we've moved deeper into the labyrinth." She looked up, pointing out the trees and unusually tall hedges had crossed from either side of the path to form a tangled canopy.

Geilt passed the women as they looked up at the extensive awning of greenery. He bent low, studying the ground, grunting loudly to himself. Cathleen and Starla soon crouched on either side of him, as he pointed out two sets of boot prints clearly dug into the dirt in several places. Some were partially obscured by the superimposed prints of something Cathleen identified as non-human. Cathleen held her hand over the boot tracks.

"I'm certain Jason and Will made these. I can only detect a faint trace of the Historian's magic, but I definitely sense Jason."

The Medicine Woman stood up, still scanning the ground.

"What made the other tracks? It was large, from the depth of the marks in the loose dirt. Whatever it was, it appears to have several legs. You can see a pattern of its prints all over the ground moving toward where the two men stood."

Using her Inner Eye, Cathleen leaned closer to the scattered pattern, picking up a long black hair from the ground, stiff and trailing a stringy goo.

"Spider," Geilt pronounced in his deep baritone, as he got to his feet. "Big spider!"

He was pointing at the tattered remnants of what must have been an enormous web strung across the trail and attached to the tall hedges and trees. Cathleen pointed out there was only a single set of boot tracks past the broken webbing. She didn't want to speculate on what that could mean. She was lost in the thought of disaster when she felt a shiver run through her body.

"Jason! He's nearby!" she whispered turning her head slowly to peer into the shadows.

She moved off without another word. Starla and Geilt followed close behind, looking up as often as down. Geilt ducked his head under stray limbs or trailing vines of the heavy canopy. He had to tuck his arms close to his body to avoid another mishap with the red thorns, turning sideways from time to time. He dragged his club at his side, wiping out their prints as he brought up the rear.

Starla heard him mutter, "This will be a long walk.

Chapter 20

Will knew his magic was useless as long as the titanium-infused webbing held him. Jason's attack on the creature interrupted its casting of silky threads, so it was only able to cover him with enough strands to keep him from escaping. His head and shoulders were free of the tight binding. The spider rolled Will's body until it was close to its hairy underbelly as it dragged him through the almost impenetrable tree canopy. As unnerving as it was to be pressed against the monster's bristly round belly, it did protect his face and eyes from the thorns and branches they crashed through. It moved quickly on its eight legs. The Historian began to think they were outside of the maze. The spider dropped him abruptly onto a hard surface. Will rolled twice before coming to rest against something that yielded when he bumped into it. *Another prey?* Will guessed there would be others, and he prayed to the Mother, Cathleen and Starla wouldn't be among them.

He heard the soft splash of water dripping onto the hard surface, somewhere in the depths behind him. Except for a weak, ambient light, outlining what he assumed was the opening to this place, it was black as pitch beyond. Without access to his Inner Eye he could only guess, but it seemed likely he was in one of the many small caves Jason told him were scattered throughout the vast area of the Mirage Compound. As Will tried to orient himself to this new situation, the spider shuffled off a few feet and began making a series of chirps and clicks. *Is it communicating to a mate?* Will dreaded the thought of a pair of these creatures hunting the labyrinth. The calls from the beast went unanswered. He watched as the vague shape of the creature scuttled away, the scratching of its many feet telegraphed its movement across a stone surface. Will remained perfectly still until it was completely silent and he knew he was alone.

Not able to make out any features on the tightly wrapped bundle he landed besides, he tried to study the form. *Non-human*, he thought much relieved. He flexed his legs slightly, finding enough give in the binding to scoot closer to what he believed was a way out. Leaning on his elbows as much as possible, he moved like a worm on his belly, until he reached the edge of the watery light. He guessed correctly; it came from the opening to the arachnid's lair and now he knew how he would escape.

The Historian wriggled his way toward the front of the cave, looking around until he spotted it. A jagged rock shelf extending out from the cave wall would provide him the sharp tool needed to free himself. Five minutes of rubbing his back against the flinty edges was all it took to free his arms. He swung onto his back and moved his legs over the rocky teeth until the webbing fell to either side and he jumped to his feet. The Historian felt a familiar surge rush through him, electrifying his body. He knew his powers were fully restored to him. Able to use his Inner Eye, he saw he'd been placed in a shallow grotto at the base of the mountain. Besides the unfortunate bundled animal lying next to him, no humans had been captured by the spider. Moving low to the ground, he began making his way down a slight incline. Spread out before him when he reached the bottom was a golden sea of tall, wild grasses. The field looked innocent of any threat as it rippled gently with the shifting breezes. After the experience of being pressed against the coarse middle of a giant spider, he couldn't help but feel some relief. This was followed quickly by the sobering thought that anything could be hiding in the lush grassland. He felt a sense of urgency in what he needed to do next.

Will Farley was not just Historian for the Council of Green Wizards; he was a living repository of the ancient magic from the dawning of the Green. Like Cathleen, he was one of the few Green Wizards trained as a Spirit Traveler. He'd have to use this dangerous method of travel to reach Cathleen without exposing himself to being recaptured. He moved into a thick clump of sword grass. Like everything else, it had grown to unnatural heights and hopefully would dissuade any prowling animals with its sharp edges. He waved a hand, making a spot for himself to avoid the wide serrated blades of grass. Laying down, he began relaxing with a form of self-hypnosis. His breathing slowed radically until his broad chest barely moved, and he entered into a kind of catatonic state. He sensed his Spirit Body rising, leaving his physical self behind among the crushed weeds outlining his ridged form. It was only two hours until sundown. Will needed his Spirit Body to return to him before darkness, or risk being lost among the shadows. Death would then claim his mortal body within hours. Time was of the essence.

The ghostly messenger fastened itself to the gentle winds sweeping around the field. It would return to the maze and locate Cathleen O'Brien and lead her to Jason. Will feared for him, knowing he now faced Mirage's traps and monsters alone. Within the span of a fading hoot of an owl somewhere in the surrounding woodlands, the Spirit Body hovered over the snaking trails of the Labyrinth until it spotted the Protector, but it hesitated a moment. Her only expected companion was the Medicine Woman. A hulking figure loped behind the petite Starla, dragging a heavy looking club at his side. The Historian's spirit being immediately recognized the figure of an old ally of battles past. Geilt, Wildman of the Third Plane.

Below, Cathleen's hand shot up and they all stopped. She was searching the darkening trail because she detected a powerful magic nearby. She raised her head slowly and the Historian's incandescent Spirit Body came down to stand in front of her.

"Will! You've sent your Spirit Messenger. But...where is Jason?" Cathleen's voice was laced with concern.

"Listen closely, Protector. My time is limited. Jason can be found just ahead of where you stand. I will mark the way for you. Move quickly, the architect is advancing toward Jason, bringing Demon Dogs on their leads."

Cathleen started to ask a question when the Historian lifted and moved off with a stiffening breeze. She saw drops of iridescent green begin to spatter the ground, marking a trail for them to follow. She turned to her companions realizing neither had responded to Will's sudden appearance as a translucent body. Both stared at her until Starla asked, "Who were you talking to, Cathleen?"

"I'll tell you later. Jason is just ahead of us. The glowing marks on the ground will lead us to him. Hurry!"

Cathleen set a fast pace through the twisting pathways. Her internal connection to Jason was on full alert as the familiar tingle of his nearness grew stronger. Just as they were rounding a narrow curve in the trail, the iridescent drops ended abruptly.

Cathleen looked around herself and was beginning to panic when Geilt shouted, "Something is wrong with these hedgerows! They shimmer like the wings of a dragonfly."

When Cathleen came back to where Geilt stood staring into the greenery, she exchanged a quick glance with Starla. The Medicine Woman was nodding her head in agreement. Cathleen held a hand close to the hedge, immediately feeling a searing cold. They had already seen the thick borders along the paths shifting-around, but this was a different phenomenon entirely. *It's like touching part of the fabric of outer space* Cathleen thought. She pushed her hand deeper into the tangle of vegetation, using a mumbled spell to protect exposed flesh. She gave an involuntary gasp when she jerked it out.

"This isn't really here. Which means we've been following a non-existent wall of hedges for several minutes."

"But you said you could feel your husband, Cathleen," Starla reminded her.

"I still can, but we've moved into a place that doesn't exist inside the maze and only the Mother knows where we are now!"

They instinctively moved closer to one another, silently searching the gathering shadows. Off in the distance the sound of baying dogs was carried on the winds. Geilt had his head tilted upwards, sniffing at the cooling air.

"Three dogs," he announced with calm certainty.

Cathleen felt a shudder pass through her. It was as if she'd touched a pulsating heart. Closing her eyes for a moment she thought, *Hold on my love. I'm coming.*

Chapter 21

Except for the Arch Wizard's signet ring, Jason was basically unarmed. It heated-up a few times, but nothing of the supernatural reared an ugly head. He kept a steady pace on the trails despite the subtle shifting of their living walls. These almost invisible changes sent him in new directions if he wasn't alert. He started to fear his sense that Cathleen was closer, was another illusion. Jason didn't doubt for a second that Mason Mirage could manipulate anything within the maze, including his own instincts. He would have to be a powerful user of the Dark Arts to have taken his wife prisoner. *Still, her escape and rescue of the Medicine Woman proved her an adversary to reckon with!* That thought gave him some comfort as he moved on along the contrived pathways.

The close-fitting canopy of trees and foliage thinned out and Jason stopped long enough to study the overcast sky. A heavy line of rain clouds moved in the direction of the labyrinth. They hung like a dark curtain, waiting to be opened in another act of a bleak play. "Great. Rain," he mumbled and walked on.

Though Jason searched for signs of the giant Orb Weaver that took Will, it left no trace of its lumbering movements. With every passing minute he became more anxious about Will's survival and made a snap decision that would give away his position. *Let's see what I stir up,* he thought, raising his hand. Directing the signet ring at a nearby cluster of hedges he focused his mind to bring it to life. A green bolt shot directly into the woody heart of the knot of limbs. The tops of three or four trees exploded with green flames. The signal fire wouldn't spread to the surrounding greenery.

Jason was accustomed to controlling burns like this, tapping into something within himself to govern the fire. Cathleen called it magic.

He called it will-power. The fire would be a beacon to notify Cathleen of his location within the damnable prison. It would also alert the monsters, but there was no choice. He needed help to find Will. The flames swayed in the darkening winds, their fiery grip on the bunched trees shed an eerie limelight below. Jason felt Cathleen's presence earlier. This signal fire would act like a lighthouse to guide her to him.

Watching his handiwork, a familiar sound filtered through his thoughts. *Dogs? Here?* The excited sound of hunting dogs was as common in these mountains as finding played-out coal mines. The baying of hounds drifting on the cooling air of evening, brought two thoughts to Jason's mind. *What if some innocent hunter has wandered up here and gets caught up in this mess? On the other hand, what if those dogs are like that spider?* Jason was familiar with the hunting habits of the small population in the County. He was sure there hadn't been any locals hunting this track of wilderness since the start of the compound. That left the other option. A pack of demon dogs, hunting the easy prey meandering maze.

The howls got closer. The excited yapping bounced off the high privets. He needed a plan to defend himself against the approaching pack and decided to create a barrier between himself and the oncoming beasts. Turning his ring he sheared off the burning treetops, letting them fall onto the path. It was quick work to add several more branches to the already roaring fire. He backed away from the intense heat, assuring himself it was safely contained. The last thing he wanted was to set the whole Labyrinth on fire with no exit in sight. He moved as fast as he could, his pace slowed by the constant jogs and dead-ends. After he was forced to turn back for a third time, he stopped to listen. He still heard the sounds of two, possibly three dogs. It was as if he hadn't put any distance between them and himself.

"They were closer than I thought," he muttered with a rising fear as he started moving down a new trail.

This one butted up against the hedges, with the trail splitting in both directions. Without hesitating to weigh options, he committed to the right turn. He smiled tightly when it looked like he'd chosen an unbroken trail. *Maybe I'll find the end of this creepy place. Still have to find Will though...* The smell of burning wood was heavy in the air. Jason hoped his fire wouldn't burn through the stack of limbs too quickly. The sounds of barking, growling and yammering continued unabated as he ran from the fiery blockade. Now, his only concern was finding a way out of the Labyrinth of Lies and searching for Will.

The hedges were lower along this trail, allowing Jason a better view outside. A quarter moon floated like a lopsided smile on the face of a darkening sky. He was almost jogging on the clear path, going toward what he suspected was the exit. The pale light reflected off of something straight ahead. Not wanting to walk into an ambush he slowed his pace, moving at a crouch close to the side of the trail. A familiar sound poked a hole in his thoughts. Jason froze. *Someone just cocked a riffle and I'm the only target!*

"While you are a mere human, you'll do nicely as a doggie treat, Sheriff Tate!"

Jason frantically considered his options. This maniac was there to stop his exit, while the pack moved in on his location. Suddenly it dawned on him how quiet it was, or he wouldn't have heard the gun being readied to shoot. *The dogs were stopped by the green fire,* he thought. Relief flooded his cramped body. He had to get out of this box. He called to the man with the gun.

"Are you the predator, Mason Mirage? Or only his lacky, the Architect? Heard all about you two weirdos," he said tauntingly.

"My associate would not be pleased with your description of him, but it's true, he's in my service. In fact, right now he is acting as my beater, and has effectively moved you ever closer to my gun."

"That makes you just another sociopath, and not the superior hunter you think you are. You need your lacky, so the only hunting you actually have to do is find the trigger on your gun! Makes you look like a wuss to any of the real hunters around here."

This torrent of insults was met with stony silence. Jason started to worry his strategy wouldn't work, but if he understood the psychology of the narcissistic personality, his words should wound the unbounded pride of the man.

"I shall give you a sporting chance, Sheriff. You may exit the Labyrinth, it's a few short yards ahead, but the Architect shall be in full pursuit while I attend to more colorful prizes. Your lovely wife for instance."

The shadowy figure melted away and Jason saw a clear path out. He knew this could be just another way to lure him into the open, but his gut told him Mirage would leave him as slim pickings for his minion. He broke from cover and ran. He slowed long enough to check for a trap. He sent a thin beam into the waiting darkness, nothing. He paused just long enough to burn a circle in the trail. *Just in case someone else makes it this far.* Keeping his ring at the ready he passed through the last of the hedges and charged into a wide expanse of tall Saw Grass. He was grateful for his faded blue jeans, as he waded his way through waist-high, sharp blades of grass. Bending slightly to keep from becoming a clear target, he came to a spot where the grasses had been trampled down by a large body. Getting down for a closer look, he was able to read the depression more closely. *A big man laid down here. It had to be...*He jumped to his feet and spun around when a heavy hand grabbed his shoulder.

"Will! You nearly took a shot to the mid-section!" Jason relaxed his hand from the tight fist and gave the Historian a bear hug instead.

"Are you all right, man? How did you escape the cocoon? I figured the mutant spider spun it with titanium, or you would have zapped it with magic.

The Historian smiled at Jason's enthusiastic greeting but kept his explanation brief. "We need to eliminate some of the monsters roaming the maze Jason. I saw your fire when I escaped the spider's lair, and I would assume, so has the Protector. She is likely on the way there now."

"Yeah, and they'll run right into the Architect and his hunting dogs. I think my burning barrier has stopped them for now, but depending on where she is, Cathleen and the others may reach Bledsworth before the barrier burns itself out and he passes through.

"We must hurry then. This time we have a good target waiting behind the fire you created. We'll deal with him and his beasts first.

<h1 style="text-align:center">Chapter 22</h1>

Cathleen spotted the green fire when it erupted above the tall hedges. She watched for a moment as the jagged flames stretched their grasping fingers toward a darkening sky, but how many rows over? She was certain Jason set it as a signal for her, which meant he wasn't captured by the mutant spider. While she was concerned for Will's safety, she couldn't help the sense of relief that washed over her. Refocusing, she became aware that all around them had gone eerily silent. The aggressive baying of a pack of dogs abruptly stopped. Cathleen guessed the hunter was after Jason. He and his mongrels were likely stopped by the unexpected fire line, which meant Jason was only minutes away. Inside the twisted paths of the labyrinth, which might mean hours of aimless searching, while they passed one another on either side of the hedgerows. While she considered their quandary, her peripheral vision picked up movement. She glanced up at Geilt. He stood as silent as a dark monolith, waiting for her to verbally recognize him.

"What is it, Geilt? Have you detected more than the wild dogs up ahead?"

His low voice was filled with alarm when he said, "The hounds call to the woman Starla. I fear she will answer their challenge in blood, Protector."

Cathleen had no idea what he was talking about. She looked over at Starla, whose back was turned to them. A spasm ran through the Medicine Woman and she hunched over. She crouched down and was immediately surrounded by the red mist. Cathleen knew better than to interfere with the shift and placed a restraining hand on Geilt's arm. They watched while the mist thickened, swallowing Starla's body inside a swirling funnel cloud. A hair-raising howl cut its way through the dull red haze. A muscular, fur-covered arm punched through the mist, followed by the body of the shifted Healer. Ignoring the two witnesses, the creature bent its powerful legs, launching itself several feet into the air. It grabbed a sturdy limb, swinging itself through the thinning canopy until it cleared the space above Cathleen and Geilt. It looked down on them, barring its teeth. Cathleen couldn't suppress the chill that ran down her spine, knowing this monster existed in the petite, soft spoken, Star Fire. The wolfish beast swung out of sight before Geilt spoke.

"The Medicine Woman has readied herself to fight the Demon Dogs."

"Yes, but there is likely a hunter with that pack and Starla can't fight his bullets."

They hurried along the path toward the area where the green flames burned brightly. Cathleen listened for the sounds of battle. The Werewolf would find the hounds and their handler quickly, moving through the trees. Cathleen also tried to pick up a trace of Jason's whereabouts. *He might have moved further down the trail after setting the barrier alight. That would keep him safe for the time being.* Another fact nettled at her. Without the Historian though, Jason must fending for himself in the dangerous jumble of trails. He'd already encountered a giant spider. *Is that what got the Historian?* A stillness settled inside the maze, as if even the twisted trees were holding their breath for the clash of Magical beings.

The peace shattered.

A pain-filled howl followed by growls chilled Cathleen's heart.

The wild dogs were under attack, and at least one badly injured. Cathleen and Geilt exchanged a look, hurrying their steps through a sharp turn in the trail. This ended in front of another shimmering barrier.

"It's not real Geilt, but the Werewolf's need of our help is! Follow me, and don't breathe until we are through the void."

Cathleen ran at the tangle of brambles and vines. She disappeared instantly. Geilt filled his lungs and followed close behind. It would never occur to him to question the Protector, even as the searing cold bit at any exposed skin like sharp-toothed Elfin Banshees. They reappeared on another path and Cathleen wondered if she made the right decision crashing through the negative space. Looking down the path, she had her answer. The architect stood with his back to them as they materialized several yards away.

He was still dressed in khaki hunting clothes, his curly hair sticking out like a slipped hallo from under a pith helmet. Cathleen still felt the deep cold after crossing the void, but with the enemy so near, she had little time to consider what that meant. Being a magic user didn't make her impervious to mortal pain, but it did mean she had the discipline to ignore it as long as possible. She shot a look at Geilt who mirrored her movements and stood slightly behind her. She noticed his heavy club. At her signal, Geilt to move to the Architect's left while she moved right. The hunter appeared rivetted to the scene unfolding in front of him. The Werewolf was tearing into the second of three dogs. Their chain leads dragged in the dirt, giving them total freedom to engage the enemy. The torn body of one mongrel lay sprawled and gutted at the architect's booted feet. It used the last of its life's energy to crawl back to its master. A third dog attacked the wolf creature, circling it as it fought the other hound. It dove into the fight with vicious, tearing bites, sinking razor sharp teeth deep into the werewolf's exposed legs.

The Werewolf had the advantage of powerful arms and a conscious strategy. Charging its opponent when they separated momentarily, it wrapped its arms around the mongrel's mid-section and took it to the ground. The Werewolf sank its teeth into the wild dog's vulnerable neck, suffocating a long howl by crushing its throat in a killing bite. With another of its pack destroyed, the remaining beast gave a wider berth to the Werewolf as it stood over the twitching body, panting and exhausted. With blinding speed, the third dog hurled itself at the enemy with a ferocious roar. Cathleen acted instantly, directing Green Fire into the ridge of fur bristling along the dog's back. The flames didn't stop it from clamping its huge jaws around the Werewolf's thigh. She heard the unmistakable sound of breaking bones. The Werewolf landed hard, a scream of pain erupted from its bloody jaws, sounding to Cathleen as if it were ripped from the bowls of the earth. She was momentarily stunned by the Werewolf's possible defeat. As if sensing this fate, the creature began to fragment, breaking into particles that were caught up in the swirling red mist and swept away. Free of immediate concerns for the Medicine Woman, Cathleen intensified her Green Fire. The flames rooted themselves in the thick fur of the confused beast, sending it howling down the path and out of range of her attack, letting her turn back to the architect.

Cathleen registered Geilt's grunt when his club came down on something making a soft, crunching sound upon contact. She rushed over to the spot where the architect lay face down, the Pith helmet, several feet away.

"Geilt, I needed some answers from this man."

"Cathleen O'Brien, this being is no more, and he is not the architect."

Using a boot, Geilt rolled the body over. The sightless, yellow-brown eyes of Bledsworth looked back at her, but she knew Geilt was right. He hadn't killed the architect.

"You're correct, Geilt. This is the Labyrinth of Lies and reality is constantly being altered. I can feel the power of Dark Magic around this body."

Cathleen stood over the corpse using a spell for discernment. The contours of the face begin to alter like clay under a potter's hand. The black aura surrounding the still form began to tremble and began to shrink, beginning to look like desiccated animal.

"This was a guard," Cathleen breathed in surprise. "I saw them roaming around the grounds when I arrived at the compound. I remember thinking how alike they looked," Cathleen said, studying the figure closely.

"And now I understand why they all appeared so lifeless. They have been brought here by Mirage from where they languished for their crimes against The Green Mother."

Geilt didn't speak for a minute, then asked, "Are you saying this is one called from the Dark Pit of the Sleepless Dead, Protector?"

"It is very likely, Geilt."

Cathleen couldn't shake the feeling the Labyrinth itself was listening to every word and feeling every breath they exhaled.

Jason knew he was getting closer to Cathleen. He and the Historian back-tracked through the shadowy trails of the Labyrinth, zeroing in on a wavering column of smoke. It dissipated quickly in the stronger breeze that moved through the maze. He snatched an upward glance at the night sky when he could. The stars were mere pricks of light, and the quarter moon hung useless in the advancing threat of the storm clouds. He felt a strange heaviness push down on him. The tight enclosure seemed to press against him. *I'm not claustrophobic*, he thought, as he tried to understand a rising panic.

"Will," he whispered, grabbing the big man's arm to stop him. "Something's happening to me."

Explaining this sudden feeling of suffocation, his friend called on a calming spell to reduce the effects of the primal fear humans felt in the night. Jason's feeling of becoming unhinged, began to fade, replaced by a warmth that melted the chill he felt settling around his heart.

"It's Dark Magic at work in this vexing place, Jason. You aren't going mad, I assure you. I have been trained to fight such evil machinations, yet I too, could feel the fear nibbling like fish at my entrails."

Will moved down the path when Jason calmed. Only a smudge of green smoke hung in the moist air, but it was enough to mark their target around the next curve in the trail. The path jogged right, angling sharply into another section of the labyrinth. This part was covered by a heavy canopy of branches and thick vines, effectively erasing even the feeble light. The two men cast no shadows on the ground because the darkness was so complete along the narrow trail. Jason was tempted to ask Will for a small flame, but controlled his impulse, understanding this need was triggered by manipulations of his mind inside this corrupted environment. They proceeded slowly but stopped at the sound of voices coming from the inky darkness directly ahead.

"The Protector and that annoying Medicine Woman have picked up an ally it would appear, Bledsworth."

"Yes, sir. Geilt is somewhat more formidable than the two small women."

His words had a mocking tone that didn't go unnoticed by Mirage. "You underestimate the females! Cathleen O'Brien is not named the Protector of the Green for naught. She has as many wiles as a mongoose. And the woman, Star Fire, is a powerful Shaman. She has already slipped our noose, and I might add it was your failure, Bledsworth!"

Jason could hear Bledsworth tone stiffen as he tried to deflect any criticisms of his botched attack with the wild dogs.

"Geilt is likely no more than the shaggy beast he resembles, sir. You'll have no trouble taking him down."

He was groveling to the unpredictable Mirage.

"You'd best be certain of that Bledsworth! Keeping them in the Labyrinth won't be easy, now that they've discovered some of your little ruses can be gotten round. No. We'd best take no more chances on losing two prizes I want for my wall!"

His voice had an almost dreamy tone as he added, "Geilt will make a fine specimen of raw power in a subspecies, to my mind. I've already picked the best spot in my room to display him. I was thinking of having my taxidermist cut..."

The last of this conversation trailed off into the tunnel of darkness as the two hunters moved away from their unseen audience. Fearful his words would carry on the weird wind, the Historian whispered close to Jason's ear, "Jason, we need to split up long enough for me to get ahead of those two. They likely believe the spider has done for me. You will use your ring from behind and as soon as they begin to engage with you, I will my attack from their rear."

Jason murmured his agreement, turning his ring until a greenish glow floated out of the dark. He asked the Historian if he could provide a kind of mobile Dome of Protection until he got within range of the enemy. "There's nothing to hunker down behind on the trail, and I'd like to survive any beast left prowling."

Jason crept forward like a determined tortoise inside his new shell. The Historian watched his friend for a moment, making certain he was moving with ease under the awkward Dome. When Jason faded into black, Will raised his arms. Using an Unbinding spell, he caused some of the thick vines to unknot from around the tree limbs overhead. As each branch sprang back to its natural place, the force of their release caused them to vibrate for several seconds. Will called a Wind Charm, using the restless winds inside the maze to carry him up, rising through the new opening he made. From above the twisting hedgerows, he was able to search for the pair of hunters. *There! Directly below.* He drifted several yards ahead of his targets. He'd stay floating until they were stopped by Jason's attack. *When they've turned to confront Jason, I'll make them sorry they'd ever drawn breath.* While he continued to hover, Will could hear Mirage still scolding the Architect for his clumsy handling of the wild dogs.

"They should have torn that lot to ribbons," he said to Bledsworth, the sneer clear in his tone.

"The Werewolf came out of nowhere! I knew it was the Medicine Woman of course. The clan member that pointed her out to me told me she could *shift* into any animal, or even take on the likeness of another person."

"You are proving very quick with your excuses, Bledsworth, but slow with your successes! You're starting to annoy me, architect. Need I say more?"

Will heard Bledsworth contritely mumble, "No, sir" just before a flashlight was turned on. Mirage held it in his fleshy hand, directing its beam to the end of the path. They quickened their pace, the light bouncing along the ground. Will heard a soft scuffing sound. The wall of hedges shifted slightly, allowing the two men to take a different trail. His plan wouldn't work unless Jason could follow their route. Will spotted a blurring motion on the trail below. *Jason must have seen the movement of* the *greenery,* he thought, watching. Still inside the Dome, Jason made the jagged turn onto the new path. The Historian gave a sigh of relief and sped up the wind gust to get ahead of the hunters. He was hovering above the pair when Mirage held up a hand. He was swinging his flashlight in a slow arc along the tangle of hedge and trees. His voice sounded agitated when he spoke to his companion.

"Byron, I want to lay more spells around the Labyrinth, and see what we've already caught in our traps. I'll collect the Historian's head from the spider's lair while I'm at it," adding with a self-satisfied smile, "He was a nice little bonus on this hunt, don't you agree?"

Turning the flashlight on the architect, Mirage laughed when Bledsworth shielded his eyes, stepping back from the suddenly bright light. Ignoring the discomfort of the other man, Mirage kept the flashlight directed at Bledsworth's squinting eyes.

"I want you to deal with the Protector's annoying husband. The fool has been following us for some time. He seems determined to get himself killed, and you shall accommodate him!"

Will was taken aback when he heard Jason would not have the element of surprise on his side. *Thank the Mother he asked for the Dome!* The architect began to argue with this plan, putting his master into a seething rage at his audacity. Mirage turned his imposing girth around to loom over the slight man.

He was almost inaudible when he hissed, "How dare you question my reasoning in this, or any matter? Do as you are told or join the others in my collection! I don't have the head of a magic using architect...yet!"

The other man's voice sounded shaky as he pleaded, "But sir, I'm not able to beckon one of the Zombie Guards again, unless you join me in the summoning spell."

"That is no concern of mine, Bledsworth. You'll have to use whatever powers a mere underling has at his disposal. Too bad you wasted your wild dogs back there. However, even *you* should be able to overcome a mere human like the backwoods Sheriff!"

A second later Jason moved onto the trail occupied by a lone figure whose form was little more than a darker shadow inside the gauzy gloom. He was careful to keep inside the Dome while it drifted along. The man on the trail ahead couldn't see the Dome's translucent walls, even so, Jason crouched lower. He wondered if Will was able to pass over the hunters unnoticed, and if he was already in position. *Where'd your partner go and why'd he bug out on you?* Jason wondered, studying the solitary figure. He was about to turn his signet ring toward the hunter when a soft rustling movement stirred the air inside the Dome. Jason spun on his heels to see the Historian squatted beside him.

"Change of plans, Jason. That's the architect up ahead. We'll drop the Dome and take him prisoner. We need to know if there are other magic users being held captive."

A quick nod from Jason was followed by Will's few words in the Old Tongue, and the shield vanished. The two were about to move when a shrill whistle pierced the silence. It rose in pitch until Jason no longer heard it but felt the vibration of its keening sound inside his head. The green glow from his ring became brighter as the ring heated up.

"A Bone Whistle," Will said through gritted teeth, "likely from a dead Sorcerer."

Abandoning any effort at surprising him, Will called out to Bledsworth, "You are outnumbered and your magic will never save you. Surrender, or suffer the Mother's wrath!"

"Save your threats for the friends I've called to snack on your bones, Wizard."

Jason whispered, "Maybe he doesn't know I'm here."

"Oh, in case you feel neglected, *Sheriff Tate*, these friends have huge appetites I can assure you!"

The architect's laugh was the last thing they heard before the hedges on either side of them opened like gapping mouths. Almost before they could register what was happening two Zombie guards burst through the openings on either side of them. The men looked back at Bledsworth in time to see him vanish down the trail. Jason spun the signet ring toward the charging figures coming straight at his exposed flank. The first laser-thin bolt missed the leading guard when he deftly feinted toward the left. It tore into the Zombie following close behind, however, shearing off his arm at the shoulder. Jason knew his scream was not due to excruciating pain, because these creatures were beyond that. He understood this foe was maddened with the driving force of unbridled hate. This was all it could ever feel. As the other Undead shuffled closer to him, he saw it swing a long-handled ax in a wide arc, letting it fly. Jason felt the wicked blade shaving off part of the shoulder of his jacket, gauging a deep cut in the flesh of his upper arm. Feeling a gush of warm blood quickly soaking through his shirt and dripping down his arm, was like adding coals to an already hot fire. The ring on his finger became iridescent with heat. The next beam hit directly into the ax wielder's mid-section in a sawing motion, cutting it neatly in two. The one-armed creature still moved unaffected by the lost limb. It appeared confused and began to kick clumsily at the torso of its fallen comrade. Jason was quick to dispatch it before it could attack again. When he turned toward the Historian, Jason saw both Zombies lying at his feet like corded wood. He guessed Will dismembered them so there wouldn't be any chance they could rise again to do the architect's bidding. While he watched, the Historian opened the ground under the parts of the corpses and returned them to the earth for a final burial.

Looking back at Jason he said, "These two have been neutralized. I'll do the same for those," he added, walking over to perform the same task on the brutes Jason destroyed.

The men stood together for a moment, speaking in quiet tones. They speculated on where the architect disappeared to after his Zombie Guards answered his call.

"I suspect he'll be somewhere outside the maze by now, Jason. Try to find the Protector as I go after Bledsworth and become the hunter for a change!" he said, baring his dazzling white teeth in a tight grin of satisfaction.

Without waiting for comments on his plan, and unaware of Jason's injury, Will shot through an opening created by the guards. Jason watched a ripple in the air above the maze where he exited, and he knew his friend was out. He took a deep breath, feeling exhausted by tension, and tried to ignore the wound so he wouldn't be slowed down. He probably should have told the Historian about it but finding Cathleen took over his every impulse.

<h1 style="text-align:center">Chapter 24</h1>

After the last of the wild dogs was destroyed, Cathleen's main concern was to find the Medicine Woman, Star Fire. Starla was badly mauled while fighting the great beasts in her Werewolf form. Cathleen wondered if that triggered her retreat into the red mist, as she tried to escape further life-threatening injury. Not very familiar with Shamanistic Magic, Cathleen could only guess at how quickly she would heal. *I need to find her to help heal the worse of her wounds.* She opened a hole in the trail and buried the remains of the Demon Dogs.

Geilt came up beside her.

"They won't know we've won this round." The big man nodded his shaggy head grunting in agreement.

With a wave of her hand, she gathered the smoldering limbs into a small pile. Narrow wisps of smoke rose from the heap, causing green smears on the black sky. Cathleen was certain this was Jason's handiwork, feeling his ring's magic over the pile. She was turning toward Geilt when a strange vibration tickled at her eardrums. An extremely high whistle.

"The puny hunter calls more beasts, Cathleen O'Brien," Geilt said, looking around warily.

"We'd better hurry. This place is becoming very crowded with masters and minions," Cathleen responded as she picked up their pace.

Moving along the paths, Cathleen still felt the penetrating tremor and it seemed to be getting stronger. After a quick glance at Geilt, she realized he wasn't feeling the effects of the sound. *Maybe his thick hair shields him,* she speculated. She rubbed gently at her ears trying to minimize the buzzing. After a minute of discomfort, the high-pitched wave abruptly ended. The stillness that followed was torn open by the sound of screams that might have come from the Pit itself. Geilt moved protectively closer to Cathleen's side, his huge club raised and ready. The smell of burning flesh drifted over high privets to where they stood rooted and listening. There was a distinct undertone to this odor that Cathleen was familiar with; it was the odor of an Undead being consumed by Sacred Fire.

"Geilt!" she hissed into his ear as he stooped down to her.

"Jason and the Historian are using the Sacred Fire! They must be nearby and under attack!"

"What is it you want of this Geilt, Cathleen O'Brien?"

After she explained her spur-of-the-moment strategy, Cathleen murmured a few words and reaching out, touched the heavy club Geilt carried, transforming it into a razor-sharp, double-edged ax. Geilt began to chop at the wall of thorny bushes and trees, moving his powerful arms in a constant rhythm of destruction. After the first hard whacks of the blade, a moaning sound erupted all around them. It was barely audible, then rose in volume with each stroke of the ax's sharp edges. This painfilled sound was worse than a bone whistle. A horrible guilt clutched at Cathleen's heart to hear it. She nearly placed a restraining hand on Geilt's arm but reminded herself this was a maze dedicated to machination.

"Keep going, Geilt!" she forced herself to order him, when she saw his arm slowing and his determination waning.

The hedgerow gave a drawn-out groan as limbs, twisted under thick vines and brambles, collected around Geilt's feet. A hole was punched through to the parallel trail. Cathleen's breath stopped in her chest when she looked through, seeing Jason's surprised face looking back at her. Geilt dropped the ax and taking a hand-full of greenery yanked hard, widening the hole enough for Jason to pass through to them.

Cathleen leaned into Jason tight embrace.

She smelled the coppery scent of blood and pulled away. Looking him up and down for possible injuries, she spotted the blood on his ripped jacket. Calling a strong healing charm, the three watched as the flesh closed around the wound.

While he waited, Cathleen said, "We were afraid the Historian was taken captive by the spider."

"He escaped before I found him outside the maze. Somehow, I stumbled onto the exit from this place. We split-up a short time ago so he could chase down the architect."

Jason took a breath and looking over at Geilt gave him a nod and wide smile. Turning back to Cathleen he asked when Geilt joined her. "And where did Starla go?"

"Geilt was capture during one of Mirage's hunts. I found him in Trophy Room after I sent Starla to find you and Will. Starla was in her shifted state, when she was badly mauled by one of the wild dogs you must have heard. We've got to find her before she can be recaptured. She's in a weakened state and won't be able to defend herself."

Jason took the lead them since he discovered the way out of the Labyrinth. The scrap of moon rode higher in the inky heavens but gave only scant light. Every shadow could hide a new threat, but as long as the signet ring remained cool on his finger, Jason felt secure, just focusing on locating the exit. He turned slightly toward Cathleen who walked close behind.

"I marked the exit trail with a circle in the dirt in case you got this far. I think we're almost to the spot."

While Geilt followed the Protector and her mate, he only half listened-in when they spoke in their whispered conversation. His attention was focused on studying the seemingly endless dark wall of hedges along the winding paths. Earlier, he spotted something moving within the tightly woven branches--something small enough to make only the slightest wrinkle in the foliage. Suddenly, Cathleen was beside him and Geilt knew she sensed that ripple as well.

"Geilt," she whispered when he lowered his head to her. "Do you have any idea what's been tracking us?"

In the gloom of the path, she could barely see the shaggy head moving side-to-side. Before she left Jason to speak to the Wildman, she told him to stop. *He must not have heard me*, she thought anxiously as she looked back in time to see him walk around a corner and out of sight. She moved to go after him when the sound of Geilt's roar of distress from behind froze her in place. A quick look in his direction and even in the low light, Cathleen saw the giant was covered from head to toe in a living blanket of insects.

"Fire ants!" she blurted on closer look.

She knew this was a particularly vicious type of this species. Geilt was beating at the parts of his body he could reach. He was scooping up tiny bodies and flinging clumps of them onto the ground only to be replaced by countless others. Cathleen couldn't use Green Fire to eradicate the attacking army, and they bit and stung Geilt relentlessly, finding a route into his nose and ears. In desperation Geilt flung himself onto the ground and began to roll in an effort to squash the tenacious creatures.

It finally dawned on Cathleen how she could stop the attack. Shouting a spell used to bind like things together, she watched as the Fire Ants were pulled by this new magnetism into one seething mound.

The squirming Geilt leapt to his feet. His face and arms were already swelling with the venom from countless bites. Cathleen spoke a charm for healing, repeating it over and over. When she was certain her friend was safe, she turned her attention to the pile of vibrating insects. Turning her Green Fire into a wide sheet of flame, they were reduced to fine ash.

Geilt confirmed he was fine, but Cathleen saw how embarrassed he was to be felled by such a small enemy.

"We have to catch up with Jason. I'm not sure why he didn't stop, but like everything else in this foul place, it can't be good."

Chapter 25

Cathleen picked out Jason's tall figure moving slowly among the shadows. She was tempted to call his name but was wary of disclosing their location to any Zombie Guards roaming the trails. She had to admit, the apparent ease Mirage displayed in turning the aggressive fire ants into his own killer army showed remarkable cunning. He was clearly warping the living *and* the dead to his will with the Dark Arts. She hurried along the trail coming within touching distance before calling out.

"Jason, why didn't you wait?"

He stopped and slowly turned toward her. His face was in shadow, but the red glow of his eyes shone out of the dark like burning coals. Cathleen was shocked as a hideous face broke into a leering grin. She stepped backward directly into Geilt coming up from behind. The stranger gave a low snort of laughter, sending the stink of its breath into the cloying air.

"This mate isn't right, Cathleen O'Brien," Geilt said, leaning down. His observation sounded like the tolling of a death bell.

"Where is the human you try to impersonate, Demon?" Cathleen demanded of the grinning imposter.

A voice as dry as a desert wind creaked out from between the Demon's black lips.

"Why, dead of course. He was needed long enough to lure you to the exit of the labyrinth. Now this hunt can truly begin for my Master."

Cathleen believed only one thing this creature said. Mirage would move his hunt to the wild mountain country outside the compound. But Jason was not dead. She could feel his life force though it felt weaker, indicating he was no longer inside the maze.

"This is the Labyrinth of Lies and you are a pathetic liar, creature!"

The Demon's face had the vaguest touch of humanity, and his utterly deranged look made him more terrifying. Cathleen knew her mocking words enraged him as he took a step toward her. She felt Geilt shift so he was clear of her and could move in with his weapon. She hadn't changed the ax back into his club and saw a dull glint of moonlight bounce off its razor-sharp edges.

"Your beast is no match for me, human!" the Demon growled in its raspy voice as if reading her mind.

"That is the second of your three mistakes, Demon. This is Geilt, Lord Ruler of the Third Plane, and fearless Champion of the Mother's Protector."

The Demon gave a contemptuous snort. His black tongue darted out between black lips as if tasting her physical presence.

"And tell me my *other* mistake before you both die, witch," he drawled as if bored by the conversation.

"You have failed to identify me as the Wizard who will send you back to the Dark Pit! I'm certain the Council of Green Wizards would approve that punishment."

Cathleen took a step back, raising her hands. Jagged streams of Sacred Fire shot from her fingertips, but in a lightening response, the Demon caused the air around it to harden into an opaque shell. Her fire fanned out to either side. Cathleen shouted a spell causing spikes to penetrate the hard cocoon he'd wrapped himself in, driving into the Demon's torso and legs. The shock of unexpected pain ripped a scream from the impaled creature. It shouted strange words while pulling free from the spikes and closing off the gapping but unbloodied wounds left behind. Cathleen was ready to use her second line of defense.

Geilt had been waiting for her to give him the order to attack. She motioned to him to come in behind the Demon while it was still occupied with a healing enchantment. She charged the creature while murmuring her own spell. As she got closer, she realized he was no longer using a healing incantation, but was summoning another Demon.

"Geilt! Behind you!" she yelled.

A monster strongly resembling a flat-faced Fu Lion materialize out of the darkness behind the Wildman, immediately dropping into a deep crouch. Cathleen knew the Fu Lion was considered an Imperial Chinese Guardian. She had a shock of insight remembering her encounter with the Dark Sorcerer Li Shaoweng back in the Mirage mansion. *Is he back in another form?*

Before she could wrap her head around that possibility, Geilt was facing-off with the new challenger. The beast hunkered lower, its massive chest sweeping the ground as it readied itself to attack.. Cathleen heard a rumble from deep in Geilt's chest. *He's laughing*, she thought, incredulous, but she knew Geilt liked nothing better than a good fight, and he was about to get one! The Fu Lion sprang as if catapulted from a canon, its claws were fully extended, as it flew toward the large target Geilt presented.

Cathleen turned away to leave her friend to fight this battle. Too late she realized the Demon had taken advantage of her distraction. He was waving his hands over the hedges causing several thick vines to detach themselves from the tangle of hedges. Cathleen watched the ropey vines slithering toward her but missed one coming from behind until it twisted around her legs. The animated vines weren't responding to her unbinding spell.

The Demon must have anticipated my magic, blocking its effect.

She burned the first one off, only to have three more heavy creepers drop onto her from above. These were quick to tie her arms to her sides. Cathleen struggled to keep one arm free when the Demon suddenly stood a foot away. He spoke in the bleak language of the Dark Ones and before she could shout out to Geilt, she was sent hurtling out of the labyrinth. She watched dumbfounded as the ground sped by beneath her. The last she saw of Geilt, he was dangling the Fu Lion's severed head from his outstretched arm. He appeared lost in an adrenalin-fueled battle haze, and likely hadn't registered her body being jettisoned from the maze.

The Demon vanished.

Narrowly missing some boulders dotting the ground, Cathleen landed on a sharp incline among several scrawny pines, their needles cushioned her body as she rolled perilously close to the edge below. The heavy vines absorbed much of the jolt to her body, and after she stopped moving they immediately relaxed their grip reverting to their natural state.

Getting to her feet and trying to orient herself, her mind raced. *I'm at a higher elevation on the mountain, somewhere above the Mirage Compound*!

The scent of rain was strong in the clear mountain air, looking up Cathleen saw a line of slate-gray clouds rushing toward the bluff. A second later the rumble of thunder echoed off the hard surfaces of the mountain, lingering like some sleeping giant's snore. Instantly reminded of the Gelt, she took a deep breath. She trusted he would find his way out of the labyrinth, and back to her side. He was as dedicated to her service as any knight of old. More thunder in the distance roused her to move. Half crawling up the steep slope, using rocks and roots to pull herself higher, Cathleen made it to flat ground and several massive boulders. They leaned on one another like drunken partygoers, forming a wide gap that she easily passed through. She hunkered down to await the storm. The thunder was closer and lightening crackled ominously among the racing clouds. The wind was considerably stronger at this elevation, sweeping up any loose debris and carrying it off in its cold grip.

Thinking about Jason as she scooted closer to the solid rock, she knew he'd be searching for her and the others of their scattered group. Sitting with her knees drawn up to her chin, her thoughts settled for a moment on the Medicine Woman. As Starla White she appeared fragile, but as Star Fire she was a mysterious Skin Walker, capable of shifting into a fearsome creature.

"Where is she now?" Cathleen murmured as if the rocks would answer.

The brewing tempest rolled in full of fury as it lashed the exposed ground. It sounded like a storming army to Cathleen, huddled in her stony shelter. Winds pounded at the scrawny trees and scrub plants clinging tenaciously to the side of the mountain. She moved as deeply as she could into the cleft formed by the boulders, but a few chilly drops managed to drip on her head, running like icy fingers down her neck. The claps of thunder growled all around her. She watched with the primordial fascination of humankind, while lightning strikes probed the darkness, searching for vulnerable targets. Cathleen strained her hearing for a second, when another sound crept under the heavy rumble of the storm. Moving back toward the opening of her shelter, but unwilling to show herself, she spotted a figure standing near the edge of the cliff.

"Starla!" she blurted out, but her voice was lost inside the next peal of thunder.

She wanted to run to the woman but had to be certain this wasn't a ruse to draw her out into the open. The storm raged on, growing in intensity with each passing moment. The rain was mixed with hail, small white balls bounced as they pelted the ground and the unyielding surface of the rocks. Cathleen was ready to dash out to Starla who appeared indifferent to the storm that raged around her. Her back was to Cathleen. *Why isn't she moving?* she wondered frantically, moving to the edge of her shelter. *Dear Mother! Is she dead?* She bolted from the shelter and grabbed Starla's arms to turn her. The Medicine Woman was stiff and unresponsive. Cathleen half-carried, half-dragged her back to the shelter, pulling her inside as far as possible. Able to see clearly without the rain and hail pounding down on them, she was relieved to find a glimmer of life in the cold body as she gently lowered her to the ground.

"Starla, I've got you now. You must return to this body. It's safe for you to come back."

Cathleen looked at the deep wounds Starla suffered battling the wild dogs in her shifted form. Though she looked completely human, it was possible the injuries prevented her from reclaiming her life force from her Spirit Warrior before she disappeared into the red mist. Cathleen had an unsettling thought. *What if Starla's life force somehow fragmented during her escape. This would leave her human self barely alive, while keeping her shifted self a dangerous threat.* If her theory was correct, there was a Werewolf roaming freely somewhere on the mountain.

"Starla, can you hear me? It's Cathleen. I need to know if the Werewolf is still alive. Starla?"

The Medicine Woman's eyes drifted shut as she slipped into a deep sleep. Cathleen took off her jacket to lay across the still woman. The chill of the mountain and the ice storm quickly seeped into her. She'd been fighting the impulse to leave Starla to find Jason, but she had to locate the Historian first. She needed his magic to make Starla's human spirit, whole again. She tried to settle her thoughts so she could think clearly. *Can't leave her,* she thought looking down on the vulnerable figure. *There is another way though.* She would resort once more to an out-of-body messenger to contact Will. She began to clarify her thoughts out loud, vaguely hoping the sound of her voice would comfort the sleeping woman.

"Will's likely figured out that the real hunt will be on the mountain. As soon as Mirage verifies that we've all escaped the labyrinth alive, he'll have to send the architect back to the barracks to organize the rest of the Zombie Guards for the hunt. I'll start in the mansion. I'll be back here in less than an hour, Starla. Don't be afraid. I'm leaving wards around the boulders and a stronger one at the entrance to this shelter."

Having shared her plans with the sleeping woman, Cathleen leaned back against the cold rock and closed her eyes. She had to ignore the roaring winds and drumming of the rain and hail. She was shivering in her thin sweater but put herself into a deep state of unconsciousness. It was only a matter of some deep breaths for her to accomplish a separation, sending her animated life force out of the rock opening into the dark arms of the storm.

Cathleen's spirit body moved swiftly, zeroing in on the Magic Signature she recognized as the Historian's. Just as she predicted, he was in the Magical Treasures room where she'd found the other captives. She floated over to stand behind him. *Will Farley turn around!* she called in a whispery voice. The Historian spun around, jumping back a few feet. He was holding his long-knife in one hand, ready for an attack.

"Protector! You've sent your spirit messenger. Speak quickly then. The architect is nearby. I fear discovery."

Cathleen explained that Starla was badly wounded, but more importantly, she was not completely reunited with her human nature.

"You are needed now! Use a Time Thread to follow me"

Cathleen's ghostly-self watched as Will called for a Thread to travel to the place where he'd find both Cathleen and the unconscious Medicine Woman. Giving her a nod after attaching it around his waist and hand, the two vanished leaving only a soft popping sound behind. The door flew open just as the air settled in the space Will occupied seconds before and Bledsworth stepped inside. His eyes narrowed and his nose twitched as if he could smell an enemy. Using his Dark powers, he sensed a presence had newly passed through the room.

"I'll find you, Historian. You shall be my personal triumph in this hunt. Even that bloated pig Mirage will be impressed."

Chapter 26

As Jason became aware of his surroundings, he found himself somewhere in the rugged terrain above the compound. He brushed his thick hair back from his forehead as he tried to dislodge an important memory. *I was on a trail inside the maze.* That thought was the trigger for him. He'd been leading Cathleen and Geilt toward the exit. Cathleen called for him to stop. When he turned back to join them, they were both gone. *And now I'm on the side of the mountain.* He guessed Cathleen and Geilt would be out of the maze too. *But are they on the mountain with me?*

The wind was much stronger and carried a bone throbbing chill. Looking up at the vast expanse, he saw dense gray clouds moving like stampeding horses across the night sky. The sliver of moon was powerless to lighten the night against the gathering storm that would soon arrive. As if thinking it brought it on, huge drops hit the ground like bullets. The fat drops turned into a deluge, coming down in slanted sheets, drenching him through in minutes.

Jason needed to find shelter and fast. He knew the lightening was as dangerous as the wind-chill. He climbed higher, recalling the area he'd scouted when the heavy equipment began to roll through the backside of town. *There are large boulders scattered around at this elevation. Better under one of them, than out in the open.* In a flash of lightning Jason spotted a cluster of huge rocks up ahead and climbed as fast as he could to reach them. Icy pellets now mixed with the rain and he slipped a few times on the slick rocks. He was almost at the top of the deep incline when a different kind of chill went through him. *Cathleen! She's up there somewhere!* The boulders he spotted in a flash of lightening were bunched closely together. Jason managed to scoot far enough between them to get out of the battering storm. Wiping the water from his eye and swiping his hand over his dripping face, he waited for the next flash to look around the pitch-black space. In the next bright illumination, he spotted Cathleen propped-up against one of the tented rocks. Starla was stretched out close by, Cathleen's jacket thrown over her. Jason crouched low to get to Cathleen's still figure. His first impulse was to scoop her into his arms, but something warned him against it. The lightning revealed her breathing was shallow, but steady. He sensed she had placed herself into some sort of magically induced stupor. He was about to touch her face when a deep voice came out of the turmoil behind him.

"Better not touch her, my friend. Her spirit needs to be returned to her body before she can be disturbed safely," the Historian warned.

Before Jason recovered from the shock of hearing Will's voice, a current of warm air ruffled his hair as it passed overhead to hover over Cathleen. A barrage of lightning strikes close by, revealed Cathleen's fragile spirit-being. The Historian brought a small flame of Green Fire to hand. He and Jason watched as the spirit floated down and covered Cathleen's body until it was absorbed. A roar of thunder shook the ground followed by another dazzling flash of lightning. Cathleen bolted upright, taking a deep gulp of air.

"Jason! Thank the Mother we found you!" she said grabbing his arm. She rushed to explain how she found Starla.

"She's in a catatonic state, but I think it's self-induced so she can properly heal. The wounds inflicted by the wild dogs were life-threatening. My concern is that somehow, when she shifted back, her life-force split between her human and Werewolf identities. That's why I searched you out, Will. I'm hoping together we can reunite Starla with her Spirit Warrior. If Starla's human self should die, the Werewolf will be free to roam these mountains unchecked by human conscience."

Hunched under the low rock ceiling, Will nodded his head. Without speaking he moved his hands in a sweeping gesture, stepping aside to float the Medicine Woman a few inches off the cold ground to the opening of the shelter.

"Are we working outside in this storm?" Jason's voice reflected some doubt as to the wisdom of such a choice.

"We'll be able to harness some of the Mother's energy lashing around us to enhance our powers," Will responded.

They were all outside, with Starla's body floating higher inside the small circle they created by holding hands.

"We need to lock her inside our sphere of magic in case the Werewolf tries to overcome her human nature and take over," Cathleen said, answering Jason's questioning look.

The ground around the impromptu shelter was covered with a quarter-inch of ice. The winds raged unabated on the exposed mountainside. The black eye patch over Jason's left eye was saturated and stiffened with freezing rain. A biting chill probed like a bony finger into the empty socket. He tightened his grip on Cathleen's small hand to center his thoughts and ignore the discomfort. The Historian spoke a few words in the language of the ancients, calling for the Werewolf beast to show itself. On his third call into the howling winds, a guttural sound answered his summons. It rolled under the thunderclaps and through the wet air. This was the moment that would bring the Medicine Woman back to full humanity, or see her human nature snuffed out of existence by the powerful spirit creature that was part of her. Jason had no role to play in this dangerous ritual but didn't break his place in the circle. His companions began chanting an incantation, while Starla floated between them, a thin sheet of ice beginning to cover her body. Jason noticed icicles forming off her deerskin dress. Her hair was no longer braided but hung in a black cascade to sweep the icy ground.

Another snarl flung itself at the three, along with the battering winds and rain. Cathleen and the Historian stopped their spell casting. Dropping their hands, they turned their backs on the levitated body, and moved further away from her. Jason was quick to realize this expanded the safety perimeter for the vulnerable woman. He was about to follow their actions when the gold signet ring sprang to life with an intense cold-heat. *The beast is near*, he thought. He checked to be sure the stone faced outward. A prickly sensation stirred the hairs at the back of his head while he looked down. A hot breath touched his neck and cheek, filling his nostrils with the coppery smell of blood and rancid meat. There was no time to call out. With only a vague notion of what he'd be facing if he looked to the side, he dove for the ground and rolled until he was near the cliff. Springing back to his feet he saw Cathleen running toward him.

"It's attacking Jason!" she screamed, as she ran toward the hunched form of the beast.

In a blur of speed, it already covered the distance and closed on Jason who scooted sideways trying to avoid falling from the precipice, into an abyss he couldn't survive. The beast stopped advancing on him when Cathleen shouted her warning to Will. Jason's ring was hot and pulsating with green energy. He knew if he used it on the Werewolf creature, he'd likely destroy Starla as well. This was a dilemma only his wife's Celtic powers could solve, but the Werewolf wouldn't be waiting for that resolution. The Historian arrived just as the Werewolf lunged at Jason, long, muscular arms out-stretched to capture its victim before tearing out his throat. Cathleen was screaming a Freezing Spell that was barely audible over the roaring storm. The beast stopped mid-air just as it reached its curved claws to grab Jason and swipe at his exposed neck.

"Jason! Get next to Will," Cathleen shouted. "I need to reunite the beast with Starla before we lose her."

Frozen like an ice carving, Cathleen turned the spirit beast, and sweeping her arm, floated it to hang in its menacing gesture above Starla's body. She could see the drops of saliva falling steadily from its open jaws, hardening into ice crystals on the woman. The warm drops proved that the beast was still animated with a part of Starla's life-force. Cathleen began a spell to reunite the Werewolf with its host, weaving a healing charm inside its purpose. She was using some of the lightning to aid her transformation of the beast. The electric strikes seemed to increase and the two men clearly saw the wolf-beast begin to dissolve, appearing like tiny pixels in a grainy video. Gradually, the Werewolf lost its shape, pouring down onto the unconscious woman in a rainbow of lights.

The Historian rushed over to Cathleen's side. Breaking his own spell, he released the Medicine Woman into his arms and hurried back into the shelter of the rocks. Jason stepped to Cathleen's side when he understood her work was finished.

"Will her wolf-spirit be under control love?"

"Until she needs to release it again."

Following Will, they crowded into the rocky compartment as Starla slipped into a natural sleep. They were all aware they still needed to focus on defeating Mason Mirage. Without a doubt, he was still hunting them and his main prize... the Witch of Appalachia.

Chapter 27

There was no doubt in Geilt's plodding but thorough mind. He'd find Cathleen O'Brien higher up on the rugged mountainside overlooking the puzzle box he just escaped. He'd seen her catapulted out of the Labyrinth of Lies like a Wooly Mush Melon. He definitely sensed her Magic signature radiating from somewhere above his position. He'd found his own way out of the maze after dealing the death blow to the Fu Lion Demon. He knew being out of the tangle of trails didn't mean he or the Protector were any safer. *The Protector knows I will come to her*, he assured himself as he found his footing among the ice-slick rocks, climbing higher still. Looking back over a fur-clad shoulder, he spotted a small light. It slowly cut through the sludge of blackness in the maze he just escaped. *Someone still wanders there.* Geilt shrugged off the discovery. His only concern was finding Cathleen O'Brien.

A heavy storm burst out of the tumultuous skies just as Geilt knew it would. He pulled up the leather hood attached to the fur vest he wore. He knew from experience his thick body hair, and his furs and leathers, would keep him warm enough. The rain pelted his face, rapidly forming tangles of frozen rivulets in his long beard. For a scant minute he listened to the noises carried inside the howling winds. Somewhere in that frenzy of sound, he heard the voice of a woman screaming into the tempest. *Cathleen O'Brien.* Geilt, like the Sacred Yew, was born to his life of service and magic. He easily recognized the words, snatched away by the fingers of fierce winds, as part of the mystic language of the Ancients. A few clear words rode the turbulent air, blown to where he clung to half-buried roots, below a prominent over-hang. Knowing the winds could toss words like the fluff of a lion weed, he hesitated before moving higher. He wrapped his hand more tightly around the sturdy root, grabbing another, deeply imbedded between rocks and dirt, as it was exposed by the next flash of lightening. He set his feet to haul himself up and over the rock face. Struggling to pull his large frame and weight over the slick surface of stone, he pulled himself over the lip of the precipice. He was rising to his full height, when a lightning flash revealed rain-blurred movement among the bulky shapes rocks several yards from where he stood. Not wanting to give himself away, he squatted low to the ground. He picked out the figure, and after watching its movements, a thought crystalized in Geilt's mind. *This is not one of the Protector's friends. This is the small hunter.* He tried to pin-point the location of the Architect who appeared to be moving among the larger boulders and scattering of scrub brush and spindly pine. He began to rise, wanting to move from his vulnerable position near the drop-off, when he heard the distinct thwack of a loosed arrow. This was followed by a sharp pain as the bolt pierced his upper thigh. Muffling a cry to deny the hunter knowledge of his success, Geilt reached down and broke the shaft just above the entry wound. He couldn't chance it catching between rocks and causing more injury. The Wildman was well versed in the ways of an expert hunter. His long life in the untamed Third Realm was secured by his innate survival skills. Over more cycles than he could recall, he'd faced every dangerous creature with teeth and poison. In the end, he ate them and then wore their skins and furs. He was made strong by nature and the Mother's Magic made him fearless.

Ignoring a dagger-sharp pain from the lodged arrow, he crouched so low his beard swept the wet earth. Geilt scuttled in this manner toward a cluster of undergrowth he spotted during the constant barrage of lightening. He dove deeply into the brittle tangle of winter starved trees and shrubs, knowing the raging storm would conceal any noise as he pushed deeper still. He was not very successful at protecting his injured leg, and felt the arrow move slightly as it grazed the frozen ground. Again, he smothered a cry of agonizing pain. There was movement to the left of his hiding place and Geilt heard another arrow in flight. It landed with a resounding thunk a few inches from his head. *This is not a good place for Geilt* he thought. He shifted his weight onto his good leg and slithered like a water leech until he was out of the stiff brush, and close to the remnants of a rock fall. The hunter seemed to sense Geilt's new position. Rather than shooting another arrow at him, he called out boldly.

"Wildman, you are injured. I can smell your blood on the wind, and your trembling fear as well," the architect's voice dripped with arrogance.

"You shall not escape my arrows. I have only been playing with you, like a cat does the vermin it hunts. My arrows have been made into the perfect instruments of death by the Dark powers. Have no doubt...they will find you *wherever* you breath."

Geilt knew it was past time he himself called on more than his brawn if he was to prevail in this high-stakes game. He placed his broad hand over his wounded leg, whispering an enchantment as old as the mountain he bled on. The arrowhead was lodged deep in the muscle and flesh of his leg. With the last word of the charm, it began to move until it, and the broken shank, exited the back of the fleshy thigh, falling with a soft thump onto the ground. He immediately began another spell to staunch the quick flow of blood, and temporarily close the wounds. Free of the arrow, Geilt could do his own hunting. He called for a Shadow Wrap as Cathleen O'Brien had taught him to do in another battle for his life. He decided the architect was hunkered down among the boulders where he first spotted his movement. Geilt moved toward the vague outline of the huge rocks, wrapped in his own darkness. As he neared the would-be assassin's hiding place, he stopped, waiting for the next lightening flash to reveal his exact location. A yellow bolt crackled through the dense night, uncannily striking the exact stand of scrub Geilt had just vacated. The big man felt the earth shudder beneath his feet. The smell of wet burnt wood swirled around him.

"Ah, ha! You have been struck by another kind of bolt! I'll finish the job and hang your head myself among the trophies!"

Bledsworth stepped from behind the boulder and moved toward Geilt's last hiding place, expecting to find a weakened victim.

"I can still smell the blood you left behind Wildman. It must have been burned by the electricity when the bolt found you shivering on the ground."

Geilt froze as Bledsworth passed within touching distance. The architect disclosed his movements when he switched on a flashlight, playing its beam over the scorched ground, and then around the scattered boulders. He was obviously searching for signs of the injured Wildman. The crossbow he carried was prepared, another arrow nocked and ready to let fly. Unarmed, Geilt mouthed another spell and called his club from among the trees below where it was stashed before his climb. He knew he'd have to move fast to outmaneuver the architect's crossbow. The club answered his call and flew into the open hand Geilt had thrust out of the Wrap at the last second. The hunter spun around when he picked up the odd slapping sound. The yellow beam of his flashlight crawled slowly over the ground and surrounding rocks.

"Have you ventured out of your hidey hole, Wildman? You are unarmed as I recall and gravely wounded now. Why not show yourself and let us end our game?"

Geilt was ready to spring from under the Shadow Wrap when a high-pitched voice cut through the fury of the storm. Suddenly, the huge boulders above them were ripped from the earth where they'd been birthed eons before. They began to roll down the slope, picking up speed and debris as they hurtled relentlessly toward them. Instinctively, Geilt jumped to the side, losing the Wrap completely. He saw the oncoming avalanche had a sure path to the architect. In a cascade of lightning, Bledsworth appeared momentarily confused by the unexpected rockslide coming directly at him. He threw away his crossbow as he twisted his body into a dive, away from the oncoming gray death. Geilt heard Bledsworth give a shrill cry, watching as the small man struggled to lift his legs. It was clear a Binding Spell had been used to hold him fast to the ground. His efforts were cut short when the lead boulder smashed into him as it rolled toward the precipice, disappearing in its dark flight. Even if the architect survived the crushing weight of the first boulder, the place he fell quickly filled with the following torrent of rocks and uprooted vegetation. Bledsworth was buried under six feet of mountain when the avalanche churned to a halt.

Geilt stayed on his belly until the last of the rockslide settled into place. He got to his feet slowly, trying to shift most of his weight off his injured leg. The rain had begun to slacken, but still pelted his face, making it harder to pierce the shadows for other threats. Whoever created the landslide had used nature to destroy the Architect. The voice calling the incantation was definitely not female, or was it? The gale force winds distorted most of the sounds around him. It may have been an echo, called from somewhere higher still. He approached the ledge overlooking the Labyrinth of Lies. The outline of its odd shape was clearly illuminated in the lightning strikes. He searched for the light he'd seen moving through it earlier. There was only blackness below him now, but he wondered if the being carrying the light was the same Wizard who caused the avalanche.

The Wildman still felt the Protector's presence somewhere higher on the mountain. "Time for this Geilt to climb," he murmured as he turned away from the dark valley that felt like a bottomless hole. He attached his club to his back with a leather strap where it gave him comfort as he and began his climb. His goal was to find Cathleen O'Brien and her party, and lend assistance in destroying the last hunter, Mason Mirage.

The storm was still raging as if stirred by a mischievous Sidhe child of the Mother. As he gradually made his way to a higher elevation,

Geilt's sense of Cathleen became much stronger. *This is good*, he thought while blocking the pain the climb was causing him. He didn't have time to perform a proper healing, and a thin stream of blood trickled down his thigh, matting the fur lining of his boot. The noise from the storm grew louder as he went higher. He was grateful for the ragged lightning bolts, as dangerous as they were. They helped guide his unsure feet over the ice-covered mountain and helped him find secure hand and footholds to hold his weight. Geilt was tiring from the steady loss of blood and he knew he had to stop to tend to his healing, or risk falling off the side of the mountain into oblivion. In the next barrage of lightning, he saw he'd made it to a wide area with more scrub and only a scattering of scraggly pine. Studying the scene before he made a move, the next bolt proved him correct. He'd spotted an animal den tucked into a dirt and rock mound.

"Move over, bear. Geilt shall be joining you," he said into the biting gusts.

His words were flung into the howling winds and brought to another's vigilant ears. Mason Mirage stood over another mound of earth and boulders marking the burial spot of the architect. Raising his hands over the pile, they shifted and rose into the swirling wind, to hang there until Bledsworth was uncovered. Mirage spoke a string of harsh sounding words, looking down at the mangled body.

"Get up, fool! I offer you this last chance to please me. Do not fail this time!"

The architect's eyes snapped open as he scrabbled over the site of his recent internment and bowed low to his Master. He looked whole, right down to the sharp crease in his pants. He flicked off some dirt and followed Mirage like a chastised pup.

Chapter 28

Geilt crawled into a low-roofed den and became immediately immersed in the pungent scent of the black bear he expected to find there. A flash revealed the animal, curled up, its great round rump to Geilt and the barely adequate opening to his lair. If it was aware of an intruder, it appeared reluctant to leave the deep slumber of its winter hibernation, and the Wildman had no intention of waking it. Stretching his wounded leg, Geilt leaned his back against the cold stone and began murmuring a healing spell. The unstaunched bleeding was slowed in the cold, but he was considerably weakened. Lost in the cadence of his words, gently rocking back and forth to their comforting rhythm, a snuffling sound broke into his concentration, stopping his hand over his leg. Geilt knew it was a matter of days before the natural creatures of the First Realm roused themselves from their winter dreaming, and feared he'd stumbled upon another creature touched by Dark Magic, while in a vulnerable state. The inky interior of the den lit up every few seconds with the strobe effect of lightning that continued to scour the night. The Wildman was convinced the bolts had been unleashed by a crazed god.

He didn't move a muscle or twitch a bushy brow. The injured leg was fully extended, his hand stopped above it like a puppeteer ready to pull some strings. He knew he could never escape the den before the bear pounced. The deep snorting sound was closer. *By the god's beards, he's sniffing me!* Geilt felt a growing panic creeping into his body. He had to make a choice. Turning to face the beast bare-handed or waiting to see what the bear would do to the intruder he found in his den trussed up like his first meal. Moving only his eyes, peripheral vision picked out the creature's hulking body in the next flash of light. It was behind his right shoulder, the hair on his neck stirred with another loud sniff and huffing of rancid breath. Geilt's own furs likely carried strong memory scents from the many animals covering his body. The Wildman prayed to the Mother that the foreign smells might concern the beast enough to dissuade an outright attack. The sharp blade of his charmed club, was secured to his back leaving him without a weapon to hand. There was a rustling sound, and he caught the movement of the great beast as it began to rise above him.

This is no animal, he thought, confirming his suspicions in the next lightening blast. He looked down and saw two hairy but distinctly human-like, feet. The hairy antler wearing Celtic god, Cernnos, flashed in his mind's eye. This was the deity most associated with animals, forests and fecundity. *Could this be…* As if answering the unspoken question, a huge arm swung out, connecting with Geilt's back and driving him onto his side. Geilt coughed-up his breath, while he reached behind and grabbed hold of the heavy club, ripping it free of the leather tie. Before his assailant could respond, he rolled out of the den into the battering winds and sleet, gaining his feet in one fluid motion to face the enemy. His arm was raised to slash into the oncoming creature, when a woman's voice rang out over the crashing of thunder and howling winds.

"Geilt! No! This is a god of my people, come to our aid at my petitioning."

The small form of the Washee Medicine Woman, Starla Star Fire, materialized out of the turmoil around him. She looked as she did before she turned into her spirit animal, savaging her enemies. There was a silvery aura surrounding her that clearly protected her from the raging night.

Still wary of the huge being standing at his full seven feet and more, Geilt had no doubt this was a deity as Starla had named him.

The woman showed no fear of the silent god while she moved to stand between him and Geilt. "This is Chiye-Tanka, Geilt. He is called Big Elder Brother by my people."

The Wildman studied the god closely. He was as shaggy-haired as a mountain goat. Long strands of braided beard concealed most of a massive chest covered in dark hair so thickly matted it would likely stop a knife thrust. His huge head was encircled with a band of golden vines, decorated with feathers and small bones. His only clothing was a roughly made loin cloth of heavy fur, cinched around wide hips with a thin leather belt.

The Medicine Woman watched Geilt closely. She released her held breath when he relaxed the tight grip he had on his club and it dipped slightly toward the ground. She continued to speak to him in a calm voice.

"Many cultures have seen our god as he travels the different realms and studies the many tribes of people. Some have named him Bigfoot, others, Sasquatch, but he belongs to Lakota alone."

The god made no effort to speak until Starla Star Fire became silent, slightly bowing her head. When she moved to stand beside Geilt, he raised both hairy arms and the fierce storm quieted until only a gentle mist swirled around them in the gentle winds. Geilt looked around himself, realizing they stood in a bubble of tranquility. A tall-backed chair constructed of tusks, antlers and bones from unknown creatures, materialized behind the god. A thick cushion of woven grasses appeared on the unwelcoming surface, and the god plopped down with a loud harrumph. He looked as if he held court, clasping the arms of the chair with wide, hairy hands, as his small yellow eyes studied the Wildman. Geilt noticed he wore a single ornament of jewelry on his index finger below the hairy knuckle. It closely resembled the gold ring worn by the Protector's mate. After a moment, Chiye-Tanka spoke. To the Wildman, the god's voice was like an echo that softened as it flew by his ear.

"You are not of this realm, but I have seen you during my travels to the many planes where life exists. You are called Geilt and Wildman. I too am seen as untamed, not unlike this storm that I brought down upon this sour place. There is much here that is evil and unnatural. It needs to be swept from this realm!"

Geilt brought his club down with a loud thump. The sound was clearly his prelude to an introduction to the god seated before him.

"I am of the Third Realm and Master of all that roam that wilderness. We seem much alike Chiye-Tanka. Yet, I am not a god, but blessed by the Mother with Her Green Magic."

"I know of your Green Mother, Wildman and of Her awesome power of light. I have answered this daughter's call, to aid in the removal of the Dark Ones. They prowl and plunder Her worlds and make sport of hunting those gifted with Her Magic...such as you."

Geilt bowed his head slightly to acknowledge this alliance. The god waved his hand for Starla to approach him. Geilt also moved closer to the giant's throne as he viewed the spectacular chair. The god's voice changed as they neared. It was rich and deep like the fertile valleys of the Third Plane. The sound gave Geilt a contented feeling of the familiar. He stood near the horned chair like a confident General awaiting his orders. He swept a look over to the Medicine Woman standing at his side. The white streak running through her black hair shone silvery under the scant moonlight. Not for the first time, Geilt felt an odd attraction to this woman in spite of knowing the creature she harbored within.

The god Chiye-Tanka reached out a hand to each of the mortals. Instinctively, the two responded by extending their own hands, palms up. The god murmured a few words in his smooth baritone voice and placed a pale lizard on each open palm. Geilt watched as the small creature circled as a dog would, before flopping down and curling up in his hand.

"These Lizard Phantoms will be your familiars as long as you are hunted by the Dark Ones. They are the same, yet different, just as you are. Do not be deceived by their size. They have been enchanted and hold enough power to defeat any Demon. Hunt well daughter, Star

Fire. And you, Geilt, assure the Celtic Wizard that the Green Mother has many allies in the battles ahead of her."

A blast of wind made the Wildman lower his head, blinking furiously. When he looked back up, the god of the wild things had vanished along with the bone chair. He felt Starla move closer to his side. She had to yell above the tempest that raged on as before.

"Geilt, place your Lizard Phantom in a secure place. We need not share knowledge of our familiars with the others. These are gifts for our use alone."

"What of your wolf spirit, Starla Star Fire? Has it been banished by your god?"

"No, my friend. My familiar is only with me for a brief period of time, but the wolf creature will stir within me as long as I draw breath."

Geilt opened his fur vest, slipping the creature into a deep inside pocket. It settled down to lie quietly until called upon.

"I hope you are as powerful as you are gentle, little one," he whispered as he refastened the bone posts and closed the garment tightly against the storm.

Chapter 29

Their reunion was brief, but the relief was obvious in the glow of a small flame waiving in her hand. The storm had quieted to a ruffling wind and the moon and stars shone more brightly, giving off a mellow light to hunt by.

Cathleen said, "We need to locate the portal Mirage used to bring his Demons across from the Fourth Plane, back at the mansion. His power source is somewhere in the *other* labyrinth he created in the wine cellar."

Jason stood next to Cathleen, looking down at her and quietly added, "I'm coming with you."

She saw the determined set of his jaw and there was no time to argue. She gave a quick nod. Turning to Starla and Geilt, she asked them to return to the grounds surrounding the house. "At one point, I picked up several cold-energy sources gathering near the outlying buildings, likely from the Undead guards. They'll converge on the mansion to protect Mirage when he summons them. With the architect dead, Mirage will probably retreat below ground and its maze of rooms. That will give him a chance to summon Demon Spawn from the Dark Pit and increase his defenses. You must intercept any creatures appearing outside the walls of the building before they have a chance to answer his call."

Starla looked over at Geilt. Seeing him nod his shaggy head, she reached for his hand. A dense red mist rose from around their feet until it swirled around them completely. In the eerie glow of Cathleen's flame, the others watched as the blanket of vapor vanished, taking with it the Wildman and the Medicine Woman.

"Protector," The Historian said, his brows knit into a deep frown. "I believe I should accompany you and Jason into this madman's stronghold. We can divide the cellars between us and work toward one another as we sweep the many rooms for the portal you spoke of. This will need to be sealed, and there's a good chance there will be more than one."

"Agreed! But before we start our search, I need to ask you about the mysterious Magic Signature I sensed when Starla returned with Geilt. And also, the odd surge of power that made my hair stand on end just before the storm subsided and they rejoined us."

"I too felt this new magic, but I'm uncertain of its source, though it felt very close by."

Jason's voice broke into their exchange as they tried to identify this possible new threat.

"Both Geilt and Starla were hiding something on their person. My ring heated up when they returned, but cooled down almost at once, as if it had already identified the source as friendly. I think whatever they had hidden is another magical force, but no threat to us. I felt the same connection to nature as the magic of the Green," he assured them.

His companions both had surprised looks on their faces. The Historian recalled how Jason stepped away from the group after Starla and Geilt rejoined them, only giving a nod to acknowledge each of them. Now he understood; he was appraising the strange energy source, deciding if it was a threat. He gave Jason a quick thump on his back. "Glad you could clear that up for us, my friend. We have no need of any new enemies. And the thought of Star Fire...and Geilt...falling under Mirage's evil influence, would be too awful to consider."

Cathleen didn't miss the note of anxiety in the Historian's voice when he mentioned the Medicine Woman. *He has genuine feelings for her,* she thought, as they began to move.

The three stayed together long enough to get closer to where the mansion was a brooding presence below them. Without the Inner Eye his companions used, Jason had to rely on the pale light from the grinning moon. It was enough for him to make out the shapes and silhouettes of the many buildings, and the ungraceful bulk of the huge stone house, rising three stories into the unsettled night sky. It was decided the Historian should travel ahead. His task was to search the meandering halls of the wine cellar, searching for any magic users caught in Mirage's net. He'd also hunt for any Portals a fiend could use if summoned. Giving his companions a nod, Will pressed his arms close to his sides and vanished.

Cathleen called for a Time Thread. She told Jason she didn't want to use the Trans-Location charm Will just use and end up too near to his arrival point. "Those charms are prone to follow each other like lemmings, if not separated by a good bit of time," she explained.

She knew Jason hated Thread travel, but he never objected, just grabbed hold of the iridescent rope and wrapped his free arm around her waist. They disappeared as if a large eraser had stubbed them out of existence. When Jason recovered his equilibrium, he had the sensation of being surrounded by something dense and solid, knowing they were below ground. His eye adjusted to recessed lighting discreetly inserted along a sound-proofed ceiling. Each spotlight formed a flat pool of yellow along the stone floor. *Looks like we'll be following breadcrumbs* he thought uncomfortably. He waited while Cathleen scanned the area before they moved ahead. Cathleen waved her hand over each door as she hunted for signs of concentrated magic, this would indicate a functioning portal from the Fourth Realm like a subway from the Dark Pit into the First Realm. Jason's signet ring was cold until they turned a corner. Although it wouldn't burn him, it suddenly felt like a hot iron around his finger. He bent down.

"Something coming our way."

She nodded and whispered, "Straight ahead."

The light was barely enough for Jason to spot a bulky shape as it exited a room at the end of the hall. It appeared to turn, clearly meaning to block them. They came to a halt, each studying the form. Jason leaned again to Cathleen's ear, whispering one word, "Guard."

Cathleen stopped using her Inner Eye when they made their Thread jump. She slipped back into it now, proving Jason's remarkable sight with a single eye. *Surely the Mother has gifted my husband in ways unknown to me,* she thought, turning her own enhanced sight to the obstacle. The guard hunched over, positioning itself to tackle them both. She scrutinized its death-ravished body, but it was the face that made her draw in a deep breath. Besides being shriveled, it was riddled with holes, black worms moving freely in and out, feasting on what was left of rotted flesh. It wore a permanent grin, its lips long ago eaten away, displaying rows of crooked, and broken teeth. This was truly an animated nightmare. For all its appearance of physical corruption, Cathleen knew these Zombie Guards were filled with an evil energy that made them formidable opponents. She made preparations for the inevitable charge. A few words and a Dome of Protection slammed down over them just as the creature charged them. It displayed the shambling gate of the Undead yet crossed the distance separating them with remarkable speed. As it rained heavy blows on the shimmering skin of the Dome, Jason sent thanks to the Mother they were spared smelling the stench of its death.

"Cathleen," he said, barely moving his mouth. "We need to dispatch this beauty so we can continue our search. Got a plan?"

The thumping continued while the Guard shuffled around the Dome, cocking its shrunken head, searching for a weakness. Cathleen called up a tiny flame. The creature stopped while it studied the green shoot leaping on Cathleen's open palm. It shifted its gore matted head in a quizzical fashion, trying to figure out its significance. Cathleen kept an eye on the Zombie, as she softly warned Jason, "Be ready to jump out of its reach." Trusting he'd understand her plan, Cathleen began to reverse her spell. The Dome vanished and Jason threw himself to the side as Cathleen transformed the tiny flame into a blow-torch, directing the intense column of fire directly at the Zombie's mid-section. The flames took root inside the rotting cavity of its lower torso and spread upward into the hollow chest. The screams coming from the Undead Guard made the hairs on Jason's neck stand on end. Looking down he saw the signet ring was shimmering with its own heat. He pointed it at the upper legs of the creature, sweeping his hand in a sawing motion. The narrow beam cut through brittle bone and morbid flesh. The top half of the Guard fell backward while the severed limbs stood planted on the floor, burning like candles. Jason got to his feet while Cathleen held her hands over the remains of the Guard. She'd send it back to whatever grave it occupied before Mirage animated it. She felt no compassion for the men he'd turned into Living Dead, knowing they were evil long before he called them to his side. Finished, she turned to Jason.

"We need to hurry. The Historian should have covered the area further ahead. He'll be moving toward our position, unless he ran into one of these creeps too."

They crept as silently as the two shadows moving up the walls of the winding hallways. Cathleen continued to open the scattered doors with flick of a hand, until they turned a corner and found themselves staring at a wall.

"Dead end," Jason grumbled softly.

"Jason, this wall isn't real... but I'd bet what lies behind it is very real!"

Cathleen raised both arms, putting her palms against the rough surface of the wall. Closing her eyes, her body stiffened before she jumped back, as if she touched a live wire.

"Cathleen, are you OK?" Jason said, grabbing her around in time to keep her from falling.

"There's a Portal here, behind this wall! I have to break through the wards placed around it, to expose it."

"I'd bet even the Architect, didn't know this was here," she added excitedly.

"And you'd surely lose your wager Protector. Just as you're about to lose your life without my help!"

The architect, Byron Bledsworth, stepped through the solid concrete as easily as a shark moves through water.

Chapter 30

The Historian reappeared in a starburst of pulsating colors. He landed somewhere in the gloomy halls of the mansion's wine cellar. The air was chilly, with a delicate trace of fruity aromas. His mission besides searching for any captured magic users was to locate and close any Portals to be used by Demons crossing over from the Dark Pit of the Sleepless Dead. He stood in a shadowy passageway, taking a minute to reorient himself to gravity after using the Trans-location spell. His acute hearing suddenly picked up a noise coming from somewhere ahead. *Sharp claws... moving this way?* The thought flashed through his mind.

Listening intently, he knew whatever was making that clicking noise on the stone floor, was getting closer. He looked back over his shoulder into a tunnel as dark as despair. The recessed lighting along that route flickered off and on, as if sending out a code to lurking creatures. Since that was the only way of avoiding a confrontation with whatever skulked in his path, he had little choice. He considered calling for a Shadow Wrap but rejected that plan. *I need to move faster than is possible while trying to stay concealed.* Moving in the opposite direction of whatever approached, he was forced to take a sharp turn left when the passageway ended in front of a storage area.

A few weak lights sputtered along the ceiling; any glow almost smothered by the weight of shadows clogging the narrow hallway. Will believed Mirage planned this sort of ethereal atmosphere to disorient any trespasser. He listened closely before committing himself to the blackness of the passageway. Not hearing the echo of claws across the floors, he thought he confused whatever it was by reversing course. He skidded to an abrupt halt when the raw scent he remembered from the spider's lair struck him in the face like the haze above a cesspit.

His hand moved down to his thigh, stopping at the hilt of the charmed long-knife in its sheath. He called on the Mother's protection against the Demon lurking in the bottomless blackness at the end of the hallway. Whatever it was, its form was mound shaped, even to Will's Inner Eye. *Got to move, or I'll be forced to give up the hunt for the Portals.* That thought put his risk in perspective. He knew he had to act. The hall was suddenly filled with the Historian's velvety baritone voice, calling out words from Druid ancestors. Green Fire created a flaming barrier between the lurking creature and Will, hopefully preventing an immediate attack. The moment the green flames fanned out to lick at the walls, Will had a clear view of the beast lying in ambush. He hadn't imbued the fire with its awesome destructive capacity yet, wanting to identify the revealed beast in its glow. The humped- back form of an enormous Black Bear rose up on hind legs the size of stout tree trunks. The shaggy body stretched until the small, tufted ears scraped the ten-foot ceiling. The fore legs dangled in front of a massive body, displaying thickly curved claws, as long as the knife Will gripped in his hand. The bear cocked its head to the side and gave an ear shattering roar. The fury it displayed at the fire reverberated up and down the corridors. The black cavern of its gaping jaws flashed rows of long, yellowed teeth, made for ripping apart food and enemy alike. It violently shook its huge head in a snarling denial of the flames, spraying thick saliva out of its blackish-purple mouth. The foamy globs showering the floor and splattering the walls, left deep runs on any surface.

"You are an enchanted beast, I see," Will murmured.

His words were lost when another roar erupted from the ghastly maw of the creature. In its heightened ferocity, the bear swiped forcefully at the flames. The beady black eyes glittering over Will's undulating wall were fierce with rage.

Will saw a moment of hesitation when it jerked back the paw it swept through the flames. Except for its wicked looking claws turning a fiery red, the beast was unharmed. Will was quick to finish his spell and summon the fire's destructive powers. He knew this beast would charge him any moment in spite of the burning barrier and would clear the space separating them in seconds. As Will summoned the full harmful elements of Green Fire, the bear dropped to all fours backing up several feet from the flames. Will wondered if the beast was quitting the field before the real battle commenced. As if answering Will's surprised look, the bear gave another horrific roar. Lowering its massive head like a battering ram, its weight adding to its momentum, it pushed through the flaming wall of Sacred Fire. Only Will's incredible speed saved him from being mowed down. The Historian streaked backward down the hallway never taking his eyes off the massive beast in pounding pursuit. The sound of its deadly claws echoed like mechanical chisels as they left a trail of deep grooves in the stone floor. Green Fire burrowed deeply into the bear's thick pelt was fanned by the bear's lumbering pursuit of its prey. The huge head was covered in fire, but the demonic beast seemed unaware.

Will increased the speed of his backward flight in the face of this catastrophic failure in his magic. In desperation he called out an incantation to arm himself with more than his long-knife. The bear's heavily muscled body began to slow. The Historian was now armed with a long spear. He wondered if the magic used to produce such a creature allowed it to recognize his weapon was charmed to find its pulsating heart.

It stopped completely, and once more rose on its hind legs to its immense height. Its bulk blocked the hallway and its shadow snuffed out much of the sparse lighting. Will knew this was an intimidation technique. Its black eyes glittered like shards of the night sky as they fastened on him. The bear suddenly exploded in hungry green flames, yet it appeared none-the-worse for the conflagration. Will guessed his magic had somehow been weakened in the cellars, but not quite defeated. The beast's head burned like a stubby hunk of tallow, without consuming the flesh beneath the flames. He had to vanquish this possessed creature before it could charge again. He wasn't sure how he'd do in close combat with such a magically enhanced leviathan. Stepping back on his left heel and carefully balancing the weight of the long spear, Will hefted the lethal shaft above his shoulder. The hallway resonated with the shouted invocation of a Druid warrior calling upon the Green Mother for killing accuracy. Will could only follow the spear by using the Inner Eye because of its phenomenal speed. He saw the shaft hit the giant beast squarely in the chest. It pushed through fur, fat, muscle and heart and kept going until it penetrated the hunched back. The beast was picked up with the force of its velocity and pinned to the wall at the end of the corridor. The Green Fire vanished from the impaled bear the moment the spear pierced its heart. A surge of relief and then regret, flooded the Historian. He was cautiously approaching the body when a voice circled around him from the shadows.

"Ah! You make a fine adversary in my hunt, Historian. You managed to destroy my dumb beast, despite my slight modifications to it. Bravo! I thank you for the surprising entertainment. I have so little of it in these savage places. But the hunt must go on! When next I see you, Historian, it will be to place your noble head on my wall of trophies."

Will dropped among the shadows at the sound of the voice and searched the hallway for Mason Mirage. Dark powers were used to change a normally shy creature into the monster he was forced to kill. Mason Mirage was behind this sinister tampering with the Mother's creatures and the inevitable end that followed. He studied the gloomy hallway for any clue to the madman, finding only emptiness. Will raised his hand, calling the spear back. The enormous body slumped to the floor, spreading out like a wide pool of blood on the floor.

"Child of the Mother, what has been done to you is a perversion of all Her laws." The Historian murmured a last charm and moved past the fury heap as it began to evaporate. *Must find those Portals from the Dark Pit,* he thought as he jogged down the open hallway. He hoped he would meet Cathleen and Jason somewhere along the way. There was a sharp feeling between his shoulder blades that someone watched, but he dared not slow himself by taking on a concealment. Heading toward the area he should find his friends, he felt waves of Magic washing over the passageway like a red tide. *A portal is near...I feel its evil in the air itself.*

Chapter 31

When Byron Bledsworth stepped through the solid wall, Cathleen and Jason backed up several feet. Jason's gold ring pulsating with heat at the nearness of Dark Powers. Cathleen laid a restraining hand on Jason's forearm preventing him from aiming the ring's deadly ray at the architect. As Bledsworth moved a step closer, she whispered, "Wait until we know how he's here."

The architect's unimposing physique was deceptive. Cathleen could feel a powerful aura surrounding him like a black sun.

"I wonder, Bledsworth. Does your master know you've been hunting on your own?" Cathleen called out.

"I have no master and can hunt as I please! I am unlike anything else here you see. I am a free-willed being."

"As long as you invoke the Darkness to yourself, you are never free of its hold over you, and you are a fool to believe otherwise!" she shot back.

"Your friend the Wildman would tell you differently. He saw me die under an avalanche of stone and yet here I am!"

Jason was quiet as his wife and the architect traded barbs, but he was finding it hard to control his urge to blast the smugness off Bledsworth's face.

"Cathleen, let me take him out," he murmured.

"No need. He's just an Astral Projection, which means his real body is hidden away somewhere. He might not have that long before he has to be reunited with it."

They never took their eyes off the architect, seeing him fade in and out, until he vanished completely.

"Well love, he knows we're in the wine cellar, so it's just a matter of finding his body, right?" Jason asked.

"It's more important we find those Portals, honey. The Historian should be closer to our position by now. We need to cover our portion of the search before we meet up with him."

The hall they followed jogged left, but before they could move on, Cathleen quietly said she felt a presence nearby. Jason leaned in, asking if it might be Will since his ring was still cold.

"Not his Magic Signature. It's possible we've inadvertently boxed something between us. But I admit, it does have a familiar undertone to its power. Let's use a Wrap, and wait to see who, or what, crawls out of the dark."

When they were well concealed, they pressed tightly against the wall where it curved off into another hallway. Jason glanced at his ring, realizing he'd been unconsciously rubbing the emerald. As if that was a kind of magical trigger, he became ridged and was no longer in the web of hallways in the wine cellar. He blinked rapidly trying to fight the deep sleep that enveloped his mind. His eye closed and he became aware he was in the dead space between reality and the unknown. He saw Cathleen beside him, snugged up against the wall, and then he heard a piercing scream. He watched as Cathleen held something up to her mouth. She began to blow into the holes of some kind of whistle. Sharp jarring notes swam around his head. Something began to materialize out of the murky shadows. He was so shaken he nearly fell out from under their dark camouflage. Cathleen's hand was gripping his arm tightly when he finally came out of his Waking Dream.

"Jason! Sweetie you had one of your dreams. Do you know what's coming toward us?" Cathleen asked in a rush.

"No time to explain. Do you have your mom's finger bone from the Forest Hag?"

"No, but I can summon it. Should I..."

"Call it to come to you. Now!" he told her, urgency ringing in his voice.

Cathleen didn't hesitate. After a brief incantation, a dazzling light flashed inside the Wrap, and a long finger bone lay across her palm. The relic had been hollowed out, blow-holes made along its length. Cathleen felt the uncomfortable charge of power it carried. Unlike the Green Mother's creative force, this power existed only to destroy. The hand it came from belonged to the Forest Hag, an evil being who relished the suffering she inflicted upon her victims. The finger was ripped off during a battle with Cathleen's mother, Brighid, while she served as an Outlander Wizard Scout. Cathleen knew the Forest Hag was among the worse of the Demons. She lived like a hermit in the most remote forests, and rock-strewn hill country of the Emerald Isle. This area had been patrolled by the Outlander Wizard Scouts since formation of the elite, secret group. They were tasked with preventing incursions from the Dark Pit, but the Hag always eluded their traps, and bested their wards. Cathleen's mother Brighid, used the Hag's own superior art of camouflage, to trace her back to her lair. Brighid battled the Hag for hours. In the end, the Hag was able to wrench all, but her gnarled index finger out of the Binding Spell used to hold her.

Cathleen let the Shadow Wrap slip back to its natural state to use the bone flute effectively. She held the charmed whistle to her mouth. Jason saw her cringe involuntarily as she placed her lips over the end. She began fingering the holes at random, blowing several notes. The shrill sound left their ears ringing, but she blew again and again, using different combinations of holes, and producing more bleating notes from the bone. Jason waited nervously, an arm's reach from Cathleen. The narrow hallway started to fill with a swirling, dark vapor. Its mass appeared to be spun by the invisible cacophony of notes bouncing around in the dead air of the passageway.

The Forest Hag began to materialize.

Jason watched as the Hag's shape began to stain the mist with her ragged black gown. His signet ring sprang to life the instant the Hag became more substantial. Cathleen played a series of staccato notes with a flurry of finger movements. Suddenly the Witch stood before them. She was hunched over, leaning heavily on a rough walking stick, as if too fragile to move on her own. Cathleen knew the Hag had no such impediment, and could spring like a rattle snake at a blink of the eye.

"I heard my tortured digit calling out to me. I see it has found a new use by the daughter of the Outlander Wizard Scout, Brighid...she who tore it mercilessly from my hand!"

Cathleen brought a shoot of fire to her left hand, holding the finger bone close to the dancing flame.

"You would do well to show more respect to Brighid and her daughter, Hag. I am Protector of the Green, as you well know, and will destroy you and your wretched finger as easily as it was used to summon you."

"What is it you want of me then, a decrepit old woman, snatched from her cozy hearth, to visit this dank stone palace? You already possess my finger and use it cruelly to force my presence!"

"Quiet, Hag!" Cathleen hissed through clenched teeth. She knew this creature's black heart and wasn't taken in by her mewling tone.

"You are old as dirt, this much is true. But all the rest you spew of your sweet cottage hearth are falsehoods, seeping like the juice of the hemlock from your foul mouth! You have been summoned to do my bidding, Hag, and do it you shall, or suffer more than the loss of a single digit!"

Cathleen put out the tiny flame in her left hand and began to blow on the bone whistle. Jason spotted a ruffling under the Hag's tattered gown. He blinked, jerking his head back when a small leather shoe with a silver clasp fastened around the top, sailed by his head. It clattered against the stone wall to lay somewhere in the well of shadows. Cathleen stopped playing. The Forest Hag was squinting down at her scrawny, naked foot.

"Ack! You are as cruel as your Wizard mother!"

"Next thing you lose is the foot, Hag," Cathleen answered calmly, making her words even more potent.

"Nay! Tell me your request that I may give it you, and be gone from the dampness of this stone that seeps into my poor bones."

Cathleen reverted to the Old Tongue, knowing full well the Forest Hag was conversant in the language of the Druid Mystics as she was with most Fey dialects. Cathleen spoke only a few words and the Hag vanished into the same dark mist that carried her there.

Jason came closer to his wife asking, "What did you order her to do, love?"

"A little housekeeping chore in the Magical Treasures room. I kept feeling there was another source of magic there besides the magic users Mirage held, but I couldn't think what it could be. Now I'm certain it was a Portal I sensed. With the titanium so prevalent around the room, my own magic would be too diluted to do the job of closing it off. The Forest Hag won't be affected by the titanium since her own magic is of the Dark."

"So, she'll seal it off, and then what? Is she free to return to her ancient forests?"

"Until I need to call on her again. Jason, you realize it was your Waking Dream that revealed the need for the whistle? Thanks for always having my back." Standing on tip-toe Cathleen pressed a soft kiss on his mouth, ignoring the stubble on his unshaved face.

"Let's get moving, honey. The Historian must have covered most of this long hallway by now."

Chapter 32

After his encounter with the demonically altered Black Bear, the Historian discovered and sealed-off two Portals between the Fourth Realm and Mirage's stone stronghold. Seeing first-hand, the bleak effects of the evil moving freely among the Mother's own creatures, Will's search became even more urgent. The hallways running through the wine cellar twisted and turned under the massive stone mansion, like a snake pinned under a heavy rock. Will was accustomed to roaming freely over rocky hills, open fields, and untamed woodlands. Working through the confines of the passages and rooms felt oppressive. He had just stepped back into the hall after searching another of the endless storage rooms, when he picked up a keen vibration in the air. He felt another tremor passing over him, and was able to trace the quivering sensation to an alcove he'd spotted earlier. It appeared insignificant, and he didn't explore it further.

Will slipped his long-knife out of its sheath; the feel of its handle comfortable in his hand. As he began to move, he conjured a small ball of fire to float ahead of him, lighting the heart of the alcove. The flame hung inside the depression like a single star barely reflecting off a mud bog. Its light was greatly diminished in the swamp of shadows. As Will approached, the slight vibration he'd felt turned into a humming sound that became stronger and louder. The interior of the cubicle remained unreadable, but Will's senses were throbbing with anticipation of an enemy. He began to form a larger fire ball and was about to toss it into the murky recess when a familiar voice rang out to freeze his arm.

"Hold, Historian! It's the Protector's champion and Starla Star Fire!"

Will held his ground until he saw the giant Wildman and the lovely Medicine Woman stepping out of the funnel shaped opening developing at the center of the cubicle. The pair quickly related how they had stumbled upon a Portal outside the building, following it until they found its twin opening leading from the alcove, into the Fourth Plane.

"We have sealed off this entry Historian," Starla was saying, "but we aren't certain if a gigantic Black Bear was able to get through beforehand."

"It has been dispatched and returned to the Mother," he assured them grimly.

Turning to Geilt, Will said, "Well met, my friend," while slapping the Wildman's broad back. "It is good to find friends among the deep shadows of this stone fortress! We must hurry on ahead to join with the Protector and Jason. They should be nearing this point any moment."

Speaking in hushed tones as they hurried along the hallways, Will told them of his encounter with Mirage, following the destruction of the magically altered Black Bear.

"Mirage is possessed. His spirit became tainted when he immersed himself in the Dark Arts. He can no longer be perceived as a natural being. Our goal must be to terminate him from this life cycle and prevent any other cycles to follow. He intends the same end for us, and our kind," he concluded soberly.

The others came to a sudden stop when the Historian held up a hand and turned to them saying, "I can feel the Protector's Magic Signature. They're close."

The trio began passing rooms with bronze plaques above their doors. These designated the origins of the trophies on display inside. Cathleen never mentioned this part of the cellar, and likely didn't know of its existence. Geilt stood in front of a plaque reading *Creatures of the Third Realm,* a growl rumbling deep in his throat.

Starla walked slightly behind the Historian. Will thought she was speaking to him until he realized she was whispering in a rhythmic language, totally foreign to him but laced with magic. He gave a cursory glance over his shoulder at her. Her head was slightly bowed. The starkly white streak in her lustrous black hair shown in the poorly lit hallway like a rare white rainbow. This woman was a mystery to him, but a mystery he found himself drawn to. He tamped down thoughts of her beauty and refocused on finding Cathleen and Jason in the infernal stone cage. After a few minutes of what seemed endless hallway, Will picked out a rippling movement in the shadows ahead of them. In this section of the wine cellar, only an occasional recessed light shone at the ends of the corridors.

The poor illumination produced deep inky wells close to the walls, creating the illusion of a narrowing hallway. Unconsciously, the three drifted toward the center of the passageway. The Medicine Woman's voice rang out, "This Demon is for me!"

Will spun around to face her, catching a blurry glimpse of her slight figure as it hunched down, her Spirit Warrior emerging rapidly. The wolf beast pushed past the stunned Historian, knocking him back against Geilt who moved forward when she blurted her warning. Both stood transfixed for a breath. Snarls and guttural roars filled the confines of the hallway, as the adversaries came together somewhere in the impenetrable darkness surrounding them.

Just as suddenly as the battle began, a flash of Sacred Fire lit the area behind the combatants. Two fire balls were lobbed directly at a Zombie Guard engulfing the creature until its skeletal body burned like a dry stalk inside the green flames. Cathleen and Jason stepped out of the gloom, behind the smoldering remains of the Guard. The Werewolf gave another roar, turning on them, clearly enraged at being deprived of its victory. Jason's signet ring shot a thin bolt at the oncoming beast. It penetrated its mid-section causing it to howl in pain as it collapsed. The others watched, shocked at what transpired, watching as Starla morphed into her human form.

They all rushed forward to where she lay, curled into a tight ball, her arms wrapped around her knees. After a minute she began to relax and uncurl until she was able to sit up. There was no sign of injury though all had seen her hit squarely by the green shaft.

Jason was shaken, kneeling beside her. "Starla, I'm so sorry. I tried to minimize the bolt's force, but you were lunging at Cathleen."

"There is no fault in your actions, Jason. I am healed, and just need a hand up."

Cathleen came over and asked why her healing process was faster. "When you were injured by the Demon Dogs it was much slower."

"My gifts are enhanced a little more after each shifting. My Spirit Warrior takes more and more of my human energies to itself."

Jason was shocked at the implication and asked if that meant shifting would prove dangerous to her grip on her human nature. Starla gave him a thin smile.

"Only the Old Ones can answer that question."

Chapter 33

Back together again, Cathleen was able to fill her friends in on the architect's surprise appearance, and his use of some form of astral projection.

"There's no doubt his death on the side of the mountain was somehow manipulated, but I'm not sure if it was his idea at the time."

They all heard Geilt clear his throat, as if a bone was lodged there. He was obviously angry at being fooled, as well as being injured by the small hunter. Leading them to the elevator she used with Mirage after their interview, Cathleen quietly shared some thoughts on strategy.

"We have to lure Mirage out of this stone maze and into the open. His ego won't permit him to doubt his safety from our attacks in any environment. He believes himself invincible. By now, the architect has returned to his body, likely hidden somewhere on the grounds. By the way, there's a good chance he's been hunting on his own. He made it clear he was more than capable without Mirage's help. Like Mirage, his ego will prove his downfall."

She turned to Geilt as the lift opened with a whisper. Jason held the door as Cathleen spoke to him. "Geilt, I ask you to hunt down the architect. He has helped capture many innocent beings from the Third Realm, and he conspired to capture you. As the Mother's appointed ruler of that domain, the task falls to you. Find this evil creature and remove him from this realm forever."

The Wildman gave a deep bow to the Protector and melted into the shadows. They all bent their heads as a gush of wind swept through the corridor. Cathleen looked at The Historian and Starla. The soft, yellow lighting from the elevator gilded their expectant faces.

"While we've effectively sealed the Portals we discovered, it's clear Mirage brought more than just his Zombie Guards into this Realm.

When Geilt makes his move on Bledsworth, Mirage will likely be alerted. Not wanting to lose his reliable lacky, Mirage ought to come to his defense. And that's when Jason and I will make our move on him."

"And what of Starla and myself? What would you have us do, Protector?" Will asked.

Cathleen told them she was sure the rest of the Zombie force was scattered over a wide-ranging area of the forest, and mountain range surrounding the compound.

"You need to ferret out any Guards and send their spirits back to the Dark Pit. They were already lost when Mirage summoned them and deserve no mercy now."

The Historian and Medicine Woman disappeared into the red mist Starla conjured. Jason and Cathleen watched until the last of the swirling vapor blinked out of sight taking the pair with it.

"Let's take the elevator to the roof, Jason, and see if we can spot some flashes of activity now that we have more night light."

When the door slid open, they realized they were at the opposite end of the roof from where the helicopter sat in the pale light. Jason whispered it was like stepping into a different world as they moved into a roof garden. Tall, clay pots, filled with exotic ferns, and plants with broad, fan-shaped leaves were placed at intervals creating the backdrop of the garden. Several glass tables and lounge chairs with pillows and umbrellas, dotted the area. The whole scene felt contrived to Jason as he looked around, half expecting to see a chattering crowd of sun bathers with gin and tonics in hand.

"It looks like the architect tried to instill some kind of warmth in this mausoleum," he remarked.

He walked over to the vine-shaped wrought-iron railing that appeared to encompass the entire roof. He turned back to Cathleen and saw a red dot on her mid-section.

"Down!" he shouted.

A thunderous blast tore through the air.

The high caliber bullet missed Cathleen by a fraction when she dropped to her stomach. Jason crawled over to her. Cathleen turned her head, looking back to where she stood just a breath ago. Fragments of a clay pot were scattered across the patio and the fern lay in ribbons as if it had gone through a paper shredder. Jason scuttled back to the low railing, hoping to get a glimpse of a reflection off the shooter's scope. Cathleen stretched out beside him. He moved his eye in a methodical scan of the area, trying to spot the flash of a gun.

"I can't pick up any signs, but it's a sure thing he's trying to get a fix on his next target," Jason said.

Cathleen thought for a minute then said, "Let's narrow it down. We can't stay here indefinitely. The shooter is likely one of the guards, acting as a snipper from a blind in the woods across from us. Remember, we passed several on the mountainside coming in here."

"How can we get him to expose his position?"

"Easy. I'll use an old trick of my mother's."

Cathleen conjured several long mirrors, raising them to stand in a semi-circle. Her reflection appeared in all of them. A red dot targeted the middle one and a shot rang out. The mirror shattered into thousands of tiny slivers.

Jason shouted over to her when he spotted where the shot came from. "Five o'clock! Behind the boulder!"

Cathleen jumped to her feet and hurled the fire ball she formed while waiting. It streaked through the air, smashing into the rock. The boulder blew apart like confetti from a piñata, taking the Zombie Guard with it in a rain of stone and bone. Jason was relieved to see Cathleen had dropped back to her stomach, guessing the Zombie Guards might operate in pairs.

"Can't wait to locate any others, Jason. I've called a Thread."

Jason recognized the low humming sound hovering slightly above Cathleen's head. He sighed, knowing he'd have to endure another unpleasant shift. He scooted close to her while she wrapped it around the two of them with a quick hand gesture. He immediately felt himself being swept off the roof garden. Cathleen's hand squeezed his tightly. They landed on their feet among a thick stand of Balsam Pine. A White Tail deer was bedded down nearby, but the popping sound of their arrival made her bolt from the area. Cathleen used her Inner Eye to peer into the fading night shadows. Jason leaned toward her ear.

"Don't move. We dropped behind a blind." He used his chin to point toward a cunningly concealed hunting shelter.

"That doe didn't even sense it," he murmured.

"Let's see if anyone's home," Cathleen whispered back.

Raising her arms and making a spinning motion over her head, she conjured a powerful tornado, putting the hut at the center of its whirling funnel. They watched as the winds clawed away at the roof and sides of the blind. The structure resisted, no doubt with the help of some charm placed upon it, Jason thought, but the battering force made short work of bringing it down. He gasped when he saw the pitiful figure of Byron Bledsworth standing in the middle of the ruins. Jason trained his ring on the architect the second he saw his dazed looking face. Cathleen dropped a Net of Nettles over the stunned looking man before he could bolt. She and Jason approached from either side of the rigid figure.

"Don't even breath heavily, Bledsworth, or suffer the pain of the poison berries surrounding you. We didn't expect to see you hiding like a rabbit out here. It appears your boss has abandoned you to your fate."

"Cathleen," Jason said softly, watching the architect shrink into himself, looking even more defenseless. Jason took Cathleen's elbow, moving her a short distance. "This whole scene has the feel of a goat being staked out in the jungle, hoping to lure the jaguar to an easy kill. I don't li..."

The shot rang out even as Cathleen lunged at Jason, taking him down to the ground. They lay among the debris of the deer blind trying to orient themselves to the new threat. Cathleen raised her head just high enough to see that the Net of Nettles had been pulverized, along with Byron Bledsworth. The bullet pierced the Net, triggering an explosion of the deadly berries. Bledsworth never screamed out, but Cathleen knew his death would have been excruciating from the effects of the poison. She vaguely hoped the bullet finished him off first.

"Jason, I'm dropping a Dome over us until we locate the shooter."

Jason pulled up his legs, feeling the sphere take root around them. He got to his feet, reaching for Cathleen's hand. They scanned the area until Jason nudged Cathleen. He was right; the hunter clearly used the Architect as bait to draw his intended victims into a trap. A gray, predawn light revealed Mason Mirage as he stepped away from a small hill, directly in line with the destroyed body of the architect. He must have used a voice magnifying charm because his arrogant words slammed against the Dome like hammer falls.

"And now, I shall conduct my hunt without the irksome nattering of the weakling, Bledsworth. Ready boys and girls?"

His laugh echoed inside the Dome, reminding both of them that his powers were fearsome and his conscience nonexistent. When he vanished, they could still hear his mocking laughter float through the unnatural quiet of the woods.

Chapter 34

Geilt watched the brief and somewhat confusing attack on the architect's position. He'd tracked the little man to a thickly wooded area where a deer casually nudged the fallen pine needles before lying down. As he prepared to move in on his unsuspecting prey, Mason Mirage stepped out from behind the sweeping limbs of a nearby fir.

Geilt pulled back into his cover and waited to see what would transpire between the master and his servant. He shifted his position just enough to hear their conversation without revealing his presence. Bledsworth acted both surprised and alarmed by his master's sudden appearance. His rifle was raised and pointing at the big man's midsection. Geilt heard Mirage scold the architect for being so easily discovered. A look of hate passed over the small man's face, quickly concealed by his bowed head.

"Byron the Bumbler!" Mirage said, looking intently at the cringing man.

The taunting words had a strange effect on the architect. His head jerked up, and a blank expression replaced the hate Geilt saw earlier. His eyes were dull and vacant of any emotion. Geilt had seen this kind of magic before. Bledsworth had been put into a mesmerized state by his master.

"You will now enter the blind and send out a charmed vibration as I've taught you. That will make your magic detectable, while I will watch for the appearance of my next trophy. For surely, she'll find such a pathetic creature as you, Byron!"

Geilt understood the architect was to become a lure to attract the Protector. Bledsworth nodded, allowing himself to be put into the shed with a shove from Mirage's meaty hand. *This is a good thing,* Geilt was thinking. *Now both will be sent to the Pit by Geilt!* Before the Wildman could act on his thought of attacking the pair, Mirage faded like a wisp of smoke. Geilt immediately felt the air humming with a vibration that radiated from inside the lean-to. Birds in nearby trees took flight, disturbed by the unnatural stirring in the early morning stillness of the woodlands.

Still in the deeper shadows, Geilt was trying to decide if he should destroy the architect as the Protector had ordered. If he was patient, Mirage would reappear and he might take the master along with the minion. He was still pondering this action when a violent wind rose up, coiling itself around the blind. The sound of its roar was deafening as it tore the hide to splinters leaving a trembling architect standing in his shredded khakis in the middle of the debris. Geilt sensed the Protector's magic, and when she showed herself, she'd be targeted by Mirage. To shout a warning would give away his position and he'd be of no use to her. He almost jumped out of his furs when a Net of Nettles bristling with deadly berries settled over Bledsworth, nearly bringing the man to his knees with its weight. Geilt felt relief when Cathleen and Jason stepped out of the trees where they must have been hiding. He decided to listen without revealing his presence. Jason warned the Protector of a possible trap and the next instant, she was flying into his side, bringing him to the ground as the gunshot Geilt dreaded exploded the air around them. Bledsworth, standing passively under the heavy Net, was hit squarely in the chest. The bullet's force lifted him off his feet, slamming him to the ground where he was punctured a thousand times by the exploding berries. His body quickly dissolved into a lumpy, purplish soup.

Geilt saw the Protector drop a Dome over herself and her mate when the bellowing voice of Mason Mirage burst from a small hillock across from them. Geilt could no longer hesitate. He needed to intervene before his friends were attacked. While they were under the Dome, he knew Cathleen's magic was useless. To drop it would mean exposing the two of them to Mirage's killing gunfire.

He melted into the forest. In spite of his size, he moved as silently as any wildlife alert to danger. Even his shadow was concealed when he used the wide fans of fir limbs and gnarled branches of barren Dogwoods to cover his presence. At first glance the small hill looked deserted, but when Mirage shifted his gun, the barrel shot out a spike of light. Readjusting the trajectory of his attack, Geilt moved in a running crouch behind a small stand of pine, coming in behind the hunter. Taking a minute to judge the enemy's strengths, he decided the only real weapon he'd face was the rifle aimed at the Dome. Geilt charged from behind, hurling his heavily muscled body at Mirage, his mouth stretched in a ferocious warrior's cry. Mirage moved with surprising agility, pivoting at the sound of the howl, his gun aimed at the Wildman's mid-section. Even with the speed of his trigger finger, he was no match for the blinding speed of Geilt as his body slammed into him. The gun discharged, but the crack of the discharge was muffled between the two bodies.

Cathleen and Jason watched Geilt's surging attack and heard the chilling sound of his war cry. Although the report of the rifle was muted, both heard its unmistakable sharp report. They froze, waiting anxiously to see who had been struck by the discharged bullet. Cathleen's fear for their friend overwhelmed her and she yelled, "I'm dissolving the Dome!"

The Dome vanished and Cathleen bolted across the ground, Sacred Fire shooting from her hand, blowing back a spray of green sparks as she ran toward the combatants. She was a short distance away from the grappling men when Jason caught up. A bright flash, followed by another explosive boom, shattered the air with enough force to bring them both to their knees. Geilt was down on all fours and Mirage had vanished. Jason reached to pull Cathleen up.

"Mirage used some kind of magnified sonic energy!" she shouted as they ran toward Geilt.

The Wildman was kneeling, making no effort to stand. Cathleen and Jason crouched on either side of him. She saw his normally ruddy complexion had gone a pasty white under the thick beard. He dropped back on his heels, wrapping his arms around his middle.

"You've been shot my friend," Jason said in a calm voice. "Let me take a look."

Geilt made no objection when they helped him to his side and then to stretch out on the ground. They discovered his fur vest was saturated and matted with blood. Jason carefully moved his heavy arm, exposing a large hole filling and emptying with blood.

"This Geilt has...failed you...Protector," the big man whispered haltingly. His words were edged with the pain that twisted his face into a deep frown. Cathleen took one of the Wildman's rough hands saying, "You have never failed me, Geilt. You are a most stalwart Champion and awesome warrior."

The wounded man gave her a tight smile before squeezing his eyes shut as another wave of pain washed over him. She looked over at Jason trying to gauge his damage assessment. He gave a slight shake of his head.

"Protector," Geilt's voice was weaker and faltering.

"I ask...only...you defend...my Realm...from...the Dark Ones. I fear...my cycle is finally...at...its end."

Cathleen's eyes filled with unshed tears. She held them back not wanting to confirm Geilt's acknowledgement of his coming mortal death. Knowing he would pass into the Second Realm of Spiritual Renewal and Peace was little comfort in losing the Wildman's friendship and unfaltering loyalty. Geilt's large frame shook in a last spasm as if struggling to hold fast to life. His eyes opened wide as he appeared to gather his remaining strength to shout his final words.

"This Geilt is yours...Green Mother!"

Chapter 35

Cathleen and Jason knelt beside their fallen friend, their faces etched in shock and sadness as they watched the seemingly indomitable Geilt quiver a last raspy breath. Jason waited for what would follow with his last breath. Above the bloodied fur vest, a swirl of silvery mist began to take shape. This rose slowly above the cooling body of Geilt, spreading out until it was as wide as his broad shoulders. The shimmering cloud hovered over the Wildman like a galaxy of tiny stars. Jason had seen this solemn passing of the spirit with other magic users, as they left the Realm of the Natural, and passed into the Realm of Restoration where spiritual energies were revived. What awaited the Green Mother's loyal children could be compared to the Heaven most humans sought in one form or another. Jason felt honored that he could witness his friend's spiritual transition. They watched in reverent silence as the last of the glittery spirit was gathered up into the floating mass. This island glowed for a second before blinking out of their space in time.

Jason reached for Cathleen's hand. The tears she struggled to hide from her mortally wounded champion slid down her cheeks, falling unchecked onto his blood clotted furs. Jason was holding her hand when they both snapped their heads in the direction of the familiar popping sound of a Thread's arrival.

"The...others," Cathleen murmured, as she struggled to regain her composure.

The Historian and Medicine Woman dropped with a thud behind them. They each held something resembling ears, but as they neared, Cathleen saw they were the insignia from the uniforms of the Zombie Guards. Starla knelt beside Geilt's body. The Historian stood close by, his eyes automatically scanning the area for other possible threats.

"Cathleen, how did we lose this fine warrior?" Starla asked. Her voice held the shock of seeing the formidable Wildman taken from this life.

"Mason Mirage shot him during a struggle. Geilt must have discovered his hiding place and attacked him before he had a chance to ambush Jason and me."

The Historian, his eyes still darting around the area, said, "Protector, we need to send our friend's remains back to the Mother and leave this area. We are far too exposed here to another attack."

Nodding her agreement, Cathleen whispered *The Prayer of Passage* from the Sacred Druid Book of Silence. The others stood apart from her, watching as Geilt's body vanished into the dark earth beneath it. The ground sealed itself once more leaving no trace of his burial behind. Cathleen turned away from the empty spot and looked into the solemn faces of the Starla and Will, recalling the patches they held in their hands.

"Why do you have the insignia patches off the Guard's uniforms?" she asked.

"We discovered the badges keep the Guards animated. Mirage used the Black Arts to infuse them with the energies needed to give his Undead a second life that he controls," Will replied, adding, "We took them from the guards we destroyed."

"Drop them in a pile," Cathleen directed, immediately incinerating the stack.

Jason spoke softly, knowing the others could still hear his words. "There are several Guards tucked in behind the boulders at the tree line above us. They're only watching, but I picked up the glint off several weapons."

"Time to move out," she said calmly, careful not to look in the direction of the skulking Undead.

The Historian was pensive as they began to leave the area. He was eager to see Mason Mirage punished for his crimes, but his mind was occupied with thoughts of other duties. He was anxious to return to the Emerald Isle and his position of Master of the Outlander Wizard Scouts. These intrusions from the Dark Pit were seemingly increasing, as powerful Sorcerers like Mirage summoned demons from the Fourth Realm to bring chaos and death to the other realms

"Power lust," he murmured to himself.

Cathleen was carefully setting her feet on the next rocky outcropping and picked up the comment. She was going to ask what he meant by it, when suddenly the air filled with a buzzing sound. Jason yelled out a warning from his rear position in their downward trek.

"Arrows!"

The four threw themselves against the rocky incline, easy targets strung-out as they were and without cover. Cathleen raised an arm toward the fast-moving clouds. Streams of crystal blue currents shot from her fingers in long, jittery tendrils as she captured any electricity lingering after the passing storm. She directed this vast energy mass at the cliffs above, relieved to watch incoming shafts explode upon contact. The Historian used a spell to form a long sheet of thick ice to cover them. The feathered missiles raining down unabated. The arrows bounced off the hard barrier in volley after volley.

"Protector," Will shouted from several feet below her place on the rough ground. "I will attend to the archers. I detected their movements just above us."

"I will assist!" Starla added, a red mist already beginning to materialize, vanishing seconds later along with Star Fire.

The Historian quickly followed suite after mouthing his spell. Staying under the ice shield, Jason moved down the slope to Cathleen. Her eyes were drawn to the gold ring, glowing a deep green on his finger.

"Jason your ring is sensing a new danger. Something other than the archers?"

Another volley was loosed upon them. Will's charm held firm, shifting like disturbed pond water. They huddled closer studying the immediate area until Jason hissed a warning. "There!"

Cathleen made a quick visual check around their position, counting the Guards that must have crept into position while they were occupied with the archers.

"Only six that I can find, but they're spread out, cutting us off from going down or up. If I drop a Dome over us, we'll be stuck here until they give up and--"

"And we both know that's not happening! These guys may be deadly, but they're pretty slow too. I'll take out the two strung-out on our left. Wait until I can join you to attack the rest."

From the corner of her eye, Cathleen saw Jason exit the improvised shield during a brief lull of the deadly shower. She murmured her spell while she shaped green flames into burning javelins. A high screech bounced off the boulders from the direction Jason took. Leaving Jason o his own devices had become second nature to Cathleen. His growing skill in using the signet ring reflected his innate instincts in using magic. Cathleen believed that her husband had the makings of a true Wizard. A scream closer to her position alerted her to a second Zombie destroyed.

Time to do my thing! Cathleen searched out movement among the Undead guards. They were very adept at fading into the landscape. *There!* Two were crawling like insects directly toward her. Hurling the burning lances at the creatures to cover her next move, Cathleen darted into a patch of stunted firs. Crouching low, she watched as Will's ice roof dissolved, no longer deflecting the hail of arrows. She was becoming uneasy, wondering why the lethal rain was undiminished, when abruptly, the dark air became silent as the buzzing assault ceased. *They neutralized the archers, she thought,* relieved. She turned her attention to searching for the last two Undead she needed to destroy. A piercing howl came from behind her. Cathleen guessed Jason stumbled across an uncounted Guard. *He must have joined my two after hearing their screams* she reasoned.

With her targets still mobile, she drew the inky puddles under the trees and boulders to herself to create a Shadow Wrap. To confuse the enemy, Cathleen decided to create a hologram of herself with a green flame in her hand. This would attract their attention while she circled around behind them. The Guards appeared to operate in pairs and she was pleased to spot the last two moving toward her slightly shaky three-dimensional form. From the way they stopped to study her ruse, she guessed they detected something different about this human.

"Come on, boys," she muttered impatiently.

The largest of the two Undead began to move out of the trees to investigate. She noticed as the stiff branches swept across his face they ripped away some of the lose, gray skin, from the corrupted body, leaving the cheek bones exposed and creating an even more hideous face. She cringed in spite of herself. *I hate Zombies,* she thought moving into striking range. The Guards each carried a bulky black weapon across their shoulders. Cathleen couldn't identify them until they fired point-blank at her hologram. *Flame Throwers? Well, let's fight fire with fire as they say."* A long stream of orange fire from the big Guard's weapon squarely hit the crouching image of Cathleen and passed through, immediately lighting some nearby brush. Rather than cease the futile assault, the Guard signaled his companion, and they both fired, sending a river of orange directly at the unscathed figure. After a continuous stream of flames, Cathleen caused her hologram to stand to face the pair.

They both charged.

Their mouths hung slack, drooling foam in their blood lust as they moved toward her figure like scuttling beetles. She waited until they were upon the phantom figure before she unleashed her own withering stream of Sacred Fire. The Guards were engulfed completely. They thrashed futilely, trying to dislodge the consuming flames. Their weapons fused with their hands and arms before they could be dropped and quickly melted into black puddles covering skeletal remains. Cathleen was watching the conflagration when she heard Jason's warning whistle. For a second, she thought she'd miscounted the number of Guards, until out of the green gloom stepped Mason Mirage. His riffle was tucked in the crook of one arm as he calmly walked toward her. She immediately regretted dropping the Shadow Wrap. She figured he'd seen the whole attack and waited to see the outcome before showing himself.

"Stop right there, Mirage, or I'll give you a warmer reception than you expected."

"Well, aren't you the spunky one? Why not kill me now? You know I wouldn't hesitate to take your lovely head. But, truthfully, I'm having too much fun to stop now. There are only four left of your party, with the demise of the hulking specimen you called Geilt."

"Your idea of fun is as warped as your opinion of yourself as a great hunter. I'm curious. Why did you allow your henchman, Byron Bledsworth, to die? Was he no longer any fun to play with?"

"I no longer desired his services as my servant. But you, my dear, will make a fine replacement. You see, I've decided that once I kill your mortal body, I shall revive you as my Wizard slave."

Mirage suddenly lifted up his free arm. A sizzling bolt of energy shot from his hand in Cathleen's direction. She dove to the side, narrowly escaping the massive electrical charge. She heard it crash into a boulder sending shards in every direction. Throwing up a quick shield against his next assault, Cathleen realized the mad man wasn't aiming at her at all. With a quick glance over her shoulder, she saw Jason lying beside the blackened hole now occupied by large pieces of the shattered boulder.

Chapter 36

Starla never questioned the Historian's strategy as she watched him vanish into the woods. His plan to disrupt the hail of arrows would give Cathleen and Jason the chance they needed leave the protection of the ice shield, and get below to the Compound. *'It all began and ended there,'* he said, before he faded into the dull night to lay traps for their quarry. She trusted his instincts as a hunter of these kinds of creatures. As leader of the Outlander Wizard Scouts, she knew his position was as revered as her own as clan Shaman. There were such hunters of rogue Skin Walkers among the many tribes of the Indian nation, but in light of Cathleen's high praise, none surpassed the Historian's cunning use of magic. Starla realized this ruggedly handsome man, impressed her deeply, and she couldn't deny it wasn't just because of his magical skills.

The Zombie Guard's outpost was below her. She and Will spotted three of the Undead archers, but likely one other was keeping them supplied with the charmed shafts. It appeared their mission was to keep the humans pinned down under a constant barrage. Starla pressed against the boulder's cold surface, dwarfed by its immense presence. She inhaled deeply. The sharp scent of stone helped restore her connection to the natural world, rooting her in that bond before she entered the place of the mystical. She began chanting softly, her words weaving themselves inside the moving air. Losing awareness of her surroundings, she slipped inside the mesmerizing drone of her chanting voice. Her eyes drifted closed and she became completely detached from the present. She felt the magic she conjured begin to take shape, and subconsciously reflected on what was to come, the Great Golden Eagle.

Among her people the legend of the eagle was as old as the mountains it soared above. In the Before Times, the famous warrior,

Nayenezgani, slayed a feathered monster terrorizing the people. This beast roosted at the craggy top of Wing Rock and after Nayenezgani destroyed it the warrior discovered two offspring, alone in their bone-filled nest. Rather than slay them, the warrior used his power to turn the youngest one into an owl, and the eldest into an eagle.

As she stood rooted inside the sound of her incantation, Starla felt the brush of a feathered wing sweep gently across her cheek. Her eyes flew open. In the scant light of predawn, her black pupils reflected the noble head of the giant raptor. Using the magic that infused the air around her, Starla leapt onto the bird's back. It stirred beneath her but remained in place as if waiting upon her signal. Starla looked around for the Historian, sure she felt him nearby. There was a shimmer in the air slightly above her upturned face, just before Will materialized and gently dropped down behind her.

"Time to hunt, my Lady Star Fire," he said in her ear.

She felt a smile in his voice, and it warmed her deeply when he wrapped his muscular arms around her waist. The enormous bird stood on a small outcropping, but with one quick run it was airborne. They flew upward in tight circles until the eagle gained enough altitude to dive-bomb the archers still relentlessly working their bows below. Starla was amazed at the silence, hearing only the air rushing by them as they streaked toward the Undead.   She felt the Historian glide his lethal long-knife from its sheath when they came out of the steep dive. The giant eagle opened its yellow beak wide, emitting a shrill cry like death riding the winds.

Starla wrapped her long braid around her neck to prevent it from wiping Will in the face as they hurtled down on the guards. Just as they guessed, there was a Guard manning the arrow supply for the other three. He looked upward at the screech of the rocketing bird. Starla recognized the far off look she'd seen earlier in the eyes of these beings, just before the great bird pulled up and grabbed the creature in sharp talons.

She heard the snapping and breaking of bones before the eagle dropped the mangled body and landed a short distance from the archers. She thought it uncanny, but the three Undead guards appeared oblivious of the attack. They kept up a robotic barrage until they ran out of arrows. The biggest of the three, swiveled his head almost all the way around, signaling for more shafts from their supplier with a harsh grunt. The crumpled body of that creature lay several yards away. The big Guard's death eaten face, registered nothing when he spotted the mangled body of the other. Only the presence of a giant golden eagle seemed to alert him to a threat.

The Historian leapt off the Golden Eagle before it came to rest entirely. The momentum carried him close to the big Zombie, still staring at the bird's sudden appearance. In one sweep of his long-knife he took the Guard's head off its shoulders. The Undead Guard immediately dropped to the ground, its dead eyes staring over at its own corpse. The other two archers dropped their crossbows and rushed toward the boulder on their left and the semi-automatic rifles stacked there. Will barely registered a Guard pointing a gun in his direction when Starla jumped between them. Before the Guard could react, she threw a red powder in his pitted face to distort his sight. The Guard shuffled around swiping at his eyes, obviously confused. His riffle was still pointed in their direction, but he began moving backward, away from the impossibly contorted targets. Starla shifted her other weapon from her left hand. The obsidian blade was said to have been made from the black heart of a powerful Shaman eons before. The knife made a huffing sound as it disappeared into the throat of the Undead creature up to its bone hilt. The remaining Guard was taking aim at Starla when Will used his blade to sever an arm and then the head.

"Well done, Starla, but I expected no less. Give me a minute to return these four to the sludge of The Dark Pit and we'll rejoin the others. We will be needed to make a final assault on Mirage's stronghold."

"You expect him to be well intrenched there, Will?"

"Like a barnacle on a ship."

As he began murmuring the secret words of his incantation, Starla moved back, leaving him to the bleak task of removing the Undead from the First Realm. She walked closer to the edge of the woods, visually measuring the distance as only a few meters, before they would be off the mountain. Then, they would enter the valley where the Compound waited like a cancerous growth to be removed from the Great Mother's fertile body. Her mind was drifting when a sound trickled through to her like water seeping around a branch in a stream. She flung her senses open to the half-night, and what it held beneath its cloak. The rustling of the nocturnal animals was filtered out by the Medicine Woman's disciplined ear, until she found the sound that had penetrated her thoughts. *The Protector and Jason!* She ran back to Will as the last of the Zombies vanished. He turned to see her clearly distressed face.

"We need to leave here and go to Cathleen's aid. She and Jason are under attack!"

The Historian saw the magnificent eagle had become very agitated, scrapping at the ground with its sharp talons, and moving its great head from side to side. He asked Starla why the bird seemed so frantic to be away.

"It is a warrior as much as you are one. It will not stand by during our next encounter."

"Good. Let's give it an enemy!"

Chapter 37

Straddling the back of the legendary Golden Eagle, Will and Starla circled above the denser forest that edged the valley floor. They made wider and wider turns, searching among the thicker growth for signs of Cathleen and Jason. No sounds reached them at their current altitude. Using her knees Starla urged the giant bird to drop lower until it lightly skimmed tree tops with its broad wings.

"There!" Will shouted, leaning close to Starla's ear. "Scorched earth and fragments of blackened rock, clearly marks of recent battle."

The Medicine Woman leaned close to the majestic head of their enchanted stead, thinking she communicated with the great beast telepathically. Refocused on the ground below, he saw there was little open ground near the charred scene. He wasn't sure how the massive bird would land without breaking a wing or spilling them off their perch at a neck-breaking speed if it tried to push through the trees. He unconsciously tightened his arms around Starla's waist as he prepared for the dive to come. For her part, Starla shared none of Will's apprehensions. She knew the great bird's abilities went far beyond that of any raptor he'd encountered in the wild.

As if they flew in a small jet that just stalled-out, Will experienced a heart-stopping silence while the creature tucked in its wings close to its body. Within a breath, the flying leviathan began to drop like a stone, but now his chilling screech was colored in the orange flames shooting from its open beak. Plunging toward the earth was unnerving enough for the Outlander Wizard Scout. He was used to climbing mountains and staring out at the wild borderlands from their summits, but this was a whole new experience to his earth-loving nature. The fire blew back harmlessly at the pair of riders along with the death bringing scream of the Golden Eagle. They landed with a soft thud. Will slipped into his Inner Eye as the great bird settled in place.

"Over there! He grabbed Starla's arm to focus her attention on two figures huddled under a shimmering Dome of Protection several yards from the scorched site.

When Cathleen spotted the descent of a fire-breathing eagle, she covered them in the hastily conjured Dome. As soon as she saw the Historian and Starla sliding from the back of the feathered creature, the opaque shelter dissolved. She leaned down to speak to Jason and hurried to meet them.

"I feared this was another of Mirage's corrupted beasts!" she said in a rush before telling them what happened. "We've been under attack almost since you left to destroy the archers."

Cathleen turned toward Jason where he leaned gingerly against another boulder. She read the tightening of his mouth as the pain took hold. Turning back to the pair her face was drawn with concern.

"Did the Spirit Eagle do this to your husband, Protector?" Starla asked, clearly distressed with the possibility.

"No! It was Mirage. He surprised me when he used a Fire Splitter charm. He was clearly aiming at Jason, but his ring gave him some warning and he dove behind the boulder that was blasted. He was badly burned on the back of one arm and down his side."

They hurried over to Jason, Cathleen noting he'd slumped further onto the ground. He had one leg drawn up, letting his arm rest there, close to his chest. He gave the approaching group a weak smile not able to suppress the rawness of his pain.

"How goes it my friend?" the Historian said softly as he crouched down to look over the wounds.

"Guessing I've lost my taste for barbeque chicken for a bit," Jason responded with a chuckle, quickly followed by a grimace.

The Medicine Woman stood apart, watching the woods while the others spoke softly together. Finding no imminent danger, she turned to the Golden Eagle, its wing lifted while it preened itself with its sharp beak. As she approached, the eagle lifted its massive head focusing glittering golden eyes on her, making a small cry of recognition.

"You are released, noble one. You honored me with your presence and did me a great service."

Starla bowed deeply to the regal bird. It sprang to its splayed feet, the yellow scales flexing over taught tendons before it launched itself into the pearl gray sky, vanishing among the dusty stars.

She hastened back to the others. Jason's blackened shirt lay beside him as Will applied a healing balm. Starla watched the immediate affect the clear ointment had on the awful burns. The charred skin on Jason's arm began to slough-off revealing new, healthy skin beneath, while the cream soothed the blistered flesh along the ribcage and his back. Will removed his own outerwear, helping Jason into the soft linen shirt he wore beneath. He then slipped back into the dark green jacket with his Master rank clearly marked on its breast.

Cathleen felt grateful she didn't need to send Jason to the Healing Gardens, that hidden sanctuary for those in service to the Green Mother. She knew while she waited in the First Realm his healing would take months to achieve, while the Historian's balm was fashioned with much of the same restorative elements used by the Healers.

Before Starla rejoined them, Cathleen saw Starla bowing to the mythical Golden bird. When the Medicine Woman came to stand beside her, she smiled a warm greeting.

"Starla, thank you for coming and bringing Will Farley when we needed you both most. The Golden Eagle you summoned is a formidable creature."

"We would have come sooner, Cathleen, but were occupied with the Archers that had you pinned down. Thank the Great Mother Jason is healing under Will Farley's care. Will is a powerful warrior indeed."

Cathleen looked more closely at Starla, detecting more than a comrade's admiration in her voice.

With Will's help, Jason was able to get to his feet. He assured the others he was fit to move, slipping back into his torn, heavily singed jacket. The four began descending the short distance into the valley and the extensive Mirage estate.

Cathleen noted, "Mirage is a psychopath and has already proved we shouldn't underestimate his skills in the Dark Arts. Our target is the wine cellar where his Magical Treasures room is located.

Jason unconsciously turned the ring around on his finger when Cathleen said, "Jason, we'll need you to act as if you were mortally wounded in his attack. I'll place you on a litter when we reach the first outlying buildings. The Undead will report they've seen me leave you unprotected there. Mirage will likely assume I've gone in search of help from Will and Starla. Expect the Guards to investigate your condition after I'm gone. When they get close enough, blast the brutes!"

"Gladly!" he said with a quick grin.

Jason enjoyed the power that flowed through him whenever he used the ring. When it shot out its destructive beams, it was as close to feeling like Superman as he'd ever been. Cathleen noted the flare of excitement in her husband's eye, and not for the first time, wondered if he was becoming addicted to the power he wielded. A real danger in one untrained in the use of magic. Quickly dismissing that thought she turned to Starla and Will, walking close behind.

"We'll need you two to find your way into the wine cellar undetected. When you do, Starla will lead the way to the Magical Treasures room. When you get there conceal yourselves, but stay away from the cases. The titanium is still a deterrent to our magic. I'll need you to block any attempts at escape from the room by Mirage after I lure him there. He may conjure creatures to distract you. He's prepared to sacrifice all of them, to prevent me from taking him before the Council of Green."

Describing the last part of her plan, Cathleen turned to Jason once more. "Jason, when you've dispatched any Guards sent after you, you'll need to search out and destroy any other Undead patrolling the immediate grounds around the mansion. We can't risk them sounding an alarm."

Starla raised her eyebrows at the Historian, obviously concerned with Jason's dangerous role. Will commented softly, "Hunting is in his blood."

Jason studied Cathleen's pensive face asking, "What will your part be?"

"I'll make sure Mirage and I end up in the Magical Treasures room. I'll pretend the titanium in the cases is interfering with my powers, but before he can do any real harm, Will and Starla can intervene. I want to take him alive if possible. He deserves the full weight of the Council to fall on him for the kidnappings and murders of innocent magic users."

Cathleen saw Starla look up at Will, signaling it was time. He nodded gravely at Cathleen and Jason in a farewell gesture. They watched as the Medicine Woman linked arms with the Historian. A red mist formed around their feet and rose until it covered them in a crimson haze, and they vanished into the shadows clinging from the long night.

"Jason there's a great deal of danger in facing the Undead guards, and you will be safer relying on your instincts rather than trust your safety entirely to the ring."

Jason knew she was afraid for him and said, "I promise you, love, I won't ignore my internal warning system. The ring's got power, but there's nothing like the old gray matter between my ears to help keep me alive!"

Chapter 38

Starla and Will began to materialize near some open storage areas across from a freight elevator. She purposedly chose to reappear in an isolated part of the cellars, far from the Magical Treasures room. The pair stood close together and very still, while the mist dispersed.

"Your red fog is a most unusual method of transport, Starla," Will Farley whispered while beginning to scope out the area. "It is like a caterpillar's cocoon. Concealing and protective at once," he concluded in an admiring tone.

Starla smiled up at the deeply tanned face, and not for the first time felt a glow at the pit of her stomach. She quickly looked away, not wanting to display feelings she hadn't sorted out yet.

"We'll need to move quickly, Will. During my captivity, I often overheard the Undead guards reporting back to a command post at timed intervals as they moved along these corridors."

She spoke in a subdued voice, but realized her words echoed inside the close confines of the hallway. She lowered her voice until Will had to put his ear almost against her lips. A strange sensation for them both. "The Magical Treasures room is in another part of the cellar, but I was hesitant to bring us too near. Its door may be heavily guarded, since the escapes of Mirage's prisoners."

The Historian acknowledged her caution with a nod of agreement, his eyes returning to his search the gloomy area. He murmured, "Let's not become separated, these passageways likely jut off in many directions. Cathleen spoke of the possibility of remote surveillance down here as well. I suggest we use a Shadow Wrap so we can travel unseen."

"Yes. I've been thinking it's very curious that Mirage didn't stop my escape or prevent Cathleen from freeing the others. I had a sense of being watched the whole time I was inside the case, and even after I was freed."

"Mirage likely gets his greatest thrill in stalking prey that feels safe from imminent harm," Will responded, his disgust deepening his frown.

He drew in enough of the shadows to cover them both if they moved slowly, and close together. When he completed the Wrap, he had Starla move closer to his side.

"Keep pace with me, and you'll remain hidden."

Starla whispered that the Shadows felt damp and chilly against her skin.

"It's the cellar's cold air I'm afraid. But as we move, we will warm up a bit," he assured her.

By the time they reached the first jog in a long corridor, Starla had warmed considerably. Will's body seemed to give off waves of heat, and she began to focus more on the task at hand, and less on the unfamiliar sensation of the Wrap. After several minutes of snaking down corridors toward the designated target, they picked up voices echoing along the hallways. The words sounded dry and brittle, as if the speaker's vocal cords had atrophied eons ago.

"Zombie Guards!" Starla hissed in Will's ear when he crouched lower.

The Historian pinpointed the position of the Guards, whispering their position to Starla, "They are coming around the corner." He was able to pick up a few words of their guttural conversation with his sensitive hearing.

"Loreena…summoned …Master calls for her to …"

The rest was lost when the Guards moved further away from where the huddled pair strained to listen. Once the silence in the dank passage settled again, Starla spoke urgently to Will. She told him she'd never heard the name Loreena while she was held captive.

"She may be a prisoner I was unaware of, or perhaps another of Mirage's servants," she added.

The Historian was silent. Starla didn't know if the shadows played tricks on her vision, but she thought a look of deep sadness passed over Will's face before he spoke. Thinking on it, she was certain she felt his body stiffen when the name of this mystery woman floated to their ears. Will's voice sounded hesitant when he finally spoke.

"I have…my suspicions, but we can't risk that she may be an innocent Wizard, selected for Mirage's hunt."

Starla responded firmly, "We cannot abandon the part we play in stopping Mirage either. Cathleen depends on us to close the trap around the Dark Wizard."

"And you can do that nicely, Starla. You have the stealth of a wolf, and under the Shadow Wrap, you can infiltrate the Magical Treasures room without notice. I shall search for this mystery woman, and bring her to safety."

"And what if she is an adherent of the Black Arts?"

"Then I'll deal with her accordingly," Will answered with steel in his voice.

"Go now, and get yourself hidden in that cursed room to wait for the Protector's plans to unfold. Mirage will likely be close behind her after Cathleen runs into the room. I shouldn't be long in finding this woman Loreena if she's wandering these halls."

"Will, the Guard said Mirage had summoned Loreena. She may be in the same room Cathleen was held when she was first captured. If she is, she's likely secured by titanium chains you'll need to break."

He told her he would focus on finding Cathleen's Magical Signature, left behind during her confinement in that room. He gave her slender arm a light squeeze and looking deeply into her dark eyes, he murmured, "Take care Starla Star Fire." He vanished with a soft rustling in the Shadow Wrap. She hoped one day the Historian would share the spell he used to move through space and time. *Perhaps* she thought smiling.

Starla began to feel the chilly touch of the Wrap again where it brushed bare skin. She stopped moving and immediately set about twisting her waist-length hair into a long braid. While she worked, her mind flashed back to a memory of how this habit of securing her hair had become a ritual before going into battle with Dark forces.

She learned a grim lesson while still training with her venerable teacher, Red Cloud when she passed her thirteenth summer. The wind blew hard out of the north, carrying the promise of snow on its strong breath. The small cave where they worked together, echoed with strange moans. While Star Fire watched open mouthed and wide-eyed, the ancient Witch conjured a hideous mythical creature Starla knew as a Jinn. She was told this was to test Star Fire's speed, and quick thinking when fighting for her life. At Red Cloud's signal Star Fire sprinted from the cave, the thick mass of her black hair streaming behind her like the wake of a speeding boat. The stark white streak running through it, vividly marked the long mane as she dodged away from the snarling Jinn. She was outrunning the beast when one of its long arms reached out, snagging a silky handful of hair and she was jerked off her feet. She was saved by the old crone then, but there would be no one to rescue her now.

Moving gingerly under the clinging shadows, Starla mouthed her teacher's invocation to summon a Jinn. Her casting complete, she moved closer to the Magical Treasures room, but now, with a huge wolf by her side. Its iron-gray fur made it invisible under the Wrap, until it curled back its black lips, its teeth flashed in a snarl, while a low growl rumbled deep in its broad chest.

"Hush! You will be a silent hunter like the shadows around us," Starla hissed close to the huge head.

It pricked its ears, its golden eyes staring balefully at the diminutive human. His head came to her shoulder, and his fur bristled at her tone. After a few seconds of staring into Starla's unflinching eyes, the beast lowered its massive head.

"You are mine and shall fight beside my Spirit Warrior when the time comes."

Starla thought over her role in the coming battle, as the creature padded silently beside her. Six legs made slow progress under the Wrap. She knew the Protector's idea of luring Mason Mirage to the Magical Treasures room relied on her and the Historian as hidden allies. Now it would be Starla alone, hiding there with the wolf jinn. She would assist Cathleen when she closed her trap around the Dark Sorcerer. She felt confused at the Historian's decision to locate the woman called Loreena. Why did he seem agitated when they heard the Undead speak her name? Was this mystery woman known to Will? More importantly, would she prove to be friend or foe?

Chapter 39

Cathleen fidgeted behind an over-sized Grandfather clock in the Witch Hunter's den. Its wide front featured intricate carvings of wild animals in various stages of being stalked and slaughtered. She used a Time Thread to bring her back to this room, an ironic hiding place considering how she'd bent time to get there. Her plan was to get Mirage to the Magical Treasures room, confronting him would have to wait until then.

Sounds from outside of the room were muffled by the hefty leather chairs and deep-plush Oriental rugs scattered around a dark wood floor. Even the rhythmic time keeping of the seven-foot clock was muted. The dense brocade curtains were drawn, sealing off any sounds from outside, and eliminating a view of the trees, crawling up the side of the mountain like green soldiers. The only lighting in the room came from the wide fieldstone hearth covering a side wall. A newly laid fire, struggled against the oppressive shadows and chill inside the room. Taking it all in, Cathleen wondered if she just missed Mirage. She drew some shadows to the base of the clock to better conceal her presence and was considering relocating when the door swung inward. The thick figure of Mason Mirage was backlit in the muted track lighting from the hallway. He was carrying the rifle he used to kill Geilt. Cathleen fought her urge for instant revenge. This mission was bigger than the loss of a single magic user. Its outcome could very well effect hundreds of Wizards and whole communities among the Fey clans. Mirage schemed to wipe them all out, making himself all powerful. In the process he'd be filling his mansion with gruesome trophies.

Cathleen crouched deeper into the shadows clustered around the imposing timekeeper. She watched Mirage as he passed in front of her, heading to his massive desk. He laid the gun across the glossy walnut top, as lovingly as placing a baby in a cradle. He plopped down on the cushioned seat of the leather desk chair, producing a loud sigh under his substantial weight. Inhaling deeply and smiling, he spoke aloud, "Time to prepare for the lovely Loreena."

Cathleen saw him finger a button on the side of the desk. Expecting another kind of weapon, she was shocked when a square mirror rose silently in front of him. Mirage immediately began to smooth down his wiry eyebrows, and then checked his dazzling teeth. Cathleen watched fascinated as he studied himself closely, with a narcissistic admiration, turning his face from side to side, and adjusting the large diamond stud in his ear lobe. *Who is this Loreena he's primping for?* she wondered with growing apprehension. *Another hunter perhaps?* Mirage touched the button again and his self-adoration came to an end, the mirror sliding into its hidden cubby. He sat back with such a self-satisfied smirk on his face, Cathleen couldn't resist sending a hot ember from the fireplace spinning out to fall on his glossy head. She knew it would do no real harm, but grinned to see his look of arrogance vanish, as he swatted at his bald head.

Mirage suddenly bolted out of his chair, grabbing his rifle in one smooth movement. Cathleen heard it at the same time. The sound of a woman's voice calling his name echoed down the hallways. Whoever she was, Cathleen knew she was definitely getting closer. There was no doubt she was another magic user, or she wouldn't be roaming his mansion so openly. There was a slight hint of demand in the silky voice calling for Mirage to show himself.

Mirage must have heard it too. He drew back his lips in a quick sneer before he put the gun down. Cathleen felt the air in the room sweep around her hiding place when the door to his den blew open. Its hinges rattled with the force, and the heavy drapes billowed outward. Cathleen quickly called more shadows to darken the area behind the clock. She had no way to judge the woman's powers and couldn't risk being discovered. It was more urgent now to get Mirage out of there, and into the Magical Treasures room where Starla and the Historian could help deal with this unexpected enemy. Another jolt of heated air stirred the hair around her shoulders when the door blew shut with a hard thud. Standing in front of it was a statuesque woman in a one-piece, black leather jumpsuit. It shimmered along the sleek lines of her body as if she'd dressed herself in part of the night sky. While Cathleen studied her closely, the stranger raised a pale hand, tossing back a long coil of lustrous blond hair.

"Mason! It is I, Loreena. My brother Byron said I was invited to join you in some kind of unique hunt involving Wizards, or some such. This was at *your* urging I believe!"

She narrowed her large grey eyes, scrutinizing Mason Mirage as she glided in a swaying motion toward him.

"Why do you look so uncomfortable? Almost as if you feel guilty about something!" she said laughing lightly, a long finger tracing his thick chin.

Cathleen's eyes widened when she heard Byron Bledsworth's name spoken. *His sister won't be so happy when she learns what happened to the Architect at Mirage's hands* she thought, shifting slightly to watch the scene play out.

Mirage stammered out a few words of fawning welcome to the woman, casually asking exactly what Byron had shared with her about the coming hunt.

"Oh, only that part of it will be in that vulgar labyrinth he designed for you. Honestly, it won't prove much of a hunting ground! Especially when the prey is being herded like dumb beasts. I much prefer hunting creatures in their natural habitats. The result is always the same for them...and I always get my prize."

She purred the last comment like a contented cat lapping up spilt cream. Mirage was quick to compliment her prowess, saying she was akin to the beautiful goddess Diana in every way. For the next few minutes, the two laughed together over accounts of their kills. Mirage regaled her with gruesome details of his most recent hunts, remarking how the magic users were cowardly in the face of his powers, begging for mercy before he slaughtered them, until they both were nearly panting with blood lust.

Cathleen studied Loreena closely. The woman held her own crown tightly as she rubbed egos with Mason Mirage. Her only commitment would be to saving her own skin in any conflict. This made her less of a threat to Cathleen's plans. Her thoughts were drawn away from the pair for a second, when a picture of Jason flashed in her mind. Their link placed him somewhere close by on the grounds. *He must still be stalking the Zombie Guards. Hopefully, he's close to finishing his own hunt.*

Half listening to the preening pair as they droned on about themselves, Cathleen picked up a subtle change in Mirage's tone. Peeping through her Shadows, she wondered if the woman had heard enough of his drivel. She was surprised when Loreena flirtatiously stepped close to pass him, brushing his corpulent middle before perching her sleek form on the edge of his desk. He turned as if attached to some string she pulled, and placing a meaty hand beside her long leg, leaned in closer. Cathleen watched as Loreena casually propped an elbow on the massive desk, seductively tilting back. Cathleen had to admit, Loreena Bledsworth was beautiful, and she clearly knew how to use her looks as effectively as a Venus Fly Trap. The object of Mirage's heated desires, became bored with his clumsy overtures and persistent attentions. At one point, she rolled her eyes upward and yawned, but neither dampened Mirage's enthusiasm to pursue her. He was obviously trying to rekindle a spark of interest from the elusive woman when he spoke.

"Getting back to our current hunt my dear…It's moved out of the maze entirely. In fact, I'm quite certain the Witch and her friends are cringing within these very walls. They are likely planning on using their magic to trap me, but now that I have you here…"

Loreena broke into his comments, looking around distractedly before speaking.

"How soon can we begin to hunt? And where is my brother? It's been ages since I saw him. And I especially like to hunt at night. You might recall I have certain advantages in those conditions!"

Cathleen saw Loreena's wide gray eyes, fade into a murky green. *She has natural night vision!* She felt a moment of panic, knowing the shadows would only provide a slight blurring effect if Loreena spotted her behind the big clock. She needed to get these two out of the den and down to the Magical Treasures room, and fast. If she couldn't move, she'd have to make them move. Tuning out the sound of the two narcissists playing flirty word games, Cathleen called to mind a spell she used vary sparingly, and for good reason. A Green Wizard did all they could before they turned to reviving the spirit of a deceased being. But Loreena had already noted the absence of her brother, Byron, and Cathleen was desperate to move her plan forward. Concentrating on the intricate wording of the incantation, Cathleen began to experience the detached feeling of becoming lost in the magic she unleashed. Her eyes snapped open when she heard a rasping intake of breath, and she knew Mirage spotted the ghost of Byron Bledsworth. Loreena's leather jumpsuit made a ghostly whispering sound as she slipped off the desk. Her mouth opened in a soundless scream, confirming she too saw Byron materializing in front of the hearth.

"Byron Bledsworth the third...Is it truly you?" she demanded, a tremor in her smooth voice.

The shade floated closer to the wide front of the fireplace, positioning itself nearer to the fire. The flames showed in gaudy orange and red through the translucent form of the architect. His hunting clothes were hanging off his slight frame in shreds, exposing gruesome injuries. One boot was missing and his foot looked mangled and useless. Cathleen had witnessed Mirage shoot Bledsworth while he was wrapped inside her Net of Nettles. But Bledsworth's ghost chose to reappear as the victim of the landslide that he somehow managed to survive. She had to admit, seeing the aftermath of being buried under tons of mountain rock was visually sickening. She wasn't certain how the architect was caught in a rockslide, but Geilt, who was nearly swept away by it, reported hearing a male voice calling an enchantment before the boulders began to roll. Cathleen knew the culprit had to be Mason Mirage. He wasn't one to tolerate competition for primacy from an underling like Bledsworth. To an egotist like Mirage, there was no room in this world for more than himself and those who served his whims.

Though Cathleen hated calling the despicable Byron back from his deserved place in the Pit, she needed to rattle Mirage's confidence. She also had to create a rift between Mirage and Loreena, and this would definitely work.

"It is I, your brother, dear Loreena," the spirit's voice rattled in the room like the echo inside an empty barrel. "As you see, I have been ripped from life, and now I'm called here by another to give witness to my murder."

"Murder you say, dear boy?" Cathleen heard Mirage ask.

He was quick to interject his concerned voice into this perilous conversation. She guessed he couldn't let it go in directions that might implicate him in any way. The specter appeared to be breathing, but it was only the heated air from the fire moving through his translucent form. The architect's face was truly horrible in its crushed state. The nose and one ear were turned to pulp under the weight of the boulders and flesh hung from splintered cheek bones. Cathleen looked over at Loreena, who had gone as still as a tomb, her already pale complexion drained of all color. Her muscles tensed under the silky gleam of the leather jumpsuit. She appeared in every way to be coiled like a spring ready to be released to action.

"Brother mine," she barely breathed out between clenched teeth. "Name your killer to me that I may bring a truly horrible death to him!"

The shade of Byron Bledsworth lifted a grisly, smashed arm, pointing at the fleshy figure of Mason Mirage.

"The shade is confused, Loreena! Whoever brought your brother's spirit back has clearly instilled confusion into his flattened skull! I cared for him like my own brother!"

"You have no brother, liar!"

Loreena launched herself at him in one blindingly fast movement. He was quicker. When she closed on him, her long nails ready to rake his face and neck, Mirage vanished under her assault.

The shade's voice squealed, "The Magical Treasures room, sister! That's how he'll escape us!"

"Yes!" Cathleen mouthed, watching Loreena run from the room.

Chapter 40

Jason hunkered down behind some privets bordering the somber mansion, breathing hard as adrenaline pumped through him. He just finished off a nest of Zombie Guards dug-in close to the high spiked fence encircling the mansion. Those spikes were now decorated with pieces of uniforms and Zombies. His pounding heart gradually slowed as he studied the main entrance. The stone face of the sprawling three-story building was colored a muted yellow wherever thin fingers of a moody sunrise grazed its rough façade. A smidge of light showed through windows in the upper levels. He mulled over ways to open the heavy, double gate with the initials *M* claiming rights to all beyond. *It's probably sealed with a powerful ward.*

His anxious thoughts were interrupted by the sound of a gravelly voice. It came from the Guard House he'd been watching, just inside the gate. Jason guessed the Undead protecting the interior grounds would likely be the best of the bunch, likely skilled killers in their lifetimes. As Mirage's servants, they would apply those deadly talents to protecting his plump rear from any threat.

The wind stirred the crisp air, carrying with it their stench as they moved. It washed over Jason, crouching deeper in the shadows. Two armed guards exited the wooden shelter to begin patrolling the grounds. Jason watched the pair, moving in their odd, lurching way, as they passed his hiding place on the other side of the fence. The voice coming from long dead vocal cords irritated like grinding glass under a boot.

"Our Master calls us to the wine cellar. The Sorceress Loreena has over-stayed her welcome it appears."

The guard laughed in harsh snorts. Jason frowned at the mention of a woman named Loreena. The fact that she was a Sorceress made his frown deepen. *Who the heck is Loreena?* He strained to hear more.

"She has seen her brother's shade," he added with a wheezy laugh.

"Who is this creature from the Shadow World? One of us?" his partner rapped in an equally irritating voice.

"Not one of us, but we knew the brother as the architect. The Master desires us to sto..."

The rest of the garbled conversation was lost as the guards moved further down the fence. Jason knew he was missing important plans being laid by Mirage. It was time to put his magic to work. As soon as the guards were out of sight, Jason leapt up and ran to the gate. He tentatively extended his right hand to touch it. Seeing no obvious locks he gave it a shove. He was immediately thrown backwards, landing with a grunt and loud thud. He lay still, waiting to see if the sound carried to the guards.

After a few uncertain moments, he got to his feet and studied the situation. As he guessed, the gate was magically sealed. He had to work fast; he might have triggered some sort of silent alarm when he touched it. As if he'd conjured them, the two guards materialized at the end of the building and the barrels of their guns were pointed in Jason's direction. A series of quick bursts ricocheted off the fence and blasted the trees nearby. Instinctively, Jason raised his arm, aiming the ring as they lumbered toward him. Sweeping the narrow beam cleanly severed the head off the leading guard. The other grabbed for the falling body, using it as a shield as it continued toward Jason in a shambling but remarkably fast run. Jason trained the shaft on the decapitated body. Concentrating on its mid-section, it burned through the creature, leaving a huge hole before reaching the other guard. The guard stopped suddenly before its halves fell to either side. All that was left behind was a thin column of pale green smoke as the bodies of the Undead disintegrated into ash.

Jason returned to the front entrance. *Can't break through the ward,* he thought. He hoped the fence wasn't charmed and decided to burn a hole big enough to get through. He met no resistance and weakened a portion of the iron rails with his beam before pushing it out. He crossed the front lawn without incident. *Inside and now what…?* He studied the windows, set unusually high in the walls, guessing these too would be under wards. Thinking it wasn't likely the spells extended to the stone walls, he touched the cold facade of the building. Nothing. "Here we go," he murmured as he trained his ring on the thick stone wall surrounding a narrow window and outlined its shape with a hot beam. Great chunks of stone fell away, followed by piles of gritty dust that covered the grass around him. The window fell inward, its tempered glass shattered into hundreds of small, granular chunks. "Time to move," Jason mumbled, hauling himself over the lip of the chiseled-out wall and into the mote-filled air.

He found himself in the foyer, spotting an elevator nearby. While he'd prefer a direct route down, the elevator was too noisy and would give away his position. He found the staircase further along the thickly carpeted hallway. As he carefully turned the doorknob, an alarm shattered the quiet. Jason let go, realizing too late the handle was secured by magic to identify any person entering Mirage's inner sanctum below. He didn't have the luxury of thinking through his next move. He knew the Undead would storm the foyer any second. He bolted down the stairs to the lower level and flung open the door to the wine cellar. He found himself in a dimly lit corridor. *At least the alarm will let Cathleen know I've jumped down this rabbit hole.* He moved at a jog down a passageway looking for a possible place to hide. He spotted a door without a wine designation and slipped inside. He figured the arrogant Mirage would never let anyone handle his precious wines, and those doors would likely be sealed with magic. The alarm continued to boom throughout the building as Jason quietly shut the door. He was looking around himself when the shrill siren abruptly stopped. The complete silence was almost as jarring as the sound of the blaring signal. He expected the rooms down in the cellars to be chilly, but it felt like he'd walked into a meat locker. Reaching out he placed a hand on the wall. He jerked it back when he came into contact with a numbing cold.

"What is this place?" he wondered softly. Remembering his cell phone, he fished it out of his jacket. Turning in a slow circle, the phone's flashlight revealed several heavily barred cages. He wove his way carefully through these, checking for any creature unfortunate enough to be warehoused here in the dark, frigid room. The cages looked sturdy enough to hold a full-grown lion if need be. In a flash of intuition Jason knew exactly what was kept in these conditions. "Magic Users!" he said the words and knew he discovered a holding area for Mirage's captives. Likely, this was where Mirage first introduced them to his hospitality, before he transferred them into the titanium lined cases in the Magical Treasures room. The cold was probably part of the spell he used to keep them subdued, without killing or maiming them. Cathleen told him Mirage would only take prime specimens on his hunts. *This was where Geilt and the Medicine Woman would have been held at first. Like circus animals waiting to perform.* He was lost in thought about such inhuman cruelty, when voices filtered through the silence. One was clearly a woman and she sounded livid.

"Where *is* this stupid room, brother? I want to exact our revenge on the slug that lives here and leave this pile of gray rock scattered over his smug face!"

The voice that answered was flat and lifeless.

"The Magical Treasures room is more than a room, Loreena. You'll find it at the end of this hallway, but it won't be there for long...and neither will Mason."

"What? You are speaking in riddles, Byron and...Oh no! You've begun to fade! Can't you force your shade to linger here, while I hunt the murdering mongrel?"

Jason detected a strange echo in the man's voice, as if he was moving further away. He pressed his ear to the cold door hoping to learn something about Cathleen and the others. If this was indeed the Architect's ghost, it couldn't continue a stay in the First Realm, without the Mother's consent, and he was certain that would hardly be extended to the Dark Magic adherent, Byron Bledsworth.

"Loreena you…hurry! Mason will…activate the Displacement Spell he built…into the room itself. He'll…transport himself and…Undead, out of this Realm."

"Where can the creature escape to that I can't follow?"

The architect's voice had lost most of its volume sounding hollow. "…the Third Realm now…Geilt is no…"

The next sound was the woman's shrill scream of frustration. Jason waited to make sure his ring was turned outward and threw open the door thinking he had the element of surprise on his side. The hallway was empty. The architect's sister would be headed toward the Magical Treasures room where Cathleen would be waiting for Mirage, and not expecting the Sorceress-sister of Byron Bledsworth! The Historian and Starla should be there by now, but so far, this plan of Cathleen's had found every pothole on the road. Jason was running down the dimly lit hallways. His wife and friends had no idea an even bigger threat would be right behind Mirage, and she was out for blood.

Chapter 41

The Historian recognized the melodious tones coloring her voice as it brushed like silk over the stone walls of the wine cellar. Her face floated out of the pit of his darkest memories.

"Loreena," he murmured. "Your voice still holds the allure of the Siren's song, but now I understand how deadly that fascination can be."

Will carefully loosened the charmed long-knife in its sheath, insuring it would pull easily. He peered around the corner where Loreena was engaged in a highly charged conversation with the shade of Byron Bledsworth. Hearing Loreena refer to the spirit as "brother," was information Will found remarkable. After studying the fine features on the living woman, and the destroyed face of the Architect, it seemed improbable, but so was her appearance in Mirage's lair. The shade spoke urgently to his sister, saying Mason Mirage would escape her revenge by traveling to the Third Realm. Will watched and listened until the spirit faded and was no more. Loreena's hands curled into tight fist as she screamed in frustration. Will knew this was the best time to capture the conniving Sorceress. She'd be distracted and too emotional to focus. He stepped into the hall several feet away from the woman's back and called her name. She whirled around, her wide gray eyes glittered with unshed tears and unreleased vengeance upon her brother's murderer.

"Historian! How…?"

"I have searched for you since your defection to a dark as black as your heart, Loreena. It seems fitting I find you in the midst of these evil deeds and schemes. Now that I've found you, I'll send you back to the Council to stand trial for your betrayal of the Code of the Green."

He moved closer while she stood rooted by shock at his sudden appearance. His words froze her reactions.

"You do remember the most important part of the Code, don't you?" he asked quietly. "Harm no life unless it be Demon Spawn, or User of the Dark Arts. You turned your back on the Mother's ways. And now, I find you a protégé of a cesspit of a man…Mason Mirage!"

His charge ignited her outrage and heated her words.

"You don't know all the facts about me, or my life, Will Farley! You are making ill-informed assumptions about my loyalties, and they've taken you far from the truth!"

Will focused on her surprising reply and almost missed how the beautiful Sorceress shifted down the hall and closer to him. Without warning, she threw up her hand scattering a fine dust into the air between them. Its metallic luster sparkled in the dull lighting, as it rained down.

Not expecting the attack, Will realized he'd been had. "Titanium dust!" he growled as he collapsed to the floor, a fine coating of the particles covering his legs and chest. He watched as Loreena ran down the hallway and around the corner. Muttering a quick water spell before his magic was dulled further, Will was forced to wait on his knees while gallons of the spelled water deluged his entire body. His clothes were drenched, heightening his anger with himself for being so careless, and forgetting to contain the sly woman. His powers fully restored he sprinted down the hall and turned the corner in time to see Loreena duck into a room at the end of the passageway. In a burst of speed, he got there just as the door closed behind her. Will flicked his wrist, opening the door with such force it banged off the wall. Realizing he was back-lit by the dim ceiling lights, he called out a Distortion Spell to surround himself, making his body a blur to anyone without the Inner Eye. And for all Loreena's powers, he thanked the Mother that wasn't one of them.

He crouched low, crossing the threshold into the room. He spotted a pile of furniture shoved against a wall and without hesitating, he made a bee-line for it. He hunkered down just as a bolt of red flame shot out from somewhere in the room's dingy interior. The stack of wooden desks and chairs he hid behind became engulfed. Will threw himself to the side and put out the flames with a pass of his hand, smiling tightly to himself. *I know where you are now, Loreena.* The Sorceress had moved to the back of the room. Raising his arms, Will caused a howling to fill the air. It was the unmistakable sound of Banshees invading the small space.

Then he called out to the hiding woman. "It appears your close friend, the great hunter, has set his Demon Spawn onto you, Loreena. You know these Banshees are like hunting dogs and will sniff you out in a minute. It's apparent he doesn't want you spilling family secrets."

Another blast of red flame shot out from behind an overturned table. Will knew this one would be a decoy. It was well short of targeting him, but more like cover for her movements. The Banshee calls were heightened by him. To add to their ferocity, Will began throwing furniture around the room as if they searched for her. When he picked up a cabinet and hurled it behind himself, Loreena came charging out. She had a dagger in one hand and a fist full of titanium dust in the other. The Historian didn't expect her offensive maneuver and was barely able to hold her back as he surrounded her in the eerie Banshee Wind. The dust flew from her hand and quickly dissipated in the turmoil of the swirling air. Will grabbed her extended arm in a vise-like grip dragging her close to his snarling face.

"No more tricks, Sorceress! But tell me…why aren't you effected by the titanium dust?"

She smiled, acknowledging his success, and answered, "I always take precautions before I visit Mason. He would love nothing more than subjecting me to his odd…predilections! And now that you clearly have the upper hand," she said, looking down on the large hand squeezing her arm, "what will you do with me? Your friends will be needing your assistance if they are to destroy Mason and his Undead. If you take the time to bring me back to those old fogies on the Council, you'll likely miss all the fun here!"

Will studied her face. She was mocking him, but he sensed something false in her glee at his predicament.

"You have a point, Loreena, but not one you can stick into me like that knife you're holding behind your back."

He twisted her around and grabbed the dagger out of her hand, spinning her back to face the depth of anger in his eyes.

"You were once a lovely, caring woman, Loreena. The Darkness has surely seeped deep into your spirit and rotted it completely."

The Sorceress became very still when she said, "I am not the woman you think me, Historian."

He was breathing heavily with his exertion of holding her when he added, "And so, you shall reap what you have sown." A few words in the Old Tongue and she fell into a deep sleep. He flung her limp body over a broad shoulder. Stepping back into the hallway, his sole mission was to locate the source of all this evil and eliminate it. He began his search for the Magical Treasures room.

Chapter 42

Jason thought back on Cathleen's description of the hallways he moved through. They ran like a network of dark veins just as she described. He located certain vintages she mentioned as his markers and confirmed he was taking the right hallways to find the Magical Treasures room. Cathleen was getting ready to trap Mirage but was unaware of the mysterious Sorceress Loreena. There was no way of knowing if Byron Bledsworth's sister was as powerful as his wife, but Jason was sure that would be tested soon. He hoped Cathleen would neutralize Mirage before Loreena could join forces with him.

He slowed his steps, figuring he was getting closer. He'd already set off one alarm, likely sending the Undead guards into action scouring the premises. Luckily the alarm was triggered on a first-floor door. It would take time for the guards to check out the countless rooms on the upper floors of the rambling mansion, before they could get to the basement level. As he moved through the shadowy passageways, he tried to come up with a plan to get inside the Magical Treasures room without dying in the process. He'd all but given up trying to use stealth. His presence was already telegraphed throughout the building. He was ruminating over and discarding strategies, when he spotted the plaque he was looking for when he reached the end of the hallway.

The brass sign above an iron-clad, wooden door read *Magical Treasures*. Jason was struck by the brazenness of advertising what lay within. He turned the heavy gold ring on his finger, getting ready to blast his way inside. He decided on this as his only option. Reaching for a dagger shaped handle, he stopped when he heard a humming noise. *Elevator!* This was quickly followed by the muted sound of several leather boots, scuffing along the passage and approaching fast. *They've begun to search down here!* Jason couldn't risk being caught in a crossfire from inside the room and have the guards coming at him from behind. He sprinted around the corner and kept moving, searching for a place to hide.

He began to panic when he spotted a large, square metal door, set mid-way up the wall at the end of the hallway. He ran to it, yanked it open, and stared for a second at a big pile of dirty linen. *A laundry-chute!* Boosting himself up, he squirmed inside. Grateful it was full, he quickly piled soiled table linens and bedding over himself. He left just enough space to press his good eye to the narrow slits on the door panel.

A few deep breaths later, the hallway filled with the raspy voices of several of the Undead guards, checking rooms and calling back "all clear" to the officer in charge. They hadn't reached the Magical Treasures room but were getting closer. If they barged in on Cathleen and the others, they could tip the balance in Mirage's favor and overwhelm her.

He needed to divert their attention and fast! Seeing the glow from his ring, gave him an idea. Slipping his pocketknife out of his jeans, he ran it along the top of the chute, producing a screeching sound that reverberated throughout the duct work and spilled into the passageways. The effect was exactly what he'd hoped for as the guards closed on his position. The cacophony ripping through the cellar stopped them in their tracks. Their heads were practically spinning on their scrawny necks as they turned in circles staring up at the ceiling. Their leader, a huge Zombie with hands like ball mitts, rapped out an order, propelling the others into a shambling run back the way they came.

He hoped they were returning to the main floor as he continued to use the knife, knowing the irritating sounds would travel throughout the mansion's pipes. He smiled to himself, when he paused long enough to hear the hum of the elevator.

Crawling out of the metal chute, Jason ran back to the Magical Treasures room. With silence restored, he guessed the guards would resume their search of the lower level soon. They might be Zombie guards now, but from what he'd observed, they were deadly mercenaries when human blood pumped through their veins from a beating heart. Jason pressed an ear to the thick wood once more. He clearly heard Cathleen speaking in the ancient tongue, but he couldn't identify the specific conjuring she performed. Then, one phrase jumped out of the tangle of words. *Nase plur... the binding of mortal materials in the First Realm*, he thought, recognizing it from years of hearing Cathleen's castings.

She was clearly working to hold something in place. But what? He still had his ear against the door when a jarring vibration ran through the wood and the outside walls. He lurched back and placed his hands, flat on either side of the door, he counted three more surges vibrating through the walls. He began to reach for the handle when a puff of air touched his cheek. He jumped back, his arm extended straight out, the signet ring glowing a vibrant green. A familiar voice came out of the stew of shadows at this end of the hall, followed by a deeply unsettling growl.

Starla threw off the Shadow Wrap. The petite Medicine Woman was dwarfed by the huge wolf sitting beside her. The massive head that brushed her shoulder had jaws that could tear her in half with a single bite. Cold, yellow eyes fastened like lasers on Jason, who couldn't tear his own eye away, mesmerized by that baleful glare.

He took a few deep breaths before he spoke, "Starla! Is that wolf here to help?"

The wolf moved as fluidly as liquid mercury, matching Starla's quick steps. When they reached him, she leaned toward the wolf's stiff tufted-ear, saying something Jason couldn't make out. Answering his inquiring look, the Medicine Woman simply said she'd identified him as friend. Jason looked back at the great beast, still glaring at him and wasn't convinced the beast got the message. Wanting to divert his own attention as much as the wolf's, he began explaining what he just experienced to Starla.

"Cathleen's conjuring a binding on something in there. It almost feels like it's the whole room she's trying to hold in place! There have been several powerful thrusts to pull free of her spell, coming through the walls themselves. Any idea what's going on?"

"When I was with the Historian, we overheard comments between the Undead guards. They spoke of a woman known to their Master. Her name is..."

"Loreena!" Jason finished. "I heard the Undead talk about her too. They called her a Sorceress. Later, I overheard her talking with the ghost of her brother, Byron Bledsworth."

Starla looked worried hearing the news about the Architect's spirit but remained quiet until Jason finished.

"The ghost was telling Loreena about a spell Mirage will use to relocate the Magical Treasures room. He called it a 'Displacement Spell' that would allow Mirage to escape to the Third Realm. Cathleen may be trying to prevent Mirage from turning the room into some kind of escape pod!"

"With Geilt gone, there would be none to stop Mirage from taking the wildlands with his Dark powers," Starla finished the bleak scenario.

The Medicine Woman signaled they move further down the hallway.

"We cannot enter the Magical Treasures room while Cathleen works her Binding, Jason. The guards will likely return to the cellars any minute, perhaps to join their Master inside the room. It would be wiser to find the Historian, than to engage in a battle without him."

Reluctantly agreeing with that logic, the two of them moved down the corridor, the pony-sized wolf padding silently at Starla's side. As they reached a juncture in the passageways, the signet ring began to glow a vibrant green.

"Magic user nearby," Jason whispered. He glanced over at the wolf. Its upper lip was pulled back in a soundless snarl. The wolf must have picked up a scent.

"The jinn sensed them as well. Is this perhaps the Historian your ring alerts you to?" Starla asked.

"Let's not wait here in the open to find out. We passed a furnace room. Let's double back and hunker down in there until we have eyes on whoever comes this way."

Retracing their steps, they entered the vast space of the utility room, with only the thin glow from the hallway crawling under the door as it closed behind. A huge shape filled most of one side of an open area. The single flame of the pilot light inside the gas furnace, looked like the eye of the Cyclops, unblinking as it watched them move closer. The sharp smell of hot water, and the huffing rattle of pipes, permeated a cloying air. The giant wolf was standing by the door. Jason noticed how his eyes glowed like jars of captured fireflies as it scanned the room, hesitant to move into the interior. In the low light, Jason saw Starla make a small hand gesture and the wolf moved to her side. Looking around they searched for a defendable hiding place. The wolf detached itself once more and walked behind a series of wide metal ducts shooting off in various directions to carry heat and air conditioning throughout the vast building.

"If they corner us in here, we'll have to fight our way out," Starla said as she walked around the furnace and over-sized hot water heater following her wolf.

"Jason. There's a small door behind the water heater."

He hurried over, trying to ignore the low rumble coming from the enormous creature when he pushed by to get closer to Starla. She was looking at a recessed handle fit into the flat metal surface. The door itself was a good three feet off the ground.

"This must access the duct work for maintenance," Jason was saying as he slipped his fingers into the hand grip and pulled slowly.

Relieved no grating noise followed, Jason swung the door as wide as it would go. Pulling himself up, he climbed into the gaping mouth of the pipe. He reached back for the Medicine Woman, but she shook her head.

"It would be better if the wolf and I used the mist. This creature will not travel well inside a metal tunnel. Give me a moment and we will join you."

Jason nodded and waited as Starla grabbed the fur around the wolf's thick neck, murmuring in her lyrical language. A moment later the woman and beast disappeared into a soupy red vapor. Jason watched intently as the mist came together in a tight swirl of color and entered the duct behind him. The door closed silently. Jason was immediately thrown into utter darkness until he spun his ring outward. The glow was much diminished, but still turned the interior of the piping an eerie green, giving him enough light to crawl forward. His head lightly grazed the tubular ceiling. He knew this metal trail would eventually lead back to the Magical Treasures room and, hopefully, to Cathleen's side. He clenched his jaw as he tried to send her his message, *I'm coming love. Hold on.*

Chapter 43

The architect's shade neatly carried out Cathleen's plan. He exposed Mason Mirage as his murderer, while warning his vengeful sibling the Magical Treasures room was more than just a place to display gruesome trophies. This was definitely of interest to Cathleen. She listened carefully to their exchange and was convinced Mirage would run to his prepared escape vehicle.

The architect was unaware he'd been summoned by Cathleen to walk the natural world as a wraith. She would hold him in the realm of the living, only long enough to ensure Loreena heard of Mirage's duplicity. Though the time he had was limited, Bledsworth was able to inflict the maximum damage on Mirage's relationship to the beautiful Loreena. She turned from his possible ally, into a sister out for his blood. When the room emptied of wraith and humans, it was finally safe for Cathleen to reemerge from behind the grandfather clock. She whispered a few words and weakened her hold on the Architect's spirit. He would begin to fade from the First Realm shortly and be sent on to the Dark Pit of the Sleepless Dead. Cathleen's heart remained like stone toward the spirit's deserved fate.

It was time to get on with her plan to capture the bloated egotist, Mirage. She closed her eyes, fixing the location of the Magical Treasures room in her mind. She had to be certain the Dark Wizard couldn't tamper with it in any way, before she got there. Calling up a Binding Spell, she mentally projected her voice to echo among the cases in the room as if she stood among them. As soon as she was satisfied with the Binding she placed, Cathleen began to call for the discarded shadows. She was about to exit the den when she picked-up an unusual sound. It came from somewhere above her head. Still using her Inner Eye, she looked up. Another muffled noise, but clearer this time, whatever was up there moved closer. *Someone's using the air ducts to move through the building. It feels like…*

"Jason!" she called out, pitching her voice directly at the spot above her head.

The movement stopped. Cathleen called again only this time adding their special warning whistle to identify herself.

"I'm just below you. I'm removing some of the ceiling panels, move back a few feet."

Cathleen heard a soft scuffing as Jason scooted backwards. She raised her hands, directing a series of vibrations at three of the sound-proofed panels. They shook loose, falling onto the priceless Oriental rug below, sending puffs of chalky dust into the room. Cathleen spotted the green glow from Jason's ring. He poked his head out before jumping down and pulling her into a quick hug.

"Cathleen, I know you placed a Binding on that room, but you should know, I overheard Bledsworth's shade with his sister. He told her Mirage will use the room itself to escape and transport himself to his destination…the Third Realm."

Even in the poor light from low embers left glowing in the fireplace, Jason saw Cathleen's face drain of color.

"Some of this I already heard from the shade, but I was not aware of Mirage's destination!"

Without another word, she ran from the room, looking back over her shoulder she yelled back, "We've got to hurry Jason, or risk losing him!" In a rush of breath, she added, "My Binding won't hold much longer!"

Jason worried that some of the wandering guards would hear them as they pounded along the meandering halls. When he listened, he realized he heard nothing as they moved. Cathleen must have muffled the sounds of their boots on the stone floor. When they neared the room, Jason reached for Cathleen's arm to pull her to a stop. Just barging in was too dangerous. Searching her worried eyes, he asked what she thought Mirage planned to do.

Her voice was full of urgency when she answered, "He's planning nothing less than a corruption of the Mother's Natural Laws. Don't you see, Jason? Without Geilt to protect the Wildlands of the Third Realm, all in that carefully balanced environment, will be lost to perpetual chaos and darkness."

Giving her a quick nod, they continued running down the hall, nearly colliding with the Historian when he and the woman he carried materialized out of the gloom. Will lifted his sleeping spell and gingerly lowered Loreena to her feet, keeping hold of her arm. Obviously glad to see Cathleen and Jason, he quickly recounted the events leading up to his capture of the Architect's sister. Loreena looked almost bored as he spoke, an arrogant expression on her beautiful face. Cathleen studied her closely, noting a flicker of something else in her wide, gray eyes. *Fear?*

"She can't be trusted as an ally, Protector. Even if she professes a deep hatred of Mirage. She works only toward her own ends," the Historian concluded.

"I have no doubt of where her true allegiance lies, but we'll use her to *our* ends now," Cathleen said firmly.

Loreena's eyes turned a steely gray, blazing with rage at the prospect of being at their mercy. Cathleen could see the Sorceress struggled to soften her angry response.

Loreena's voice was low and silky, "I know you as the Witch of Appalachia, Protector. I've heard tales of your exploits. Very impressive for one so very young, and shall I say, unseasoned?"

"You can use whatever words you choose, Loreena. Your opinions are worthless here.   My only concern is making sure of your punishment, and Mason Mirage's capture, or elimination."

Cathleen asked Will to place Loreena into the dead sleep once more, to insure she wouldn't try warning the enemy. They were about to enter the hall leading to the Magical Treasures room when a swirling red mist materialized directly in their path. Part of the red vapor detached itself and a slight figure stepped into the passageway.

"Well met, Starla Star Fire!" The Historian called as she walked toward them. Her hair was held back from her oval shaped face with a strip of leather, showing her high cheekbones and flawless copper skin to their best advantage. Jason looked over at the sound of Will's greeting, noting how his normal dour expression seemed to light up when he saw the lovely Medicine Woman. He gave Cathleen's arm a gentle nudge, pointing to Will with his chin. Cathleen had a small smile on her face when she looked back at her husband. Starla addressed the Historian.

"I am pleased to have found you well and safe. I assume that's Loreena Bledsworth you have slung across your back, Will. Is she dead?"

Before he could answer, the rest of the crimson haze dispersed and in its place stood the giant wolf. The Historian's reaction was instantaneous and the hiss of his long-knife was the only sound in that frozen second. Cathleen simultaneously brought Sacred Fire to her hands in response to seeing the great beast. Starla was quick to explain that this creature was a Jinn, conjured by her to join in their battle. Starla joined the small knot of people, the beast close on her heels. The Green Fire reflected in the large orbs of its yellow eyes. Starla reached down, placing a small hand on its back, and it responded to the slight pressure by immediately sitting.

"This jinn is bound to me. You have nothing to fear from him as long as I control its existence among us. Your Green flames would have no effect on this wolf, Cathleen. He was summoned by me from among the sacred spirits of my people and is not of your Green Mother's own."

Cathleen looked the wolf over before responding, "And will this beast fight beside your Spirit Warrior Starla?"

"As I've said, Protector, the Jinn and I are now bonded. What is your plan?"

As if it sensed an acceptance of its presence, the wolf appeared to relax its taught muscles and laid down. It placed its massive head on a paw, waiting on Starla to let him know her will.

While the flames in Cathleen's hand disappeared, a new fire gleamed in her eyes as she called for the total destruction of the one who was Hunting the Witch.

Chapter 44

Starla's wolf-jinn lay meekly at her feet when Cathleen asked her to use the intimidating beast to search out where Mirage was hiding. She wasn't confident he would still be found in the sprawling mansion, telling the others there was a possibility he'd already used the Magical Treasures room to escape. Privately, she thought the Witch Hunter's extensive excursions were for more than trophy-gathering. Mirage had somehow discovered how to syphon off the powers of his prisoners, before he used them as weakened prey in his hunts. Their magic was stored where they couldn't access it, even if they managed to evade his bullets. She suspected the purloined magic was inside the Magical Treasures room. She shuddered inwardly to speculate on how long the mad man had been carrying out his ghoulish expeditions, and how many of the Mother's gifted had already fallen.

Jason and the Historian, his sleeping prisoner once more dangling over his shoulder, walked ahead. While the men were alert to hidden threats, Cathleen turned over clues in her mind, searching for the elusive detail that poked at her memory. Finally, an old tale waved like a flag snagged on her pointed thoughts. Her mind flashed back to a time she was a youngster visiting Granddad O'Brien in Ireland. Among his many tales of elfin clans and Wizards, he told a tale about a room that had been enhanced with magic, and was used as a craft able to move through the Four Realms as easily as a breeze through the trees.

"That's it!" Cathleen blurted out as she came to an abrupt stop.

Her companions turned back to her with unasked questions.

"I remembered something about this room from a story my grandfather once told me. This room is not new to the Mother's Realms. Which means Mirage has been a practitioner of the Dark Arts for much longer than we assumed. My grandfather spoke of a magically transformed room, back in the dawning of the Dark Times, when the Green were empowered to fight the rising evil scourge. According to my grandfather's story, the room was used by a Dark Wizard to translocate from Realm to Realm, easily avoiding any repercussions from the Outlander Wizard Scouts, and the Council of Green Wizards."

Jason frowned, trying to do the math in his head. "That would make Mirage…"

"Very old, indeed," The Historian finished. His face reflected Cathleen's deep concern with this newly discovered information.

Cathleen murmured, "We have to hurry. This Dark Sorcerer is already capable of shifting between Realms, and this Realm is merely a refueling stop! I suspect Mirage's end-game was always to travel to the Third Realm after he disposed of Geilt. He would see the pristine Wilds as a perfect habitat to secure a stronghold against discovery, while he kept storing up magical energies unhindered."

Jason stopped her with a question as she turned to move down the hall.

"But Cathleen, why would he go to all the trouble of building this huge compound, and summoning the Zombie Guards to protect it?"

"This is another one of his illusions, Jason. He made a great show of building this place to create the impression that it is the center of his little kingdom. All along, it was only a way of diverting our attention from the murderous hunts that keep him refueling his Dark Powers."

The Historian added ominously, "And he knew this is where he'd find the Protector of the Green. He'd love nothing more than to tap into Cathleen's special gifts from the Green Mother. Think of the chaos he could bring to all the natural life in this First Realm alone, if he had the Sacred Fire!"

They all wore tight, worried expressions as they moved toward the end of the corridor, until they stood in front of the closed door with the bronze plaque reading *Magical Treasures*. Will lowered Loreena onto the floor, leaning her against the wall. She stirred slightly, but then appeared to return to a deep sleep. He looked down on the woman, placing a stronger sleeping spell on her. Something kept nudging his instincts that her current state of unconsciousness was not quite complete, though he saw no outward signs of her waking.

She proved how devious she was many eons ago when he first encountered her. Loreena's beauty was as legendary as her skills as a Wizard back in her youth. Will wondered over the years if she used a Glamour Enchantment to make him long for her as he did, those many life cycles past. But that was when he himself was a young Scout. She joined that elite force and was assigned as his partner, roaming the mountainous hinterlands of the Emerald Isle in search of Demon incursions from the Pit. She quickly became like a third hand. She automatically moved to protect his back, or to help dispatch any Demon using the Portals they unearthed. It all changed for Loreena and him when she was ordered to return to the Council Keep. Tales were circulating among the ranks of Scouts, that he knew eventually found ears among the Council. Loreena was suspected of covertly working on behalf of a mysterious Dark Sorcerer. Rumors flew unchecked about her duplicity, when she suddenly vanished after being summoned to appear before Arch Wizard Duncan inside his private Chambers. Duncan was already very old, and whatever transpired between him and Loreena was lost when he passed over. Looking down on her peaceful face, Will reminded himself how she became corrupt, and turned away from the ways of the Green. He felt once more, the cold place she left behind when she pierced his heart with her betrayal.

"Will! Will!" Jason finally brought the Historian back to the very dangerous present.

"Sorry my friend. I had to be certain she was secured by my spell," he said quickly, asking how they would proceed.

Cathleen's original plans were no longer viable in light of the translocating abilities built into the room. She turned to the two expectant men after casting a glance at the sleeping Sorceress.

"Mirage wants Loreena. That was abundantly clear to me as I watched him become a drooling idiot when she was with him earlier. I think we should give her to him!"

Cathleen saw a look of hesitancy pass over Will's face as he looked down at the vulnerable, sleeping woman. *These two have a history,* she thought.

She began speaking again, "If Starla and her wolf have been successful, she's already flushed Mirage out of hiding. He has to be inside the room, to activate the spells and recite the incantations he'll need to start the translocation process into the Third Realm. Letting him know Loreena is waiting for him here, will speed up his attempt to leave with her aboard."

"Do you intend to ask her to summon him to her side, Protector?" the Historian asked frowning down on the Sorceress.

"Not quite ask, but she'll do it. Drop your spell and wake her, Will."

The Historian rapidly reversed his charm and watched as Loreena's gray eyes fluttered opened. She looked up at him and then over at Jason who was standing just behind Cathleen. Turning back again to the Historian, she smiled.

"Am I to remain on the floor like a sack of rubbish Will?" she said holding up her arm for him to grip.

He reached down grabbing her elbow and hand to hoist her to her feet. There was a silky sound from the movement of her leather jumpsuit as she gracefully rose to her booted feet. Watching her closely, Cathleen noted how every muscle twitch could be detected in the tight garment. *She's using a glamour charm,* she thought with alarm.

"That's enough of your manipulations, Loreena," Cathleen said in a cold voice. She brought a spurt of Green flames to her hand.

"Any more attempts at using your glamour charms and I won't hesitate to use the Mother's Fire somewhere very visible on your perfect body."

Loreena stiffened and backed away from Cathleen until she was up against the wall. Cathleen shot a look at the Historian to be certain Loreena hadn't succeeded in turning him to her will. He had a determined look on his face, adding his own comment to Cathleen's.

"You are like a beautiful viper, Loreena, and just as poisonous."

Jason broke the tension when he told them the door was opening. Cathleen looked back over her shoulder. The door to the Magical Treasures room was moving inward until it was wide enough to pass through. She considered her options for a moment before telling the subdued Loreena she'd be in the lead. Loreena's face showed no outward fear when the tall cases became visible in the pale light from the hallway. She ran her hands down the side of her leather-clad legs as if checking her armor. Moving slowly toward the doorway, her shadow fell across the threshold and was soon lost in the gloom.

"There's no one in here!" she called back to the others. Her light voice sounded small and tentative.

Is she afraid, Cathleen wondered?

The others began to move forward, with Cathleen entering the room first and stopping next to a case. Using her Inner Eye, she easily picked out Loreena, standing by another of the tall cases at the back of the long room. As Cathleen passed the first few cases, she scrutinized their interiors for any new victims. Wanting to do this with all of them, she called to Loreena to stay put as she worked her way toward her. Jason and Will moved close behind as she searched. They cleared six cases when Loreena's voice carried over to them. Her words drifted off as if she'd turned toward the back wall.

"Have you seen something?" Cathleen called.

'I thought I saw…" Her last words were suddenly choked off. The three of them looked in her direction, spotting a long, tentacle-like arm, wrapped around the Sorceress' delicate neck. Her screams were cut short as the rubbery appendage constricted her larynx. Cathleen was almost knocked out of the way as the Historian began to run past her.

Cathleen forcefully grabbed his arm and Jason grabbed hold of the other.

"No Historian! I'll deal with this!" she said emphatically.

Her words and tone held the authority of her office as Protector, and the Historian immediately gave a curt nod, moving back a step. Cathleen knew Mirage would safeguard the room with some powerful wards, but now she wondered if instead, he chose his final battle to be fought in this form.

"This is Mirage's Avatar!" she murmured, knowing with a sudden certainty.

The men heard the alarm in her hushed words and braced for yet another challenge from the Dark Sorcerer.

Chapter 45

Cathleen and the others stared at the horror standing a few feet away. "This being, the Avatar, already had the mystical powers of a Demi-God when he was summoned with Dark Magic," Cathleen said, her voice betraying the shock and awe she felt. "If I'm right, Mirage bonded with the Avatar, and the creature now shares his memories...even his DNA!"

And he's lost all humanity inside this beast Cathleen thought as she inched closer to the struggling Sorceress. The twin tentacles were thick with muscle, each covered in a thin layer of a yellowish, mucous-like substance. The leather body suit Loreena wore was slick with it, preventing the beast from getting a good grip around her waist or legs. Loreena managed to remove the tentacle from around her neck, stabbing it over and over with a small blade that suddenly appeared in her hand.

Cathleen guessed it was hidden on her person the whole time and wondered why she hadn't used it to escape from Will. She also noted that the Sorceress kept her cool after her initial scream. She was calling out a stream of spells as she relentlessly jabbed at the beast. *For all their effect, they might as well be nursery rhymes* Cathleen thought alarmed. Cathleen shifted closer. The Avatar moved himself and the struggling woman, deeper into the shadows. The beast must have detected movement and immediately dropped the cursing Loreena with a loud thump. She jumped like a gazelle, running to a far wall, rubbing her throat and catching her breath while she watched the Protector approach the Demon Deity. Cathleen she barely noticed the men moved to either side. She spotted the green glow from Jason's ring, knowing he was prepared to send its bolts into the monster lurking in the inky interior of the room. When the Historian slipped his long-knife from its sheath, its hiss stung the air like the warning of an Adder, ready to strike. Even well-prepared, Cathleen's was keenly aware they were all in mortal danger. There was a stirring inside the dusky ambient light, the monster shuffled backward and was waiting. Cathleen cautioned Will and Jason not to engage until they had a good look at it. A gurgling laugh came out of the depths of the room and the beast boldly stepped into the watery light. He let them study the monstrosity they would face, adding another level of fear in their hearts.

He was slightly hunched; two hefty legs carried a body dense with muscles that rippled beneath a tight sheath of silvery scales. His feet were broad, the clicking of their curved nails pricked the air when he moved. The beast had three, deeply recessed eyes under an over-hanging browbone, they glittered as black and cold as obsidian chips. His ears were mere slits with skin flaps on either side of a face ending in a pig-like snout. His mouth was wide enough to swallow a small goat and filled with flat teeth and curved tusks at its upper-corners. He was broad-chested, and besides the two tentacles sprouting from his scaly shoulders, he had the arms of a steroid-using body-builder ending in claw-like hands.

Cathleen suspected the silvery scales covering every inch of it would act as a tightly woven body armor. The tentacles constantly moved, as if anxious to be crushing something in an embrace. Cathleen also noted that besides the scales, the massive chest was studded with spikes that jutted out and then retracted. The beast showed off his prowess to his audience.

Loreena was fortunate the beast only tried to choke her, Cathleen thought. She shot a look in the direction of the Sorceress. Her leather clad figure leaned against the side of one of the wooden cases, leaving her face in shadow. Cathleen wondered why she hadn't tried to escape while she had the chance. Her random thought was cut off when the beast spoke. His high voice held all the arrogance of Mason Mirage. Now she knew why she kept thinking of the creature as *him* and not *it*.

"You have met my Sorceress, and now I afford you the honor of meeting my *immortal* self!"

The creature continued lecturing the three humans staring at him in the same droning fashion Cathleen remembered about Mirage.

"You may address me as Gorgon. If you remember your Greek and Hindu Mythologies, you'll note I have successfully melded several deities to create my Avatar. I had to choose carefully among them, before allowing the absorption of my weaker human spirit. But here I stand before you...the next ruler of the Third Realm...or any Realm that captures my fancy for that matter! I shall establish an empire ruled by Dark Magic, filled with every manner of living creature to serve me, beginning with Geilt's Wildlands!"

This fantastic merger of two living beings, was as mad as Mirage. Cathleen began considering a multitude of spells and weapons she could bring against this abomination. Her concentration was shattered when a fierce growl surged into the stillness from the back of the room. The scaled feet of the beast scraped the floor as he clumsily turned in in the direction of the new threat. Cathleen and the others also searched the recesses of the room for the source of this new presence.

"Cathleen, the red mist on the left," The Historian hissed.

Gorgon spotted the swirling fog, and his tentacles flailed, beating against the empty space. *This is an intruder Gorgon hadn't counted on*, Cathleen thought. She wondered if Starla's wolf jinn could prevail, now that she studied the enemy closely. When the mist began to disperse, Gorgon raised both arms high above its head. The room was instantly flooded in scorching white light, while his scream bored like glass shards into their ears. Cathleen flinched as if she'd looked directly into an eclipse of the sun. The sharp brilliance stabbed at her eyes making them water and burn. Blinking furiously, she immediately slipped out of her highly sensitive Inner Eye. She caught the movement of the two men, their arms flung across their faces, trying to shield their eyes from the searing glare.

Cathleen acted while Gorgon was preoccupied with his spell. She cupped her hands close to her mouth, the murmur of her voice moved under the harsh sound of Gorgon's incantation. This hex was from her mother's book, *This and That Magic* and would be unknown to him. He jerked his large head, trying to locate the source of the spell casting, but too late. Cathleen's hands were already filled with a fine yellow powder. Bringing it close to her mouth she blew. Her charm carried every speck of the yellow talc directly at the Gorgon. The three eyes turned a bright red as he was enveloped in a yellow cloud. He waved his tentacles and arms in an effort to clear the air, but only managed to stir the fine granules into tiny funnels that flew into his open jaws with every roar. Cathleen watched closely as the snout sucked in a good dose, leaving yellow traces of powder around the flared nostrils. Gorgon suddenly stopped flailing about and the room returned to its gloomy state. Cathleen and the others had to readjust to the abrupt darkness. The creature was immobile, but his eyes blazed with rage when Cathleen stepped closer. She knew the *Fixity Potion* as her mother quaintly named it, would last exactly two minutes, and was only used as a stop-gap measure. She saw both tentacles twitched.

"We need to get him into a case. Maybe the titanium will affect his powers until we can subdue him," Cathleen said to the men.

Cathleen held her hand in front of the nearest case. The door resisted, vibrating on its hinges as her charm pulled at the magic laid upon it by Mirage. Cathleen repeated the spell with urgency in her voice. She knew the powder would be wearing off Gorgon any second. With a protesting groan, the door opened. The Historian began his own incantation when Jason noticed the Avatar begin to stir.

"Gorgon's moving!" he yelled.

Cathleen was looking into the case when Jason's warning rang out. As she turned in his direction, a long tentacle swung out like a club, smashing into her back with such force she was lifted off her feet. She crashed against the side of a heavy wooden frame, nearly passing-out with the shock of the impact to her body. Her head was spinning and something warm slid down her cheek. She was disoriented, tried to stand, but ended on her knees, waiting for the turbulence to settle. Her head was filled with ringing and Jason's shouts barely filtered through.

"My ring is barely making a dent! The scales are too dense!" he was yelling over to Will. He couldn't run to Cathleen and leave Will to fight on alone.

Cathleen's eyes were unfocused, she struggled to understand what happened when the air vibrated with a terrifying roar. *Starla and her wolf jinn*! She reached for the side of the case, careful not to touch its titanium lining. When she was able to right herself, she looked back to where the red mist first appeared. Starla's and the enormous wolf stood there looking totally unphased by the monster watching them. The wolf lowered its head, its ears were flat and the fur bristled along its back making him look even more massive. It was ready to charge, when Cathleen saw Starla lay a restraining hand on the huge head. Her lips moved, but her ears were still ringing and she only picked up a few words. Cathleen murmured a few words of healing and the ringing subsided enough to hear the last of Starla's words.

"Hold.! My own Warrior joins us."

Cathleen thought, *she's calling to her Spirit Warrior!* The Medicine Woman turned away from the men as they continued their attack on Gorgon. Bending at the waist in a low crouch, both hands flat on the floor, she braced herself for the transformation to follow. The red mist suddenly reappeared and enveloped her figure beneath its opaque vale. In the scant lighting, Cathleen watched as Starla's body began to contort. A long howl rang out in the room from the wolf jinn as he stood by. The leather dress was gone, and the crouching form was covered in a pelt of dark reddish fur. When the mist dissolved completely, the Werewolf jumped onto its splayed feet, throwing its head back with its snowy white streak. The long jaws opened in a blood thirsty roar. Cathleen was enthralled by the transformation. The sound of its challenge lingered ominously among the wooden cases. She saw Jason and Will move several steps back, each unsure, and taking a defensive posture.

This was a beast to be feared, its actions unpredictable. Cathleen wondered if Starla truly had control over this creature that existed only to kill. She looked at Gorgon. He was very still after turning in the direction of this threat. When he saw the wolf jinn and the shifted Medicine Woman, a snort of mocking laughter pushed through the flat snout. Gorgon sounded amused as Mirage's voice uncannily came out of the flat faced creature. He turned his eyes to Cathleen.

"This is a pathetic array you've gathered to defeat me Witch! A Skin Walker in the guise of a mangy Werewolf and her pet!" he said derisively. Looking over at the two men in their battle stance, he snorted again. "Plus, your weakling human mate and a *History* teacher! Is this the best you can bring to the battle? I expected better from the storied Protector of the Green!"

Cathleen laughed. The Avatar focused more closely on her. He was clearly annoyed by her nonchalant scorn. His black eyes flashed; the tentacles snapped at the floor like whips. Cathleen's voice was filled with contempt when she finally stopped snickering.

"Your overinflated opinion of yourself is exceeded only by your ignorance of those who serve the Green. I address my comments to the human part that still exists under your scales. The Mother's own gifts are *exactly* what you sought in human form. Over uncounted eons, you trapped and tortured the Mother's magic users as sport, but more importantly, you stole the power you scorn, from your victims. And where did it all bring you, these sick hunts and murders? Your enhanced Powers have fused your human spirit with this... thing...this Avatar! As hideous as any monster crawling through the slime of the Dark Pit. Your great ego is now part of a scaly beast. Even the Sorceress Loreena, who once tolerated you, is repulsed by the nightmare you've become. All that power, and no one to impress!"

Cathleen painted Gorgon as a Frankenstein of mythical proportions. Looming above these acts of magic subversion was a more sinister fact staring out of three merciless gazes boring into her. The frailty of the corrupt human personality could never control the power she felt radiating from the scaly beast.

Chapter 46

Jason winced when the Medicine Woman disappeared inside the red cocoon, remembering the Spirit Warrior that would soon be among them. When Starla last shifted into the Werewolf it attacked him, proving its unpredictable nature, not to mention how unsettling it was to witness Star Fire morph into the fabled creature. He shot a look at Gorgon who appeared riveted on the scene, though he didn't react. The Werewolf reached out a long arm, beckoning the enormous wolf closer. It laid a clawed hand on the dark fur of the massive head. Immediately a yellow current sprang to life, becoming a crackling stream between them. There was a single flash of light when the yellow current covered the wolf completely and the wolf jinn vanished. Jason saw the Werewolf was larger and more frightening. He followed the gaze of its glittering eyes and realized they were fastened on Cathleen. He moved a step closer to her and was about to take another step when Cathleen quietly said, "Stay back, Jason. The Spirit Warrior is not here for me."

Looking into the depths of those beady eyes, Cathleen called over to it, "Our enemy awaits!"

Cathleen's right hand now gripped a jagged bolt of green lightning while the other was covered in Sacred Fire as she and the Werewolf charged Gorgon. The bolt flew with such force it punched through one of Gorgon's muscular thighs, exiting, and setting a wooden case alight. The Werewolf closed with the Avatar before his howl of pain faded in the room. Jason watched as the Spirit Warrior lashed out with a powerful right arm, its claws raked Gorgon's broad chest, pulling off scales and ripping into exposed flesh and muscle. Mirage's high-pitched voice screamed from the gapping jaws, "Enough, you mangy dog!"

Cathleen suspected Gorgon had been caught off guard by the ferocity of the attack. He recovered quickly, whipping a tentacle around the Werewolf's back and pinning its arms to its sides. In this tight embrace, he began pulling the Werewolf closer to his chest and the deadly protruding studs. The Werewolf stretched its neck back and lunging forward, clamped its jaws on a tentacle, freeing an arm. It dug its claws into Gorgon's broad back, leaving it deeply scored, with oozing trenches.

Enraged with pain that reedy voice shouted chants both alien and alarming to Cathleen. Enhanced with a blending of the Magical and Demi-god, Gorgon ripped himself out of the Werewolf's grip, unconcerned with the strips of his flesh left dangling from his enemy's claws. He shuffled out of reach of the Werewolf, and another incantation rang out. It hung like a dark cloud over the watchers. The air suddenly filled with hissing vipers, twisting and wriggling around the Werewolf and Cathleen, who waited for an opening to use another green bolt on Gorgon. She reacted instantly, throwing up a shield of ice in front of herself and the Spirit Warrior, but the Werewolf, filled with blind fury, leapt over it to get to Gorgon. All Cathleen could do from behind the barrier was watch wide-eyed as every kind of venomous snake smashed against the cold wall, and a wave of vipers threw themselves at the Werewolf. Most were swatted away before they got close enough to bite. With one eye on Gorgon, Cathleen saw him lower a raised arm. The serpents immediately fell to the floor in front of her ice shield. They appeared to have forgotten her completely and moved in a slithering mass toward the harassed Werewolf.

Cathleen watched horrified as five snakes drilled long fangs through the thick fur of the Werewolf's thighs and vulnerable ankles. She heard the snap of a tendon and saw a dark liquid ooze onto the floor from several punctures. The Spirit Warrior howled. It reached down, jerking the vipers off with such ferocity the heads were ripped from their writhing bodies. The snakes curved fangs held fast creating an array of gruesome decorations. Cathleen feared if the Werewolf received more bites it would succumb to the venom.

She caught a darting movement from the corner of her eye. Loreena Bledsworth stood just outside the ice barrier, her hands extended over the undulating, snake-filled floor. The Sorceress began chanting in the Mother's own tongue. *But how*, Cathleen thought, amazed? She didn't recognize this spell but knew from some of the words it must be arcane and not even her Wizard-parents knew of it, or so would she.

The snakes slithered over one another in an effort to reach the Werewolf, biting one another in the frenzy. The Werewolf was weakened from the venom coursing through its body. Flecks of foam flew from its snarling jaws while it fought off attacks, using two snakes like cat o' nine tails. Loreena's silky voice rose over Gorgon's as he bellowed his strange incantations in his reedy voice. Vipers killed by the Werewolf were replaced by ever larger numbers.

Cathleen knew this had become a battle of spells for the life of the spirit creature standing at the center of the surging mass. She was so intent on watching the magic users, she nearly missed what was happening almost below her feet until Jason shouted, "The floor!" She looked down to see the cement floor under the writhing piles of serpents furrow like a stirred pond. The rippling spread out, stopping with a hiss of bubbling heat at the feet of the Sorceress, and barely before reaching Cathleen's ice shield. The floor became more agitated, small gray wavelets formed at the top before the cement turned into a tarry sludge. Cathleen was stunned that Loreena would know ancient magic needed to alter the composition of matter. Looking past the turmoil of the sinking snakes, she saw the Werewolf hung suspended a foot above the thick gunk. Cathleen looked back at Loreena. Her hands were steady and the look on her face determined as she held them over the floor. The Werewolf lowered when the last of the demon vipers vanished beneath the muck.

Cathleen's thoughts raced as she watched the floor return to its natural state. She was convinced after what she'd witnessed that the

Historian was holding back pertinent information about this woman. She sensed a strong emotional undercurrent between the two since she showed up flung across his shoulder. Rather than escaping when she had a clear opportunity, the Sorceress chose to do battle against the Avatar bent on killing them all. Cathleen suspected Loreena was somehow involved in the Dark Arts as was her brother Byron Bledsworth, and decided Loreena had a hidden agenda. There was no time to unravel the knotty ball of clues. She had to deal with Gorgon, but she was determined to find out what was behind this sudden change of partners in the middle of the dance.

She dropped the ice wall.

The beast must have sensed her new exposure, jerking around in her direction. Gorgon's words were sharp with sarcasm. "The Medicine Woman's Spirit Warrior appears to be having some difficulty breathing, Protector. With every kind of venom coursing through its mangy hide, there's little chance of it surviving. Tut, tut. And we know what fate awaits the Medicine Woman then, don't we?"

Cathleen felt sickened hearing Mason Mirage speaking through Gorgon. *How could he give over his humanity to such a monster?* His comment was followed by a lunatic's cackle. It echoed around the cavernous room, filling the moving air with a putrid stench from the snout-nosed jaws. *Mirage will inhabit this creature for* eternity, *or until death,* Cathleen thought. *Whichever comes first!* But this wasn't a mere taunt by Gorgon. The Werewolf had likely been bitten hundreds of times. When Cathleen looked back, Loreena was kneeling beside its body, an arm under its head. A small bottle appeared in her hand and Loreena tipped the contents into the slack mouth before getting to her feet.

Gorgon shouted out, "So feeble it can't even help itself! Pathetic! Loreena, you are a fool to abandon me for the likes of these weaklings and a plague-ridden dog!"

"I am not abandoning you, Mason. I have never *been* with you!" Loreena shouted back.

While Gorgon was distracted by Loreena, Cathleen motioned to Jason and the Historian to move closer. They could see the Werewolf's attack had injured Gorgon. Layers of scales were peeled back, exposing vulnerable flesh. A beam shot out from Jason's ring, exploding inside the broad chest in a firestorm of green energy. Eye searing smoke billowed out from the beast's mid-section, carrying with it an acrid odor. The Sorceress was closest to Gorgon and began choking violently. She raised an arm to cover her mouth and nose, moving back from the motionless Werewolf, but seemed reluctant to abandon the creature, looking down at it as she backed away. Without warning a long tentacle shot out of the dense smoke and encircled her waist. A gush of air was pushed out of her lungs as the muscular limb squeezed harder.

Jason shifted the beam toward Gorgon's upper body. The scales proved impervious to its cutting energy and held fast against his assault. Jason knew this was a god-like beast and wondered if it could ever be defeated. Cathleen and Will, arms outstretched, mouthed powerful spells, but desperation marked their faces. Loreena was going to be impaled inside the Avatar's last embrace.

Chapter 47

The Historian held his long-knife out in front, shouting his spell. Instantly, the sharp blade transformed into a flaming broadsword. The basket shaped hilt gave his hand protection against Gorgon's attempts to grab his wrist and disarm him. The Avatar seemed unaware of the Historian's presence, or his burning weapon. His focus was on the struggling woman, as he pulled her toward the chest spikes. Will wondered why she wasn't shouting her own spells. As he moved closer, the reason became horribly clear. Her mouth was stitched shut with a heavy black thread. Will's thoughts raced with dire truths. *Gorgon cast a cruel binding spell to silence Loreena's Magic. The depravity of his Magic bodes ill for her and her punishment for aiding us would be horrifying.* Taking advantage of Gorgon's deadly attention on his captive, Will drew closer. The beast curled its tentacle tightly, reeling Loreena in like a hooked trout. She fought for every inch of space between them, using her feet and legs to push back from the deadly spikes. Gorgon tried to bring her closer, to secure her with his short powerful arms.

The Historian launched himself, his sword's flames so intense the varnish on nearby cases bubbled up. He swung the burning weapon in a wide arc, but at the last possible moment the beast turned. Gorgon suddenly launched Loreena's body directly at him, forcing him to twist to the side. She flew past, missing the flaming blade by a fraction of an inch. Her scream was blunted by the seal upon her lips when an explosion of flames tuned her leather clad body into a living torch. Will heard Cathleen's voice cut through the horror that paralyzed him for a breath. The flames vanished, leaving only a trace of smoke rising from Loreena's singed jumpsuit. She received bad burns to her hands and neck. The Historian rusher over to begin a curative charm, but there was no time to do more than rudimentary healing on the scorched skin.

Mirage's strident voice brought all eyes back to the beast. Cathleen edged closer to one of the open cases. She signaled Jason to move toward the beast's side while Gorgon watched Will. The Historian half-dragged, half-carried Loreena toward the front of the room, leaning her against the wall before streaking away return to Cathleen's side. She wondered why Gorgon didn't react to the three of them positioning themselves in a loose ring, when suddenly she had her answer. A deep hum filled the expectant silence. The floor and walls surrounding them began pulsating like a beating heart. They felt a subtle shudder through their boots, like a mild after shock after an earthquake, and then the vibration increased until the whole room shook. The heavy wooden cases moved side to side in a precarious movement. One tipped to the side, hitting its neighbor, and in Domino fashion, the whole row toppled over. Will jumped clear of the unexpected avalanche moving toward him.

Cathleen shot a quick look toward the door to check on Loreena. She was gone, leaving behind her scorched leather jumpsuit in a pile on the vibrating floor.

"What in the Mother's dreaming…?" Cathleen muttered.

There was no time to figure out where the unclothed Sorceress might have run to. The hum they heard at first, had become a penetrating throb, and the sense of impending disaster gripped the three as they fought to stay on their feet.

"Cathleen!" Jason shouted above the growing din. "We've got to get out of here before Gorgon blasts off!"

There was no need to discuss abandoning their battle with Gorgon, he already melted into the shadows while his room was being readied to act as a Translocator. The three had to jump out of the way as long platforms rose up from the floor around them. Each was covered with levers and buttons glowing a sharp yellow. Cathleen realized this was the craft's control room. The three raced for the open doorway and flung themselves into the gloomy hallway. Will was the last out. When his boot hit the passageway, the Magical Treasures room began to shimmer like the gossamer wings of a dragonfly. As they watched, it became as insubstantial as tissue paper and blinked out of sight, taking with it, the Avatar that possessed the Dark Magic user, Mason Mirage. They stared into the emptiness, shocked looks on their faces. Bottles of priceless wine from the adjoining room vibrated out of their little nooks, perfumed the air as they shattered on the floor.

"Protector, Loreena can't have gotten far with her injuries. She'll likely hunker down somewhere on the compound to heal them, before trying to escape. I feel confident she still wants to avenge her brother's death."

Cathleen pointed out that Loreena was quite resourceful, and if she knew anything about the Translocator from her brother, may have secreted herself aboard to take that revenge.

Suddenly Cathleen blurted out, "Oh no... Starla's Spirit Warrior was still in that room! Loreena gave it some kind of healing potion, and there's a very good chance when it revives, Starla will be the one who wakes up!"

"And she'll find herself aboard the Translocator with the Gorgon," Will said, completing the dreadful scenario.

Cathleen's face went from concerned to determined. "We must find Loreena! She may have information about Mirage's scheme to take the Third Realm, like where he'll settle the Translocator. The Wildlands are vast and dense with vegetation. It could take years in this Realm's time to find where he'll locate his stronghold and be far too late for Star Fire."

Cathleen picked up the leather outfit shed by Loreena saying, "There's another way to locate her if Loreena is still around here."

Without further explanation, she ripped off a piece of leather sleeve, dropping the rest to the floor. Holding her hands over the pile, she mouthed a silent charm. The space around the shiny black material began to spin taking the burned leather into a whirlwind. The men stepped back a few paces. When the funnel disappeared, a large Blood Hound stood in its place. Jason was very familiar with this breed of dog, having raised several himself over the years. This was a 'scent dog' used for hunting deer, wild boar, and since the Middle Ages for tracking people. He couldn't help but admire the dog standing proudly like the best-in-show winner. Its overall rust colored fur had a splash of glossy black on its sides and back, covering a muscular seventy-pound frame. It would be easy to miss the look of intelligence behind the sleepy-eyed appearance.

Jason looked over at Cathleen saying, "Well done, love. Just what we need to find her. Who'll track with him?"

"He won't need a handler, Jason. I've attached a second spell to this beauty. When he finds her, he'll immediately change back into the House Pet I called and bring her to us. He won't have trouble finding us even if we leave this Realm. He'll retain his strong scent instincts after he's back in his true form and use his special magic to travel with her."

"Clever Protector," the Historian added. "A dog will have a better chance of approaching Loreena without undo suspicion. But is this House Buddy you've summoned prepared to subdue Loreena if necessary, once he's changed back to his natural form?"

"This is not just any conjured House Buddy, Will. This is our old friend, Parsons. He's serving the Arch Wizard, and I'm certain will be up to the task."

The dog's droopy lidded eyes looked directly at Cathleen. The large head bobbed up and down as if in agreement. Jason stepped closer to the hound and began scratching behind a long floppy ear. He was rewarded with a soft woof of recognition. Parsons had proven both brave and resourceful in past struggles against Dark Lords. Jason knew Cathleen had a real fondness for this elfin magic user as did he.

"Let's move out before..."

Cathleen's words were cut short when a bullet whizzed by Jason's head, the sound of the shot ricocheted around the narrow hallway. The Historian lunged for Jason pulling him off his feet when a second round was fired in quick succession, this time hitting a pile of broken wine bottles. The glass sprayed the area with deadly shrapnel, lodging in the ceiling above Jason's head. There was no obvious place to seek cover. The Historian immediately conjured a Dome of Protection for himself and Jason knowing Cathleen had vanished with the hound. The men searched the shadowy hallway outside the gapping space left by the Translocator.

Jason said softly, "That was a handgun. With the Translocator gone, the Guard has a clear shot from the room at the other end of this hallway."

"I agree. I will leave the Dome and …"

"No. We'll both leave! If you can fill the hallway with a thick smoke screen, I'll get close to the creep to use my ring to fry his boney butt!"

"Very good idea…and most colorful description," the Historian said smiling back at Jason's determined face.

A minute later Jason was scooting low, moving through a dense, gray fog. The Historian held the dark mist in place, staying several feet behind him. He figured the dark cloud he produced might alarm the Undead Guard, maybe fooling him into thinking the place was on fire. They weren't particularly smart, just hellishly dedicated to a task. Jason used the glow from his ring to guide his steps, carefully shielding its green light from possible detection. He was almost on top of the Guard's position at the end of the hall, when he heard a scuffing sound. He figured the Zombie Guard was shifting his position into another room. Jason continued moving, low to the floor, trying to stay inside the dark haze. He was about to advance when he heard the distinct whistle, he and Cathleen used to let the other know they were nearby. He waited for her to reveal herself when there was a gentle tug on his jacket sleeve and a faint whisper.

"Wait. I asked Will to take a Time Thread into the Third Realm. I need him there when the Hound locates Loreena. It's just us sweetie!"

They heard the shuffling noise the Zombie Guards made as they moved their stiff limbs. Cathleen leaned close to Jason's ear, telling him she just saw the guard move further down the hallway, and around the corner. As they moved, swirls of gray fog stirred around them, but kept pace providing cover. They would be turning the corner soon, entering a less used section of the huge cellar complex. The Undead Guard would be waiting in ambush nearby. Under the billows of gray mist, they made their way to the bend in the passageway. They heard the Guard just ahead. Cathleen grabbed Jason's arm.

He leaned into her, "I saw him go into the room where I was held. That's good. Outside of the marble table there isn't any other furniture for him to use as cover."

"How do you want to handle this?"

Cathleen answered, "Your ring will do nicely, and once he's down I'll dispose of him."

Cathleen got rid of the dense fog as they moved to the partially open door, but when the mist vanished, he wasn't in Jason's line of sight. Cathleen stood close to the wall on the opposite side of the doorway. Jason used an old trick, reaching into his jacket he pulled out a coin. He crouched and tossed it, hitting the font of the marble table. The guard fired three shots in rapid succession, but before the last round cleared the chamber Jason dove into the room. A razor thin beam swept across the Zombie's mid-section, cutting him in half. Cathleen shouted out her spell and they broke into dark particles floating like dust motes until they were sucked out of the room and vanished.

"Perfect Jason! Now, let's get out of this cursed place and get to the Third Realm and The Historian. He may really have his hands full if he's found the hound and Loreena"

"I guess this means a Time Thread," Jason said with the enthusiasm of a patient facing a root canal!

Chapter 48

The Historian was waist-deep in a hole filled with a tarry liquid. He'd been cursing his own carelessness, letting himself cut corners in his hurry to find Loreena and the House Buddy, Parsons. He knew relatively little about the Third Realm, and most of that from conversations with Geilt about his beloved homeland. Those were never detailed enough to warn of this kind of literal pitfall. He knew his arrival via the Time Thread would not have gone unnoticed by Gorgon and his Zombie Guards. He was able to avoid detection by two guards, but had to dispatch three others, something that surely alerted them to an intruder. He realized he allowed himself to become distracted, placing himself in this dangerous spot. A series of spells successfully lifted him, inch by inch, but he needed to hurry the process, or risk being found in this defenseless position. His last Magical boost left him in the muck, half-way up his thighs. He was murmuring another spell when a silky voice came out of the surrounding woodlands.

"Perhaps I might help you with that, Historian."

Will's head snapped up in time to see Loreena materialized out of the green miasma of the dense trees. She was dressed in the supple leather jumpsuit and not alone. Standing next to her was the House Buddy, Parsons. He had a pleased look on his face as the Sorceress placed a delicate hand on his round head, patting it absentmindedly.

"It appears you've gotten yourself into a bit of a pickle, Will. Or should I say, *stew*."

Her sweet smile infuriated the Historian, trying to ignore the woman's presence long enough to finish his extraction from the pit. He mumbled his spell. This time he added a rope around his waist that flew over to the nearest sturdy tree. His charm made the tree bend back until its top branches scraped the ground. Will shot out of the pit leaving both boots behind. He undid the spell, straightening the tree and was about the do something about his boots when the Sorceress spoke again.

"Parsons, be a dear and retrieve the Historian's boots for him."

"Yes, Mistress."

The House Buddy blinked out of sight only to reappear a moment later with Will's boots tucked under each arm. He whispered a charm known by his kind of house servant, bringing a lustrous shine to the black leather. Handing them to the scowling Historian, he remarked, "Are they not to your liking sir?"

"They are fine, Parsons," he answered, adding a deep harrumph as he glanced at the smiling Sorceress.

"How is it this House Buddy found you so swiftly, Loreena?"

The woman's smile faded in response to the Historian's stern tone. When she spoke, her honied voice took on a serious tone. "I was preparing to take a Time Thread, when Parsons, in the guise of a sharp-nosed hunting dog, located me. I knew he must have been sent by the Protector and since I wanted her to join me here, I snatched up the hound and took him along. I used the Thread, following the Translocator's energy trail as it moved through the In Between, and ended close by. When we arrived a few minutes later, Parsons was quick to slip back into his true identity and is helping me since we share the same mission."

"And what mission would that be, outside of your own selfish desires?"

"You really should address Mistress Loreena with the respect her office deserves, Historian!" Parsons said in a scolding manner.

"Her...office?"

"Yes, as the Arch Wizard's *Enforcer of The Code*," Parsons answered indignantly.

Will looked over at the woman, but she let the House Buddy answer Will's surprised look.

"When Mistress Loreena was an active Outlander Wizard Scout," the elfish Parsons continued, "the sitting Arch Wizard recruited her to spy for him. She faked her defection from the Scouts, even deceiving you Historian, her partner of many cycles. I was assigned the task of shadowing her progress and reporting back, as I do now for our current Arch Wizard. Her assignment was to infiltrate the evil world of Mason Mirage. He's been known to the Council for many eons as a Master of the Dark Powers."

Will waited for any other surprising information to emerge. Parsons shuffled back to stand next to Loreena. He studied the pair for a second then decided, "We'd best hurry before some roaming guards realize a few of their mates have gone missing. Have you already established where Gorgon has positioned the Translocator?" he asked Loreena moving ahead of her.

It felt to Will as if they never stopped working as a unit. He and Loreena slipped into a comfortable dialogue, laying out strategies while they moved through dense woods and vegetation. Loreena knew precious little of the Translocator's location, it turned out, only that it was to be tucked into a valley hidden from easy detection. Will sorted through his sparse store of knowledge about the third Realm. The valley was likely formed when the Realms were split apart by the Mother. Tales from the history before the Dark Times spoke of many cataclysmic events that would eventually separate the Supernatural, from the Natural worlds. Somewhere in this Third Realm, Gorgon managed to hide the Translocator. Find it-find him!

They walked single file through tightly spaced trees. Will noticed the nearly impenetrable forest surrounding them was eerily silent. The thick canopy of leafy branches, appeared empty of any forest creatures nesting among the high limbs. Occasionally, the trio used Wind Charms to pass over rushing rivers or deep lakes. The Historian would take Loreena's hand, as she did the same with Parsons to cross together. Their movements were coordinated, making little, or no disturbance, on land they passed through. A sharp hunter would not have known of their presence. They both slipped into Scout mode, and Parsons smiled privately at an old alliance being reformed. Stopping near a fallen tree, they took a moment to rest on the rough seat provided by the wide trunk. The Historian was mostly silent to this point.

"I hope it isn't much further to this valley. We need to be alert for guards patrolling the area as we get closer."

"As I recall from some of Mason's description, we should be within sight of the drop to the valley floor within the next few minutes, Will."

Hearing her speak his name so naturally made Will smile to himself. This wasn't glamour she used. This was a comfortable familiarity. Strangely, his spirits were lifted, but he still had a nagging feeling to be on his guard with this woman. Though she was newly revealed as a secret agent for the Arch Wizard, their relationship was badly damaged when she deserted him and her post. He couldn't help wondering why she didn't trust him enough when they were together, to tell him of this secret assignment.

Her voice cut through his random thoughts. "I know you are still unsure of my allegiance Will, but I'm sure I can prove…"

Her unfinished thoughts hung between them when the peace of the surrounding woods was shattered by a thunderous roar. To Will it sounded as if a great dam had broken through its retaining wall. The sound continued to rumble around them drowning out any words of alarm. Parsons was the first to react. He muttered a few words and reverted back to Blood Hound form, bounding off in the probable direction of the valley. The two Wizards stood away from the tree, waiting for whatever made the roaring sound to appear. Will shot a look at Loreena to try to gauge her reaction as suspicion bubbled up inside him once more. For her part, the Sorceress looked cool and calm as she began to prepare for battle. *Or is that knife for me*, Will thought.

Chapter 49

Cathleen and Jason were just above the lush Valley of Voices, Geilt once called it the seat of his kingdom. The landmarks were described vividly by Geilt for this particular place. The first was a swift flowing river, its deep waters the color of ripe plums. The other was close by, called The Harrowing Caves. Geilt said the twin caves intersected one another continuously as they meandered underground for miles. Their earthen walls held the tormented spirits of creatures that attempted to bring chaos into the Third Realm. As Guardian here, Geilt defeated any beings coveting the free Wildlands, filling the caves with their spirits, over time without count.   He described to Cathleen how, when close enough to them, the disturbing sounds of hundreds upon hundreds of souls could be heard. Their howling and screaming voices echoed throughout the vastness of the caverns.

Jason was quick to be free from the tether of the Thread, and glad for the feel of solid earth beneath his feet. Like Cathleen he began taking in the view before them. The oddly named Valley of Voices ran on for miles. Its whole expanse appeared ringed by dense forests and vegetation atop thousand-foot cliffs. The open skies above the vastness of the lowlands, were filled with all manner of avian life, gliding smoothly through crystal-clear air. Jason breathed in deeply, relishing the taste of a living woodland on his tongue, and the sweet smell of earth all around. He never relied solely on his single eye to learn about his environment, although that eye offered a sharp picture. Rather, he listened to the cries of the flying creatures first, filtering those out, he located the distinctive sounds of rushing water.

"Cathleen, the river is to our left. Past that area covered in yellow flowers I'd guess."

Cathleen gave a quick nod, and Jason took the lead. As they negotiated the downward slope toward the valley floor, she explained that the river would lead them deeper into the valley, and ultimately to Geilt's stronghold. They scrambled over shale ledges, loose rock and prickly scrub. Bright orange gecko-like lizards darted in and out of their holes, in a constant game of peek-a-boo as they passed. It took an hour of careful hiking to reach the edge of the yellow expanse they'd seen from above. The color was amazingly vibrant, presenting them with a buttery, restless sea. The flowers bobbed and swayed atop thick stems, dotted with several cup-shaped nodules. These acted as moisture collectors for each plant, Jason pointed out on closer inspection. They stood a moment, awash in the spicy fragrance of the blooms, when Cathleen stirred beside him.

Shielding her eyes, she checked the positions of the orbs Geilt had called the Jewels in the Mother's Crown. "I'm not sure how long we'll have before we lose our light with the setting of the three suns," she said, looking back at him.

Jason snapped out of his reverie. "Right. Let's head east through the field. I can almost smell the river from here."

As if confirming his instincts, a huge flock of honking birds sailed overhead in a wedge formation, almost blotting out the suns with their incredible wingspan, until they turned south. Jason located an old animal trail through the dense flora and following this they quickly found themselves leaving the golden field behind. Jason called back to Cathleen several minutes later, pointing to the glitter of the suns poking through the high grasses they passed through. Sweeping the feathery stems aside, Jason revealed the deep purple waters of the river Geilt called The Mother's Robe, because of its royal color.

"Jason, from this point we follow the river until we come to its source. That's where we'll find the Sacred Grove of Yew Trees. According to Geilt, this grove is the beating heart of the Third Realm. He told me a species of intelligent primates tend and guard the Yew trees and surrounding orchards. If Gorgon is anywhere, he'll have settled the Translocator there, trying to access the Mother's powers."

Jason thought of Starla saying, "I hope Starla has shifted from her Spirit Warrior form. I don't think Gorgon would want to mess with the Werewolf again, and he'd likely destroy it."

That somber thought lingered as they walked down-river, alert from this point onward, to running into Zombie Guards acting as outlying security in the area. It was easy moving through the high grasses along the riverbank, and Jason's mind wandered. He'd picked up the same vibes as Cathleen whenever the Historian was near Loreena. Cathleen said she sensed Will was withholding information about the Sorceress. Jason wondered if sending Will to the Third Realm on his own was such a good move.

Moving through the marshy grasses rimming the river, Jason watched the waters break over boulders that rose from its purple depths like stone temples. He speculated they likely broke loose from the cliffs, plunging them into this deep valley as the ground heaved in its formation. He was beginning to think every Realm shared a cataclysmic birth, and the violence seemed to echo throughout the worlds of Natural and Supernatural alike.

His mind meandered in this fashion until Cathleen called out. "There's a small boat tucked into the water grasses, Jason! We'll let the river do some of the work."

Jason waded in and pulled the boat further onto shore to make certain it was watertight. Shaped like a shallow soup bowl, it was fashioned from extremely thin strips of wood, likely from the heart of a tree, and the flexible reeds growing in abundance all around them. The materials were tightly woven together, then covered with several layers of some kind of resin. The coating had beaded in places before hardening, and the glossy globs of adhesive gave the boat the appearance of being decorated in exotic jewels. Jason judged that nothing could slip through the skintight seal. Looking back at Cathleen he nodded and together they lifted the round craft back into the water. Cathleen hopped in as Jason gave it a hard shove and climbed aboard as the swift-moving current caught and lifted it in a swirl before settling into an alarming bobbing motion. Cathleen handed one of the paddles she found on the wet bottom to Jason as soon as he was settled, and they began to ply the violet waters together. Jason alerted Cathleen that the boat would tend to spin if they didn't keep their strokes even and coordinated.

They didn't speak after that, quickly falling into a smooth rhythm. They looked up on occasion when large shadows passed overhead, blocking the suns momentarily. These shadows were often caused by flocks of giant white birds similar to the graceful herons that visited the pond behind their house in Iron Mountain. That life seemed far away to Jason, as he tried to wrap his head around being in another dimension, another world. They'd been paddling downstream for some time when Cathleen shouted.

"Jason! Oars up!"

Raising the paddles abruptly while cutting through the water at a good clip immediately put the undirected craft into a wide circle. They held onto the sides to keep from spilling out of the shallow vessel. When it slowed to a gentle rocking motion, Jason was finally able to follow Cathleen's gaze in the direction of the shore. Even from their position near the center of the wide river, Jason made out two ape-like creatures standing at the river's edge. *They must be huge*, he thought with some apprehension. One held what appeared to be a staff. The round boat drifted with the current, moving them closer to the figures. Jason leaned forward and spoke to Cathleen in a hushed voice, not taking his eye off the pair.

"Do you think the one with the long crook is holding a sign of rank?"

"There are symbols carved, or painted, all over it so that's probably the case,"

Even hunched over as he was, they could see this ape creature had the appearance of a resolute leader. He raised the long staff over his head, and the wind shifted suddenly, carrying the small craft closer still. They watched with growing apprehension as more of the creatures came bursting through the tall grasses. With the exception of the noise from the resisting reeds, they made no sounds. As they emerged, they lined up in orderly rows behind the motionless leader and his companion. Their ranks were deep, and Jason guessed there were close to one hundred. As the boat floated nearer to shore, they saw the new arrivals all carried throwing spears, the light glittered off the sharpened tips.

In unison, they began pounding the blunt-end of their weapons on the ground. The sound of a hundred synchronized thumps created vibrations in the still air, and a strange tremor along the gravely shoreline. This triggered the river water to stir and the wavelets created washed over the low sides of the boat. Jason noted that the ape creature with the staff, and the one beside him, *his lieutenant?* were unfazed by the controlled frenzy around them.

"Cathleen, do you know what we're looking at here? They definitely don't seem like a welcoming committee!"

"I believe these are the extraordinary primates Geilt spoke of. If indeed they're the Guardians of the Sacred Grove, they'll help us. Let's paddle closer and test my theory."

Jason looked back at the sharpened spears, still relentlessly pounding the earth. Going closer to the hordes wouldn't have been his first impulse, but when Cathleen lowered her oar into the choppy waters, he followed suit. Cathleen leaned back so Jason could hear her.

"Jason, let's stop a few yards out. I don't think these creatures like the water, and until we know they won't attack, we'll be safer."

He was quick to agree, not relishing the possibility of facing a wall of giant apes with sharp sticks. With soft, steady stokes they kept the boat from spinning-out again. The assumed leader raised a hairy arm. The thumping immediately stopped. As they drew closer, Jason and Cathleen were able to study him, and try to draw some conclusions about the role he played among these wild beings. When he lifted his head, they saw he was much taller than any of the 'soldiers' as Jason thought of them. While all of them were covered in shaggy dark fur, their leader's pelt had many white streaks throughout his head and face. In an unexpected gesture, the leader drew back his thick lips. His teeth were square and large, and even at this distance, they looked worn to Cathleen as she used her Inner Eye to study him. The leader's eyes had an intelligence and awareness as he in turn studied the humans. Using a spell to carry her voice, Cathleen carefully stood. The boat shifted slightly under her feet.

"I am the Mother's Protector of the Green, Cathleen O'Brien. This is my mate, also blessed by the Mother. I am here on behalf of your Lord, the mighty Geilt. We come to avenge him, and many others of the Mother's chosen."

Cathleen stopped speaking to let this all sink in. She wasn't even sure these beings had the capability of understanding language, but her doubts were put to rest as the presumed leader spoke. His voice boomed out like a canon shot over the water.

"You are welcome, Protector, as is your mate, Lightening Maker! I am called Old Father by my own. They are assembled here to greet you with the Thunder Clap, a greeting reserved for special dignitaries. We have heard of your many exploits alongside Lightening Maker. Lord Geilt often warms our spirits with tales of your battles during the *dead times,* when our three suns lose their way in their travels, leaving us in a bitter cold darkness."

He stopped for a moment as if reflecting more closely on what Cathleen said. "But...what is this revenge you speak of? The all-powerful Geilt has been taken from our Realm?"

"Not taken... murdered!   He died saving us from a Dark Wizard whose magic has melded with the evil Demi-god, Gorgon. In this form, he plans to usurp Geilt's position as Lord of this Realm."

"This cannot be! This will not stand! My kind have lived free under the protection of the Mighty Geilt for more eons than drops of water in the mighty Robe River! We know of no other home. We will not relinquish our freedom to any who would seize Geilt's place among us. Tell me what you would have of this Old Father and my children."

Cathleen motioned to Jason and they paddled onto the rocky shore. A burly soldier ape loped forward to help ground the boat and offer a leathery hand to Cathleen. The two walked to where Old Father stood hunched over, but still formidable. This close they could readily see his advanced years in the deep wrinkles and puckering of skin around his mouth and small black eyes.

"Let us return to our village together, Protector. You and Lightening Maker must help us make our plans."

"Old Father," Cathleen said respectfully. "We know you are Guardians of the Sacred Yews, as such you need to understand the gravity of our task. I believe Gorgon will make an attack on the Sacred Grove. He would make it his stronghold and has traveled here in a fortified capsule to achieve that end. If he succeeds, he can tap into the Mother's seat of powers for himself. All here and in the other Realms, would fall to him."

Old Father raised his staff over his head. His voice boomed out, "Home my children. The *Dead Time* is upon us!"

Chapter 50

Loreena and Will jumped off the log they'd been resting on. Standing back-to-back, they slowly turned their heads to pinpoint the source of the roar as it hung suspended inside the dense woods. Parsons immediate reaction to the ominous sound was to revert to the Blood Hound form he had when he arrived in the Wilds, and disappear at a run toward the valley below. The humans barely noticed. Will slipped his long-knife from its sheath. When she glanced back at him, Loreena saw the Historian also had a long segment of heavy-linked chain around his fist. She didn't have time to question the length of shackling iron, instead she focused on conjuring her favorite weapons. Will took a quick look over his shoulder.

"I see you still prefer your Flying Garrote and the Dazzler, Loreena."

He was looking at a whip-thin strip of steel, and Loreena's sword, Dazzler. She named it that because of its incredible speed in her early days as an Outlander Scout. They began moving in a slow circle, covering all directions of a possible assault. Loreena alerted Will with a quiet word when she caught sight of a pair of Zombie Guards moving low between the trees. She had little concern about dispatching the two, but the enormous mongrel that followed them, might cause some problems. She hastily told Will that Mirage often hunted with the beasts he formed from various parts of Demon creatures. They were fierce and decidedly difficult to kill. She glanced at the Historian to see if he'd conjured better armament for the coming battle after her comments. He raised an eyebrow and nodded that he was ready. The same roar that startled them earlier, shattered the unnatural stillness of the woods. Even though they knew the source, it had the same disquieting effect. Any wildlife within earshot would have taken refuge in deep holes, or atop the many lofty trees. The Historian speculated that the coming conflict must be new in their experience. Whatever the results, the innocence of this Realm would be lost for all time in the violence to follow.

"The Undead move more boldly," the Historian whispered. "They obviously have given up on the element of surprise," he concluded wryly.

Studying the pair of Zombie Guards as they dodged between thick trunks, Loreena commented on the opaque shields they held in front of themselves.

"I don't recall any such armament being used by the Undead guards I encountered at the compound," Loreena said in hushed tones.

"Let them get nearer, then let fly with your Garrote. I'll take the one on the right."

The Zombie Guards moved in their odd shuffling gait but were surprisingly fast none-the-less. When he was certain they were within range, the Historian shouted, "Now!" Loreena spun the wire until it was a blue blur above her head and sent it zooming toward her target. It looped snuggly around the Guard's neck while Loreena curled her fingers into a fist. The wire pulled taunt, cutting through the neck. Bones and tendons snapped like twigs and the head severed.

Loreena whirled in the direction of the Demon Dog. It hung back, still several yards off. Then, in a single thrust of powerful hind legs it cleared most of the space between them. She whipped Dazzler in front of herself, gripping it in both hands to meet the charge of the giant beast. It opened its huge jaws, spewing waves of nauseating smells into her face. She swallowed bile but didn't flinch. Planting her feet firmly on the ground, she waited for the inevitable weight of the huge monster to hit her like a cannon ball. Out of the corner of her eye she saw Will finish off the other Guard and he was beside her the next instant bracing for the attack.

The creature slowed its charge, shifted over a few feet when it saw the Historian move to Loreena's side. Will wondered why the creature changed course when suddenly it was airborne, a move which left Will and Loreena open mouthed. The beast flew back several yards. It and the attacker came down in a rush of sound as heavy bodies smashed into the ground. As the pair tried to identify this unexpected ally, the Demon Dog let out a shriek when Starla's Spirit Warrior tore into its exposed underbelly. Its death was gruesome to witness but worse to hear. Will shook himself to refocus on a new challenge. *Is the Werewolf friend or foe?* He didn't have long to consider the implied consequences before the bloodied Werewolf stood away from its kill. It threw back its shaggy head, jaws dripping the blood of its enemy. Its victory howl filled the air; a long warning siren to any other challengers.

"Will, it's the Medicine Woman's Spirit Warrior. Surely, it's no threat to us," Loreena said, as Will raised the chain still wrapped around his hand.

"We don't know if a blood lust has taken the creature. It still has a hungry look in its eyes."

The Werewolf slowly moved toward the watching pair and Loreena saw the eyes glowed a deep red and held a frightening intelligence. She raised her arm to direct Dazzler at its heart.

"Make no moves, Loreena. Not until it becomes threatening to us. The last thing we want is to destroy the Medicine Woman."

As it moved closer, they could see the shaggy creature was covered in the Wild Dog's blood. It casually flicked away some entrails from its arm, the red glow of its deep-set eyes had begun to fade until they reverted to their natural coal black orbs. It seemed to be studying them, or waiting for one of them to do something. The Historian slid his long-knife into its sheath and aside from the chain wrapped round his fist, was without a weapon. His sonorous voice broke the silence. He spoke in a conversational tone.

"Recognize us as friends, Starla Star Fire. You must reclaim your human form."

"Will, I think your words are having an effect. A reddish mist is forming," Loreena pointed out softly.

Neither of them moved, watching closely as the mist rose until it completely enveloped the Werewolf. Encased now in gauzy crimson, the creature began to spin faster and faster until it was no more than a pinkish shape against the dark backdrop of the forest. The Historian took Loreena's elbow and made her shuffle backwards, putting several more feet between them and the whirling fog.

He whispered down to her questioning face, "Until we know what will step out of that mist."

The answer was quick in coming as the fog dispersed. The petite Medicine Woman walked haltingly out of the vanishing mist and came toward them. The Historian rushed to her side as she swayed on her feet. Steadying her, he led her to the log they'd been resting on earlier. He knew her change into the Spirit Warrior was a physically draining process.

"Thank you, Will," she murmured with a sigh. "It seems to take longer and longer to recover after each shift now. I'm not sure why."

Her face was drawn and pale. Loreena conjured a flask of spring water, helping to revive her enough to share information. She told them when she shifted from her Spirit Warrior, she found herself lying on the floor of what Cathleen called the Translocator.

"I was weak, but I had to escape from that machine before Gorgon knew I'd regained consciousness. I waited until I knew the Translocator was settled and Gorgon exited the vehicle to secure the area with the Undead guards he summoned. I guess he thought me an insignificant threat in my human form, or he wouldn't have left me alone. I heard him conjure that beast that attacked you. That's when I escaped using my mist and began to search for any of our party that might encounter his monster. I thank the Great Mother I found you before you came to any harm, Will Farley."

Starla turned her dark eyes to the sleek figure standing beside Will adding, "I question your choice of traveling companions, however."

"Loreena has been acting as a secret agent and appointed as Enforcer of the Code by Sir Creighton. She has been reporting on the Dark Wizard's movements for a very long time, and now, she'll help to cause his downfall."

Starla looked deeply into the wide, gray eyes of the beautiful woman. Finally, she bobbed her head in agreement. Once Loreena's allegiance was settled, the Historian raised the issue of finding Cathleen and Jason. As he started to move toward the bluff overlooking the valley, Loreena put a restraining hand on his arm.

"What about Parsons, Historian? We can't move away from here should he return looking for us."

"The House Buddy will still have the scent of you in his memory and will track us down. Have no fears on Parsons' account. He knows how to take care of himself."

After a long hike out of the woodlands, the three stood on a high bluff, a valley spreading out like a colorful mosaic below. They were all drawn to a bright yellow field and just beyond, the crisp twinkle of water on the horizon. The Historian decided the best way to travel was by Time Thread. After he was satisfied the others were securely fastened, he fixed the yellow patch in his mind and they vanished. They were enveloped in the spicy fragrance of wildflowers the moment they set down. Will released the Time Thread and the three began scanning the field surrounding them in every direction, while golden blooms nodded their welcome.

Starla called out, "There!" pointing to a narrow path through the yellow field and suggesting that Cathleen and Jason traveled this way.

"They are likely headed to the river we spotted from above," the Historian said.

This time it was the Medicine Woman who led the others through the tall flowers, with Will protecting their rear. Starla was careful to stay on the same path used earlier by Cathleen and Jason, not wanting to leave any trace of their passage. She agreed with Will, the Protector and Jason hadn't passed through here more than an hour before, noting how the plants were already springing back up along the trail. They would effectively mask their trek through the field, covering their presence in the Realm. After a short time, they stepped out of the sunny field, walking until they found the damp shores of a wide river. They stood for a moment to take in the beauty of the plum-colored waters.

"It looks like rippling velvet," Loreena said with obvious fascination. "The Third Realm holds many beauties and…"

"And some nasty surprises if we're not careful," the Historian added. "Let's fan out and see if we can find any tracks along the damp shoreline. We need to know whether to proceed on foot to find Cathleen and Jason or learn if they somehow crossed this river to the far shore."

The Medicine Woman said she would search the surrounding area for a boat or canoe. She reasoned that if there were intelligent beings here, they would surely use the river to fish and navigate to remote areas. The Historian and Loreena went in opposite directions along the shoreline, while Starla moved around the area closer to the river's edge. Will was the first to call out that he'd found footprints pressed into the damp soil.

"They must have used a boat…their prints stop here, among the high grasses. The reeds here are bent and long-dead so I'd guess they discovered a hidden boat moored on this spot.

We need a watercraft!"

Loreena went a short distance when she called out excitedly, "Here! I've found a craft!"

They studied the odd, saucer-shaped vessel after Will dragged it out of the reeds. He pronounced it water-worthy and women boarded leaving Will to push the boat further into the water. He waited until it spun around, so he could carefully climb into the small space left for him in the middle. Loreena and Starla each held a paddle and began to row smoothly toward the center of the river. The Historian pulled a small brass spyglass from the leather pouch attached to his belt. He was trying to locate the best possible landfall for them, and at the same time, watch for any Undead guards scouting the area. He asked the women to paddle toward a patch of shoreline that looked like a safe place to come ashore. They were quick to vacate the odd craft when it scraped bottom, leaving it hidden among the tall grasses. The small group found themselves at the edge of a kind of mangrove forest, their exposed roots clustered along the shoreline. As they walked on, the trees began to resemble others they were familiar with. This forest was very dense with old and new growth trees, the air felt heavy with moister, encouraging a spongy, lime-green moss to grow in profusion. It clung to every surface, quieting their footfalls where it carpeted the loamy soil. It sprouted off the tops of large rocks and covered immense tree trunks in fuzzy green skirts.

"Geilt spoke to me of this forest when we shared another time of strife," Will said in a moody tone. "He called it Whispering Woods because of the silence created by the moss that dulls sounds."

Starla was back in the lead, leaving only a hint of a trail and her companions had to be vigilant to follow her footsteps. She looked back at one point, commenting on the lack of animal life, or even the sound of chittering or birdcalls among the branches. A moment later, she stopped. Up to this point the dense clustering of the trees limited the light penetrating from the three suns. Loreena was the first to notice many of the higher branches in the tall trees, were purposely cut back and sealed with a tarry substance, so they wouldn't grow back.

They moved ahead, following the path of this enforced lighting system. Looking around, Starla pointed out how this allowed the heat from the suns to nurture large sections of fruit bearing bushes dotting the area. Upon closer inspection, they realized there was a pattern to the placement of these miniature orchards. As they moved on, looking to either side of the lighted path, they saw hundreds of carefully tended bushes, their dark berries glistening with heavy dew.

"This has been done with careful planning and great care," Loreena said, looking back at Will. "Whatever beings live here, they are clearly able to cultivate the land."

She casually pulled two of the plump berries off the nearest bush, giving one to Will as they followed Starla who was already out of earshot.

"This would imply some sort of society, or at the very least, an order imposed by a leader," the Historian added.

They passed through neatly kept rows of various leafy plants, and species of tubers and other unfamiliar produce. As they crossed a clearly defined border surrounding the cultivated area, Starla warned in a hushed voice that they'd likely be encountering the beings responsible for this orchard, very soon.

"They would not plant and garden like this, far from their village. And there is the possibility of some type of security for the settlement as well as this garden."

The verdant life of Whispering Woods permeated the crystal air. Its unique richness clung like a green mantle overall, from the humblest wild grasses, to the magnificent towering trees. When the trio traveled a short distance from the cultivated area, Loreena's voice floated from behind the Medicine Woman. She sounded as if she'd been put into a trance. The Historian struggled to make his speech audible, saying ominously, "I feel…legs…growing heavy… focus…dim…"

Starla had been listening with half an ear to the conversation behind her, when she heard Will's comment. She spun around in time to see both her companions collapse with a muffled thump. Approaching Loreena, lying unresponsive on the spongy moss, Starla knew this had to be some kind of spell placed upon them. Looking down at the two, her question hung in the heavy air, "Why haven't I been affected?"

She watched with growing concern as Loreena's body then the Historian's began to convulse and then become completely stiff. When Starla touched Loreena's neck for a pulse, she found the skin hard and unyielding. The same condition had overtaken Will Farley. Kneeling between them her mind raced, trying to think of counter spells to restore them. Her thoughts were interrupted when she heard a rustling among the long branches above her. A few leaves showered down on the wooden bodies. She looked up. *Something is moving through the trees.*

Not wanting to be captured, and yet needing to defend her companions, Starla called to her Spirit Warrior. She crouched low to the ground, letting the green smell of the prickly moss fill her senses as she waited for the Werewolf.

Chapter 51

Growls and snarls pushed through the moisture ladened air inside the woods.   Any predator moving through the trees would know, something unafraid was waiting for it. The Spirit Warrior's keen sense of hearing informed its next move. The threat was coming from overhead, inside the darkness of the interlaced treetops. The Werewolf threw its head back, its intelligent eyes scanned the foliage. Some of the branches were just snapping back, as if they'd been used like slings. A hairy arm poked through the screen of leaves and knotted vines. A large beast covered in a dark pelt swung out of the canopy, grabbing hold of a limb just above the Spirit Warrior's head. The Werewolf snarled, showing a mouthful of sharp teeth. The hairy animal seemed undeterred by this display, or by the size of the muscular man-beast waiting below. In a smooth jump the creature snagged another limb. Pushing off from a sturdy tree trunk, it dropped to the ground a short distance away.

The Werewolf and Old Father stared at each other like boxers in a ring before a fight. While the Spirit Warrior was inferior in size, it had incredible speed and caught its opponent off guard. The force behind the move brought Old Father to the ground in a body slam.   The Werewolf was about to tear into the exposed throat of its enemy when a voice shouted from behind it.

"Stop! This is no enemy! Starla Star Fire, hear me and return to your natural form!" Cathleen commanded.

The Spirit Warrior twisted its shaggy head to see the speaker, still gripping Old Father so his throat was exposed to its long incisors. It must have sensed something familiar and non-threatening about her and loosened its grip. Cathleen held her arms out and using a cushion of air, pulled Old Father out from under the distracted Werewolf, floating him back into the higher limbs of the canopy. Before the beast could react, a Dome of Protection slammed over it, not for Cathleen's safety but for that of the shifting Star Fire. Cathleen watched as the beast pitched forward beginning the transformation. She knew these shifts took a terrible physical toll on her. As Cathleen predicted, Starla seemed to rest easy on the pillowy moss, drawing her legs and arms close to her body, before falling into a deep sleep. Old Father dropped down from his perch in the canopy after he witnessed the remarkable change in his attacker. He said nothing to his rescuer, only nodded his head. They both turned as Jason and several Guardians emerged through the narrow openings between trees. He walked directly to Cathleen's side, bowing his head respectfully to Old Father.

"Cathleen, you were right in thinking Gorgon would set up his base camp near the Sacred Grove. But there's something else."

Cathleen arched a curious eyebrow and Jason continued.

"The human part of Mirage is gone. He's been completely absorbed into the being of the Avatar, Gorgon. But more than Mirage has been altered beyond recognition. The Translocator has been transformed into a living creature, covered in scales, with several openings secured by the Undead guards. The Guardians and I tried to get closer, but Gorgon has placed some kind of energy shield around the Translocator...a sort of lethal moat. We lost one of the Guardians when he tried to pass through the field."

Old Father moved to stand at the front of the Guardians while he listened to Jason. They formed into two short rows behind him. He said nothing during Jason's report, but his grunt punctuated the end, and signaled his desire to speak.

"It is time, Protector," he said in his oddly clipped English.

"The Sacred Grove cannot be sullied by such a monster as this Gorgon creature! The Great Geilt would never let this stand!"

The Guardians gave a single thump of their sharpened staffs. Responding to an unspoken command from Old Father, the troop melted like dark whisps of smoke, back into Whispering Woods. Cathleen turned toward the Dome where Starla was getting to her feet. Old Father and Jason stood by as the shimmering Dome disappeared. Starla was obviously anxious. Rather than approach them as expected, she shouted for them to follow, and ran back into the gardens where she'd left the Historian and the Sorceress. Cathleen was surprised at the speed Old Father displayed as he was first to reach the fleet-footed Medicine Women. He reached down while the others looked on and gently took Loreena's stiff hand in his leathery palm and turned it over. Dark stains were on several of her fingers. He went over to where Will was stretched out and did the same thing.

Facing the others, he said, "They have eaten of the Dream Berries, and this is the result of their action. I shall reverse the spell laid upon our gardens by our Lord Geilt."

Old Father moved his long staff over Will and Loreena doing this twice more as Cathleen and Jason watched, fascinated by the vivid green sparks falling on the rigid bodies. The Historian was the first to rouse, followed quickly by Loreena. They both sat up, looking around at the expectant faces.

"What befell us Protector?" Will asked, reaching for Jason's extended hand to get to his feet.

He reached back down and helped Loreena. It was Old Father who answered before Cathleen did more than open her mouth.

"You have both fallen under the spell of Whispering Woods. The Mighty Geilt placed powerful wards here, protecting the gardens and orchards from creatures who would eat them, or trample the tender shoots. When you partook of the sweet berries, you were unlocking the door to those wards."

"Who are you?" Loreena demanded bluntly. Old Father stared into her gray eyes for a long moment before replying.

"I am the one who saved you! By the end of the three suns' travels on this day, you would have been gnawed wood for the many types of

Forest Sweepers. It is their job to clean fallen limbs and debris from the forest floor."

Jumping in before Loreena could blurt out some kind of edgy response, Cathleen gave them a quick summary of Old Father's role as leader of the Guardians of the Sacred Grove. She told them they would help destroy Gorgon and the Translocator.

Old Father broke in at this point saying, "That is not possible, Protector! The Guardians have been prepared by the Mighty Geilt for a single mission; to protect the Grove at all costs! All Guardians will be stationed in and around the holy grounds as we implement the plan of defense outlined by him."

Cathleen was disappointed, but recognized these intelligent primates had a deeper coding for their singular task. This almost robotic response, would remain unchanged, and no amount of reasoning would alter their original directives. She bowed her head slightly, signaling her understanding. He stepped back a few feet and waited as Cathleen looked around the group.

"This may prove the last battle for some of us. As Protector of the Green it is my sworn duty to be here, but this isn't so for any of you."

Cathleen lifted a hand to silence Will who began to object.

"Historian, the Outlander Wizard Scouts have been successfully protecting the First Realm under your leadership. We cannot risk your loss and possibly disrupt the shield of magic you helped create against the Dark Ones."

"It is as you state, Protector. However, if we can't succeed here, the Outlander Scouts will eventually be overrun and destroyed by the Demi-god, Gorgon.

Cathleen didn't respond, but slowly nodded agreement and turned to the Medicine Woman.

"I am here for my own revenge as one of Mirage's victims, and that of other Shamans he took for sport. My Spirit Warrior hungers to spill his blood, no matter what form he now inhabits!" Her words rang true and Cathleen could not deny her the chance for justice. Again, Cathleen silently nodded. She looked at Loreena standing beside the Starla, she looked...*Like a black panther*, the thought flashed through Cathleen's head. Their eyes met and an unspoken message flashed between them. This woman was surely as stealthy and powerful as the big cat, but there was something else. She had a steely determination found only in true warriors, either for good or evil.

"Loreena, the Historian has vouched for your role as an agent appointed by the Arch Wizard. How do you choose your role?"

Loreena's smile was as cunning as the Cheshire Cat's and warned of deeper meanings beneath. "My particular talents will be at your disposal, Protector. I think you have an inkling of what those are. My goal to destroy Gorgon. He will not be susceptible to my glamour, but I assure you, I will prove a worthy ally with Dazzler in my hand." She patted the long sword sheathed against a leather-clad thigh.

With all of them on board, Cathleen turned to Jason. They looked into each other's eyes. "Jason, I..."

"Cathleen, you might as well stop right there. As long as I draw breath, I will fight alongside you. I'm not a wizard like the others, but my own special gift of the signet ring proves the Mother has searched my heart and found me worthy of a unique power of my own."

"I was going to say exactly that my love! You are more than qualified to wield the ring. As Lightening Maker you'll play an important role in the destruction of Gorgon."

Turning back to the others Cathleen added, "In accepting the Avatar as his alter-ego, Mirage has renounced his humanity. I have only one directive regarding his fate. He will be treated like the monster he's become!"

Will wore a determined look and gave a curt nod. Cathleen turned to Loreena who's smile became even more sinister on her lovey face. Starla clutched the totem amulet hanging around her neck. The stark white streak in her hair moved like lightning when she signaled her agreement. Cathleen looked back at Old Father who quietly watched and listened as the humans conferred like Generals before battle. She asked him to use his staff to mark Guardian defenses in the dirt, as they would be placed around the Sacred Grove. Taking a minute to study this, she addressed him again.

"Old Father, from what you show here we are within a few minutes of the Sacred Grove. My people will proceed to the Sacred Grove where you've already stationed your Guardians. Each will join the Guardians stationed at one of the four corners of the perimeter you've outlined and fight beside your warriors."

"And you, Protector? Where will you be?" the ancient primate leaned heavily on his staff and studied Cathleen's closely.

"I am the Witch he wanted to hunt and now I will give him his opportunity," she answered quietly.

Chapter 52

Cathleen and the others studied the rough map Old Father scratched into the dirt. The strategy was simple; all positions encircling the Sacred Grove must be defended! Like beads on a necklace, if one was lost, they could all fall. Cathleen and Jason would fight on their own, while the others would fight beside the Guardians. Everyone was keenly aware that if Gorgon prevailed he would have won total access to powers endowed by the Mother along with dominance over the Third Realm. Cathleen looked around at the solemn faces.

"Historian, you will be my Second in Command from this point forward. You'll carry out our mission if I am incapacitated, or killed, in the coming battle." Cathleen's face was set in a stern resolve that quashed any argument. She saw Will's jaw tighten with his disagreement, before he nodded.

Starla turned to Cathleen saying, "Protector, I can best serve if I release my Spirit Warrior, and this is not safe while among you. My red mist will carry me wherever I sense I am most needed, and I will shift accordingly. Until then, I can monitor attacks on each position, from the Sacred Grove."

The deep red fog swirled upward until Starla was covered and she blinked out of sight. Cathleen had to admit to herself, this was a safer use of the Werewolf for all of them.

Looking back at the map, Cathleen addressed Old Father to decide the best positions to array their small force. She was surprised and alarmed that there were only forty Guardians from among Old Father's clan, which were actually trained to fight. The group that met them on the river shore when they first arrived was inflated by non-fighters. She knelt and pointed to each corner, calling out the wizards defending that sector. With Will and Loreena at separate corners of the Grove, they'd help augment the thin forces of Guardians. She and Jason would take a corner alone, freeing the few Guardians to reinforce any weakened positions during the conflict. Old Father would hold these troops in reserve while he and two or three others held that corner of the map. He would regulate the movements of his scant forces and would travel behind lines during the battle if necessary, to carry out their strategy. When Cathleen worried out loud that would expose him too much to the enemy, he looked above at the thick canopy of branches and ropey vines.

"I will be well out of their reach, Protector."

"It's time to move out. May the Mother protect you all," Cathleen said quietly looking at each member of the small band.

Everyone appeared calm and ready as they jogged toward the Sacred Grove.   It was tacitly understood, they'd have to hold their positions against unknown odds and enemies, until the last among them drew a final breath. Cathleen and Jason found five Guardians already stationed at the corner of the Grove they intended to defend. She released these, telling them Old Father would reassign them.

"Let's get a better handle on our defensive position, Jason. Will you do some reconnaissance? I'd like to maintain a safe perimeter of at least twenty feet around us."

Jason made the unconscious turn of his gold signet ring, readying it for potential defense. Cathleen gave him a quick smile before he was absorbed in the green haze of the forest. She was pleased to see the ring had become a natural part of her husband's response to danger. She still didn't understand how he had acquired his control of an instrument of magic, but that was a mystery for another time.

Alone now, Cathleen was on high alert as she moved along the front of their position. The Sacred Yew Trees were several yards behind her in the center of their wheel defense. They rose gracefully above the dense hedge that formed a backdrop to the four defense sites. Old Father referred to these scrub plants as "Companions," stating they encircled the entire Sacred Grove. These were a thick jumble of stout trees, but with a stunted appearance. Devoid completely of leaves, they were covered throughout their broad limbs and stubby trunks, with hard spines, tapering into a slight curve and ending in sharpened points. Cathleen knew whatever tried to come against the Companions would leave with deep wounds, if they left at all.

She had reached a bend in the encircling barrier of Companions, when she picked up movement in the surrounding woods. Not certain she'd really seen something at first, she switched to her Inner Eye. "There you are," she murmured, confirming the sighting of two Zombie Guards. They both carried a clear shield and appeared heavily armed. They would have looked like part of a SWAT team except for the greenish flesh and pitted faces. Cathleen felt that unique chill run through her body. *Jason. He must have come up behind them,* she thought, hoping the reverse wasn't true. She watched the pair of Undead guards as they shifted position to hunker down behind a stand of broad leaf trees. She was certain Jason flushed them out of hiding like a couple of grouse and was setting them up for a quick attack. Jason would feel Cathleen's presence, and know she was waiting to snap that trap shut on the pair.

Moving until she felt the Companion trees at her back, Cathleen went into a deep crouch. She couldn't use her Green Fire for fear of damaging any part of the Sacred Grove. Instead, she'd use an heirloom spell to create a shimmer in the air around herself. This would distort the guard's view of her movements, while making her look physically more imposing than her five-foot-four. She closed her eyes, and pulled the spell from the crevices of time, almost lost under the dust of countless generations of her mother's Wizarding family.

At the sound of the last syllable, the air began to quiver around her. Cathleen only used this spell once before, while in training with her father. She had no way to judge her altered look but felt the trembling air settle like a snug cocoon around her body. Feeling that odd sensation now, her mind flashed back to the scene of her first attempt at using this spell. Her father warned her this was a dangerous charm because it altered the natural pressure of the air around you. *"You can't stay within this cone of air too long, sweet girl. It will continue to compress until you break its hold,"* he warned in his most serious tone. The memory reminded her she'd need to act fast dealing with the Guards, or risk being suffocated inside her own spell.

Jason gave the whistle she'd been waiting for. A green beam lanced the shadows where the Guards concealed themselves, its target exploding in a grisly shower. The other Undead moved away from the advancing beam, and closer to her. Cathleen saw him raise a peculiar weapon to his shoulder. She was wondering if he was going to launch some kind of missile, when a glowing red sphere, the size of a football tore through her cone of air. She shifted to her right. giving her body the elongated appearance of pulled taffy. Cathleen knew the Guard would keep up his barrage until he killed her, and that was a distinct possibility!

The tear in the cone was causing the air to compress around her body, compensating for the hole. She felt like she was inside too-tight rubber wet suit. There was another high whistle. Jason changed positions coming up behind her. He'd never witnessed this air spell before and didn't realize he would be in grave danger if he tried to come too close to her. Cathleen was whispering, "No Jason," over and over to warn him off, but knowing he'd never hear her.

She had to turn her attention back to the Undead Guard as he shifted closer. His eyes were vacant of any spark of life but held a kind of singular determination. Cathleen moved to meet the demon head-on. The vibrating swath of air moved with her as she picked up speed. The guard stopped his own forward movement and calmly placed his weapon on his shoulder. Cathleen leaned to the left just as he squeezed off another missile, this time tearing through the cone inches from her arm. She was close enough to him now for the edge of the quivering air mass to make contact. The spelled cocoon slipped off her body and sucked the Guard into its vortex. Cathleen balled her hands into tight fists, causing the air to crush the guard to fine, yellow dust. She was panting with the rush of adrenaline when Jason came up beside her.

Slipping an arm around her shoulder he drew her in close to his broad chest. "Are you alright, Magic Girl?"

"Yes, but I was afraid you might get too close to me. As you can see, that would have been disastrous!" she said looking down at the mustard-colored dust

"I know better than to interfere when you're working, love, and I heard you warn me off."

Cathleen didn't have time to discuss that extraordinary comment, but the idea of telegraphing her thoughts lit up in her mind like a storm of fireflies! Knowing other of the Undead would be on the prowl, she let that idea root somewhere in the back of her conscience. She was asking Jason to move to the area fronting the Sacred Grove when a long shriek filled the air. Cathleen searched the shadows for the source of the pain-filled scream. When she looked back at his questioning face, her comment raised a shiver through Jason's body.

"Gorgon is here, and I don't think he's alone!"

Chapter 53

The scream echoed in the shifting gloom among the trees. There were small patches of lighted areas, where the solid tree canopy allowed narrow streams of light to filter through. Cathleen judged the three suns were moving toward twilight, to be followed by the night she dreaded. Never having experienced any of a day's cycles in the Third Realm, she could only guess what strange creatures would stir in the true darkness of the forest to feed and hunt. A picture of Geilt wearing his many kinds of fur pelts popped into her head. Jason touched her arm interrupting her speculation. His voice, just above a whisper.

"It sounded like it came from Loreena's position. She may not be able to ho…"

His next words were cut off by another high-pitched screech. This time Cathleen knew it wasn't human.

She looked up at Jason saying, "That is definitely coming from Loreena's position, but it sounds like Gorgon has sacrificed another minion to her Magic. He's likely testing her defenses. We can't leave our own position vulnerable, Jason. If the Undead guards found it undefended, they could cut through here and storm the heart of the Sacred Grove. Old Father was only taking a few of his Guardians with him as a last line of defense."

Jason quickly agreed with a light squeeze of Cathleen's shoulder as he moved past and into the deepening shadows. With the light already scant, Cathleen continued to use her Inner Eye to follow him as he chose a defendable location. She watched as he dragged several fallen limbs to a wide stump, covered by mounded dirt and leaves, and crouch low behind the fortified pile to wait. Looking directly ahead, Cathleen noted how the shadows seemed to crowd in all around.

The three suns were sliding behind the purple splashed mountains that encircled this valley. There were no other screams, but Cathleen felt as if the forest held its breath in anticipation. She was about to move further along her own front when Jason gave a warning whistle. Something was stirring out there in the inky woods. Cathleen was suddenly aware of a pungent odor carried on the slight breeze. She mouthed the word cat and knew the hunters were closing in. She settled her focus on a thick stand of willowy saplings, watching them shake, then bend outward as a heavily muscled shoulder pushed through. The cat was a replica of the sleek Black Panther she'd seen among Mirage's trophies. It was preserved in all its ferocity, but she knew in spite of its courage, it fell to Mirage's arrogance. While this beast resembled that unfortunate creature, Cathleen saw it had been horribly altered by Dark Magic. A few yards from her, it crouched low to the ground.

She watched its thick tail whipping back and forth, readying itself to charge. This gave Cathleen the needed seconds to conjure a modified Net of Nettles, replacing the poison barbs with a numbing potion that would render its victim immobile, but alive. She would use one of Gorgon's weapons against him when the time came. The Net was suspended over-head. The air exploded with a roar as the giant cat launched itself directly at its vulnerable prey. Blind resolve seemed to strengthen every magically-infused muscle, as the big cat flew through space like a dark missile. Cathleen could smell the hot air escaping from its open jaws.

She faded back and dropped her Net over the creature while it was stretched out in its lunge, covering it completely. Its weight, along with the weight of the beast, took the panther to the ground. Cathleen approached the prostrate cat making certain the spell had been effective. The eyes in the huge head were dull. She studied the body from head to the tail, thinking the panther was nearly the size of a small pick-up truck. Holding both hands over the still form, Cathleen murmured another incantation. This one would create a bond between the beast and herself, as close as if she was its mother and in effect, she was.

She gave Jason the "all clear" whistle to keep him from leaving his post to check on her. He must have seen, or smelled, the big cat before she had, making her wonder for the umpteenth time about the hidden powers her husband possessed. When she finished her charm, the cat began to stir. Cathleen watched its first move, knowing this would indicate if the bonding spell was effective. She wasn't certain it would be powerful enough to override the Dark spell used by Gorgon to summon it. If she couldn't bind it to her will, it would have to be destroyed and so would her plans for it. The cat began to draw its legs under itself, and rose to its full, astonishing height. Cathleen saw the glossy coat on its sides rippling and knew the spell was working. She came closer to look into its golden eyes.

"OK big boy, I'm going to release you now," she said softly. With a hand flick, the Net of Nettles disappeared from the muscled shoulders and back of the cat. Its body twitched once, and it sat on its haunches with a thud and deep grunt. Cathleen came closer still. She slowly reached out her hand, placing it gently on top of the glossy head, lowered now to receive her attention. The golden eyes shifted to her face, but the cat remained still under her hand.

"You will now serve the Protector, beast," Cathleen said softly. "You must return to the forest to hunt the Undead Guards. Destroy all you find. Return to me with the rising of the three suns, and I shall release your spirit to be used no more."

Without hesitation, the great beast sprang up, the sound of its passing through the trees and shrubs was no more than a sigh of breeze among the branches. Cathleen knew he'd be a skillful hunter and was glad she didn't need to destroy him. *One more ally can't hurt* she thought watching as the ebony figure became another black shadow. Wondering if Gorgon was still inside the Translocator, Cathleen decided it was time to take this fight to him. She whistled to Jason and in a few minutes was explaining to him about converting the big cat to their side.

"While he's off hunting the Undead guards, we can do a little hunting ourselves," she said.

"I guess you'll want to find where Gorgon has stashed the Translocator. Do we call the others in?"

"No. There will undoubtedly be Zombie Guards and beasts moving against their positions. Gorgon wants our total annihilation, and he'll use corrupted creatures to clear his path to the Sacred Grove. I'll leave wards to prevent any from penetrating through this position."

Cathleen was anxious to get moving before full dark prevented even ambient light from getting through the canopy. Though she used her Inner Eye and saw well at night, Jason would be handicapped to some degree. They took the opposite direction from the big cat. This would lead them into the portion of Grove defended by the Historian. Cathleen didn't want a green bolt hurtling out of the shadows if Will mistook them for the enemy. She realized she needed to let him and the others know their plans had been amended. There was one reliable messenger whose lanky body and wide eyes popped into her mind. "Parsons!"

Jason looked over at her when she blurted out the House Buddy's name. "What about him, love?"

"He'll make the perfect messenger...even if he did run off when Loreena and Will were attacked earlier. The others need to stay put when they hear our attack on the Translocator and he can carry my messages to them."

Without further comment Cathleen held her hands several inches apart in a praying gesture and began her summoning charm. This was followed quickly by a whooshing sound and a small, annoyed voice.

"By the Mother's chin hairs, why am I called here?" Parsons was rubbing his eyes as if he'd been roused from a nap.

"Welcome back among us, Parsons! I have need of your services once more."

"Protector! And Master Jason! This is a delight!"

"You weren't called here to visit, Parsons, but to help us in a time of great need and peril."

Over the next few minutes, she summed up his task, explaining the reasoning behind it before the inquisitive House Buddy could pelt her with questions.

"Of course, Protector, I shall alert the others to remain vigilant at their posts!"

Cathleen couldn't suppress a smile at the elfish creature's sense of importance.

"After you've told them my plan to attack the Translocator, you may return to Verdant Keep, Parsons."

"Oh! But I'd much prefer to stay by your side as your aide-de-camp, Protector! I do have some notable talents as you know."

As soon as Parsons vanished, they began their trek to find the grounded ship, cutting through the narrow paths between the trees. The soft ground showed no trace of the Cleaners, Old Father mentioned yet. Rotting branches, piles of molding foliage and bubble-topped fungus shooting up off of massive tree trunks made the woods feel undisturbed by any life forms other than vegetation for eons. Cathleen was quiet, but Jason knew she was searching for the magic that would surround the Translocator. He felt his own senses sharpen. He wasn't in Cathleen's league, but he could detect whenever magic had been used within touching range. He wasn't surprised when Cathleen held up a hand. Jason leaned down and whispered close to her ear, "I feel it too."

They crouched within the low shadows. A few seconds passed before they heard a shuffling noise. Something heavy moved through the woods. Whatever it was, Jason had the prickly sensation of being too close to a high voltage wire, as the atmosphere around them became charged with a powerful magic. He felt Cathleen recoil as this powerful magic swirled around them. Leaning into him, she whispered, "It's Gorgon and he's got one of ours with him!"

Chapter 54

They huddled under the Shadow Wrap as the source of powerful magic moved in their direction. Cathleen felt this was Gorgon returning to the Translocator and unfortunately he wasn't alone. Certain Will and Loreena were successfully defending their positions, it left only Old Father as a possible captive. Gorgon wouldn't have wasted energy on bringing any of the Guardians back alive. Old Father's role in protecting the Sacred Grove had him moving between the defensive positions, adding his extra Guardians as needed. They all expected the guards or other Demons to come against them. None foresaw Gorgon doing more than directing his minions. His bulky shape broke from the gloomy woods not ten feet from Cathleen and Jason.

The pair didn't twitch a muscle in their enforced crouch, holding their breath until he passed. When she looked at the ground, Cathleen saw how his broad feet had shoveled the forest debris aside, leaving deep gouges in his wake. The slouching figure of Old Father stepped from the same shadows, followed by a single guard, prodding him from behind with his weapon. The ancient primate swept the woods with desperate eyes, turning his grizzled face directly to where Cathleen and Jason crouched under the Shadow Wrap. Cathleen waited until the small parade was reabsorbed into the night woods before she dropped their cover, sending the shadows scuttling among the clustered trees like blind moles. She and Jason stood from their cramped position. Jason leaned close to her ear.

"Cathleen, how can we free Old Father without giving ourselves away?"

"We can't, but I don't think he's in any immediate danger. He's likely going to be used as a pawn to urge the Guardians to surrender. But we won't let that happen, because the minute they do, the Undead guards would over-run our friends and take the Sacred Grove. I have a better idea. Come on."

They crept along the deeply rutted path left by Gorgon. The lone Zombie Guard would prove little challenge. The trail they'd been following ended abruptly. Cathleen jumped to the side, as Jason took one more step. A feeling of being lifted off the ground momentarily paralyzed him. Cathleen heard his shocked intake of breath and grabbed his arm pulling him to her side.

"Why did I feel like I stepped into a moving elevator?" Jason asked, trying to slow his rapid breathing.

"There's some sort of beam here. Look."

Jason looked down where Cathleen studied their feet. He saw a wide shaft of light, partially hidden beneath clods of dirt and leaves. He followed it to where the dull glow traveled upward into the thick canopy, tracing the beam to a point above them.

"Don't move, Jason. I need to take your hand and float us clear of this light before it carries us into the Translocator. I'm not ready for that!"

Jason gripped her hand tightly. A few whispered words brushed his ear as he stood rigidly. He thought he was imagining it, but a sudden shock of heat radiated through his heavy boots. Cathleen moved them off the beam and onto the forest floor.

"We've stumbled upon the access to the Translocator, but we need the others if we're to breech its defenses. I need Parsons."

Jason spun around when the elfish House Buddy tapped him on his lower back. He looked pleased with his abrupt entrance, bowing slightly to Jason and then more deeply to Cathleen.

"I heard your summons, Protector! What message do I carry?"

Cathleen wondered how Parsons managed to get there so quickly, but that fleeting thought was replaced by her sense of urgency. She dropped a Dome of Protection over the three of them to mute the sound of their voices.

"We need the Historian and Loreena to join us immediately Parsons. They must leave the Guardians to deal with any Zombie Guards. It's urgent they come quickly!"

"I shall deliver your orders, and return to your side as quickly as possible, Protector."

"Wait! This is going to become a battlefield shortly, and you needn't expose yourself to that danger."

"Ah! I thought you might tell me to return to the safety of my cot in the Arch Wizard's rooms. But I cannot! My place is with you, and lending my expertise to your battle strategies, not back at the Council Keep!"

He was clearly determined and Cathleen didn't have time to argue. She glanced in Jason's direction. He was looking at the House Buddy approvingly. Decision made.

"Right! Get going, Parsons, and don't be long," she said before dropping the Dome.

They headed for a patch of open ground several yards from the Translocator's beam, and then into the surrounding woods. Jason hoped they didn't trigger an alarm on board when they stepped onto the beam's surface. Looking up, he saw a narrow stream of moonlight nudging the thick matting of branches and vines and felt the heavy presence of the ship above them. As they moved deeper into the woods, he realized they would approach from behind and avoid the beam. He began considering the enemies they were about to face. Gorgon's demonic powers were now completely merged with the Darkness that corrupted Mason Mirage. Jason knew this would truly be a battle between good and evil. With a mental shudder, he stopped moving. It was a minute before Cathleen looked back to see he had gone rigid.

"Jason, what is it?" she whispered urgently, studying his face.

His eye stared into some unknown distance. The patch over his left eye glinted a flat-black in the watery light. His unresponsiveness could only mean one thing. He was having a Waking Dream. *But why now? What triggered this one?* Cathleen knew not to disturb him in this trance-like state. Another anxious minute passed before he blinked his eye and looked around. Without trying to explain he immediately began describing his vision.

"I was inside the Translocator. I saw Old Father suspended in a beam of light like the one we stepped on. He looked nearly dead if he wasn't already. Gorgon has attached something to Old Father's head. I think it might project messages back to his Guardians. If we don't get in there, Old Father will be used to lure the others to their own slaughter."

Cathleen never questioned the reliability of Jason's visions. She'd learned over the years that any future event could be altered and these were just another form of warnings of what could happen without intervention. When she was certain he was completely out of a trance state, she moved them deeper into the trees, to a large group of spiny bushes dotted with glossy red berries. From this vantage point the beam of light was quite clear, quivering like a living thing stretched along the forest floor. Cathleen vaguely wondered what unsuspecting creatures might have stumbled onto it already, and what happened to them. Jason nudged her arm. She followed his line of vision and spotted two Zombie Guards. They stepped onto the beam and like a tongue returning to an open mouth, they were pulled into the dark foliage above. That's when it dawned on Cathleen. She tugged on Jason's sleeve until his ear was at mouth level.

"This part of the canopy is a mirage! Just like in the Labyrinth of Lies, it isn't real. The Translocator is above us, hidden by a powerful camouflaging ward."

Jason was about to ask how she proposed to get into the craft, without using the beam, when they heard the familiar popping sound of an arriving Time Thread. Parsons suddenly materialized with Loreena and the Historian.

"Protector," he said softly as he approached. Cathleen was pleased he used his voice pitching technique so all could hear, without alerting the enemy to their presence. "We were surprised you took us from our posts, but the Guardians seem quite capable of dealing with any of the guards still left abroad. By the time we left, they'd dispatched five at my post and another two at Loreena's without our support."

"Speaking of our help," Loreena cut in, "What are we doing here?"

Cathleen heard a slight tone of annoyance in the directness of Loreena's question. This was decidedly a woman who chafed at taking orders. Cathleen hoped her vanity would not lead to hasty actions that could jeopardize them all.

"You will be attacking the Translocator with Jason, while I find a way inside to rescue Old Father. He's being held in a kind of motionlessness state by a beam similar to that one."

The new arrivals followed the direction of her look. Parsons lifted each of his shoeless flat feet, looking beneath. The Sorceress barked out a snort, bringing all eyes to her.

"If Old Father is on board this vessel, his chances of survival are zero. Nothing comes inside that isn't already dead, or soon to be."

Cathleen was the first to comment. "How do you come by this information?"

The Sorceress opened her mouth, but before she had a chance to speak, the Historian drew their attention to a swirling crimson mist.

"Starla Star Fire," he said interrupting any response Loreena would have given to Cathleen's probing question.

The Medicine Woman pushed through a tangle of vine-laced trees. A large stain covered one side of her deerskin dress. She walked slowly and Jason wondered out loud if she was injured. He was about to run to her to help when Cathleen's arm shot out to grab his arm.

"Remember what I said about the Labyrinth of Lies, Jason. Let's be certain of what we're seeing before we get close."

Starla stopped a several feet from the group, looking from one face to the other. She drew in a deep breath and began speaking in a strained, halting voice as if every word was a painful effort.

"The Guardians… have taken heavy losses, but …have destroyed all the Undead guards…The Sacred Grove is… secured."

She barely finished speaking when her knees buckled beneath her and she sank to the ground. The others rushed to her. Cathleen crouched down to cradle her head and shoulders in the cook of her arm. Parsons had been silent since their arrival, and his high-pitched voice startled the others.

"Your friend is mortally injured, Protector. See, beneath her arm…"

Cathleen moved Starla's arm away from her side. She uncovered a gunshot wound seeping a heavy stream of blood. Cathleen guessed she'd been shot by one of the guards after she shifted. Starla told her once she shifted, she no longer could use any other magic. She had to rely on her Spirit Warrior to protect itself. Cathleen studied the gaping wound. Parsons was right. There would be no healing this injury. She continued to cradle Starla. They all watched in silence as she shuddered, taking a last human breath.

Chapter 55

They were stunned by the death of Starla Star Fire. Her last act of bravery was to help the Guardians bring about the total destruction of the Zombie Guards attacking the Sacred Grove. Will called for a gleaming white shroud to wrap Starla's body and ready it for burial. Cathleen spoke a few words, commending the Healer's brave spirit to the Mother's care. She held her hands over the shrouded form, reaching out to the departing Spirit Warrior as well. The red mist rose in small whisps until it transformed into an iridescent crimson fountain from the center of her body, spreading out until it covered her completely.

When Cathleen urged the spirit mist to return Starla's remains to lie among her Washee Navajo family, a keening wind began to stir the silence. The watching group uneasily looked around. As the sudden gusts stirred the trees, they became aware of shadowy figures fanned out in a large circle enclosing them. The sounds of rattles and small drums were carried on the mournful breeze. The small group waited silently until the shrouded body disappeared, followed by the shadows of the Medicine Woman's sorrowful ancestors. It was difficult to break into the somber mood that settled over the small band. Cathleen saw Parsons wiping a sleeve of his rough tunic across his nose. He sniffled loudly. Loreena walked over to where Cathleen stood beside Jason.

"Protector," Loreena said softly. "I will answer your question now, about how I know so much about the Translocator."

"Yes, go on." The others moved closer to hear her explanation.

"I encountered Mason Mirage while still serving as an Outlander Wizard Scout…and Will Farley's partner. I'd been working on my own at the time, and thought I'd uncovered a new portal from the Dark Pit into the First Realm. I was hiding nearby, waiting for something to emerge, when I saw a man crawl through the murky opening. When I got to him, he was bleeding from a deep gash on his head and babbling incoherently. I helped him to an outcropping of rocks to tend to his wounds. I was cleaning the head wound, when I sensed the presence of a powerful magic surrounding us. I searched the shadows inside the overhang for signs of other life forms, believing something followed the injured man through the new portal."

Cathleen's voice cut through the air like a blade. "And that man was Mason Mirage and the power was coming off of him. Correct?"

"A much younger Mason Mirage. Before his appetites ruled him body and soul. But you are correct. The power I was feeling radiated off him in waves, and I knew he could be a real threat to the First Realm. His injury was life-threatening, and I didn't find out until later, how he sustained it. In his delirium, he spoke about needing to destroy his enemy, calling him, "That maggot, Creighton…" I realized then, this strange Mage was not escaping from the Dark Pit when I found him, but escaping into it, from the Arch Wizard, Sir Creighton! I was only able to overcome the man's powerful aura of Dark Magic because of his weakened condition. I placed him into a deep sleep, leaving him there while I used a Time Thread to return to the Council Chambers, to report to Sir Creighton. The Arch Wizard saw my rescue of Mirage as a perfect cover, and ordered me to act as his special agent. I was to insinuate myself into Mason's small inner circle and report my findings directly to him."

The Historian broke in, asking how Mirage came to be wounded by the Arch Wizard before she saw him at the mouth of the portal.

"The Arch Wizard and two hand-picked Scouts tracked him down just before I found him. Sir Creighton confirmed to me later, it was his own ax that landed what he hoped was a killing blow to Mirage before he managed to vanish and make his escape."

Cathleen said, "So, you told Mirage you were a deserter from the ranks of the Scouts and used your glamour to convince him. Is this how you came to know about the Translocator?"

"I saw him over many years, strictly to keep him in my thrall. It wasn't until he built Mirage Compound and perfected the transmutation of the Magical Treasures room into a transporter that I accompanied him on a few hunting expeditions. During my time aboard the cursed thing, I'd never witnessed anything captured by its beam come into the Translocator alive."

Cathleen silently considered all this new information before speaking.

"Then let's give him the magic user that escaped his hunt. Because Gorgon absorbed Mirage's human nature, capturing the Witch of Appalachia will continue to be a stinging failure, and like Mirage, Gorgon can't admit to losing."

"I believe I know where you're going with this plan, Protector," Will said quietly. "This would be a most risky strategy on the part of the supposed victim," he concluded.

"That's exactly why I need to do it," she said, turning to Loreena. "Loreena, this is your opportunity to prove your loyalty to the Green. I want you to present me as an offering to the mighty Gorgon. He will remember how he felt about you at one time."

Loreena said, "And he'll know how I betrayed Mirage in the end."

"Yes, but Gorgon will see that as admirable. The depth of his depravity will work in our favor."

Jason knew this plan was set in stone as far as Cathleen was concerned, but he decided to add a twist to it.

"How about giving this monster two enemies? Bring him Lightening Maker, as well? Gorgon has already felt the bite of my ring. He won't view me as being a real threat, but what if its powers can be enhanced? Some added magical juice to give it some real punch?"

The Historian was rubbing the stubble on his square chin, nodding his head in agreement before he spoke. "This can be achieved Protector, but the question is how to go about it quickly?"

Parsons had been pushing dirt around with his bare toes when he looked up from his daydreaming and said, "Why not go to the Sacred Grove? There must be lots of magic floating about that place if the monster wants it so badly!"

Cathleen and the others turned newly appraising eyes on the House Buddy. He was as imposing as a ten-year-old boy, but they suddenly realized they misjudged his simplicity as weakness. He'd proven his bravery many times over, during other battles with denizens from the Pit, but he'd never helped shape a battle plan.

"You are absolutely right, Parsons!" Cathleen stated firmly.

The others instantly nodded agreement. He smiled shyly at them, saying he knew the way. Cathleen glanced around at the faces of the others as they hiked through the woods. She read their excitement at the prospect of visiting the Sacred Yew stand. They all knew the tales of a cosmos of power residing with the embrace of the Yew Trees. Powers that were infused into every tree and stone within the wide circle of the grove. Though they'd been fighting to defend it, with it at their backs, none had ventured inside the blessed grounds. The Mother chose the Third Realm and Geilt, to guard Her precious gifts of enchantments and spells. Over countless ages, long before the Dark Times brought chaos to the worlds, this Grove's magical gifts were replenished by the Mother, and kept as a secret trove for Her chosen few. Cathleen shared many tales of the Sacred Grove with Jason. She said it was like a bottomless well to the Council of Green Wizards when they thirsted for more power to boost their efforts to defeat the Dark Ones. She and this tiny band of fighters, would harness the magic they desperately needed to defeat the ultimate threat to life in all the Mother's realms.

Chapter 56

Parsons sat on a wormy tree stump casually watching as the small party of humans advanced into the Sacred Grove. He suspected Yew trees didn't normally grow to these towering heights and broad widths, but this was the Third Realm, and everything here seemed enormous here to Parsons. Cathleen and Jason were the first to enter the center of the Sacred Grove, with Will and Loreena close behind. As the four looked around themselves, and up at the arched ceiling created by the tops of the giant Yews, the branches begin to tremble.

Parsons paid closer attention as clumps of glossy red berries and dark green leaves stirred. A thought flashed through his mind that the rough trunks were being shaken by the hands of invisible and angry giants. As he watched fascinated, and not a little frightened, several Yews began to drop a light shower of their fruit and greenery over the ground.

Cathleen's voice called out with an urgency when she asked the others to follow her example. She dropped to her knees and they quickly did the same. They formed a tight circle within the natural circle of trees. She leaned forward onto her hands, pressing her palms flat on the rich earth. The others mirrored her action. Parsons stopped swinging his feet, interested now in what would happen next after this odd behavior. He slid off the stump and carefully approached the scene, without crossing into the Grove. He didn't want to miss the next mysterious occurrence.

Cathleen threw her head back, eyes shut. Her strange words penetrated the rustling sound of swaying branches, as her chant buzzed through the trees like the sounds of insects on a summer night. They floated over to where the House Buddy stood watching. He began to rub his pointy ears and shake his round head to dislodge the unexpected annoyance. Cathleen's chanting suddenly ended. The trees stopped trembling and a breathless stillness settled once more inside the hallowed space. Cathleen rose to her feet.

Parsons sucked in his breath when he saw her body shed a strange light. The others stood, keeping their circle formation. They all had this strange glow about them. All except the Protector's mate. Parsons studied Jason closely, wondering why he wasn't giving off the strange light.

"The light you see, Parsons, is of the Mother." Cathleen called over to the shocked House Buddy.

"You read my thoughts, Protector! Is this part of the Mother's gifts to you?" he asked excitedly, inching closer.

"No, Parsons. The look on your face was all I needed," she answered smiling down at him as they filed out of the sacred grounds.

Parsons thought the humans had the radiance he'd seen in some among the fey. When he asked why Jason didn't share this glow of magic, Cathleen explained he was gifted in a very special way. Jason stood with his right hand covering his left. As Parsons came near, he uncovered the gold signet ring. The ring's perfect five-carrot emerald pulsed like a beating heart. The heat waves radiating from the stone were strong enough to stir the air with their intensity. Parsons could feel the sparse hairs on his head move as hot eddies washed over him.

"Your ring holds the heat of the three suns!" Parsons exclaimed in wide-eyed amazement.

"Not quit little Domo," Jason said covering the ring once more. "The heat you felt is very weak, compared to what I know the Mother has gifted me for this mission."

Cathleen's voice stopped the curious House Buddy from any further questioning.

"We have a dual mission now," she broke in. "Bringing the Translocator down where we can attack it...and rescuing Old Father...if he's managed to stay alive. Historian, we'll join our Magic and disrupt the illusion concealing the Translocator within the canopy. As soon as it's revealed, we'll pull it to earth and begin our attack. We'll need to create several access points into the craft, before Loreena can bring her prisoners aboard later."

Parsons listened closely at first, as Cathleen discussed plans. Since his own name wasn't mentioned, both his attention and his feet, began to drift away from the hushed conversation. Unnoticed by the others, he meandered towards the wide circle of Sacred Yew Trees. He put a toe then a foot inside and finding courage, stepped close to a tree. He was studying the enormous girth of the giant, and bravely starting to place a hand on its rough bark, when his ears pricked up at the sound of stirring within its branches. Parsons jumped away, craning his scrawny neck to see into the leafy branches when suddenly he found himself staring into the eyes of the one called Old Father. Parsons thought, *but how can this be if he is held captive, or already passed from this Realm?* He was about to shout out his discovery, when the apparition held a finger to his blue lips in warning. Parsons watched silently as the leader of the Guardians held out his hand to him. He trustingly placed his own hand into the warm grip, and together they shot up into the treetop.

Old Father whispered close to his startled face. "Fear not, tiny warrior. Gorgon must not learn he's brought an imposter onto his flying boat. I have sent one of my Guardians in my stead. He has been shaped in my form and is now aboard the Demon's war ship."

Just then, Parsons heard the Historian's deep voice rising through the heavy foliage. "Protector, the House Buddy has vanished. I saw him but a few moments ago when I glanced over. He may have entered the circle of the Sacred Yew."

Cathleen looked around before warning, "We don't have time to search for Parsons. There's a good possibility he decided to return to the security of his cot. We can't delay this attack and give Gorgon a chance to escape."

Parsons saw her look back at the Sacred Grove, but she quickly refocused on the strategy they planned. His feelings were stung slightly by the Protector's refusal to search for him. *What if I'd been snatched up like a bread crumb by some ogre?* His thoughts were reflected in his pout. Old Father placed a huge, hairy hand on his thin shoulder to give him a consoling pat.

"We'll need to take a short trip, tiny warrior," he whispered, tickling Parson's ear with his warm breath. "My imposter Guardian will likely have perished by now inside the grip of the deadly beam."

When he saw Parsons' dismay at this callused observation, Old Father was quick to add, "Have no fears on the Guardian's behalf, my small friend. He will only appear to have taken passage to the Dominion of the Spirits. My magic is strong and is protecting him by the Mother's graces."

Parsons gave him a weak smile, not quite content with that claim, but asking, "Shall we travel to the monster's craft? The Protector and Jason discovered it hidden within the canopy of this woodland."

"We leave...now!" Old Father still had a comforting hand on Parson's narrow back and shoulder. With a squeeze, he and the House Buddy were gone in a slight rustle of leaves.

The Historian had been scouring the surrounding area high and low, for signs of the curious House Buddy. He was considering the possibility he'd run into foul play when he was startled by an odd stirring in some branches inside the Sacred Grove. The soft glow coming off of him suddenly brightened. He wondered if it reflected changes in moods. He looked up, but the limbs were as still as the cathedral ceiling they resembled. He turned in time to see the radiance surrounding Loreena and Cathleen also spiked and then muted.

"The glow is a living connection between the three of us," he announced.

He returned to the others who also noted this curious phenomenon. He described seeing the rustling among the branches, and how being alarmed appeared to have triggered a change in the glow's intensity.

"I believe our enhanced powers will respond to perceived danger. It appears we are bound together with this special light," he said.

Jason had been standing apart from the two women, and like Will, was scoping out the area, searching for Parsons. He was holding something in his hand as he approached the three.

"I found this snagged on a low branch inside the Sacred Grove. I was at the east end of the stand when I saw it moving in the breeze. It looks like a strip of cloth from Parsons' tunic."

Cathleen took the piece from Jason's hand and nodded. Her face showed no emotion, but Jason knew the look in her eyes. She feared for Parsons' safety. She spoke to the others, her voice filled with unmovable determination.

"This cannot change our plans to attack Gorgon."

Each of them knew the endearing Parsons would be abandoned to his own fate, whatever that was. As they moved away from the Sacred Grove Jason took up rear-guard position. The others shed a constant glow from their bodies, as they passed like a trio of apparitions through the silence of the forest. He was fighting the feeling of impending disaster lodged like a fish bone in his throat. His senses felt sharper and more heightened, following the others in their loose formation. There were no night sounds percolating in the impenetrable quiet surrounding them. The moon still struggled to penetrate the living ceiling, with stray shafts of buttery light.

Jason was able to follow the sheath of luminosity surrounding each of the Wizards, insuring he'd not lose track of them among shadows they passed through. Cathleen led them to where they discovered the Translocator suspended amid the tangled awning that scrapped the night sky. They all knew Gorgon would use Mirage's guiles of illusion. The craft would be well camouflaged to appear like part of the jumble of foliage. There was no longer any sign of the light beam leading into it, but the trace of magic left behind was immediately felt by all of them. It was strongest in a wide clearing, filled with thin saplings and low brush.

The others gathered near Cathleen when she stopped under what she suspected was the false canopy. She whispered a charm to create a replica of the forest floor and trees, tenting it around them to conceal their presence from any passing guard, and from the craft above. "After the Translocator is pulled down, Jason will use his ring to damage the outer skin. That accomplished, Loreena will make her entrance, taking me and Jason as pseudo prisoners. The Historian must melt back into the forest as soon as the ship is downed. His absence will be explained as cowardice by Loreena. Remember, Gorgon knows nothing of any of us except what he's absorbed from Mirage's memories."

Everything was covered as far as their individual parts. The only thing they couldn't plan for were Zombie Guards, or other demons summoned by Gorgon. Cathleen was relatively certain there were no more roaming the woodlands, but that didn't mean Gorgon may not have kept a few close by. While the Historian and Loreena were making ready the various weapons they carried, she noticed Jason searching the surrounding woods.

"Jason, did you hear something?"

"I felt something earlier and that feeling's getting stronger."

As his last words hung in the still air, they all turned toward the sound of something heavy crashing through the trees from the direction they just came from. Loreena and The Historian moved closer to Cathleen. A ball of Green Fire appeared in her open hand. Jason saw the large emerald on his signet ring pulsing in time with his heart, fast and steady. They all smelled it. A pungent odor riding the soft air. Jason's voice was steady when he looked over at Cathleen.

"It's your Panther!"

As if on cue the enormous cat burst from the inky interior of the woods. It was hunting and the Historian stood in its direct line of attack. In a blur of motion Cathleen shifted to stand in front of him, holding up her left hand. The charging cat pulled its hind legs into a braking position and huge front paws dug into the soft dirt. It stopped in front of Cathleen's outstretched hand. Cathleen allowed the green ball of fire to disappear. She calmed the beast, stroking the sleek, black head and crooning soft words the Historian knew were as prehistoric as the Mother's forest.

"Protector," Loreena's silky voice broke into the odd tableau. "You clearly have command over one of Gorgon's creatures. How did this come to be?"

Cathleen sketched a few details of the earlier encounter with the possessed animal. "It appears his task of hunting down the Undead guards has been accomplished," she concluded with a tight smile.

A deep rumbling sound came from the Panther when Cathleen leaned closer to its head, whispering into a tufted ear. Jason knew she was keeping her word to the creature. Confirming his thoughts, the great beast vanished from under her hand.

Cathleen directed Loreena to hide herself among the trees until the ship was well grounded. Jason would move off as well. The Historian wasn't too pleased that he'd be named a coward, but they had to account for his absence. *No time for ego stroking,* he thought as he and Cathleen took up opposite positions to the space she designated. Even with his Inner Eye, he barely made out the outline of the Translocator under its camouflage.

Giving him a signal, he and Cathleen held their arms level, pointed upward toward the invisible craft. Loreena dropped from sight behind a screen of tangled berry bushes. Jason did likewise, waiting for the ship to be pulled to ground. He heard the gradually escalating volume of chanting. Soon the deep character of Will's voice merged perfectly with Cathleen's lighter tones, becoming a smooth-flowing stream of words. Only on the rare occasion had Jason witnessed Cathleen blend her magic this way, and never with a user of the Historian's talents. When he asked why, she said he had to witness it to understand. Now he understood. A wide arc of green lightening sizzled between Cathleen's outstretched hands, crashing into the ragged shafts shooting from the Historian's hands. The resulting blast of energy exposed the shape of the Translocator.

Jason gasped when he saw how the craft morphed yet again! It had an uncanny resemblance to the fabled Norse monster, *the Kraken!* Sheathed in heavy scales, the ship furiously waved muscular tentacles in the air when the green bolts struck it. Jason felt his ring throbbing on his finger. With the enemy exposed, the power within the emerald was building like a tsunami. He watched the living body of the Translocator fight against the pull created by Cathleen and Will. It heaved in its effort to break from the power arc that pushed downward, forcing it toward the ground. The chanting voices of the two Wizards wailed against the night until the craft slammed with an explosive boom onto the forest floor. The moment it was grounded, the Historian vanished from sight and Cathleen melted into the trees.

Jason launched his attack. The thrashing tentacles kept him at a distance, making them his first targets, methodically drilling them until they shriveled up. An oily smoke began to fill the air as Jason penetrated the scales, reaching more vulnerable parts of the living ship. He barely registered Cathleen standing close by and continued drilling holes in the outer skin of the craft. After he'd scorched every part of the ship he could reach, he felt Cathleen touch his arm.

"Enough. Time for phase two, my love."

Loreena watched until Jason ceased his assault, her signal to jump into action. Capturing the pair of them as they stood together looked easy enough, so she was surprised when Cathleen put up a fight. The small ball of Green Fire burned a hole in the sleeve of her leather jumpsuit as it flew past. A second ball scorched the ground inches from her foot. *What's she playing at?* She shouted out a spell to freeze the pair, knocking them to the ground before Cathleen could do some real damage. Coming up to them she leaned close to Cathleen, knowing she and Jason were both fully aware.

"Protector, I do hope this is real enough for you!" she said between gritted teeth. The billowing black smoke from the Translocator was rising into the shades of night when Loreena said, "Let's pay the Lord Gorgon a visit, shall we?"

Chapter 57

Jason was immobilized, but keenly aware of what was happening. A rush surged through every cell of his body from his ring. Light from inside the Kraken ship, escaped from the damage of his attack. The Sorceress floated him and Cathleen like two inner tubes, skimming the ground toward the ruined Translocator. Three tentacles came into view, reduced to withered black lumps and bunched against the scorched body of the craft. He felt certain Gorgon's living transporter was mortally wounded. Heavy black smoke coiled up from several gaping wounds and the air thickened with the rank odor of charred meat. Only moving his eye, it was enough for Jason to scan for more damage.

A heavily blackened section shimmer weakly, exposing a large, ragged opening. Loreena stepped in front of the pair, her mouth barely moving as she looked down on them.

"I'll go in first to be certain Gorgon is pleased with my offering, and explain the Historian's absence," she said.

Frowning, as if very angry, she dropped them without warning onto the hard ground. Jason registered a faint smile as Loreena moved off. Was she only slipping into her part? Jason felt the cold metal of the gold signet ring. *Is it paralyzed by Loreena's spell?* His anxiety at trusting a woman with a talent for duplicity grew by the second. *This might be a double-cross!* It felt like they'd hung suspended for hours when the Sorceress crossed Jason's line of vision. She moved to Cathleen's stiff body and with a flick of her wrist, floated her through a ragged hole. When she moved to his side, she made no effort to speak or make eye contact.

He felt himself pass from the gloom of the woods, into a dimly-lit space. A damp chill washed over him and he fought the sensation of being swallowed alive by a huge serpent. Struggling to see Cathleen, he managed a glimpse with peripheral vision. He felt the power awaken in his ring, praying it would go unnoticed until he had the chance to use its deadly force. There was a scraping sound, followed by the same intense light he recalled from their first meeting with Gorgon.

"Welcome, Protector. You must wonder at this turn of events placing you and your mate inside my living vessel."

The nearness of the monster caused Jason's ring to pulsate with a stronger urgency for release. Could he chance directing it by thought alone? He had no idea the extent of his powers. Loreena was saying something to Gorgon.

"...and she may be very useful to you my Lord, if you wish me to drop the spell holding her."

"It might be amusing to allow her to beg for her mate's life. You may proceed to release them both. The mate is little more than her lap dog, and no challenge."

Jason prepared himself for the short drop to the floor, but wasn't ready for the way he bounced. His deadened arms and legs were flailing about like a marionette whose strings were breaking. A screech of laughter erupted from Gorgon, while Loreena's giggle curled around his head like a soft purr as he came to rest on the spongy surface. The numbness in his limbs began to wear off, replaced by a painful tingle as his circulation was restored. Cathleen floated a few feet away. He fought the urge to go to her, knowing it was smarter to play the docile lap dog. He'd learned long ago it was helpful to have an enemy underestimate your abilities.

He stayed on his side and nearly bolted upright when a hard shove from Gorgon's tentacle pushed him onto his back. More screeching laughter at the spasm of surprise his body couldn't conceal. Jason seethed at being the entertainment, but his vengeance could wait until his ring's power pulsed through his body. *Soon,* he thought, curling his hands into fists.

Loreena began to speak about the value of the captives, when a long groan came from the inscrutable shadows behind them. Jason wondered if this was where Old Father was being held. He saw Loreena take a few tentative steps toward Cathleen. A drawn-out cry broke like shattering glass around them. Gorgon must have heard enough of the pathetic sounds and shifted his heavy body with a grunt.

Jason squeezed his eye as if in pain but could feel the sweep of three glittery eyes pass over him. The beast turned his considerable bulk and headed into the shadows toward the mournful cries. Loreena moved to Cathleen's side, helping her to stand. A bouquet of jagged green bolts appeared in her left hand. Jason got to his feet, careful not to bounce on the pliable surface. He saw Loreena move to create a wider front. He barely breathed, listening for the sound of tentacles sweeping the floor.

"Jason," Cathleen's hushed voice broke into his concentration. "Loreena and I will handle Gorgon. You *must* destroy the Translocator 's beam. It acts like a vacuum, sucking power and energy from any life form that stumbles into the light. If it moves into the Sacred Grove, it will tap into the heart of the Third Realm. It's likely what Old Father discovered when..."

A blood chilling scream erupted from the back of the craft. Loreena's thin sword Dazzler, appeared in her hand. Cathleen motioned for them to move closer to the craft's sides. Jason's shoulder touched the spongy wall, giving him the feeling, he'd rubbed up against a corpse. The crackling bolts clutched in Cathleen's hand shot sparks in every direction. Jason saw her mouth forming words, and soon he felt the magic swirling around them. Cathleen's ancient chant began to hum like a swaying bridge between them. The space around her quivered as a wide form began to materialize. It came to her shoulder, hunched over, with no identifiable shape. Yet, Jason felt there was something familiar. Suddenly, the form rose up and Old Father loomed over Cathleen. A rattled looking Parsons stood beside him in the dull light of the cabin.

Old Father's voice carried to Jason and Loreena. "Many thanks for guiding our journey back to you Protector. I have destroyed the portal between the Third Realm and your First World. You were correct to assume it was guarded by the last of the Undead Guards, but the Historian dealt with those. He now works to seal both ends permanently, with strong wards as you ordered."

Jason was relieved to see the Guardian's leader alive, but wondered who screamed under Gorgon's torture?   Before he could speak, Cathleen turned toward the Sorceress. Without warning, she shot a single green bolt directly at Loreena's position. The bolt passed through Loreena, drilling deep holes into the living tissue of the ship. The wall contracted violently in reaction to the incredible heat. Loreena stumbled away from the quivering mass; her body wrapped in a cocoon of green flames. Cathleen's face wore a grim expression.

Her doubts were confirmed. Loreena had been playing at her own game. The Sorceress used her impressive powers to create the body clone Cathleen just incinerated. Loreena duped them all, Cathleen thought in a quiet rage. A likely scenario flashed through her head while she watched the clone burn.

The body switch was likely made after I shared plans to gain access to the Translocator and destroy it along with Gorgon. The Demi-God must have guessed Loreena was trying to gain control of the ship. Possessing Mirage's memories, he wasn't taken-in when the clone presented us as hostages. The beast already knew that duplicity was part of Loreena's nature. Cathleen had no doubt Gorgon had taken the real Sorceress to another part of the craft where he would use magic to draw out her punishment for maximum pain. As Protector of the Green, it was Cathleen's duty to see Loreena handed over to the Council. Running over to Cathleen, Jason grabbed Cathleen's arm.

"What's happening? Why did you destroy Loreena?" trying to find a rationale for the Cathleen's actions. Another cry rang out.

"I've only destroyed her body clone! I suspected her of duplicity, but when I realized she was using a clone, I was convinced. She pretended her alliance with Mirage, then Gorgon, and lastly, us. She planned to take over the Translocator and syphon-off the magical powers of this Realm for herself."

Old Father looked into Cathleen's eyes as if searching for an unspoken answer. "You will have us rescue the Sorceress, will you not Protector?" It was more statement than a question.

Cathleen nodded, "We can't allow Loreena to remain Gorgon's prisoner. Her punishment for betraying him will be unimaginable."

Parsons moved closer to Old Father, a stunned expression on his round face after hearing Cathleen's indictment of Loreena. He was obviously struggling to understand this turn of events when he spoke up. "Perhaps Loreena is still acting as a Secret Agent, Protector. She has woven an extremely intricate web for the purpose of taking this ugly craft for herself," he said, his eyes wide as he looked around.

"No more time for talking, Parsons," Cathleen snapped.

She directed the three to stay put while she moved further into the craft to locate Loreena.

"Don't follow until you hear our whistle," she called softly to Jason.

Jason peered intently into the gloom that absorbed his wife when he heard her signal. Using the muted light from his ring, he and the others crept through the craft. He realized even its size was an illusion, it was roomier than it appeared. He whispered over his shoulder to Old Father and Parsons, directing them to stay close to the wall as they moved. He thought the shadows might give the skittish Parsons a feeling of safety, though he knew this was just another deception. Parsons pressed into Old Father's back as they moved deeper into the new landscape of the darkened craft.

Without warning, Old Father's hairy body backed into him, flattening the House Buddy against the spongy wall. He gave a sharp yelp, causing the Guardian to jump, grunting loudly. Jason hurried back to the pair, the last thing he needed were noisy companions. Before he could ask what happened, a dumb-struck Parsons pointed to the large form stepping away from the wall.

Chapter 58

The Historian chose one of the strongest wards in his arsenal, confident the Portals between Realms were sealed for all time. While he worked, he had the nagging feeling he had to hurry and get back to the downed Translocator. With his task completed, he summoned a Time Thread, placing the position of the craft in his mind as his destination. Earlier, Cathleen privately outlined her plan to him, out of earshot of both Loreena and Jason. Being handed over to Gorgon as prisoners would be perilous to them both, but using it as a ploy to test Loreena's loyalties made it doubly dangerous.

As soon as his feet touched ground, Will could feel Cathleen's magical signature, and the more subtle influence of Loreena's. He studied the outside of the craft. Jason's ring left its own signature, very distinctive from the Wizards of the Green. Passing a discerning eye over gaping holes in the side of the craft, he thought, *Jason has done some fine work here!* A dull glow radiated from one of the larger holes, and he was certain this was their entry point.

Will needed an effective concealment spell so he could pass unseen through the blown side. He scrutinized the outer skin and the thick layers of spongy wall. In a flash of insight, it dawned on him, the Translocator was more than a Time Shifter, it was an extension of the Demi-God, Gorgon. Thinking of the ship's physical environment, Will placed a hand on the exposed interior surface, whispering his spell. He was pulled into the body of the Translocator until he became absorbed into an interior wall. He moved toward the darkness beyond, a mere ripple beneath the wall's covering membrane. He was making slow progress, when something sharp poked into his mid-section. He recognized the scrawny elbow of the House Buddy. Parsons yelped upon contact, and this was followed by a deep grunt.

A loud whisper floated back to him that Will identified as Jason. His perfect camouflage melted away as soon as he lost contact with the wall.

"It's just as well Parsons' arm jabbed me. I felt the ship's life-pulse, and it is steadily weakening. I'd be in grave danger if it succumbed to its injuries, absorbed into the ship's fabric as I was, I would suffer the same fate."

Jason told Will about Loreena's scheming, and her current plight as Gorgon's double-dealing prisoner. The dull glow from his ring colored the mixed emotions of disappointment and anger as they crossed the Historian's stern face.

"She has shown her true nature at last," he said with the grave finality of a judge.

Old Father was silent to this point, but when Parsons said something about a second prisoner besides the Sorceress, he spoke up.

"I allowed one of my Guardians to mimic my appearance to gain entry here. It was surely his agony you first heard, Lightening Maker. I shall release my brave child from the body Gorgon destroyed and by the Mother's graces he shall be whole once more."

Jason glanced over at Parsons. He wasn't sure how to protect the little guy during a confrontation with Gorgon. The Historian must have shared his fears, suggesting Parsons' return to Sir Creighton to carry news of their current situation. Parsons looked relieved and the familiar popping sound meant one less problem in Jason's mind. The emerald stone continued to give off a subdued glow, carving out a narrow tunnel of light as they moved deeper into the ship. He speculated that Gorgon might possess a kind of Inner Eye like Cathleen and Will.

He began to feel a downward slant to the floor, indicating it led to a lower deck. *Does this craft even have a below decks like other ships,* he wondered? That thought was barely formed when he jolted to a stop. Gorgon's broad back filled the entrance to a recess in the wall they'd been following. Loreena cringed on the floor in front of him. Pulling back into the shadows, and turning his ring into his palm, the three listened as Gorgon raged at Loreena.

"You've had ample ways to prove your worth to me!" he roared.

"I was loyal to Mason! You possess his memories and know this to be true!" she protested weakly.

"I have no more need of you, human, and I'm weary of your protests!"

Loreena's screams made Jason think of the sickening cry of a rabbit caught in a snare. He stretched his neck to see what was happening. Gorgon held a tentacle above her, while holding her down with the weight of the injured one. Jason watched horrified while every drop of moisture was pulled from her body, rising like a waterfall in reverse. The creamy skin on Loreena's lovely face began to pucker and pinch. Her entire body was dehydrating, altering her sleek form into shrunken flesh over protruding bone. Standing close to Jason, Will watched, the heat of his rage radiating from his tense body.

Forgotten by the others, Old Father looked around until he spotted a large gap where it penetrated through to the upper level. The humans were totally absorbed by what they witnessed, and Old Father rose soundlessly through the opening, disappearing without a word. He peered down on the scene, ready to spring. Jason turned his head slightly. From the look of Will's tightly clenched jaw, he feared his friend might attack Gorgon before they had an advantage. He grabbed his elbow to try to restrain the fury that flared in his dark eyes. Suddenly, the shadows concealing them were garishly lit by a bolt of Green Fire.

"Down!" Cathleen's voice magnified in volume and crashed against the walls. She could be anywhere, making it impossible for the enemy to counter-strike with any accuracy. Bolts were being launched from several directions. Several hit Gorgon squarely in his broad back. The exposed areas where he'd lost his scales in their previous encounters, began to smolder under each salvo.

Gorgon awkwardly twisted his body, trying to avoid the next shaft. The bolts were followed by a wide ribbon of Green Fire. It sizzled as it flowed over the floor of the craft. Gorgon was beating out the nests of fires rooted under his scales and missed the liquid fire. The lava-like flow raced in, covered his splayed feet and rose like a charmed snake up his muscled calves. The liquid fire immediately cooled and hardened, leaving the beast encased and unable to move. He bellowed his frustration.

"Attack!" Cathleen shouted.

Jason felt his ring's thirst for demon blood. He concentrated its razor-sharp rays into Gorgon's side and back. Will suddenly appeared on the other side of the creature. The slashing of his charmed long-knife was so fast it created its own howling wind, blowing back his long hair. Jason checked on Old Father and realized he was nowhere to be seen. He was about to call out to him when he dropped through the ceiling. His heavy body landed squarely on top of the struggling Gorgon, taking him to the floor. Gorgon had one functioning tentacle and swung it upward to pick the Guardian off his back, tossing him aside like a piece of lint. Jason was directly in line with the flying body and collapsed under Old Father's weight. They struggled to untangle themselves when a deep rumble shook the Translocator, making its living flesh quiver like shaken gelatin all around them.

"The craft is dying!" Will shouted.

The Historian's warning brought Gorgon's tirade to a halt, allowing him to take advantage of the human's distraction. He lashed out with the lone tentacle, wrapping it with blinding speed around Will's chest. The Historian tried to call out a spell, but his words were stopped in his throat as the appendage squeezed like a vise, tighter and tighter. When Jason and Old Father regained their feet, Gorgon was swinging Will, increasing the pressure on his throat. Jason aimed his ring's beams at Gorgon, but couldn't blast it without hitting the Historian.

Giving in to desperation, he shouted, "Cathleen! Need a little help here!"

Cathleen materialized out of the gloom, directly behind the monster, but only long enough for Jason to spot her before she ducked back under a Shadow Wrap. Gorgon's malevolent powers were in clear view as she passed the desiccated figure of Loreena on the floor, her body reduced to an empty husk. Cathleen knew her own fate would be worse if she failed to destroy the evil creation of Demi-God and Dark Wizard. The rock-like substance that partially encased Gorgon was only a temporary inconvenience to one as powerful as he. She vaguely wondered why he hadn't summoned other demons to fight beside him until he freed himself. Cathleen guessed his arrogance blinded him to any need for additional help. She prayed to the Mother that ego would prove his undoing as she crept up behind him. Cathleen faced the same dilemma as Jason.

She couldn't attack without causing Will grave harm. The masking shadows muffled her voice, but Gorgon obviously heard her call his name. Making her presence known had the intended reaction. Gorgon crouched as low as his encased legs allowed, presenting a smaller target for Cathleen's fire. Gorgon was still hampered by the stone-like substance and unable to turn his body fully, while still holding the struggling Historian. He relaxed the tentacle, dropping the Historian with a dull thud while he searched for a more important enemy.

Jason shifted carefully to get closer to Will. He saw how he struggled to breathe, his chest rising and falling in ragged gulps. He decided on a bold move and slipped the heavy ring off his finger. Balling up his jacket, he created a ledge for the ring. He turned it toward Gorgon, willing the ring's powers to life. An immediate barrage of saber sharp bolts pierced the monster's upper body. Gorgon howled in pain as the shafts drilled through previously weakened areas on his body. Jason squirmed on his belly, reaching for Will's outstretched arm. He brushed the Historian's hand just as the Translocator heaved violently under them. He gasped in shock as he felt himself lifted, as if he rode the crest of a giant wave. He hung suspended, digging his fingers into the spongy floor to keep from being tossed further from Will. A rumbling sound filled the dark air inside the craft with palpable intensity. Jason was certain it came from every fiber of the living ship.

The Translocator is in its death throes, he thought frantically. When he was finally lowered after another heaving sigh from the ship, he blindly reached for the Historian's arm, only to find he'd also been shifted by the undulating of the dying vessel. He tried to stand, but it was impossible with the continuous bucking beneath his feet. The green shafts from his signet ring were shooting off in every direction. Jason knew the ring was rolling around after being dislodged by the violent movements. The ship was taking all the hits, but he had to secure it, before it hit him or Cathleen. He crawled back to where he left his rolled jacket, hoping the ring would be nearby.

Feeling around in the chaos of shadows, his fingers brushed against a piece of cloth. He grabbed it tightly, feeling something inside. In a flash of green from several bolts tearing through the ship, he saw he was holding what was left of Loreena's leather jumpsuit and a desiccated arm. Flinging it away, he felt a keen horror at touching death's work. He quickly reversed course and started crawling in the opposite direction. The deadly shafts appeared to be trained on one spot and Jason scuttled along the heaving floor to get there. There was a lull in the spasms within the body of the craft. Jason jumped to his feet. The green shafts were still visible, making it easy to locate the ring where he found it was lodged against the still body of Old Father.

Chapter 59

Old Father's eyes were a dull black, the spark of life gone. Jason knelt beside him as the touch of another's eyes stirred the hairs on his neck. He slipped the ring on his finger, turning it to his palm to stifle its pulsing light. The Translocator rippled beneath him in another spasm, a low keening filled the craft with the sound of its impending death. A current of air ruffled his hair, and he rolled until he hit a quivering wall.

"You scurry like an insect, human!" Gorgon scoffed in his whiny voice.

The searing edge of panic hit Jason as it occurred to him his wife might have lost her battle with Gorgon. Any light inside the cabin shifted as the Translocator heaved in its death throes. Jason barely noticed the beast move, but couldn't miss the gleam of satisfaction in the three eyes as he studied Old Father's shattered body. In any other circumstance, it would be comical hearing Mirage's screechy voice coming from the bulky Demi-God.

"Your friend succumbed to my attentions, but soon I'll have worlds filled with others to entertain myself."

Though Gorgon had sustained some serious injuries, Jason knew he remained a formidable foe. There was nothing he could do for Old Father, but he would use his death to poke the Demi-God's massive ego.

"You're no great threat, Gorgon, unless you're killing ancient beings like Old Father. Probably because Mason Mirage, a mere insect, controls you."

"What drivel you spew, bug! Mirage was no more than my gateway into the Third Realm. I allowed his thirst for power to be slackened by his hunting games. Watching him toy with you and the others in his labyrinth proved amusing. Disposing of the architect was an idea I planted in Mirage's ego-ruined mind and destroying Geilt only happened with my superior powers. I was generous with Mirage, allowing him to some glory, otherwise, he was less-than the magnificent Translocator I created!"

Mentioning the dying craft renewed rage in the creature. Jason felt the tremors weaken under his feet and Gorgon would too.

"You and the Protector will enjoy terrible deaths, for your destruction of my craft!"

The Demi-God raised his arm. Jason felt like he'd been hit in the gut, seeing Loreena's desiccated body dangling loosely below. Gorgon brought the shriveled head close to his flat snout like a lover leaning in for a kiss and huffed a stream of rank breath into the ruined face.

"Breath, Sorceress! Your time has come to serve me!"

Jason watched in fascinated horror as the beast held the withered remains of the traitorous Loreena out to the side, suspended from a thick coil of her blonde hair. The destroyed body began to writhe like a skewered snake. Jason watched as the sunken eyes in the puckered face snaped open, their luminous gray lost in twin pools of clotted blood as they shifted in the grisly head. Loreena had joined the ranks of the Undead and would not hesitate to kill any of her surviving companions. Gorgon released the newly made Zombie, letting her drop, cat-like, onto all fours. She froze where she landed, moving her head slowly to scan the shadowy space.

The clotted dead eyes found Jason crouched against a wall of the trembling ship. He covered the pulsing signet ring with his left hand, holding back its lethal shafts until the last moment, hoping for the element of surprise. A shriek like a thousand souls crying out in torment erupted from Loreena's withered mouth. Her desiccated body blurred in a streak of speed as she launched herself. Jason unshielded the ring, his body absorbed in the pulses of hot energy. Bracing himself as best he could against the trembling wall, a razor-thin shaft exploded from the emerald stone.

Riding the echo of the ungodly screech, it slammed into the Undead Sorceress in an explosion of bone shards and bits of black leather. This was followed by another howl, as the Zombie scurried crab-like over the floor, trying to reattach her lower torso. Unlike Mirage's guards, Loreena was given more powers of recovery by Gorgon. She would carry on her attack relentlessly even if she had to do it in pieces. Jason was aiming his ring at the scuttling creature, when Gorgon roared his impatience with her failure.

"Stop, fool! You're of no use to me!"

Gorgon shifted to where the Undead Loreena tried to reassemble her body. He brought his heavy leg down on the upturned head and twisted the scaly foot until it came away with the dust of her skull. Jason was sickened by the sheer callousness of the act, knowing there would be no mercy when Gorgon's evil was directed at him. The ring was sending urgent rhythms of energy throughout his body. *It senses this is a fight for my life*. Jason felt ready when the monster made a lumbering turn toward him. Three fierce eyes fastened on him where he stood unsteadily on the rolling floor. Gorgon shifted himself, the dead weight of the tentacle hindering his movements. Jason noted this weakness and hoped to use it against him. He felt the wall behind him give gently when he pressed his back to it. He pressed harder, feeling the pliant membrane sink in deeper. A few more pushes, and a deep cleft formed to surround him. Gorgon's slow progress toward his position gave Jason time to try to locate the Historian, hoping the Wizard had recovered. He made out a slight movement among the shadows. Gorgon was nearly upon him when he stopped short. The beast opened his massive jaws, laughing manically.

"Well, isn't this convenient for me? You've sought to hide inside the flesh of my own creation."

"And if you attack me here, you'll destroy your precious craft as well. How long will it take to create another?" Jason snarled.

"It will take the Demi-God millions of life cycles. Isn't that right?"

Cathleen stepped out from under a Shadow Wrap, the Historian at her side. Will stood with his sword glowing in his hand.

"That's because he must find another Dark Magic User like the despicable Mirage, who'll assist him in its creation. Mirage's bloated ego made him susceptible to Gorgon's manipulations and promises. Gorgon is a parasite, needing a human host to survive in the Mother's Realms. Without a host, he is destined to spend his eternity as an untethered evil, nothing more than a putrid smell floating in the abyss between life and death."

Gorgon screamed, "Your mate will make the perfect host Protector! Even now he unwittingly feeds my magnificent ship!"

Jason had forced himself deeper into the wall for protection, but Gorgon's words focused him on the gelatinous material, moist and smelling like an unearthed corpse. Until Gorgon said Jason was feeding his ship, his only concern was staying alive. He looked at Cathleen and caught the Historian placing a restraining hand on her arm. *Maybe this wasn't such a great idea…* Jason tried to move a leg, immediately experiencing shooting pains. He was able to lower his head enough to see the vein-like tendrils attaching body-piercing suckers to his lower body. If he used his ring, he would be injured along with the ship. His eyes were brought back to Cathleen as she stepped to her right, the Historian mirroring her movement moved left. The space was immediately filled by the imposing figure of Old Father. His presence had the desired effect on Gorgon, who shuffled his bulk to move a few steps backward.

"What is this trickery, Protector? This thing was destroyed by me! It is well-known your kind are forbidden the art of necromancy. Have you caused an illusion such as you encountered in the Labyrinth? Before I completely absorbed him, Mirage would have appreciated this…toothless tiger!"

Jason watched Old Father closely. The old Guardian hadn't moved a muscle. *Maybe he is an illusion,* Jason thought. He was nearing panic as the tendrils crept upward toward his torso. He knew he had to save himself. Still able to move his arms, he pushed his ring hand into the fibrous wall, directing its powerful beam into the spongy mass. The result was a cataclysmic event inside the body of the Translocator. The craft shuddered violently, the floor pitched and rolled.

Jason saw Cathleen and the others scrambling on their hands and knees. He tried to wriggle out of the contracting wall, but felt the energy leaving his body as the tendrils, in spite of the upheaval, stayed attached to half of his body. He was about to shoot another beam into the quivering wall when Cathleen reached inside and he was being pulled free.

He was clutching her hand, and trying to slow his breathing when Cathleen shouted, "Historian! Kill this beastly ship!" Will rose a foot above the bucking floor and began to spin until his body was distorted by speed. He made thrust after thrust into the walls as he spun past, until the shuddering weakened and finally stopped. A last gasp poured from every surface of the ship's body. Gorgon opened his wide jaws, emitting an ear-shattering scream.

"By all the Dark Fates, this shall not go unpunished!" he bellowed.

As he moved sluggishly toward them, it dawned on Cathleen he'd made no effort to heal himself and suddenly she knew why. He had to rely on the Mother's powers while in Her Realms. She now understood why the Sacred Grove was so crucial to the Demi-God's plans. He needed the energies in the Sacred Grove, controlling that, he would have absolute authority over the Realms, including the Fourth Realm. In that Realm of unbridled evil, he'd have dominion over every creature from the Dark Pit of the Sleepless Dead.

Old Father was all but forgotten in the battle to free Jason from being absorbed into the living fiber of the Translocator. Now, he flinched under the malevolent look in Gorgon's eyes as he lumbered toward him. The ancient Guardian was closest to the Demi-God and within easy reach of the beast's clawed hands. Gorgon might have viewed him as easy prey because of his enfeebled appearance. *You are badly mistaken,* Old Father thought. As Gorgon reached out to grab him, Old Father used his long staff as leverage and vaulted over the monster's huge head. Gorgon was left staring at empty space. A hiss of foul breath was snorted from the flaring nostrils of his snout.

Leaving Will to free Jason from the tendrils, Cathleen rushed to Old Father's side. Standing beside the ancient one, she began moving her hand in wider and wider circles in front of them. Her charm caused the rank air to stir until she felt like she was drowning in a putrid stew. The soft words of magic were lost under Gorgon's own shouted threats as he lumbered closer. He hesitated before reaching the wide coils, studying the circling currents.

Cathleen looked into the trio of unblinking eyes. They were covered with a thin, moist membrane. She'd seen the same in other creatures of the Third Realm, including Geilt. He'd explained to her once, saying the film was needed to protect his sight from the strong light of the three suns. This unique characteristic in Gorgon meant he was already adapting to his new world. She wondered why his eye shields were activated now, in the shadowy belly of the ship.

Continuing to widen the circles she drew, she felt Old Father move closer to her side. Her peripheral vision captured a flash of light. A quick glance revealed Old Father's staff of authority was transformed into a solid gold rod, covered in ancient symbols. When their eyes met, the Guardian curled his blue lips in a hint of a smile. Though the sheer beauty of the Guardian's staff was impressive, she was unsure of its magical worth in battle. As if reading doubt on her face, Old Father spoke in a confident voice.

"Fear not Protector. The beast shall feel the Mother's own wrath!"

Old Father lowered the staff like a javelin until it was parallel to the floor. He murmured some unrecognizable words, but Cathleen felt their power scintillating around her, making her hair stand straight out from her head in its presence. When the dead ship was bursting with the cracking sound, Old Father slammed the golden shaft to the floor. An intense boom shattered the fragile walls of the Translocator, blowing fragments of skeletal structure into the shadows of the forest. Using the light from the night sky, she searched for the others. She spotted several lumps of scaly flesh. These gruesome parts hung from spikes of fractured bone protruding from the floor and walls of the vessel.

"Do not be fooled into believing the evil Demi-God has been removed from this and every life cycle to follow, Protector." Old Father had come up beside her so silently, she involuntarily jumped when he spoke.

"What do you mean?" she asked, alarmed.

"The Mother allowed me to be instrumental in the destruction of Gorgon's present form, but alas, he lives. As all Evil lives, he can be found in the hearts and minds of even some of Her own. He will search out the next desirable being and use their own wickedness to lure them into becoming his living host. Then, as he did with the human Mason Mirage, he will consume them body and soul."

Cathleen was looking around the broken ship when she heard her name.

"Jason! Are you alright?" she asked, rushing over to him just as he pulled away from the last of the blackened tendrils. The Historian was sliding his sword back into its sheath.

"I feel a little light-headed, but I think it's the effects of the tendrils."

"They were sucking off your energies like vampires, my friend," the Historian said, joining the pair. "The Translocator is dead, Protector, but I believe we need to destroy every vestige of it in the Third Realm."

"Agreed. Jason, are you recovered enough to help blast this thing to the Mother's back door?"

He smiled broadly as he answered, "Nothing I'd like better!"

Old Father added a few sobering thoughts. "Through my eyes, and that of my imposter Guardian, I witnessed many strange powers I never suspected Gorgon possessed. His mere presence in this Realm disrupted the cycles of our days from our nights, and turned passive creatures into blood hunters in the Whispering Woods."

"Calm your fears Old Father," Cathleen said, seeing distress deepening the furrows on the ancient brow. "Every particle of this evil beast will be found and destroyed."

Old Father nodded his head in hopeful agreement, as he returned the gleaming shaft into his humble crook. He turned away from the humans, moving toward the Sacred Grove. As if a thought just occurred to him, he stopped abruptly. Looking back over the deep slope of his shoulder, his voice carried a dire warning.

"Something else you must understand before you begin this eradication. The Demi-god, had the ability to revive the smallest fragment of a victim and bring them back to live as an Undead slave. Be vigilant my friends."

The three silently watched the ancient being use his staff to launch himself into the brooding silence of the tree canopy. Cathleen looked over at the men, realizing they were weighing the implications. Without conversation they began looking around themselves at the carnage, pushing debris aside with their boots. Cathleen's voice broke into this grim effort.

"Historian, I leave it to you to recover all of Loreena's remains. We shall return them to the Council to be buried under their strongest wards so none can disturb her sleeping spirit."

"Thank you, Protector," he said quietly.

Cathleen could see Loreena's traitorous behavior still stung him, but placing her remains where Gorgon couldn't revive her, seemed to encourage the Historian's search.

"Jason, you and I will locate and destroy every piece of Gorgon's scaly body."

They set about marking the debris-strewn grounds with a grid created by the Historian before he went off on his own search. The roughly drawn lines floated inches above the ground and after each area was searched thoroughly, the lines vanished along with the detritus, blasted from existence. Cathleen could see this job would take an impossibly long time. After conferring with Jason, it was decided they needed an expert in searching. A few minutes and one spell casting later, Parsons stood with them in the form of the Blood Hound. The big dog dropped to his rump, panting rapidly. His doleful eyes rolled around and he shook his floppy ears as if to clear them. Cathleen crouched in front of him.

"Parsons, we need your special talents finding the missing. This time you need to locate every piece and scale of what is left of the body Gorgon inhabited.

The hound tilted his head to the side, appearing to listen intently. Jason heard the dog whimper when she mentioned the Demi-God.

"He's nervous, love. These dogs like to run in their pack, or with their hunter. How about letting me team up with him? I'll use my ring to incinerate everything he finds, and you'll be free to concentrate on removing the remains of the ship."

Cathleen was quick to agree. The last she saw of them, the Blood Hound's nose was pressed close to the ground, his head sweeping side-to-side. They moved off into the thicker stands of trees, where she saw the constant flash of green marking Jason's work. The last shaft was aimed high into the trees, reminding her to check above the scene of carnage, as well as ground zero.

The three suns had begun spilling warm colors onto patches of bare ground by the time the small party of humans and the hunting dog met up. The Blood Hound flopped down, his sides heaving.

"Parsons had to chase after a large slug-like creature, trying to make off with a scale. He caught it before it made it back to its hole."

The Historian walked up to his friends carrying something under his arm. It was a wooden box covered in symbols and latched with a heavy iron lock.

"Loreena's remains, including her clothing. I've placed my own wards upon it, until it can be entombed safely by the Council. Our next task will be cleansing this polluted ground."

The Time Thread Will called to transport the remains was wrapped like a pulsating shroud around the oblong container. The expression on his face was somber but determined when it disappeared with its burden.

Chapter 60

Cathleen and Will stood back-to-back; their arms held out as they turned like spokes on a bicycle. The purifying of the site would take only a minute to complete, but its compelling intensity made it feel like hours to him. The effect was immediate and a sense of relief settled over him. He glanced over at the Historian as they moved through the trees toward to the Sacred Grove where they would report on a successful cleansing to Old Father. Will appeared calm and focused. Jason hoped he was coming to grips with Loreena's ultimate betrayal. *Sending her body back to Sir Creighton should give him some peace of mind,* Jason thought, though he wondered if Will's feelings once ran deeper for the beautiful Loreena than he'd admit even to himself.

They were moving through Whispering Woods, when the colossal Yew Trees seemed to spring up like green mountain tops. The three suns had risen directly behind the Sacred Grove, creating deep, inky pools within the wide expanse of the circle of giants. Cathleen felt the nip of apprehension as they neared. She brought a tiny shoot of Fire to her hand, hiding it inside her closed fist as she walked toward the murky center of the Grove.

When she stood in the middle of the Grove, she picked up a low humming sound clearly coming from the rustling leaves. A feeling of complete serenity came over her, replacing the uneasiness she'd been feeling as she approached. *What had me so jumpy?* She looked around using her Inner Eye to pierce the cloaking shadows. *There!* Standing at the foot of one of the trees was the Blood Hound.

"Parsons!" Cathleen called over to the big hound. "It's time to shift back, little man."

The hound didn't move, but his droopy eyes were fixed on her as she came closer and she heard a low growl. Cathleen stopped when she was near enough to confirm her suspicions. One of the sharp scales that covered Gorgon was deeply imbedded in the dog's muzzle. The hound's mouth twisted into a snarl and he bared his teeth menacingly. Cathleen felt a thrill of alarm shoot through her when she saw the back of its thick neck was covered in the same over-lapping scales as Gorgon's body had been. From the look of it, the scales were beginning to form around the sides as well.

"This won't be easy to fix Parsons," she said softly to the creature that looked ready to tear her throat out. The Blood Hound responded by making a head-long charge at her, his growl filled with the fury of the possessed. Cathleen used the small flame nestled in her palm, waiving her hand in a fan motion to create an instant sheet of fire. When the big hound tore through it in his crazed lunge, she spun the fire into a tight webbing that carried the heavy dog to the ground. The Blood Hound was on its side, thick gobs of frothy saliva drooling from his jaws. Cathleen began a spell to pull the scales from its heaving body and the one lodged in his snout. There was profuse bleeding and the creature howled in distress and pain. When she was certain none remained, Cathleen quickly staunched the blood flow and removed the webbing.

"If I got this right, Parsons, you should start to shift right about..."

The hound's body convulsed as if hit with an electric shock. When its trembling stopped, Parsons lay on his side, his eyes squeezed tightly shut.

"Parsons, you're safe now."

Parsons raised his long fingers to his nub of a nose and felt around. "My nose feels a bit tender. Is all well with your expedition?"

Jason and Will came up to them just as a group of Guardians streamed out of the trees. They marched in tight formation directly toward the small group, striking the ground with their spears, to create a cadence as they moved. They halted a few feet from Cathleen and the others, splitting to create a corridor. The humans watched Old

Father pass through the columns of Guardians, his own head, well-above the tallest among them.

"Well met, friends," he said solemnly. "You have brought us the peace promised by our illustrious leader, the Magnificent Geilt! The Sacred Grove remains unsullied by the evil visited upon us. Your bravery will preserve the Mother's most awesome gifts."

The three humans and Parsons, stood in a loose line as they listened. Parsons stood straight, stretching his thin neck until he added an inch to his height. Old Father seemed pleased with their respectful composure and continued.

"The Great Geilt expressed his devotion to the Mother by using the prodigious powers She granted him, to protect and provide for our world. With his passing from this life, we Guardians of the Third Realm became vulnerable. When the beast ship carried Gorgon to the Whispering Woods, his darkness stained our world with chaos and death. This history, and your own parts in shaping its outcome, shall be recorded in *The Book of Shadows and Light*, telling our history for all time."

Having delivered this long and impassioned speech, Old Father turned and walked back through the lines of Guardians without a single glance behind. His tall figure disappeared behind the wall of their closing ranks. The Guardians turned in a perfect wheeling motion, and thumping the ground once more, vanished into the heart of forest. A deep silence followed the departure of the Guardians and their leader. None of them doubted that Old Father's speech signaled they had completed their mission in the Third Realm, but it was Parsons who pointed out they'd been dismissed.

"It appears our services are no longer needed, or wanted, Protector. Does this mean we're free to return to our own homes?" he asked.

Jason saw the longing in Parsons' round eyes and appreciated that need for normalcy, whatever shape it took! Without answering

Parsons' question, Cathleen walked away from the others, reentering the towering circle of Yews. When she reached the center, the trees began glowing. Cathleen pressed a hand to the illuminated ridges of bark on the nearest Yew. The radiance enveloped her body and the tree appeared to physically absorb her, drawing her in until she became a natural outgrowth on the wide trunk.   Fear for Cathleen stopped Jason's heart, until she closed her eyes. Jason realized she was in prayerful communion with the Mother.

In his reverie, he thought on this strange mission, until he recalled the destruction of Gorgon. This meant Mason Mirage was also wiped from existence. Mirage's boasting as a great Hunter of Witches, was just another illusion. When the Historian placed a hand on his shoulder, Jason was brought-back to the present in time to see Cathleen coming toward them.

"Our work is done here," were her first words.

She looked and sounded like Cathleen, but Jason wasn't sure what to expect after such a uniquely magical experience.

"The Third Realm's safe and I've placed stronger wards around the Sacred Grove to protect it from any incursions by the Dark Ones. But there is one last concern that must be met. Old Father has already served countless eons here, and I've been shown his cycle is coming to its natural end."

Cathleen turned the intense gaze of her hazel eyes onto Will saying, "With the loss of the Great Geilt, a void of leadership from a human Wizard was created. For in reality, Geilt was as human as any of us, though he carefully seeded the imagination of others by naming himself the 'Wildman' of this Realm. Historian, you have acted with honor and valor in defense of the Sacred Grove and our mission in the Third Realm. Through me, the Mother offers you a rare and noble reward. The title of "Mystic Protector" is to be granted to you, Will Farley. If you accept, you will act as Guide and Ruler of the Third Realm, shielding it from the Dark Ones as you did in the First Realm."

The Historian looked stunned by this offer and the implications of accepting it. His dark eyes were drawn to the Sacred Grove as he considered his next words.

"If this is the Mother's calling for me, I shall answer and am ready to serve."

A sound came from the circle of Sacred Yew. The four saw a figure rising from the middle, slowly turn and face them.

"Star Fire!" Will Farley said, gasping at the vision of the beautiful Medicine Woman.

She wore the long, deer skin dress they remembered, but it shone like the sun on new snow. Her glossy black hair cascaded loosely down her back, the stark flash of white running through it appeared like a sprinkling of stars woven into the night sky. Starla moved directly to the Historian. The others stepped back and watched as she reached out to take his hand in hers. Will looked into her upturned face with unbelieving eyes.

"Are you real, or phantom, Star Fire?" he asked while covering her small hand with his.

"I have been granted this life force to join you, Will. I have known from before our first meeting that I was destined to become your mate. My own Spirit Guide showed me your face in my grandmother's fire during my Blessing Ceremony. You, Will Farley, were marked as a blessing before we ever met."

The Historian's weather-worn face broke into a broad grin.

"It's time for us to leave this Realm, and for Parsons to go back to his cot in front of Sir Creighton's hearth," Cathleen said warmly.

Cathleen and Jason spent the next few minutes saying their goodbyes to the man who had proved over and over, his friendship and courage. After they each embraced him, Parsons, swiping at fat tears, stood in front of the Historian. He was managed to throw his scrawny arms around his waist in an awkward hug. He received the usual hair tussling in return. When all was quiet between the friends, the Historian reached for Starla's hand and they entered Whispering Woods, following the path of the Guardians he would one day lead. He turned a last time, holding up his hand in a final farewell and vanished with Starla into the fastness of the forest.

Parsons and Jason were still watching when Cathleen's voice cut into the pensive mood. She noticed Parsons wringing his hands and looking apprehensive. "What's wrong Parsons? Aren't you happy for our friends? They've been given this beautiful place, and each other to care for over many life cycles."

Parsons looked at Cathleen and then at Jason before answering, "I don't know if my welcome will be as warm in the Council Chambers when I tell Sir Creighton that the Master Scout has left his post permanently! The Scouts are leaderless now! If a Demon breaks through our defenses, they will head straight for the Green's Keep slaughtering us in our sleep!"

Cathleen had no idea Parsons lived with such fears, but he was a creature of habit and order. To his mind, the Historian's leaving the elite Outlanders meant his safety and that of his world, depended on the wizened Council members and a smattering of leaderless Scouts. She used her Calming Voice and explained how there was already a leader in place on the wild borders of the First Realm.

"Parsons, you'll find Sir Creighton has filled the Historian's place with a fine Wizard named Willa Farley; the daughter of Will Farley and Loreena Bledsworth."

Jason, shouted, "What? Will had a daughter with…?"

"Yes. The child was raised away from both parents in an effort to protect their secret. She was trained in the Magical Arts, while learning valuable skills in the Healing Gardens. Our Healers were her loving teachers and surrogate parents. She displayed extraordinary skills early in life, becoming a Wizard of the highest order by the time she was twenty. It is she the Council has chosen as Master Outlander Wizard Scout."

"Wow! It was easy to see there was something between him and Loreena at one time though," Jason said as he gazed off into the woods as if he might see his friend standing there.

Parsons squared his shoulders saying, "I suspect Sir Creighton will be needing me after such a long absence Protector. He will be wanting my full oral history of this adventure no doubt!"

"Then let's go home!" Cathleen said, smiling at his enthusiastic recovery.

Parsons was so excited at the prospect of returning to his safe and pampered life, he was unable to grab for the Time Thread summoned by Cathleen to carry him.

"Parsons, you've got to calm yourself and concentrate!" she admonished calling up a third Thread.

After several minutes of futile attempts and eye rolling, Cathleen was at last able to fasten the dancing rope around Parsons' thin waist.

"Remember, when you return to Verdant Keep Parsons, you must seek out Sir Creighton and give him a full report."

"I'll be off then, Protector. Farewell my friends! Until the next time you call upon my assistance, may Mother bless you both."

As he vanished from their present time, Cathleen looked over at Jason. He hadn't said anything since his comment about Will and Loreena. Studying his face, she asked if he was missing his friend.

"I'm fine, love. There's just so many surprises and changes to process in my head. I've been gnawing on one worry though. Is Starla just another type of Undead. It doesn't seem natural for her to return the way she did."

"It isn't natural in *our* world, sweetie. But here, in the Third Realm, the Mother can endow life where She sees fit. Starla's spirit is intact and pure. The only change will be in her Spirit Warrior. She can no longer shift into the Werewolf. Her new powers are no longer linked to her role as Medicine Woman, but to her standing as Will's mate."

"I'm still trying to wrap my head around the fact that Will has a daughter, and now he has a mate!"

They continued discussing their friend's new life while they headed back toward Mother's Robe River. They hoped their odd-shaped boat would still be moored where they tied it. Unspoken between them was the wish for one more chance to float on its magical waters. They saw the wide body of deep-purple water, shimmering like a satin sheet under the brightness of the three suns.

The trip across was sped-up by the sweet breeze Cathleen captured, stirring the current's swift flow. They watched together as the shore faded behind the morning fog clinging to the marshes. Jason shot a glance at his wife, watching her pensive face relax. He reached out to stroke the curve of her cheek. When she turned to face him, he leaned in and kissed her deeply. They only took a breath when the round craft beached itself, shaking them apart.

"Going on these missions seems to inspire a bit of passion in you, husband," she laughed and gave him a kiss on his rough stubble.

He smiled sheepishly and jumped out into the high marsh grasses, pulling the round boat further up onto solid land. He secured it to a large rock and they found an open area where Cathleen called up a Time Thread. She held the dancing, luminous rope in one hand, looping it securely around her waist and watched as Jason did the same. The results of dropping from a Time Thread were beyond unimaginable, and she always scrutinized his security.

"Are we really going home, love? You know, it's just a few days until Hunting Season opens, and I wouldn't want to miss it!"

His laugh was lost in a rush of air and the popping sound he dreaded. The pressure on his chest felt like an elephant sat there. He could swear he heard Cathleen's laughter in his head. *How can I hear her?* They landed with muffled thumps as the Thread set them down in the silent woods behind their house. Cathleen undid the Thread and it disappeared immediately.   They walk hand-in-hand down the well-worn path to their kitchen door. Jason's thoughts of home brought a stirring of desire and he squeezed the hand of the woman he was deeply in love with.

Cathleen chuckled beside him. When he looked over, her gaze was fastened to him when she spoke. "There is *one* more gift the Mother granted me, sweetie, that I probably should have told you about…"

Francesca is part of a large Italian family where she discovered early on that a love of reading was as much a part of her DNA as her mother's skill at baking. Growing up in a house filled with laughter, screaming, banging pots, fighting and loving family bonds, shaped her life and heart.

Having moved from the east coast where she was raised between New York and New Jersey, Francesca left for the mid-west where she spent several years outside the Chicago area raising a family of three children, completing her college degrees and writing introspective poetry like other young mothers.

Francesca has worked in local television, a small city zoo, founded a non-profit tutoring agency for an inner-city neighborhood which eventually served local school districts, worked for an International

Evangelical Television and Radio Station and for a non-profit organization serving challenged adults.

Francesca Quarto resides in a small town outside of Indianapolis, Indiana with her husband Patrick. She still has a great love of the written word and while she enjoys her E-Reader immensely, she still treasures the excitement of turning the next page.

Tell-Tale Publishing would like to thank you for your purchase. If you would like to read more by this or other fine TT authors, please visit our website:

www.tell-talepublishing.com

www.ingramcontent.com/pod-product-compliance
Lightning Source LLC
Chambersburg PA
CBHW061040190726
48286CB00006B/1535